I0646394

THE AVIATORS OF XIBALBÁ

by

Carlos H. Cantu

The Aviators of Xibalbá

By Carlos H. Cantu

Published by

Mystic Buddha Publishing House, LLC

www.MysticBuddha.com

First Edition

Printed in the United States of America

Edited by Roger Cantu

Copyright © 2011 Mystic-Buddha Publishing House, LLC
All rights reserved. No part of this book may be
reproduced in any form or by any means, electronic or
mechanical, including photocopying, recording, or by any
information storage and retrieval system, without
permission in writing from the publisher.

Library of Congress Control Number: 2010929869
ISBN-13   978-0-9820505-5-2
ISBN-10   0-9820505-5-0

ACKNOWLEDGMENT

My gratitude goes to...
> The Giver of Life.
> Was it my father?... Was it my mother?...
> Was it the Father Creator?...

To whomever it was that gave me life, goes my gratitude because being alive I can write, and through writing I can give birth to my own microcosms in which I breed multiple children. These children I can situate in their own realm to ensnare them with temptations to see how they behave; to see them grow, making decisions based on the dictates of their conscience or their heart...

Thus, I bear children that are good and noble, and deserve reward; or bad and covetous, and must be chastised; generous, selfish, beautiful, ugly; courageous, or fearful; children of all conditions, but all of them children of my entrails... children of my fancy.

So, I express my appreciation to whoever gave me life, because being alive I can create.

TABLE OF CONTENT

PREFACE

Green... a lush green... green from its beginning to its end.

Seen from above Xibalbá – the jungle – looks like a solid arboreal carpet, beaten flat on earth by the weight of heat and humidity.

It is a hushed river of sap throbbing through the arteries of the sacred Mayan forest that Gucumatz – divine Heart of Heaven, Mother and Father of all There Is – brought forth at the creation of cosmos to be the domain of Balam, the tiger, and shelter for Zaquicaz, the serpent; to ensnare in its foliage the buzzing of Xan, the mosquito, and the cry of Caquix, the macaw. It was the place for Xzul, the centipede, to trace paths with its manifold feet, and to have Vuch, the buzzard, keep the brush clean for the enjoyment of Coy, the monkey.

Gucumatz conceived the pristine forest as a den for animals large and small, but never intended it to be a dwelling for men because, for humans Xibalbá, the jungle, is hell itself. Nevertheless, consumed by greed, men invade its boundaries looking for the treasures therein, but unfailingly stumble onto a collective frenzy that binds them to the roots of its forest, preventing their escape before their time is due.

Seen closely, the jungle frightens. When men dwell in it, they turn into beasts that scorn kindness and surrender all virtues, submitting to wickedness. How can integrity be preserved while living in hell? For the jungle is Xibalbá, hell itself, the abode of demons.

What do men look for in Xibalbá, besides searching for a pathway that may lead them to wealth; if to live there they must be willing to leave behind not only their lives, but also their souls? Perhaps what they really are in quest of is absolution because, regardless of where they all come from, when the masks of greed they wear are stripped off, the real purpose of their journey is revealed.

They are fugitives running away from a conscience that chases them – seeking retribution for their transgressions. They start from points nearby and remote to come to Xibalbá because, once there, they know. Xibalbá offers atonement. They can be absolved of their remorse... their guilt. But to do this, they must journey into the treacherous land of the ancient Mayan jungle, known as Xibalbá.

PREAMBLE

In the Yucatan Peninsula the ebbing glimmer of the sun, setting behind the wooded horizon of the Mayan remote forest, touches the lowly shacks of the Xkantak Gum Concession Central Depot.

Aircraft mechanic Ricardo Quel opens the lid of a magneto casing to examine it, and swatting the mosquitoes that hover around his face, tells his assistant:

"Look, Neto; this armature is busted. Go and fetch another one from the storehouse."

"But , maistro; there are no more electric spare parts left since a week ago."

"¡Máre! You are right! Now the Robin will remain grounded!"

"And why worry? The airplanes are not flying anyway…"

Wincing, Ricardo retorts: "The airplanes must be airworthy all the time, ninio! I do not want to have to make excuses because I neglected my duty."

"And who will reprimand you, maistro? The boss is dead, and his widow is not working the concession anymore."

"Doña Estelita is a resorceful woman, bosh. She is not working the concession because she lacks money; but maybe she will get a partner, or she will sell the business."

"And in the meantime what do we eat, maistro? The storehouse is empty of staples."

"Neto, we are in the middle of the jungle; there are all kinds of fruits to pick; fowl to trap, or animals to hunt."

"I say, we should go looking for work in Campeche, or in Mérida. Before the boss got killed in the Aircruiser, I heard that Aerovías del Sureste needed mechanics…"

Ricardo looks to his left where a Curtiss Robin, a Travelaire and two Bellanca Skyrockets, are lined up alogside a dirt airstrip in front of their shed, and candidly states: "I could never do that, Neto; those planes, old and battered as they are, remain my responsibility while doña Estelita does not release me from my word to take care of them."

"So, what will we do then, maistro?"

"Appeal to our gods' mercy. The gum harvesting season is almost over, so we will have nothing to do until the new season begins next September. Today, I will offer a sacred Saka ceremony to the thirteen Mayan levels and spheres of life, requesting their blessings. I will harvest some Saka leaves, the best corn and the purest wild honey, to present the potion to the Bacabs, expressing my gratitude to Noj Yuum K'uj, the greater God, to Yuum K'aax, and all the Yuumtsilo'ob godly earth elements. Will you help me do it?"

"Anything you say, maistro."

"Very well, we will offer it tonight at the foot of the mound north of the landing strip, which was a pyramid in Mayan epochs and, even covered by grass and bushes as it is today, it still is just as sacred as it used to be!"

"Say, maistro, and what good will this ritual fetch us… if any?"

"There you go again with your doubts, Neto! Have I ever told you a falsehood?"

"No, maistro; although sometimes your stories, or mythology as you call them, about Mayan gods and what they do, are too wild to believe…"

"Look, this ritual will provide us with good fortune, healthy gum crops next season, and protection against all the evils concocted by the evil Lords of Xibalba.. With this sanctified safeguard, whoever comes to run this concession, no matter who he might be, or where he comes from, shall prosper, and that will be good for us. Now, put the tools away. We shall be on our way, as soon as doña Ticha cooks us a bite to eat on the way… "

PART I – Berlin, Germany - August, 1939

Chapter 1 – Colonel Maximilian "Max" Görzten

"Heil Hitler!" The arrogant orderly salutes, extending his right arm stiffly.

Luftwaffe Colonel Max Görzten fastens his steely eyes on the young man standing before his desk, and ponders: *"If I withheld my reply, the stupid bastard would remain frozen in that stance for the rest of his worthless life!"* The youth must be younger than fifteen, but his bearing reveals the fanatical National-Socialist conviction embedded in his brain by *Hitler Jugend,* the compulsory five-year youth training program. *"He is proud to be a bloody Nazi!"*

Reluctantly, with his elbow resting on the desktop, Max raises his right hand and replies, "Heil Hitler."

Those two words break the spell. The orderly clicks his heels, turns around smartly, and marches out of the office.

As the door closes, Max looks at the sealed envelope lying on top of his desk. It has disturbed him from the moment he saw it appear from the pouch held by the youngster. *"Why had it been brought by an orderly from the Ministry of the Air,"* he wonders, *"instead of arriving by regular official channels? Why is it sealed?"* Picking it up, he weighs it in his hand, turns it over, and stares at it. *"This is no ordinary communiqué, I could behead myself if it does not bear the signature of Reichmarschall Hermann Göring."*

He sighs to relieve his increasing restlessness and grasps the Damascus dagger he uses as a letter opener but a peculiar, rumbling vibration, catches his attention. Behind him, the glass panels in the panoramic window rattle slightly. Swiveling his chair around, he looks outside across the neatly clipped lawn, where five Junkers Ju 87, Stuka aircraft, roll on the adjacent runway taking off in a tight "V" formation to climb skyward at a steep angle.

"Splendid!" Max rates the performance of the brand-new Stukas, while his gray eyes follow their flight into a bank of low clouds. The intriguing envelope calls his attention again but, wanting to overlook it, he turns to glance at the enormous aircraft factory, scanning the vast hangars that are already insufficient to shelter the aircraft being assembled in the adjoining plant. His eyes are drawn back to the envelope. *"I better open it and put an end to my misgivings."*

Taking the dagger, he tears a corner of the envelop as the door to the office opens to admit Lieutenant Freda Leber, his secretary.

"*Herr Oberst*, Major Heinz and *Oberst Leutnant* Dorr are here."

"Send them in, *Leutnant*," he replies, concealing the envelope under the leather writing set that bears his name, rank, and a swastika hanging from the Luftwaffe emblem.

Freda reappears and stands aside to allow in two Luftwaffe officers. Major Ludwig Heinz and Lieutenant Colonel Hans Dorr who walk in and salute, "Heil Hitler!"

"May Satan trash his corpse!" Max replies, standing from his desk to extend his arm toward Dorr, who, startled, darts an uneasy glance at Freda. Following his gaze, Max detects a playful grin in her full lips and, shaking hands with the Lieutenant Colonel, remarks: "Do not fret, Hans. Fräulein Leber would sweeten the coffee of the *Small Corporal* with a lump of arsenic, if she had the opportunity. See that we are not disturbed, *Leutnant*."

"*Jawohl, Herr Oberst!*" she replies, shutting the door behind her.

Moving toward the red leather sofa that imparts a relaxed touch to his spacious office, Max invites them, "*Setzen Sie Sich, Herren.*"

Still uneasy, the lanky lieutenant colonel asks, "Are you sure about her, Max?"

"I would place my hand over fire for her!"

Winking, Heinz says, "It must be rewarding to have such a close relationship with someone who cannot hide her assets, even under a vapid uniform."

Scowling, Max replies, "Let us mind our business, Ludwig," but it is obvious that the remark made by Heinz has gratified his ego. "What is new?"

"We are attaining remarkable progress, Max," Heinz replies. "The Opposition is unifying. Goerdeler came back from England to lead the civilians."

"Karl Friedrich Goerdeler, ex-mayor of the noble city of Leipzig; the everlasting Nazi regime opposer!" Max scorns, offering them cigars.

"Do you consider him untrustworthy?" Heinz asks, furrowing his forehead.

"He is a congenial man and has always countered Hitler, but his scant seasoning hardly qualifies him to lead a divided civilian population, especially if he pursues the theory that Hitler will fall under his own weight. Pacifism will accomplish nothing! I have it from reliable British sources that neither Prime Minister Chamberlain, nor Lord Halifax – in spite of their appeasement policy – took his speculations seriously. People like Goerdeler hinder our plans."

4

Heinz objects: "But now he insists on direct political action, and has contacted Generals Beck and Tresckow to organize the coalition between civilian and military groups."

"He is succeeding," Dorr cuts in, "in unifying the opposition parties: Christian-Democrats, Social-Christians, Socialists, and Social-Democrats, even the Communists, are willing to collaborate in overthrowing the Nazis!"

Staring at the tip of his cigar, Max asks bitterly, "And how do they plan to do it?"

Dorr is taken aback by the bitter tone uttered by Max, and replies with slight conviction, "General Beck suggests that every conscientious officer refuse to obey commands that come directly from Hitler, making it impossible for him to start another world war."

"I agree that total war must be averted," Max asserts. "If that lunatic assaults Czechoslovakia or Poland, Germany shall confront the world and we are not ready to do that. However, refusing to obey orders is not the solution and does not befit German military honor. Most officers will obey." Max pauses, and then asks: "What will the civilians do?"

"They depend on us," says Heinz.

"On us?" His stern face reddens and the veins in his neck swell. "On a pack of idealists who believe that the Nazis can be overthrown by parlor intrigue? Moreover, what do we represent in the gigantic apparatus of the *Wehrmacht*? How much influence can we exert over our fellow officers? Answer me that!"

Heinz and Dorr look at Max apprehensively. His steel-gray eyes are cold and mean. The ashen crew cut topping his sturdy head turns him into a sledgehammer, ready to pound. His excitement makes him look taller and stronger.

"Calm down, Max," Heinz says. "The *Non Aggression Pact* that Hitler recently signed with Stalin gives us a respite. I do not believe hostilities will break out just so."

"Oh, no? Hitler himself has induced Poland to reject his absurd proposal to guarantee the German-Polish border! Why do you think Poland and England signed a safeguard treaty just two days ago? And what about the so-called *Pact of Steel*, which is nothing but an alliance between the Nazis and the Italian Fascists? Only the blind cannot see that Hitler is ready to attack!"

Weighing those assertions, Heinz admits: "Your logic is sound, Max. We must urge the men we have in key positions to action."

"That is where we have to be very cautious. Who are you sure would support our cause?"

"Well, we have general Trescow in General Staff; Admiral Canaris in Intelligence; Nebe in the Gestapo; Oster, Kleist, and many other high-ranking officers in the Army."

"And how will those illustrious gentlemen detach Hitler from government, before he pushes Germany to ruination?"

"They will force him to resign!" Dorr asserts.

Max strikes the desktop like a thunderclap. "Who dreamt up such stupidity? Each and every day he suffocates groups that oppose him. Have you not noticed how he has removed the nobility from high ranking posts in government to weaken their clout? Do you not realize that with each one of his ploys, he becomes more of an absolute dictator? Hitler will never resign!"

Gazing at them intently, he announces the solution that he has been mulling over for months: "Hitler must die!"

His utterance shocks both officers, who stare back at him, unable to speak.

Moving closer to them, Max lowers his voice to a secretive whisper. "The stupid notion *Reichmarschal* Göring has that he can win the war by utilizing Stuka aircraft as a key weapon, has him swollen like a bullfrog, so he will bring the *Führer* to this plant tomorrow. The chancellor will walk along the assembly line shaking hands with the workers and, when he stops to admire the Stukas," his eyes shine with the anticipation of triumph, "everything within twenty meters around him shall blow up in pieces so small that not even his memory will remain to be buried."

Dorr and Heinz look at each other in disbelief.

"This must be kept in absolute secrecy. Only you two and I know about this possibility."

"*Um Himmels Willen!*" Dorr mumbles, and then exclaims: "What you say is inconceivable! What will happen?"

"With Hitler gone, Germany will be secure!"

"Yes, but what about the government? There will be chaos!"

"Moreover, the Nazis will try to remain in power!"

"That, we can prevent. There is no one else with the cunning or personality to replace Hitler. We will organize a coalition government while things go back to normal."

"But we would have to tell someone," Heinz objects. "This is something that cannot be done impulsively. We would have to get ready for it."

"Ready we are, but if anyone knows about this plot beforehand, we shall fail. What I need you for is to inform those who participate that the plan has succeeded as soon as I confirm it. Our essential people already know what to do in the event that the government is dissolved. I will see you tonight at my home to work out the details. Now you must excuse me, I have to inspect the assembly line in fifteen minutes, and run test flights on some of the new Stukas. *Lebewohl, Herren!*"

He leaves them no alternative. Still dazed, Heinz and Dorr march to the door...

Chapter 2 – On the Edge of the Razor Blade

Brushing aside the Damascus dagger, Max hastily tears the envelope open and takes out a parchment-like sheet with the Ministry of the Air monogram at the top and the signature of *Reichsmarshal* Göring closing the bottom of the text. As he reads, his features become ashen, his stiff fingers go limp and the communiqué falls from his hands. A defeated man, he sinks in his chair.

Freda Leber comes in minutes later and finds him still feeling vanquished. "*Herr Oberst*, it is time to – Max, what is it?"

"All my plans have been upset," he says, indicating the document lying on the parquet floor.

Freda picks it up and quickly scans the first lines. Then she reads aloud:

"Judging by your valiant demeanor, masterful flying, and heroic deportment fighting the Republicans in Spain, this Ministry informs you that the Luftwaffe will be proud to have you back among its leading officers and anticipates you will serve as an example to be emulated by our novice pilots. I would appreciate your having all matters readied to transfer your appointment as *Oberaufseher der Produktion* to the administrator this Ministry will designate, begging you that at your convenience, but not later than three days, you report to the Reichenau Base to take command of Fighter Wing Jg. 22, subordinated to *JAFU 2* (General Von Doring), commanded by the 2nd. Aerial Corps (General Kesselring).

Looking up from the letter, Freda exclaims in disbelief, "Reichenau Base is at the Polish border! You are being sent to command a fighter wing!"

"Yes, *liebling*; it is war. The *Small Corporal* is already deploying his toy soldiers."

Shaking, Freda sinks down in a chair.

"Calm down," he says, crossing the room and taking her in his arms. "This may disrupt my plans, but it does not finish me off. There are other means to attain power, even from the war front. I promise you."

"Forget that. All I want is to be by your side. Take me with you to Reichenau. I can still be your secretary."

"No!"

"Max, please?"

Neither her beauty nor her tears move him. Her undeniable devotion, however, makes him reconsider. "All right! You will come with me."

"*Danke,* Max. *Danke schön!*"

"Enough! We have much to do." First, locate my father. He must be at the factory in Bremen, or in the Hamburg office. Tell him it is imperative that his chauffeur drives him here tonight. Then make everything ready to turn the office over tomorrow. Call the flight line and have a *Junkers 52* ready for immediate departure from tomorrow morning on. Call Heinz and Dorr and tell them that our meeting for tonight is cancelled, and not to try to see me until I get in touch with them. Do not let them or anyone else know about my transfer. Ah, and send a memorandum to Personnel Command advising them you will continue to be part of my personal staff in Reichenau. *Schnell!* It is already two forty-five and I still have to make several phone calls."

"Who shall I connect you with?"

"Do not bother. I will use my private line."

Wiping her eyes, Freda leaves and Max opens a drawer in his desk to take out a telephone and dial a number.

Seconds later a male voice answers: "*Schlageter Staffel Hundert und Ein.*"

"Get me major Schultz-Hoysen."

"*Bitte, ein minute.* I will see if he has landed yet."

Max notices another document within the crucial envelope. It is a carbon copy of the official communiqué from the Ministry to the Chief of Staff of the Luftwaffe, General Jeschonneck. He perceives there is something odd in the way his transfer is being processed, but cannot quite figure out what it could be.

There are connecting noises on the telephone line and then a familiar voice: "Shultz-Hoysen here."

"This is Max, Harold. The Ministry is transferring me to command a fighter wing in Reichenau. I have to know who gave the order and why."

"I understand, Max, but it is late. I doubt I can find out today who did it and why. I will call you tomorrow as early as I can. Is that agreeable with you?"

"Try to do it today, Harold. It is of utmost importance."

"I will do my best."

Max hangs up and ponders for a moment. Then he dials another number.

"Chancellery Automotive Maintenance Shop," a lively, booming voice answers.

"Hello, Halem?"

"Yes, this is he."

"This is Max, from the lathe shop; to let you know that the part you ordered will be ready for delivery tomorrow sometime in the morning."

"Tomorrow? Are you sure, Max?"

"Absolutely! There will be no further delays!"

The voice in the telephone breaks. Almost breathless, Halem replies: "I – have the motor ready to assemble, so I will be expecting that part...."

"Advice me as soon as you have assembled the motor, *lebewohl*." Max pauses for a second considering if he should have told Halem that setting up the explosive device in the assembly line to blow up Hitler, will be a deed worthy of a true patriot, or somehow encouraged him; after all, his action will safeguard the future of the Görztens' enterprises; however empathy is not in his nature. He replaces the receiver softly in its cradle, mulls over what additional precautionary measures he should take, and picks up the telephone again to make a long-distance call.

"International Operator, Berlin...."

"Bitte, *Österreich. Graz*, four two, six seven. A person to person conference with Baronin Olga Scheuermann. Colonel Maximilian Görzten calling."

"Allow me to verify if there is any delay, *Herr Oberst*."

"My priority number is one six one one, Operator. Connect me immediately!"

His well-trained mind works with the intensity needed to coordinate his activities for the next few hours. That bloody order has disarranged his meticulously thought-out, long-range plans to become one of the most powerful industrialists in Germany, so he is not going to let a last-minute contingency ruin his future – not for a single moment. He reacts to a voice in the telephone.

"Hello, Baronin Scheuermann here."

Annoyed, Max asks: "Will you ever be Fräu Görzten?"

"*Mein liebe* Max! This is a surprise! I did not expect your call today. Will you be here for the reception Gräfin Ziegler will offer tomorrow?"

"Listen to me!" he interrupts her brusquely. "I have just been ordered to a combat command post. I want us to spend two days in the mountains before I leave. I will be there tomorrow or the day after."

The line is silent for a few seconds. When Olga speaks again, her voice sounds shaken. "Is it the war, Max?"

"Yes, but maybe it will not interfere with your social calendar, if I can prevent it."

"And if you cannot?"

"It will break out in a few days. Take only one suitcase and do not tell anyone where you are going. Did you understand clearly?"

"Yes, Max."

"*Auf Wiedersehen*!"

Max checks in his mind if there is anything left for him to take care of. Satisfied, he speaks into the intercom: "*Leutnant* Leber, call the flight line. Tell them to ready the aircraft that I must test today."

"*Ja doch, Herr Oberst!*"

Chapter 3 – Reminiscences

Nothing unwinds Max more than the time he spends flying. He flies at a level of eight thousand meters, where the problems that plague him on the ground simply vanish. Flying boils down his world to that cockpit, where there is only a complex instrument panel, a robust command stick, an engine control pedestal, the weaponry triggers, and the levers to actuate the air brake and the flaps. It is a world in which the Maximilian Görzten involved in politics does not exist. The roar of the 1,200 hp. *Junkers Jumo* engine overcomes his feelings, which sink down into the slime of passion and ambition spread over the surface of the earth. If he did not have to go back to that, how different his life would be!

Possessed by the euphoria of flight, he pulls the throttle back, and pushes the Stuka nose down. Gradually, the dive-bomber picks up speed and the rush of air flowing around its W-shaped wings magnifies its noise. The drag created by the fixed undercarriage and the surface of its angular tail increases, as does the pulse in his temples. Although the Ju 87 B-1 is sturdy, a new aircraft is never exempt from structural failure, and breakage of a wing is always a possibility.

Despite the cold generated by altitude, his forehead grows damp. To feel every slight vibration travels from the fuselage to the stick control, and then through the glove to the palm of his right hand, is as exhilarating as it is awesome.

When the needle of the airspeed indicator sweeps past 250 kph, he pulls the stick control gently but steadily until the dive-bomber is upside down; then he releases the rearward pressure on the stick allowing the nose to drop and, seconds later, pulls back on the control again to level out. With minimum effort, the Stuka has drawn a perfect loop in the sky. With similar ease, Max performs an Immelmann turn, snap rolls and slow rolls, four and eight-point barrel rolls, and regressions – the whole range of aerobatic and combat flight maneuvers, trying out the technical perfection of the dive-bomber.

Perfection in flight gratifies him deeply.

He has always been an excellent pilot, the best in the sailing flight school in Westphalia. His skill is rooted in his zealous demand for flawlessness. He always bid for the smoothest gliders and, even during off-duty hours, when his comrades relaxed and had fun, he relentlessly drove the mechanics to keep his sailplane in top flying condition. He struggled fiercely to attain his first goal: to become a pilot.

The ashen haziness suspended over the horizon takes him back to those pristine days, the bitter days when the Allied victory in 1918 cut off the wings he was starting to grow; then, the subjugation of Germany and the ban imposed on it to manufacture military aircraft occurred. Nevertheless, he and his classmates –- all young and eager to fly – resorted to sailplanes to glide through the air in powerless flight, scattering their love and dedication to the art of flying all over the barren steppes of Börkenlerger, and the red rooftops of Westterholt. They built, maintained, cracked up, and repaired the sleek vessels in which they began to discover the secrets known only to the eagles soaring at those heights. Subsequently, although he hated it, he joined the military as the only means to become part of the Air Force, whenever there was a Luftwaffe again.

Suddenly he realizes only six years have elapsed since the coveted opportunity materialized. *"When was it, March, April, 1933?"*

In hiding, behind the backs of their British, French, and American guardians, the Luftwaffe began to sprout again through the pilots who survived the war, and the novices that sprung from all over the untamed *Vaterland.*

Although his face was not so young anymore, the fresh features of Galland, Dittmar, Opitz, Reitsch, Spate, and his other comrades-in-arms, rise up in his mind. They secretly had trained in Italy to become proud air warriors.

Finally, real war arrived in the middle of November, 1936. Disguised with the garb of tourists over the Nibelung coat of mail that wrapped their hearts, 370 volunteer German pilots sailed from Hamburg to Spain to constitute the Condor Legion. Under the command of General Hugo Sperrie and with Wolfram von Richthofen as their chief of staff, they were to serve Francisco Franco during the Civil War. Spain would be the warfare laboratory where they were to test their latest combat weapons against weakening Republican Forces and a defenseless civilian population, earning them distinctions and promotions

Against the hazy horizon, Max envisions the unforgettable gilded fields of the Vitoria Base, relishes in the remembrance of the warm lips of the Spaniard women, and experiences again the excitement of the air battles where he attained 38 certified kills. Almost as many as those of Werner Mölder, the top-notch German ace. He had rated his Messerschmitt Bf-109b against Russian

Polikarpov I-16 fighters, fine aircraft flown so skillfully by Soviet volunteers and Spanish Republican pilots, that German pilots were no match for them when steering their older Heinkel He 51s.

He learned to disregard the value of human life flying strafing missions in his Henschel Hs *123*. His orders were to back up Franco's Nationalistic troops from the air while they pushed on to Santander. He simply had to shut off his emotions and press the trigger on the control stick. The bullets spewed by his machine guns decimated the faceless bodies scurrying on the ground. To develop and improve the blitzkrieg, he perfected air tactics that earned him the Iron Cross. With each new experience he earned even more medals to enliven his gray Falangist uniform.

"Maybe that is really why I am being sent to a combat command."

Although those past experiences were foggy in his memory, he has to admit that, in the estimation of the Ministry, he is a hero; a role model for novice pilots. His assignment is justified after all. *"But I'll be damned if that is a comforting thought!"*

He glances at his watch and realizes he has been in the air longer than his tight schedule allows. He has to land to face his problems.

"I have but one problem! That lunatic whose only notion is waging war!"

In a fit of anger he steers toward the strafing training area, pulls a small yellow lever deploying the spoilers, and shoves the stick forward slanting the Stuka in a vertical dive. Seconds later, over the drone of the engine and the scream of rushing air, he hears a loud howling coming from the left strut of the landing gear. It is a small propeller-driven siren devised as a psychological weapon. That dreadful shriek will announce the lethal presence of the Stukas over the enemy lines.

The ground crew assigned to set up targets on their pedestals hears the *"Trombone of Jericho,"* as the siren has been nicknamed by the Stuka pilots; but not having shooting drills scheduled for that afternoon, they go on about their tasks until the rumbling of the double MG 17 7.9 mm. machine guns scatter them to scramble for the safety of the steel-sheltered hideouts.

His rigid right fist folds around the command stick in an iron grip. As in Spain, his eyes become components of the electronic sights that aim the weapons at the target. His thumb presses the red button and the aircraft shudders as it fires the double machine guns, just as he trembles with rage.

The scene at the firing range field is bedlam.

Max levels out the Stuka. Having spent his fury, he steers toward the airfield and, reluctantly, takes the microphone to call the control tower to conjoin with the other world and the slime that saturates it.

Chapter 4 – Death Stalks

Autumn starts extremely humid. The sky has been overcast since early afternoon and a persistent drizzle makes the Berlin cobbled streets slippery. Max grips the steering wheel firmly feeling every bump in the boulevard. This makes him proud and confident. Few people in Germany own a Mercedes 540 Sport Roadster like his, with its handmade leather and hardwood interiors. It has a souped-up, eight-cylinder 225-hp engine, individual suspension coupled to torque shafts set on pneumatic shock absorbers, and a hydraulic-assisted steering mechanism of his own design. This coupe is the result of his inventive shrewdness, backed by an affluent bank account. Money makes everything possible.

He observes people running through the rain, skipping over puddles to catch their collective motorcars, but he does not pity them. Most of them are content with earning a meager salary that barely supports their trivial lives. They are the sheep induced by the political rants of the Führer into believing they are the Aryan master race, destined to rule the world some day.

"Imbeciles! A superior race would be made up of people like us, who are creating an industrial empire to give you well-paid jobs and better living conditions."

Connecting these thoughts to the problem of war, once again reaches the same conclusion: none of his manufacturing plants can be converted into wartime production factories. Who will want refrigerators, stoves, water heaters, or electric fans, in the middle of a war? What would they manufacture that could be used in war? There is the possibility of stamping metal sheet to build aircraft fuselages or truck or tank bodies, but that would require a conversion of their plants at an out-of-proportion cost. War means disaster for him. It must be prevented.

Although sunk deep in thought, he drives carefully. Approaching the Hafenplatz, he slows down, looks in both directions of the boulevard and, although his view is distorted by the rain spattering on the windshield, he makes out the headlights of a heavy vehicle coming directly at him. His first reaction is to brake, but he notices that the truck, obviously out of control, is about to ram his auto. Shifting down in gear, he floors the accelerator but the rear tires skid on the muddy surface producing only partial traction. His Mercedes is hit on the right rear fender and spins around twice before coming to rest on the promenade of the plaza. The hefty truck swerves to the left and collides head-on with a lamppost, which comes crashing down.

Max is stunned. His head smashed the side window, but the cap he wears softened the impact. Peering outside, he sees a man running away from the truck to disappear in the rain.

Getting out of the car, he moves aside the onlookers gathering around the truck and approaches the wreck on the left side.

"This soldier reeks of gin," says a corpulent man peeking inside the cab of the truck.

"Is he hurt?" Max asks.

"I would say he is dead," the man says, and noticing the insignia Max wears on his trench coat he asks, "Are you all right, *Herr Oberst*?"

"Yes, I think so."

"Well, you were fortunate. These brutes accelerated as if they had wanted to run you over intentionally."

"They? Then, there was another man!"

"Oh, yes. Another soldier. I saw him run away. He also seemed to be hurt."

"What happened here?" asks a policeman, elbowing his way through the crowd…

Chapter 5 – The Fallen Idol

In spite of her anxiety, upon opening the front door of the stately mansion, Freda Leber is a vision of sensuality in her night apparel.

"What took you so long, *lieben*? You had me worried!"

"I was involved in an accident. Nothing serious. Did my father arrive?" he asks, handing his trench coat and his kepi to Johan, the elderly butler.

"Your temple, Max! You are bleeding!"

"Tell me, did you find my father?"

"He waits for you in the library," she answers, and then asks the butler, "Do you have a medicine cabinet, Johan?"

"Yes, Madam."

"I will get something to dress that gash," she tells Max, who is already walking toward the library door.

Lifting his tired eyes from the finance report he reads sitting at the massive Edwardian desk, Herr Gustav Görzten asks his son as he enters: "What is so urgent that you had me dragged over here in the middle of the night?"

"I have been transferred to Reichenau to take command of a combat group," Max says, dropping heavily onto the overstuffed sofa.

"I know, Freda told me," Herr Görzten says, and adjusting his glasses on his nose, he notices Max bleeding wound. "There is blood on your temple."

"A stupid drunkard rammed my car at the Hafenplatz." Staring beyond the crystal chandelier that illuminates the library, he muses. "I assume that my transfer is a ploy. Somebody wants me away from Berlin."

Herr Görzten shuts the binder he holds in his hands and, annoyed, gets up from the desk to move swiftly, despite his seventy-six years, revealing the abundant stamina stored in his lean body. Walking the length of the room, he faces his son to scold him as if he were still a child.

"If this is true, you have no one to blame but yourself!" he states. "Tell me, how many people know about your plans to depose Hitler?" The glance in his eyes is fiery.

"Only those people who collaborate with me."

"What about Freda? Do you think she will not turn you in, just because she is your lover?"

"Father!"

"*Dummkopf!*" Herr Görzten exclaims in anger. "You have never grown up enough to become a sensible man!"

Getting up to walk away from his father, Max shouts back, "If we do not act at once and with determination, we shall be ruined!"

Freda enters the library, bringing iodine and bandages. "Allow me to dress your wound."

"Forget my wound!" he snaps. "Give us some cognac."

Herr Görzten wants to add something but he holds back, distrustful of Freda.

Max stands by the window watching the storm brewing over the city. Lightning intermittently illuminates his face. At length, he speaks. "Germany is plagued by too many insignificant political parties engaged in constant bickering. Nothing can be expected from them. We have to behead the enemy. Hitler must be removed!"

"With the Nazi Party in power, what do we gain by changing the leader?" his father asks, taking the goblet Freda offers him.

"No other Nazi could resist the impugnation of a conjoin opposition."

"Only that the opposition is made of one per cent of the eighty million Germans who subscribe to National Socialism. You just said it!" Herr Görzten retorts, adding: "In your opinion, who from the opposition could instantly take control over eighty million minds that think differently?"

"A coalition government!"

"And you assume that a coalition government could survive without the economic support of the Krupps, the Thyssens or the Kindorffs, and other industrialists who have increased their profits tenfold by manufacturing weapons for Hitler? Who do you think sustains his regime?"

Max remains silent, thinking.

Watching both, Freda addresses Herr Görzten. "There is one thing that maybe you have to take into consideration, sir," she says softly in her full throaty voice. "The contacts Max has established with the opposition leaders, including notable officers in the Wermacht, make him a key figure in the future of Germany. He can become Economy and Commerce Minister, for instance, and you would be the first to profit from that."

Herr Görzten regards her intently. Her voice sounds convincing, but he still does not trust her. Her features, very much those of a Middle Eastern princess, reveal limitless ambition and a yearning to see herself showered with the treasures that only abundant riches could provide. Her aspirations can either keep her faithful to his son, or compel her to betray him.

"Think of the stature Max would acquire if he were credited with eliminating the Führer."

"I can imagine it, and understand its importance, but that does not mean Max must announce his intentions publicly," then, turning to his son asks him sagely: "What will you do now, away from Berlin?"

"I am hungry. I have not eaten since noon."

"Dinner must be ready. I will see about it," Freda offers, leaving the room.

Once they are alone, Max walks toward his father and almost whispers, "As you will see, there are certain things I keep to myself. I have had an emergency plan ready for months, known only to me and to the man who will carry it out. Tomorrow, the Führer will appear publicly for the last time!"

"What do you mean?"

"A bomb will send him to hell when he visits the aircraft assembly plant. It is a risky plan, but very simple. You know the perpetrator, Otto Halem, the chancellery mechanic who has worked on my cars. The imbecile is willing to become a martyr for the Vaterland. If he is found out, he will commit suicide."

"That man is almost retarded!" Herr Görzten splutters. What will happen if he cowers, or if he panics and backs out?"

"There is where the risk lies. The Gestapo would make him denounce me, but by then, we would be in power."

Dejected, Herr Görzten removes his lenses to rub his face. When he speaks again, there is sadness rather than anger in his voice. "Two serious flaws spoil your personality, my son. One of them is possibly caused by a belief I embedded in your brain – that money is almighty. The other evolves from wealth itself: you are incorrigibly egocentric. These two blemishes instill in you a sense of hollow heroism that will destroy you. Actually, you do not hate Hitler – you love yourself too much. You want to eliminate him not for the sake of our country, nor for our own economic gain, but to take his place in the eyes of the world, even if you have to bear the consequences."

"That is not true, Father!" Max protests.

"You dare to contradict me?" Herr Görzten asks bitingly. "There is an incident that you have obviously forgotten. When you were a child I was striving to create a position for our family, working my life away in a small shop manufacturing galvanized tin buckets and iceboxes. Being my only son, I wanted you to establish important

21

connections that would benefit you when you grew up, so I sent you to a school favored by wealthy families, some of them close to Kaiser Wilhelm. Your mother, a simple, faint-hearted woman, opposed this idea. Maybe if I had listened to her, you would be different today. Do you remember what happened?"

"What the devil is he talking about?"

"You were expelled from that school!" continues Herr Görzten. "To prove that you were, if not the wealthiest, then at least the bravest of all the pupils, you answered to a reproach the Headmaster made to you, by throwing an inkwell at his face!" He stares hard at Max. "Is that what you intend to do now? Throw an inkwell to the face of the Führer so that the world knows you exist?"

Max restrains himself. His father may be right, but he hates to admit it. "I will not permit his madness to wreak havoc on my future. I will kill him personally before that happens."

The old gentleman regards Max with a brief gleam of pride in his eyes. "If you called me to approve your plan, you wasted my time. However, I have to admit one thing: misguided as you may be, you are a brave man, my son. If you go to war, I know you will come back a hero. If, however, your attempt on the life of Hitler succeeds, every German, including myself, will be in debt to you."

Taking his report from the desk, Herr Görzten puts it away in a briefcase. Before leaving, he looks one last time at his son and says, "Anyway, may God bless you, son!" Then the door to the library closes softly behind him.

Rooted to the center of the room, Max holds back for a few seconds and then yells at the door in rage, *"Feigling!* You are as cowardly as everybody else!" And staggers to the sofa, where he collapses with a vacant gaze in his eyes.

"Is he right?" he wonders, feeling his stomach tighten. *"What will happen if Hitler dies tomorrow? I would have to wield my authority over men of recognized experience and prestige. What if I am relegated to a minor position? And what if the attempt fails? Maybe it would be better to leave things as they are now. As a commanding officer, I would be promoted quickly; seniority would easily lead me to the Ministry of the Air. Should I call off the attempt? What should I do?"*

Freda re-enters the room and observes him quietly. He is too overwrought to think clearly. She has to stir his senses, or change his mood, to pull him out of his dazed condition. Once relaxed, he will be able to climb back on his pedestal.

Going to the record player built into the bookcase, she carefully selects a record. Mozart affects him, but he needs the intensity of Beethoven to stimulate him. From several hidden speakers, the library is flooded with music spirited enough to beguile his senses and create a diversion.

She checks her make-up on the burnished surface of a gold-plated aeronautical diploma hanging on the wall. Her fingers slide along her soft black hair falling over her bare shoulders and then they smooth her soirée gown along her slender waist and enticing hips.

Sauntering in counterpoint to the music she stands before Max and, moving with feline grace, performs a slow and highly erotic dance. Without interrupting her movements, she slips off her shoes. The magic embedded in the Persian carpet permeates her bare feet causing her oscillations to expand in breadth.

Initially, she dances before a man deprived of feelings and physical sensations. His gaze is upon her but fixed, unseeing. However, as her gyrations deepen, his eyes begin to follow her movements, beholding her breast firm within the vermeil silk, and reveling in the alluring cadence of her oval hips and the smoothness of her limbs, encased in the tight dress. He finds in her hazel eyes a lascivious glitter that captivates him and finally arouses his desire.

Her womanly instinct tells her she is being successful in titillating his libido, but not enough. Her left hand pulls the zipper on the back of her dress and, arching her shoulders, she frees her breast from her strapless brassiere allowing her gown to slip down to the carpet, revealing her exquisite figure.

Max swallows the cognac in one gulp. Although unemotional, he is easily seduced by passion when it is so tangible. The unusual dance is a fervent offering that excites him more than the sensuality emanating from the alluring flesh. The laced garter and dark silk stockings make her thighs look whiter and more appealing. The nude breasts, lithe but firm, are crowned by dark coral nipples rising in defiant erection. Her eyes, shaded by lashes that fall under the weight of their own lushness, and her full lips parting to bare clenched teeth, create a mounting sexual desire that evokes in his mind distant memories, filtered by the haze of time of a long-forgotten scene akin to the one he watches now....

Through the keyhole to the door of her room, Helga, the youngest chambermaid of the household, is seen bathing in a tin tub. She is slowly rubbing lather on her small breasts, on her belly and between her thighs, a portion of her body that conceals a secret that, although unknown to Max, sets off in his brain a lustful craving that distends his manhood with the vigor of his thirteen years. As he becomes overestimulated his heart throbs in his temples and, when he experiences the thrilling surges of a maiden ejaculation, suddenly feels on his back the violent blows of a metallic cane held by his mother, and hears her shriek cries: "Schwein, schwein!" The strikes hit him repeatedly while her shouting pieces his eardrums, and his seed of life spurts away for the first time in his life.

Abruptly, a groan cuts off her mother's screams and an agonizing panting supersedes them. Her wrinkled face grows stiff and pale, then blue, and finally static and cold. When he looks up, he has Helda, the young maid, before his eyes half covered by an old towel, giving out terrified screams that resound through the house....

Arousing from his reverie, Max opens his eyelids to find in front of him a nude Valkyrie pouring out the liquor of her sensuality for him, inviting him to wander off with her into the limitless pleasure of all the senses, to have him die as a hero scorched in the ember of her burning passion. He pounces on her and, with his usual abruptness, becomes quickly spent, remaining ready ready to rest in order to function intellectually, unaware that, as a man, he has failed once more in satisfying a woman.

Although her femininity has been betrayed again, Freda buries her resentment in the same dark nook where she keeps her previous frustrations. Dejected, she covers Max with a fur mantle and leaves him asleep on the sofa...

Chapter 6 – The Elusive Target

The telephone rings several times before Max gets up drowsily from the sofa to go to the desk.

"Yes?"

"Max?"

"Yes."

"Shultz-Hoysen here. Listen, I have contradicting information about your assignment. The Ministry does want you at Reichenau, but my contact in the Gestapo told me they received orders from high above to eliminate you... in the shortest term."

"What?" This news yanks away his last veil of slumber

"The order was issued yesterday. You have two options: leave for Reichenau immediately, where perhaps you will be secure, or flee from here. In about three hours, I can send you enough currency and a forged passport. Considering that your best alternative is to seek Russian guardianship, I already advised our contacts in Hungary and Rumania to help you across the border. In Odessa, important Communist Party members will welcome you. *Glück*, Max."

"Wait, Har. Do you know when exactly was this order issued,?"

"According to our contact, around four-thirty yesterday."

"Har, you have photos of my wife in my dossier, correct?"

"Yes."

"Have another passport made for her and send them both to my office. I must follow my daily routine to avert suspicion, but I will leave as soon as everything is settled."

"It would be easier if you went by yourself."

"I know. This is just another precaution."

"I will be in touch. *Glück*, Max."

"*Danke, Har. Lebewohl!*"

Deep in thought, Max replaces the receiver and looks at his wristwatch, 5:30. He has enough time to bathe, have breakfast, and plan an alternate escape before he is due at the office.

Brushing soap on his left cheek, he notices the bruise on his temple and muses on the incidents of the previous day. The Gestapo received the order to assassinate him at half-past four, and the traffic accident was staged at seven-fifteen. They move quickly, no doubt, but they are being too obvious. Many prominent men have died recently in all sorts of accidents, especially high-ranking Army officers who openly opposed the Nazi regime. It was logical. If the Nazis carried out arrests or executions on alleged charges of treason or sedition, they would simply be feeding martyrs to the opposition fire.

What he needed now was to predict how and when they would make another attempt on his life. To have another go was an easy task for them; however, even if they had been able to discover some of his activities they cannot guess the extent of his actions, regardless of his father's opinion. He has cohorts in all the parties willing to help him. How could the Gestapo suppose, for instance, that having fought against the communists in Spain, the German Communists were helping him escape their wrath? Such were the pledges he had made the dumb bastards! Nevertheless, fleeing to Russia is the least attractive of his options.

However, everything can change during the course of that day, when Halem sends the Small Corporal to hell. Regardless of his perilous situation, he feels confident.

Johan, the butler, approaches the terrace table with a glass of prune juice and the *Berliner Zeitung*, and leaves to fetch the rest of the breakfast service.

Opening the newspaper, Max finds a brief article at the bottom of the front page, merely a few remarks under the headline: Fire in the Automobile Department of the Chancellery. Blame for the blaze was placed on mechanic Otto Halem who, carelessly, had been smoking while fueling an automobile. The blast had killed him instantly. The vehicle was slightly damaged.

This information, however scanty, was significant. He knows Otto Halem suffered from emphysema and did not smoke. His plot to assassinate Hitler had been found out!

He remains stunned for a few seconds, feeling an increasing throbbing in his neck. The imbecile had failed! Another hope lost. The prospect of immediate triumph vanished. What else can he do? For instance, he has enough clout to be introduced to the Chancellery and into the private office of the Führer. He can still put a bullet between his eyes, but throwing an inkwell directly at his face would be suicidal. He wants glory, but only if it is associated with power, not as an epitaph for his tombstone.

Angrily, he sweeps the silver and crystal service from the table and swears endlessly, damning the man who ruins his life. Then, suddenly, emerging from the frenzy that threatens his sanity, he remembers another fact in the article that jumped out at him. Picking up the newspaper, he rereads: At fifteen minutes past four, the explosion rocked —-

"No! That is not possible!"

At 7:35 am, the Administrative Building in the Aircraft Assembly Plant is still vacant. In the anteroom to his office, Max goes to the desk of his secretary, opens the lower drawer and finds an earphone connected to a remote line. Although he had anticipated the possibility of a betrayal, this reality causes him a bitterness that angers him more than the exposed disloyalty. He does not have to trace the earphone wire to know it is connected to his private line.

The voice of Freda comes through the office intercom. *"Herr Oberst,* a messenger with a personal communiqué for you, is here."

"Send him in."

An orderly from the Air Ministry comes into his office and salutes crisply, extending an envelope. "From Major Shultz-Hoysen, *Herr Oberst!"*

Taking it, Max says dryly, *"Danke.* That will be all, Soldier."

The messenger salutes and marches back to the door. Max feels the envelope, and pushes the intercom button: *"Leutnant* Leber, I want no interruptions until my successor arrives."

"Ja doch, Herr Oberst!"

Max rips open the envelope and dumps its contents on the desktop. Two Swiss passports catch his attention. He opens one and finds his portrait duly stamped and, under it, his fake name: Max Wolff. In the other passport, the picture of his wife is identified as Ingrid Wolff. Leafing through the documents, he finds visas for most of the European countries and seals of entry and departure on various dates. They are perfect. Nobody would question their authenticity.

Also included in the packet is the metallic Gestapo seal used to authorize documents. There is stationery from several ministries signed by high ranking officers, five thousand Swiss francs in different denominations, and a document containing precise instructions to get him to Russia, according to the wishes of the German Communist Party.

He swings his chair around and looks toward the second large hangar where a hefty *Junkers 82 trimotor* is parked. Two officers loaf under its left wing. Its pilots, he guesses, and turns back to the desk to read the instruction sheet.

"Herr Oberst, a commission from the Air Ministry is here to see you," Freda announces over the intercom, startling him. He did not expect them so early.

"Bitte, show the gentlemen in, *Leutnant,"* he says, putting the passports and the rest of the items in a drawer.

The official vehicle stops by the trimotor and an orderly hastens to assist Freda down.

One of the pilots approaches Max. "Karl Halder, at your orders, *Herr Oberst*!" he salutes, and turns to the waiting mechanics. "Place the baggage on board!"

"Wait, Hauptmann Halder," Max says. "What is your estimated flying time to Reichenau?"

"It will be a one hour plus thirty-five minutes flight, *Herr Oberst*."

"Humm, it is almost five now. I do not want to arrive after dark." Max sees a group of mechanics pushing a twin-engine *Junkers 88* light bomber into the hangar, and calls the man in charge. "*Sargeant*, is that airplane ready to fly?"

"*Jawohl, Herr Oberst*. You flew it last week,"

"Is it fueled?"

"*Jawohl, Herr Oberst*, full tanks."

Turning to the pilot, Max says, "Hauptmann Halder, we will take that airplane and reduce flying time by half. Dismiss your copilot and have my baggage placed in the bomber."

Halder hesitates for a split second, but immediately replies: "*Ja doch, Herr Oberst*!"

As soon as the pilot moves away, Freda asks. "Why did you switch airplanes, Max?"

"Hostilities are about to break out. I would not want to risk your beautiful neck if we attract anti-aircraft fire from a nervous gunman."

"Risk my – but I am not going with you. We would violate regulations; furthermore, I do not have my baggage. I will join you as soon as I receive clearance from Personnel Command."

"I believe my rank allows me a few privileges," Max smiles, "such as taking the aircraft best suited to my needs, and the personnel I cannot do without. Remember, I am going to the battlefield and this may be the last night I have to enjoy your delightful company."

"But, Max...."

"Come, come. If you are worried about clothes, I think we will be able to buy all you need before war breaks out."

"We may leave when you give the order, *Herr Oberst*," Halder says from a discreet distance.

"Climb aboard, *Fräulein* Leber," Max says, helping her through the hatchway.

Max looks through the aircraft storm window. The idea that he might be seeing Berlin for the last time bothers him. He turns to

Halder, who is flying as copilot, and pointing at the control yoke, says. "Take over, Hauptmann. Climb 200 meters per minute and level out at three thousand."

He looks down again at the suburbs of the city that rapidly disappear under the evening haze, and ponders. He wants to be certain his next action will be justified, so he reviews all the events that occurred over the past twenty-four hours.

He feels the airplane level out and looks at the altimeter. They are at exactly three thousand meters above sea level. Taking a round-faced flight computer, he calculates the remaining flying time according to their true airspeed: thirty-five minutes. Then, out of the corner of his eye, he looks at Halder. He is young; flies with extreme ability, and his alert features reveal a keen intelligence. He should understand.

"Hauptmann Halder, do you have a family?"

The unexpected question cajoles the pilot. "*Jawohl, Herr Oberst*! A boy and a girl!"

"You are a fortunate man, I do not have children. Are you happy with your wife?"

"Very much so, *Herr Oberst*. She is a wonderful woman."

Max regards the young man, who is beaming. "Tell me, Halder. What would you do if you knew today was the day marked for your death?"

Halder thinks he heard wrong. "I... do not understand, sir."

"A courier in a motorcycle came to the flight line this afternoon. Did he bring a package for me?"

The young man blushes. "I... promised not to tell you, *Herr Oberst*. The courier said it was a present from the Air Ministry and I was supposed to give it to you upon arrival at Reichenau."

"A farewell gift?"

"Yes, precisely!"

"That package, Hauptmann Halder, contains a bomb activated by an aneroid barometer, similar to those in our altimeters. Upon reaching a certain altitude, we were going to be blown out of the sky. Auspiciously it remained in the trimotor."

Gaping, Halder stares at Max. "A bomb! But, why, sir?"

"To eliminate me. You and your copilot were going to be mercilessly expended, like many other young men will be when war frenzy breaks out. Do you understand that?"

Halder is so bewildered he has allowed the aircraft to deviate thirty degrees from its course. He looks at the gyrocompass, corrects his bearing, and asks in a thin voice, "Are you with the Opposition, *Herr Oberst*?"

"Not exactly, but I do think we should not start a world war."

Halder continues to fly like a robot.

"I am certain that, before this happened, you never questioned the orders you received from your superiors But tell me, how do you feel about it now?"

"I... do not know, *Herr Oberst*. I sincerely do not know."

"We flew over the Oder River two minutes ago. This is a well-traveled area. If you parachuted out, how soon would you get back to Berlin?"

The pilot considers the question, looks at the inquiring face, and smiles. "I would get lost in the woods, *Herr Oberst*, especially at night. I would have to wait until daylight to get my bearings."

Max looks away nodding. He wants to believe Halder is being spontaneous and loyal. "I wish you a safe landing, Hauptmann Halder."

"*Danke Schön*, sir." Halder says, already sliding over his shoulders the straps of the parachute he sits on.

Max moves the stabilizer wheel forward to make the airplane nose heavy, before engaging the two-axis autopilot that holds the course and altitude steady. Unbuckling his safety belt, he leaves his seat. "I will meet you back there," he says, going toward the bomb bay in the ventral cabin.

Freda, who sits by the central machine gun position, is startled by the unexpected appearance of Max in the ventral cabin. "Is something wrong?"

"Nothing, *liebling*. You look frightened, why?"

"I... I had never flown like this."

"I am sorry I could not extend to you the comforts of the trimotor."

Her distress increases when she sees Halder exiting the cockpit. "What is happening, Max?"

"Nothing, relax. Hauptmann Halder has decided to go back to Berlin," he says, and goes to the side-port sliding hatch, where Halder now stands. "Is your parachute in good order, Hauptmann?"

"*Jawohl, Herr Oberst*."

Max turns the lock and slides the hatch open. The wind, combined with the roar of the engines, is deafening. The pressure differential created by the slipstream sucks on the hatch opening, pulling toward the void. Max braces himself on the bulkhead.

Halder moves to the opening and looks into the expectant eyes. "*Glück, Herr Oberst!*"

Max pats him on the shoulder.

The young man holds onto the hatch frame and dives into space.

"His parachute opened all right!" Freda says, peering through the side window. "Why did he jump, Max?"

"Because I do not want anyone to know where I am going."

"Are we not going to Reichenau?"

"Have you forgotten I told my wife I would meet her today or tomorrow in Graz?"

"I did not know that, Max!"

"No? You did not know either about my plan to blow up the Führer at the assembly plant? Then, what use did you have for the earphone connected to my private line, if not to listen in on my conversations?"

Freda opens her eyes in shock. Her throat closes. Only her left hand opens and closes spasmodically.

"I found it this morning in your desk, before you came to work."

"It was the Gestapo, Max!" she finally cries out. "They hold my parents hostage. Please understand, Max. We are Jewish!"

"You are Jewish! *Um Himmels Willen!* When did you start spying on me for the Gestapo?"

"Since the *Crystal Night*, last November, when Göbbels unleashed his campaign against the Jews. My parents and I were arrested. It was horrible, Max, I swear! When the Gestapo agents found out I worked for you, they threatened to kill my parents if I did not keep them informed of all your activities. They already suspected you, Max. I was released, but I had to report immediately any outstanding action on your part."

"Ten months!" During those ten months he had crusaded to drive a wedge into the Nazi Party. In person, by mail, and by telephone, he had been in touch with various opposition groups. Now he understands why his plans failed all the time. "*How many good Germans are going to die, or have already died, to preserve the lives of two miserable old Jews?* And his plans, his hopes, his future? When he grasps the extent of the damage her betrayal has caused, he loses control.

"It was a trap! All of it feigned! Your love, your loyalty, your dedication, your moans in bed! A whore from the Postdammer Platz would have been more faithful!"

His solid fist strikes her cheek and her head hits and bounces off the butt of the machine gun. Spitting blood through her broken lips,

Freda lashes out with accumulated hate, "Of course everything was feigned! As a man, you are worthless! You could never earn the respect or loyalty of a woman, much less her love!"

Her scorn bites deeply into his pride. Leaping on her like a wounded beast, his blows pound her flesh and shatter bone until she loses consciousness. Still enraged, he drags her to the edge of the open hatch and shoves her out into the void.

Clutching the hatch frame, he gapes at her figure becoming smaller as she whirls in space. Then, exhausted, he slides the hatch shut.

Once back at the controls, he plots a new course on the navigation chart, disconnects the autopilot, and turns the Junkers to a heading of 182 degrees. In two hours, flying mostly over Czechoslovakia, he will arrive in Graz, Austria.

Chapter 7 – Exodus

The cold gin settles his upset stomach. At this time of night, there are no more commercial flights and the small bar at Graz airport is empty except for Max, who sits on one of the bar stools, dressed in civilian clothes.

The fat barman twists his Prussian mustache, wishing his customer would leave. Looking at him over as he wipes a glass, he asks, "Would you want another drink, Herr?

"*Nein, danke.*"

"I will be closing the bar in ten minutes."

"All right, give me a last one," Max replies, annoyed. He called his wife Olga when he arrived, almost an hour ago, but she has not arrived to pick him up.

There is movement on the platform deck; the fuel truck is driving away from the Junkers after filling its tanks. Max figures that, with six hours worth of fuel on board, he can easily reach Denmark, Sweden, the Middle East, or Africa, and from there South America. He can go anywhere, except back to Germany. Someday, however, he will return to assume a high position in a new regime when the Nazis are overturned, or, if they force Germany into total war, they will be defeated and the opportunity to rule and rebuild will come to those who had opposed Hitler.

The two hundred and fifty thousand American dollars he was able to obtain from his ready assets give him a feeling of solid confidence in the future. To that sum, he can add the amounts he has regularly deposited in the personal account of his wife, which must tally up a considerable balance by now. First thing in the morning, they will go to her bank to liquidate all of her assets.

Through the panoramic window that opens toward the ramp, he watches the fuel truck driver as he strides toward the passenger terminal with the fuel ticket. Suddenly, two military vehicles appear from the north side of the ramp and grind to a halt by the propellers of the Junkers. A dozen Austrian troops jump from the trucks and surround the bomber.

Max recognizes the black uniform of the commanding officer as belonging to an SS captain. His first impulse is to flee. Obviously, the Gestapo has been advised over the aeronautical communications network about his escape. However, his reflection in the mirror behind the counter of the bar eases his apprehension. The Nazis will be looking for a Luftwaffe colonel, not for Max Wolff, the Swiss merchant dressed in civilian clothes, sitting at the bar waiting patiently for his wife to pick him up.

He takes a drink of gin to restrain his anxiety and waits for the fuel attendant, all the while trying to figure how to evade the Nazis.

"It took one thousand, four hundred and fifty liters, sir. That will be four hundred and eighty francs, Swiss," the old fuel man tells him.

Max places a generous tip on the counter, "Give this man a drink," he tells the bartender. "I will be back with the money in a moment."

Both the attendant and the barman beam gratefully. Watching the SS officer, Max hopes he will leave only a few soldiers guarding the Junkers. Maybe he will find some way to trick them.

"Did you find anything in there?" The gaunt Gestapo captain asks his men, poking his head inside the aircraft hatch.

"There is no one on board, Herr Hauptmann, but there are blood stains on the floor, and three suitcases."

"Bring them down," the captain orders and turns to the sergeant that waits by his side. "Albrecht, take five men and watch the airplane from a discreet distance. If that colonel we look for shows up, arrest him and take him to Major Innes in the Command Post."

"*Jawohl, Herr Hauptmann!*"

When Max sees the soldiers carry away his suitcases, he feels the floor sink under his feet. One of the bags contains his two hundred and fifty thousand dollars. However, there is no time to mourn over that fact, because the SS officer is heading toward the terminal. Maybe he has his description and, anyway, without the money he cannot use the aircraft any further.

Walking out of the bar, he bumps into his wife.

"Max! Is it really you in… "

"Shut up and act naturally," he whispers in her ear, pretending to kiss her. "If anyone asks, I am Max Wolff, a Swiss merchant, and you are my wife, Ingrid."

"But, Max...."

"Shut up and walk!" He says, taking her arm to stroll along the terminal corridor. Two more SS officers enter from the street through the main door. Max chats with her as they pass among the Nazis, who pay little attention to the civilian couple.

Once outside the building he sees the Duesenberg his wife drives, parked by the curb. He opens the passenger door for her, walks around to sit behind the steering wheel and, seconds later, the powerful *SL* convertible disappears into the night.

The first light of dawn hurts his eyes, and his upset stomach feels worse. Driving from Graz to the Swiss border town of Fledkirch, along a narrow winding road in nine straight hours, has proved to be exhausting for Max and his wife. Nevertheless, they have crossed the border safely and are now having breakfast at the open terrace of a café in Sarganz, one step away from *Lucerne, Zurich,* or *Bern,* three doors open into the world.

Still excited about what she considers a romantic escapade, Olga raises her smiling violet eyes from her cup of tea to look across the table at her husband. "You know, *lieber* Max, I never imagined you were the audacious kind of man. I like you better this way, you know? Now that we are in Switzerland, away from the thousand-and-one perils I have envisioned, can you tell me what is happening? All this is very arousing, but illogical. It does not befit your austere personality."

"Shut up, I am thinking!"

"How rude and also unbecoming of you, Max! What are you up to? You dragged me away from the reception given by Countess Ziegler, in this soirée gown, and then abducted me like a desperate lover. And why did we run away from those Gestapo agents who were waiting in my house?"

Max remains silent, trying to concentrate.

"How long will we be staying in Switzerland? I must buy some clothes in Bern and, from what I gather, you will also need a wardrobe. You know what? I think this is the first time I have ever seen you wearing civilian clothes. My, you look odd. Have you resigned from the Luftwaffe?" she asks, laughing playfully.

"What are you laughing at?"

"At how bizarre you look out of your elegant uniform. Come on, *lieber,* finish your breakfast. I feel too uncomfortable in this evening dress, with all this junk jewelry on me. People must think I fled from the Venetian Carnival."

"Your jewelry!" he exclaims, looking at her heavy necklace and bracelets. "How much are they worth?"

"These? These are worthless, *lieber,*" she laughs. "The genuine set is worth half a million marks, but with the many robberies we have had in Graz lately, nobody risks wearing the authentic ones, not even to a celebration such as Countess Ziegler offered!"

Overwrought, he unleashes his resentment on her. "Only one thing surpasses your beauty, Olga. That is your stupidity!"

"Max! What is the matter with you?"

"You want to know what is happening? All right! The Gestapo is out to assassinate me! We cannot go back to Germany, or to Austria. We have to flee as far as the five thousand Swiss francs I have in my pocket will take us!"

"But why, Max? What have you done?"

"I attempted to kill Hitler!"

"Oh, Max!"

"Let us go."

"Go where, Max?"

"We shall see, come on!"

"No, Max, wait. I will not go with you!"

"What!"

"I will not be subjected to the consequences of your frenzy."

"Do not act like an idiot! You have to come with me. You are my wife! The Gestapo will arrest you to find out where I am!"

"Only I will not know where you are. Besides, I am an Austrian Baroness. Those gorillas will not dare to bother me!"

"Maybe they will not at this time, but as soon as they have more power, they certainly will, and I do not even want to think about what they will do to you."

"And what is it you want to do? Drag me into poverty? What can we do with a paltry five thousand francs?"

"We will go somewhere safe, to South America maybe. You have credit in Bern. We will transfer funds from your accounts in Graz and, if we cannot do it, we shall embezzle, cheat, or do whatever it takes to obtain enough money. Do you understand me?"

"*Du Bist Ja verückt!* You are utterly crazy!" she repeats, getting up to run toward her car parked below the terrace, but he moves swiftly around the table and grabs her by an arm.

Struggling, she starts to cry for help when a waiter runs out of the kitchen shouting at the few customers eating breakfast. "The war! The war has started!"

Startled by the alarming shouts, Max and Olga turn around to hear the news. "The radio said it! The Germans are invading Poland!"

Olga goes pale.

Max releases her arm and says dourly, "Now the gorillas have all the power!"

He places a five-franc note on the table, and walks slowly down the steps of the terrace. Sitting at the steering wheel of the Duesenberg, he stretches to open the opposite door and wait.

Olga looks toward the east, toward the blue mountains of the Austrian Tyrol, and her eyes moisten. An unusual feebleness pervades her body and soul; her will, just as her legs, goes numb. Step by step, leaving a trail of sadness on the loose gravel, she walks back to the car.

Max starts the engine and the heavy Duesenberg raises a cloud of dust behind its tires…

Flying in Xibalbá

PART II – Mexico City – September 1939

Chapter 8 – José María "Chema" Ortegón

Chema knows that if he arrives home early, he will not be able to resolve his predicament that evening. So he rather ambles home from work…

…and I wish it were farther away, so I could have more time to think things over…

The sky darkens over the rained rooftops, dimming the green in his eyes already weary by the bustling rabble crowding the sidewalk.

…these people run round and around the same hole like blind roaches that cannot find their way out….

His eyes grow blurry.

…Pérez is right. The women I live with fasten my shadow to this frigging shantytown as if they were iron shackles….

The Peralvillo neighborhood has been his prison since infancy.

…how long have we lived in that hovel…

He and his family have dwelt for eleven years in a street secluded east of the heart of the La Lagunilla marketplace, that some teaser named Mariana Rodríguez del Toro Viuda de Lazarin.

…such a frigging long name for a back alley, only one block long….

An opulent district during the 19th Century Spanish Viceroyalty, Peralvillo was demoted by an excessive influx of refugees who fled the provinces to escape the ravages of the Revolution, and to hold on to the hope of life they were losing.

Chema stops before crossing an intersection. He stiffens and relaxes his leg muscles to loosen them, and looks at the package he holds in his right hand.

…if it had been one peso more expensive, I could not have afforded to buy it….

Raising the eyes, his gaze scans the freestone façades which remind him of the diatribes that Erasmo Torres, his fifth-grade history professor, uttered against the Spanish conquerors. "Those front pieces were designed by illustrious Italian architects," he had said, "but they were carved by native Xaltocan artisans, while their backs were flogged by the whips of their uncouth Hispanic masters…."

…uncouth, what a frigging refined word….

The residences, once stately, have been transformed into human beehives sheltering meager repair shops, and their sidewalks have been crammed with portable stands that turn the streets into motley bazaars where used wares are sold or traded.

...and as a child, I used to think that those buildings were inhabited only by people of royal blood....

Age has enlightened him. He notices that those walls hide fissured columns and monumental stairways with worn-out steps eroded away by human weight and the passing of time. Patios bound by broken down balustrades that seem to smile with the tragic fatalism of toothless elders, as they gaze at clotheslines flapping in the wind multicolored rags, flags depicting destitution.

...what royal blood? There is nothing there but a bunch of pot-bellied kids born from wretched mothers, to grow up playing in dark corridors, splashing soapy puddles and breathing an air that stinks of refried beans, chili, and grime....

Heavy gates and daintily carved doors enclose such depressive settings, that compel one to escape, to run away, but that are so oppressive they sap any fighting spirit left in its inhabitants.

...only we dumb-asses go on living there. We work our asses off all week, and Saturday comes around to find us just as dejected by our many debts. At least, I bring home my paycheck. The really poor bastards are those who are compelled to look for temporary oblivion, spending their salary in cantinas or bars, given that, anyhow, their wages would not have been sufficient to feed their children...

A bony, shaky hand, appears before Chema to take in its palm a two-cent coin he spares.

"May God give you more, my child!"

...child!... When was I a child...? How long have I been a man? And for all instances and purposes, maybe a man without a future....

Just like that old beggar, resigned to meet her fate. Or like the young women learning how to submit to an existence of destitution, ailments, drudgery, and unrelenting pregnancies. Or like those boys with their greasy hairstyles; kids who, emulating their boxing idols, beat at each other without gloves in drab alleys.

"And you, which john? Do you think yourself the 'Monkey' Casanova, or what?"

"My proof goes as testimony... I do not saunter around the barrio acting as if I were the next 'Kid Azteca.'"

"Then how about a short bout to shut up your big mouth, you sad-assed ox!"

Or like those other lads kicking around a ball made of rags and paper, dreaming that some day they will be in the roster of the

Necaxa Eagles. Or like those poor girls that emerge from dark nooks as starving ghosts, hiding their blemishes and blots with cheap cosmetics to seduce a boyfriend who, instead of rescuing them from misfortune, will abandon them with a new life throbbing in their entrails.

So, still ambling along, Chema goes by the barbershop owned by Don Tacho, and stops to say hello to the old man. Wearily, he goes inside and takes the same small rickety chair where he used to sit down years before, when he was the barbershop *chicharo*, to wait for customers to shine their shoes.

Watching his image in the stained mirror covering the front wall, he goes over what occurred that morning at work.

Chapter 9 – Revelation

Around ten in the morning, amid the din of banging, clanging, blaring from a radio, and shouting that encompassed the mechanical shop, Chema heard a drone in the sky. Craning his neck, he looked for its source and, when the buzzing grew louder, he spotted the gleam of a large twin engine airplane as it slid by between two clouds. Shading his eyes, he followed its flight path to the east as it flew toward the airport.

"Pass me the seven-eighths"…

Cringed, as his boss was under the hood of an old Ford, Chema did not hear his voice.

"¡*Oh, joder*! Are you deaf, Chema?"

"What?"

"I said, hand me the seven-eighths wrench!"

"Here you go!" Chema replies, his eyes still glued to the flight of the airplane.

"¡*Epale*! You almost plucked out my eye!" Pérez snarled, emerging from under the hood. "Are you dim-witted, Chema, or have you never seen an airplane before?"

"Never seen one that big, *maistro*!"

"This mulish carburetor seat is all crooked, that is why I cannot adjust it right. Come on; hold it straight so the screwdriver does not slip. I bet you do not even know what it is."

"What is what?"

"That airplane, you clod!"

"Ah, no. How would I know?"

"Well, so you start learning, that is a Boeing 240, it has two 575 horsepower Pratanjuitni engines, carries ten passengers at 130 miles per hour, and takes two pilots to fly it! How is your eye now, eh?"

"Move over a bit so I can grab it."

"Do not do me any favors!"

"Oh, come on, *maistro*! Do not twist my words. I meant grab the carburetor! And now, where did you learn so much about airplanes, *maistro*?"

"Maybe I do not know much, but how about my brother Lencho?" Pérez says, ducking under the hood again. "He is an aviation mechanic in the Southeast. Grab it good, you hear?"

"You mean that one all dressed up, that I took for a client yesterday?"

"That very same, he.... ¡*Ay, recabrón*! I bust my thumb! You see, you dimwit? All because you are distracting me! I told you to grab it good!"

"Make up your mind – did I distract you, or did I not grab it good? Is it my fault the screwdriver slipped because you are a donkey... is what my godfather rides on Sundays!" He laughed, while Pérez grew annoyed.

"Instead of pretending you are so smart, go get me the peroxide bottle and a clean rag from my chest," Pérez grumbled, getting up to sit on a stool under the shadow of the shed, blowing on his left thumb.

Chema came back with a peroxide bottle and a clean rag. "Here, clean it real well."

"I did not do number two."

"I meant cleanse your thumb, not your thimble, if you do not want to catch tetanus."

"Do not cast any curses on me! Come on, while I open the gash, you pour in a little peroxide."

"Listen, *maistro*.... Does your brother Lencho make a lot of money, or what?"

"Just imagine.... ¡*Ay, recabrón*! It burns worse than alcohol! Just imagine, he took the airline all the way from Villahermosa, with his wife, to spend their honeymoon here!"

"¡*Ah, chirrión*!

"He easily takes in double my box office every month, although here I own the circus."

"Listen, *maistro*, and how did he learn about aviation mechanics?"

"¡*Ay, jijo'e la guayaba*! Pérez moaned, blowing on his thumb. "Well, let me tell you; he was the kid brother, so he had a chance to get a little schooling. Then he was my apprentice here and, later, when he found out that he could make a lot more money working as an aviation mechanic, he left for the Southwest where everything is transported by airplane."

"And did he know a lot of mechanics when he left?"

Pérez rubs his thumb, "As much as you do now, I guess."

Thoughtful, Chema bows his head.

"And now, why do you hush up?"

"It is just that my wages stretch only so far!"

"How many people do you have at home now?"

"Four, all of them women."

"No wonder! I cannot make it with just one woman, and now you with four!"

"No, *maistro*, do not think evil thoughts. Not that kind of women. I have my mother, two sisters, and now a cousin who took shelter with us."

"I know, you dimwit! I was just kidding. Anyway, it is a lot of curves to cover with fine tatters."

"¡*Achis*! And why should they dress nicely?"

"¡*Uh, Chema*! Do you not know that I realized you are one of those well-to-do chaps that the Revolution left in the middle of the street? All one has to do is look at your face!"

"What is with my face?" Chema glowers.

Pérez understands he has touched a sore spot, and makes amends. "With your face, nothing! What I meant to say is that you are not just any ape like the rest of us. I know because I was raised in a *hacienda* where my father was a peon. Once in a while I saw the 'masters' as my pa called them. Those people were like you, and not like the swarthy new-money guys who now bring us their cars for repair. What is more, I see that you work like an ox, and I know you do not drink or squander your wages with the painted-eye girls, like the other mechanics do. So, I ask myself, what hardship is eating up Chema, that he needs more money?"

Chema looks around slowly. The "shop" takes up most of an elongated vacant lot. A wooden framework holds a galvanized tin roof along the north end, protecting the eleven mechanics from sun and rain. The gravel-covered ground, compressed with burnt engine oil, becomes a muddy mess when it rains. Placed on top of timber workbenches, several broken-down tool chests hold rusty utensils. Cans brimming full with used bolts and nuts, dishpans filled with blackened gasoline, and worn-out tires piling up in every corner, are just some of the symbols of paucity Chema wants to escape from.

"Is your mother sick?"

"No, *maistro*, thank God!"

"Then, what is your problem?"

Chema looks into the bulging kind eyes of his boss. His concern is genuine. He may be grumpy and gruff, but he always tries to help his workers when they are in trouble.

"You were right, *maistro*." To buttress up his revelation, Chema squats to prick the dirt with the screwdriver. "I mean, what you said about us being rich before is true. The problem is that my mother is always bragging about it, and fantasizing about what she had. I do not even remember the places we lived in, the stores we had, the hacienda and all the rest, and I do not even know if all of that is true, or my mother already learnt it by rote. Anyway, I feel... I do not know, like a compulsion to give back to her and my sisters what we had before."

"I have seen your mother only once, when she came in to demand that I gave you a better salary, but that was enough for me to know that she means what she says."

"Maybe, but then if there is noise in the building, she complains. If there is no running water, she complains. If something smells bad, she complains and nothing is right for her. Yet, I know it is all because I never learned a good trade and I do not earn enough money to move out of that dump we live in."

Pérez never took his eyes off Chema's face. "Then, that is your problem."

He nods.

"You know what, Chema? Your problem has nothing to do with giving your mother back what she needs or had before. What you really want is to get rid of your chains. Do you understand?"

Astounded, Chema says, "You think so?"

"I have told you this before, Chema. To be tied down to their skirts is not favorable. Look, maybe I am giving you the wrong advice, but you will be the judge to that. Leave them behind! Go your own way! Look for your own life!"

"*Chirrión, maistro.* I will not deny that sometimes my mother gets on my nerves and I feel like doing just that. But they are women, and they depend on me. How can I desert them?"

"Do they really depend on you, or on the money you provide?"

Chema scratches the scar on his cheekbone. "I.... I really do not know."

"When I say you should leave them, I do not mean you should walk out on them. You can send them money from wherever you are. What I am saying is, do not live with them anymore!"

"But if I go live somewhere else, I will double up my expenses."

"Sure, but you will also be making more money."

"But, doing what, *maistro*?"

"¡*Ay, Chema*! Do not pretend to be an ox, because then the horns will be in your way. Look, when my brother Lencho comes by this afternoon, we will ask him if there is any chance of you going to the Southeast to work where you can make more money than you make here."

"On your word, *maistro*?"...

Chapter 10 – The Uprising

Pondering on the matter, Chema switches his gaze from his face, reflected on the cracked barbershop mirror, to the package he holds in his hands, wrapped in newspaper.

"That Lencho is a garrulous one. I do not know if I should believe what he says. I wonder if he really makes that much money fixing up airplanes. Will he really keep his word to help me get a job?"

"I am ready to close shop, Chemita." Don Tacho pats his back.

"So early, Don Tacho?"

"What early? It is already seven. Come, come. Go on home; otherwise your mother will get on my back for keeping you so late."

Chema smiles. Nine years have elapsed since he worked as *chicharo* for Don Tacho, but the good old man seems unaware of things like the passage of time.

"All right, Don Tacho. I will go now. Have a good night."

He steps out of the barbershop and feels the cold dew on his face, just as he did when, as a boy, he used to leave the shop jingling in his pockets the coins he had earned shining shoes during the day. Sauntering down the República De Chile Avenue, he arrives at the intersection with his street, and reluctantly looks toward the building where he lives.

"¡Carajo! No wonder my mother pesters me so much. There is nothing in this alley but roving musicians, burglars, buyers of stolen articles, junkies, and prostitutes. ¡Ah, no! There is also us, the decent family in Number 17."

"Ah, but you have to do it just to annoy me! You know how I hate it when your supper gets cold, because I have to warm it up again. Go on, wash up and sit down!"

"Yes, Mother," Chema says, and goes to the sink.

Still angry, Doña Laura examines him further. "And just look at your clothes! I have told you a thousand times not to bring home all the oil in which you wallow!" Then, going toward the masonry charcoal stove where she does the cooking, she asks, "And where were you? Why were you so late?"

Scrubbing carefully under the nails, he says, "I walked from work, Mother."

Doña Laura holds the ladle full of beans in midair. "You walked? Have I not told you not to roam in this neighborhood after sundown?"

Her questioning amuses him. "*Has she forgotten I used to roam the streets selling newspapers until one in the morning when I was a kid?*"

"Hurry up, José María!"

"*José María! José María! If she only knew how much I loathe that name!*"

Being a combination of male and female names, his given name constantly reminds him that he lives surrounded by women. He wants to be called by its diminutive, Chema, because Chema has a manly ring to it. Chema is a popular *charro* character appearing with his *Juana* in the songbooks given away by the Picót effervescent seltzer. Chema, having the right solution for every digestive problem, is very *macho*, while his chums suspect José María is a sissy due to his good looks.

The small scars on his left eyebrow and his right cheekbone attest to the price he pays for his comely countenance. He has a long record of school and street brawls lasting for fifteen of his twenty-one years of age, triggered by his compulsion to prevent derision or slander because of his looks.

His mother believes him to be an incorrigible brawler, thus she uses a horsewhip on him to amend his ways, unaware that because he looks so much like her, she is the cause of all his fights. He has her oval face ending in a cleft chin, her green eyes shaded by thick lashes, her fair skin, and her light wavy hair.

The contrast between his face and the swarthy, ape-like features of the hoodlums populating the nooks and alleys of the dungeon-district, spark the fights. That is why he brawls, and it is also why he has built up a strong physique and big heavy fists. That is how he has received those scars that turn his effeminate features into those of a man.

And above and beyond, he is a man.

Twelve years before, during the bloody religious counter-revolt backed by the Catholic Clergy against the Mexican Government, known as *Revolución Cristera*, his father, a wealthy landowner from Jalisco, and supporter of the rebellion, was shot by Federal troops in the outskirts of Ocotlán, while the defiant war-cry, "Hail Jesus Christ!" vibrated in his throat. All his properties and assets were confiscated by the government. Thus, looking to distant relatives for support, Doña Laura had moved to Mexico City, to the Peralvillo district from where they might never leave, although they do not belong. She became a seamstress, and embroidered linen and clothes for relatives and their friends, but whatever little money she made was barely enough to pay for rent and to keep hunger at bay.

Chema soon understood that, at the tender age of eleven, he was the man of the house and had to face his responsibility as such. As a *chicharo*, he had swept the hair off the floor of the barber shop, and shined shoes for the customers. As *coime*, he kept the pool tables clean and the urinals watered at the billiards hall down the street. He sold the evening newspapers: *El Gráfico*, *Ultimas Noticias*, *Variedades*, and *El Redondel* by the doors of the *Garibaldi* variety theatre. During the day, he attended grammar and later secondary school.

When he turned fifteen, he peddled candy and popsicles inside the theatre trying to conceal the constant manly urge that the chorus girls' nudity caused in his manhood. Despite his youth, his handsome features and his sturdy build appealed to the dancers, who loved to tease him and, at times, even locked him up in their dressing room to have fun with him. Finally, at sixteen, he had placed himself as apprentice in the automotive shop of José Pérez, on Matamoros Street, almost at the intersection with República Argentina Avenue, some three kilometers from home.

He shakes his hands in the sink and then squeezes himself into his chair, crammed against the corner of the small kitchen that also serves as dining room.

"Why do you not you answer me, José María?"

"What, Mother?"

"You make me so mad, I have already forgotten what. Do you want rice and beans?"

"Is there anything else?"

"You know very well there is not!"

"Then?"

Looking at him sourly, she asks, "Then, what?"

"Nothing, Mother. Please serve me some rice and beans."

He feels, deeply in his soul, how sterile and barren their relationship has turned. That icy coldness grates his bones, and the hostility in her silence offends him. The only intimate warmth comes from across the table when his eyes meet the sweet gazes of his sisters, or those of his cousin *Magdalena*.

Although it is not in his character, Chema restrains his temper before his mother. Her puritanical hysteria and incessant demands overwhelm him. Crushed by norms of blind family loyalty and obedience, he endures her reprimands and unfair confinements. He is only free when he is at his work.

His sisters do not enjoy even that relief. At fifteen and seventeen years of age, respectively, *Carmen* and *Margarita* are pretty and lively, but forced to restrain their laughter due to their convent-like upbringing. Their only outings are to church on Sundays and holidays. Doña Laura persists in the belief that she is a wealthy landowner raising them in propriety and the ways of God, to turn them over one day, chaste and diligent, into the hands of worthy men who will marry them. The girls have grown to believe that too, and are docilely being consumed in that sterile flame of hope.

Chema feels sorry for them. He recognized that delusion for what it was at age fifteen, and since then has directed all his efforts to make that mirage come true. For that purpose he hoards his paltry savings, depriving himself of candy as a child, and, as a man, even from the cheap caresses his friends buy from the prostitutes working at the Organo Alley. He wants to save enough money to relocate his sisters to a decent neighborhood where they can find husbands. What he really wants, although the mere thought fills him with remorse, is to rescue them from the polished claws of their mother.

Furtively, he looks at the almond-colored eyes of Magdalena. For two months now, she has also been permeating his thoughts. She is another victim who has fallen inside the invisible gates of Peralvillo. Although she is a second cousin, the daughter of his recently deceased Aunt Teresa, Magdalena has arrived from Zapotlanejo to stir his dormant male instincts – instincts he has been trying to suppress. She is another victim waiting to be released, but for a different purpose.

Gulping down the last of his coffee, he gets up.

"Where are you manners? Can you not wait for us to finish? Where are you going in such a hurry?"

Chema looks at the floor and then, slowly, turns to look at his mother. Her lanky figure does not look as impressive sitting down. "Which of all your questions do you want me to answer?"

"What! All I need now is your disrespect!"

"It is not disrespect, mother. It is that you ask too many questions at the same time."

"I asked you, where you are going."

"Nowhere."

"Then?"

"Then, what, Mother?" he sighs, concealing his exasperation.

"Why do you get up from the table?"

"Because I have finished eating, and I want to read for awhile."

"Read? What are you going to read?"

He tightens his fists to hold back the violence that is about to gush out through his mouth, and walks out of the kitchen. He returns seconds later unwrapping a book that he drops on the tabletop in front of his mother.

"That is what I am going to read. Do I have your consent?"

Doña Laura props her lenses up her nose to read aloud, "Aviation Engines. What is this? Who gave you this book?"

"No one gave it to me," he says with deliberate honesty. "I bought it for eighteen pesos."

The surprise momentarily mutes Doña Laura and causes the girls to look up and stare at Chema.

"Eighteen pesos, you said?"

"Exactly!" Suddenly, he feels a strength that he has never before experienced. "Do not say it! I know you need that money for many other things, but do not even think I pinched one cent off my salary. I have had those eighteen pesos saved for a long time, in case of some emergency."

Doña Laura regards him sternly. Finally, she overcomes the stiffness in her lips to ask with malice, "Did you have that money a month ago, when I was ill?"

He feels like he is about to be struck by the mythical lightning that punishes offspring who commit crimes against their parents. Despite this feeling, he asserts, "Yes, Mother."

"Then to you, a book is more precious than the health of your mother!" she concludes. Getting up to leave the kitchen, she adds, "Raise crows and they shall pluck out your eyes!"

Chema cannot avoid the pang in his gut. Annoyed as he is, he cannot ignore the fact that she is his mother.

"But why her lack of understanding?"

Turning to his sisters, who still stare at him, he says, "No one dies from a common cold!" And fixing his gaze on the almond eyes of his cousin, he declares, "If we want to get out of here someday, I have to study so I can make more money!"

Chapter 11 – The Offering

To label it a parlor is a pompous statement. Actually, it is the workroom where Doña Laura and the girls embroider and sew. Chema has always disliked its stuffiness, and it is not because of its outdated furniture or the cheap porcelain figurines that top each piece. It is, perhaps, its exaggerated tidiness – the countless knitted mats covering every flat surface, or the mended Persian carpet that hangs on the central wall, a reminder of better times. Idly, he tries to reason why that room bothers him so much.

Suddenly, he finds the reason. "*I know what it is! So many hours of brainless labor. So much energy wasted trying to hide the destitution we live in. It is like my mother wants to dress up poverty with rags, so it does not look so grim!*" If he could not stand that room before, now he abhors it.

The unexpected arrival of Magdalena had deprived him of the privacy provided by his own bedroom, which, although dark and gloomy, was a sanctuary where he buried his dejection and nursed his hopes. To have a room for himself was a privilege bestowed upon him by the excessive modesty evidenced by Doña Laura, who would rather crowd herself with her two daughters in the other room than risk him seeing them in their undergarments. But the arrival of Magdalena had robbed him of that privilege as now she and Margarita share his room, and he has to set up a cot every night in the hated parlor, as his mother vainly calls it.

His eyes itch. The colored prism shade encasing the light bulb hanging from the ceiling makes reading an arduous task.

He gets up to turn the light out and while he waits by his mother's door to get used to the faint light entering through the grimy skylight, he hears a loud snore in the bedroom. To realize it is his mother who utters the ridiculous sounds makes him smile. Walking around the furniture, he goes back to his cot to lie down.

Kneading the hardened wool in the pillow, he lays his head on it and strives to hear the snoring, but the thick walls and the sturdy door keep the sounds locked inside. It is better that way. The carillon at the tower of the *San Lorenzo* church strikes the half-hour.

"*Half-past what? Is it two-thirty in the morning?*"

Reading about aviation engines had fascinated him. He has never stayed up so late. He is falling asleep when he hears a faint noise. It sounded like bare feet sliding over the cold wooden floor. One floorboard creaks; but a long while goes by without even a rustle in the air. Suddenly, another noise: the slow stretching of a worn-out spring and the friction of a rusty hinge. Clear and definite noises, but so soft they have the air of covert activity.

Chema opens his eyes and looks around him. The door to his old bedroom is closing and a figure clad in white moves forward to stand by his side. Astounded, he realizes it is Magdalena, who slides down to kneel on the floor and place her face very close to his.

"Magdalena!... What are you doing?"

Sealing his lips with warm soft fingers, she whispers in his ear, "I love you, José María."

From this revelation rushes a radiant light that ends confusion and brings forth awareness. Its tender silence conceals a burst of joy and the uninitiated couple discovers carnal knowledge.

There is rubbing of lips that relish in the breath of another mouth. Soft hands that grip rugged manly skin in their warmth; and rough hands that avidly discover budding breasts and the fearful tremor of maiden limbs; and a muffled cry of pain smothered by tears of happiness.

Anguished struggle between puritanical anxieties shouting: "Sin!"

And jubilant feelings rebutting:

"No, it is love!"

"Sin! Sin!"

"Love! Love! Love!"

Silence...

San Lorenzo's carillon strikes three lonely bells. Chema beholds, amid the maindenly thighs, a flower that draws out its crimson petals on the floor. He wipes the symbol of the offering with his sheet and thinks of a place to hide it, but his mother will certainly miss it and ask about it. He has to have an answer.

He stands up slowly, cupping in his hands the warm moisture enwrapped in the sheet, and mutters, "No, I will never have to have an answer again!"

Within those walls, a woman and a man have just been born.

Chema stops in the middle of the Zócalo square and looks at the clock of the cathedral. It reads 4:35. He wavers for a moment, but the voice of José Pérez rings clearly in his mind: "Leave them behind! Look for your own life!"

With a cardboard suitcase in his left hand, and the right one deeply buried in his pocket clutching a small wad of crumpled bills, he walks briskly across the square toward the corner of Pino Suárez and Corregidora, to go into La Merced District, where he once saw the Southwest bus depot.

The coolness of dawn makes him shiver, but he still feels on his lips, and maybe forever, the chaste warmth of the gift Magdalena had presented him with. It is the only memory that, maybe someday, will prompt him to come back...

PART III – Miami, Florida – September 1939

Chapter 12 – Captain Robert "Bob" Calver

Sighing wearily, Vince Califano throws the Dalton flight computer inside his flight bag and scribbles the last leg of aerial navigation data on a pad. Tearing off the sheet, he passes it over to Willy, who sits in his cubicle across from the instrument panel of the Boeing Stratoliner aircraft. Stretching his short arms, he yawns and says, "This is how far the mule farts. If you want a voice on the radios, wake up *Sleeping Beauty*." Turning off his personal lamp, he crosses his arms over his work table, rests his head on them, and gets ready to nap while the rest of the intercontinental flight comes to an end.

Willy reads the data and extends the slip of paper to Jim, the copilot, who steers the four-engine airliner. Jim winks away the mesmerizing effect caused by the instrument panel's phosphorescence of the piloting instruments, and turns around to shout at Vince, over the four engines' drone, "The magic spell needed to wake him up is a love kiss. Will you volunteer, Vince?" After reading the slip of paper, he adds, "I hate to interrupt his sweet dreams."

"Bah! Wake him up so he makes at least a buck's worth of the fat salary we earn for him!" Willy snarls. "Don't pamper him so much!"

"I thought he was your favorite skipper," Jim replies throwing a sidelong glance at Bob, the flight commander. Reclined in the pilot's seat, he resembles a human question mark. Running along the floor, his left leg disappears under the rudder pedal, while the right one points its knee at the ceiling, making a straight angle. His foot rests on the throttle pedestal, concealing several engine instruments, and, shading his face, his cap only reveals a blissful smile. Jim extends his arm, but before he can touch him, Bob speaks:

"Don't you dare wake me up, James Jones! Right now I'm dancing at the *Miami Yacht Club* with Betty Grable, while she's proposing to me!"

Jim raises the cap to uncover Bob's smiling blue eyes, now wide open. "And tell me, Skipper, do you dream in Technicolor?"

Pretending crankiness, Bob straightens up and looks outside through the windshield. "Party pooper! I hope those crystal-clear waters below are the Caribbean, and not the Mediterranean Sea. Traveling with such inconsiderate and unromantic guys, anything can happen."

Jim whistles, Willy reads a manual, and Vince gives a thunderous snore. Bob unleashes his cynical smile – the heavy artillery he uses to tame women and secure friends.

"Okay, you cattle rustlers," he says. "According to the ADFs, we're going direct to... where? What is our mysterious destination, and how much longer until we arrive there?"

"If the spaghetti didn't get tangled in Vincenzo's computer, in thirty-two minutes we'll be in Miami. We'll arrive at sunrise, four minutes ahead of schedule."

Between yawns, Bob babbles, "Uhfff! What a long night! How wearing these night flights are!"

"Yeah, too much sleep is really tiring," Vince grunts drowsily from his cubicle, clustered with radio and navigation equipment.

"Vince is right! Remind me not to let you all sleep so much next trip," Bob jeers.

Jimmy looks at Vince, who throws his arms up in the air.

"Quit making lewd gestures you think I can't see, Grumpy! And you, Willy, adjust power for a long slow descent. How far back did we leave the hurricane?"

"East-southeast of the Lesser Antilles."

"Great! That means it'll go straight north and we'll have good fishing weather in Miami this weekend."

"I didn't know you like fishing!"

"I love fishing... on the sand!"

"Oh, for mermaids!"

"You're catching on, young man. Use the stabilizer to lose altitude with finesse so you don't wake up the passengers."

"How considerate of him. Obviously he is sympathetic to those who sleep." Vince grunts again.

As the engines' sound diminishes gradually and the aircraft's nose dips to begin descent, Bob says, "Call Miami Center, Jim, request a VFR letdown and get the terminal weather report." Then he punches an overhead button three times.

Stewardesses Joan Stevens and Maureen O'Leary are putting away the service equipment when a soft bell rings three times in the kitchenette, above their heads.

"Oh, Jesus!" Maureen sighs in dismay. "I just threw away the last cup of coffee!"

"You should know by now that as soon as he opens his eyes, the first thing he asks for is coffee, and second.... Did you know they call him the Roadrunner?"

Maureen looks at her with reproach.

Joan shrugs her shoulders: "Well that's what I heard. Check with the girls in the back, maybe they still have some, or take him tea or instant coffee." Joan suggests.

"Are you nuts? He'd throw it in my face!"

With the coffeepot in her hands, the petite redhead considers if she should brew a fresh pot, but she recalls something that makes her Irish temper flare. "Come to think of it, that big ape doesn't deserve to be worried over. If he doesn't want instant coffee, he can use the hot water to soak his butt!" she concludes, and pours hot water into a cup.

"Did he make another pass at you?" Joan's perfect lips smile knowingly.

"A pass?" Maureen's eyes flash. "From the time I met that man five months ago, as soon as he has me within reach, he tries to lay me down on the first available horizontal surface, even if it is a pool table!"

Joan regards the pretty freckled face. The glitter in her eyes is of a special sort: "You know what? Your labeling him an ape sounds to me like a love call."

"What! Are you implying I'm in love with that conceited, irresponsible old bachelor who throws away all his money on binges?"

Still smiling, Joan nods.

"What you're saying is that I'm getting in line behind all his other love-sick puppets!"

"Since he dashes after you, I haven't seen him chase any other girl," Joan answers calmly.

Maureen stares at her sternly but, unable to restrain her elation, she admits, "Yes. You bet your lace panties it is true! Only I'll kill you if you tell anyone!" She threatens Joan by shaking her small index finger under her nose.

"Hey! How long has this been going on?"

"From the day I met him! But the worst part is that I think he knows it. The no-good son of a goat!" The bell sounds again, insistently, reminding her of what she was doing. She hastily places a bag of instant coffee in the cup and rushes along the aisle of the first class passengers' cabin, where some fifty travelers still sleep, and enters the flight deck.

The cup of coffee appears before Bob's eyes so abruptly that some drops land on his shirt and tie. Craning his neck, he looks into a pair of defiant green eyes.

"Well, well, well! Look what we have here! A leprechaun arrived from Ireland's emerald woodlands. For a moment there, I thought you had gone back to Brazil to harvest the coffee beans."

The nostrils in her upturned nose quiver, implying her animosity. "What I harvested for you is a yummy cup of instant coffee!"

Just about to sip the coffee, Bob gives it back. Lowering her voice, she says with malice, "What's wrong, lover boy? Ain'tcha so fond of instant everything?"

Bob frowns and threatens, between clenched teeth, "Listen, you little fairy, the day I catch you, you're gonna lose something else besides your pot o'gold."

"Before that ever happens, you'll have to stamp your X on a marriage license, you ape!" And jostling the cup against his hands, she swings around to leave the cockpit.

Shaking his coffee-drenched fingers, Bob shouts after her, "If that's what it takes, maybe that'll be the first thing I do when I get off this airplane in Miami!"

Her hand freezes on the doorknob. Has she understood correctly? Is he proposing? Turning around she reads the confirmation in his grinning eyes. Her body is too small to hold her joy. Running back, she hides in his outstretched arms.

Jim, Willy, and even Vince, arisen from sleep, watch them kiss for a long while.

Chapter 13 – Doubts in the Wind

Willy holds Bob by an arm while Jimmy and Vince leave the cockpit and start down the gangway. "Hang on, buddy. Let me ask you something. You weren't kidding Maureen, were you?"

"Jesus! Under the fatherly cloak always looms a sermon!"

"Were you kidding, or not?"

Bob's gaze wanders around the cockpit, searching for an answer, and then finally settles back on Willy's friendly wrinkled face. "No, I guess not."

"You guess? Aren't you sure?"

Although well-meaning, Willy's probing annoys him. "It's not uncertainty, shit! Try to understand, Will. I don't know how to put it in words... Okay, listen. I know what you and everybody else is gonna say. That it won't work because I'm a forty-year-old man and she's just turning twenty."

"Don't get me wrong, Bob. We've known each other... what? Ever since we started flying to Havana, twelve years ago. Back then you were the right age to be a footloose playboy, but now, twelve years later, what are you? Your peers are all married, some of then even have teenage kids. What have you got besides your Long Beach apartment and your sports car? Money in the bank? Investments? How much longer can you fly, considering the way you drink and the life you lead? Another five, ten years maybe? Maureen is a nice kid, maybe the only decent girl that has stepped on this deck, so she doesn't deserve to be hurt."

Bob drops his flight bag and, turning his back on Willy, looks at the command controls.

Willy takes Bob's arm and holds it in a friendly squeeze. "We've always been good friends, pal, that's why I'm telling you this. Maureen is a nice decent kid, maybe the only that has stepped on this deck, so she doesn't deserve to be hurt."

Bob remains quiet, deciding between the right thing to do and what he wants to do, even against all odds.

Willy looks him in the eye. "Ask yourself this. Do you really love her? Is she the woman you want to raise a family with? Or is she just a wonderful binge partner to have fun with, with the advantage that she wears a skirt? How long can that last before one of you gets fed up?" Willy buttons up his shirt, straightens his tie, and picks up his flight bag. "Think it over, Bobby boy! See you."

Bob stands still for another moment. He wants to shout his emotions, his desires, his cravings, but he feels embarrassed. He ponders: *"You're right, pal! In a few seconds I've gone over my entire life and it was like flying over the ocean. I saw nothing! Nothing except one-night stands with women whose names I don't even remember. And there's nothing to see ahead but the excruciating feeling that life is escaping me, and I keep only a fraction of what I could have had. When I'm with Maureen I feel like I want to live a lifetime in a few years, loving her more than I ever loved anyone. I want these last few years, when I am on my let down, to be the happiest and most rewarding. I can't be by myself any longer. Just the idea of growing old without leaving a kid behind, frightens me to death."*

"Yes, Police Precinct Eighteen, I want to talk to Sergeant O'Leary… No, no, not in Jersey. In New York. This is his daughter Maureen… Thank you, Operator." Delighted, Maureen smiles at Bob. "He'll either faint, or bellow the phone to pieces, but don't you worry. He growls to hide he's all heart."

"Tell him what a nice guy I am," Bob kids, leaning against the phone booth door.

"How much, Operator?... Bob, give me all the change you have," Maureen asks, emptying her own purse. "Here you go, Operator … It's ringing! Come inside and listen."

Bob crowds into the booth and places his ear near hers.

"Eighteenth Precinct, Sergeant O'Leary."

"You have a call from Miami, go ahead, please," the operator says.

"From Miami? Good Heavens!"

"Papa, it's me, Maureen!"

"Maureen? What is it, child? What's wrong?"

"Nothing wrong, Papa, nothing, I have wonderful news, but get a good grip on your seat, in case you faint. I'm getting married!"

"What? Getting married, you say?" O'Leary bellows.

"Yes, Papa! Isn't that wonderful?"

"The roof of Saint Patrick's cathedral caving in on me wouldn't be that wonderful!" O'Leary roars. "Are you pregnant, or what do you want to get married for? Do we know him? Listen to me, you can't get married, you're only a child!"

"Papa, Papa, I'm twenty years old, and he's the most wonderful man in the whole world!"

"I'll believe that when I get a report from Washington saying that he doesn't have a criminal record! I told your mother we shouldn't have let you take that crazy job! Who's this punk you wanna marry, anyway? Is he a bookie? Miami is full of crooks!"

Bob's face makes Maureen giggle. "No, Papa. He's no crook. His name is Bob Calvert, and he's a senior pilot in the airline I work for."

"A senior! What do you want with a dirty old man?"

Maureen bursts out laughing. "No, Papa. Senior means he's a high ranking pilot, not that he's old."

"Oh, I see. Is he a Catholic at least?"

Maureen turns to Bob, asking, "Are you Catholic, Bob?" Bob just shrugs, smiling.

She speaks into the telephone again. "Don't worry Papa. If he's not, I'll convert him. I swear you'll love him. Listen, he plays golf every Saturday, like you do. We'll come visit when we get back from our honeymoon. Please tell Mama, and send us your blessing."

"Maureen, child... God blesses you both. I hope he makes you very happy."

"Thank you, Papa. Here goes a big kiss."

"Hey, wait. Is this guy with you? Let me talk to him!"

"Okay, here he is."

Bob takes the phone, "Hello, Sergeant O'Leary."

"So, you're gonna marry my daughter, huh? Okay, listen real well. Just like any proud Irish girl, Maureen has a dowry, but we'll discuss that later on. Now, Maureen is my pet, so you better take good care of her or you'll have to deal with me, you hear?" Then his voice breaks. "Please make her very happy. She's always been an angel. May the Almighty bless the both of you."

"Thank you, sir." Bob murmurs, moved. Then he hangs up.

"What did he tell you?"

"Nothing new. He said you're a spoiled brat, and I better make sure to use a heavy hand on you!"

"Heavy, your butt! Come on, the judge is expecting us."

They run toward the airport parking lot like a couple of kids heading for the carnival.

Bob looks at Maureen intensely before ringing the doorbell.

She understands what lies behind his gaze. "I love you. I love you more than enough to make things work out."

He smiles hesitantly and looks at the sign on the door: *Justice of the Peace*. Seeing her reassuring smile, he presses the buzzer.

Nick Harper, the airline Miami base Operations Manager, covers his ears with both hands. "Okay, okay! I give up! You're gonna ruin my flight schedule for the whole month, but okay! Take two weeks off and be happy!"

Bob pats Nick's shoulder and Maureen plants a big kiss on his balding head.

Smiling bashfully, Nick asks, "Where are you gonna spend your honeymoon?"

They trade a look, and exclaim, "Hey, we haven't even thought about that!"

"Some couple!"

"We'll decide it right now," says Bob. "Look, Maureen, take this pin, close your eyes and walk toward the wall map. We'll go wherever you stick the pin on."

Everything is dream-like, a fairy tale. Maureen walks happily toward the large airways map that decorates Nick's office. Being short, she sticks the pin on its central lower portion. Opening her eyes, she cries, "Jamaica! We'll go to Jamaica!

"Great! No better place to spend a honeymoon than Kingston!"

"And how the hell are you gonna get to Kingston? Swimming? There are no regularly scheduled flights to Kingston," Nick argues.

"Do me another favor then, Nicky."

Throwing his heavy body backward, Nick slides in his chair. "No, not money! I don't have any, I can't lend cash, and I won't lend you a penny!"

"No, no. Let me borrow your airplane."

"My airplane to go to Jamaica? Are you insane? It has only one ADF to navigate with, and, besides, flying over water in a single-engine plane, come on Bob! Pick a place here on the mainland, will you?"

"Charles Lindbergh made it to Paris over the Atlantic in a single-engine plane, didn't he? If your airplane flies okay, what's there to worry about?"

"The weather! There's a hurricane roaming around in the Caribbean."

"I know. We saw it last night well above the Lesser Antilles. By now it's out in the Atlantic heading north. Maybe we'll have to detour a little bit, but what the heck. Kingston is worth it."

"Come on! Pick out some other place. I'd hate to miss you two!"

"No, sir." Maureen replies firmly. "I won't defy fate. If it said Jamaica, Jamaica it'll be, hurricane or not! Don't you trust your own pilots?"

Defeated, Nick lowers his head.

"Bye and thanks, Nick. We'll send you a postcard." Bob says on his way out, pulling his young wife behind him.

Smiling, Nick repeats, "Some couple!" and removes his glasses. While he wipes them he gets up quickly to go to the door, and shout after the newlywed. "Hey, Bob! Go by Meteorology and get the latest route forecast!"

At the end of the corridor, Bob raises his arm, waving goodbye.

Chapter 14 – Defying Fate

The ADF needle oscillates from the *Espiritu Santo's* radio beacon in Cuba ahead of them, to point at the thunderstorms on their left. Despite the moderate turbulence, the small *Cessna C-37* handles rather well, and the 240-hp radial engine responds adequately to the power setting Bob has adjusted to climb even higher. The airplane has logged only 235 hours since new, and Nick Harper keeps it in top shape.

In the right seat, Maureen dozes. A jolt wakes her up and she shakes her head.

"What's the matter, sweetie-pie?" Bob smiles.

"If you don't do something to stop this bouncing around, I'm going to end up getting sick!"

"Come on, you're not supposed to get sick."

"Not in the biggies, but in this nutshell, I can't be so sure. How much longer?"

Bob figures it out mentally, "About two hours."

"That long? Where are we now?"

"Did you ever hear about the Gibraltar Strait?"

"Jesus! Did I sleep that long?"

"The ground you see down there is Cuba. In two or three minutes, we'll be over the *Espiritu Santo* radio beacon."

"Espiritu Santo?" Taking the navigation chart, she checks their route. "What kind of lousy navigator are you? We're over one hundred miles off course. We should be over *Camagüey.*"

Maureen's jest erases his frown. "I warned you. The damned hurricane made me deviate to the west."

"Is it close by?"

"No, but its effects are widespread, causing a lot of atmospheric disturbances."

"Is it that line of thunderstorms to our left?"

"That must be its periphery."

"It looks awfully close. Do you think we'll be able to make it, Bob?" She asks a bit worried.

"Christopher Columbus made it over sailing in a caravel. Let me ask for a report," he says, dialing a frequency on the radio. "*Cienfuegos* radio, this is Cessna C-37 *Nectar Charlie, one, one, one, over.*"

Maureen watches the magnificent spectacle through the windshield, one she can seldom appreciate when tending to her chores aboard the airliners. There are clouds everywhere, huge billowing towers snowy white above, black and threatening below. They skirt their tops at thirteen thousand feet and climbing. Looking down the deep ravines between the clustered cumulus clouds, she sees Cuba's emerald surface. Far to the east, the sinister chain of thunderstorms begins firing lightning into the swelling ocean whitecaps.

Bob repeats into the microphone, "Cienfuegos radio, this is Nectar Charlie, one, one, one, over."

Amidst the cacophony of static and the blast of thunderclaps, Bob hears a distant Cuban voice in the earphones. "This is Cienfuegos radio, Nectar Charlie, one, one, one, over."

"Cienfuegos, triple ace, flying direct from Miami to Kingston, at this time over Espíritu Santo, leaving thirteen thousand five hundred for fifteen-five, due to weather. Please give me the hurricane's present position, heading, and velocity, over."

"Roger, triple one. Stand by on this frequency. I will get you the 20:00 *Zulu* information."

"Triple ace, standing by." Smiling, he tells Maureen, "We'll go on climbing. Get the oxygen masks out of the seat pockets."

Maureen reaches for the masks. Looking at them, asks amused, "Do we have to wear these?"

"Yes."

"Why?"

"Because we're already reaching fourteen thousand feet of altitude."

"We fly higher in the airline and never wear masks."

"Of course, silly elf, because those airplanes are pressurized and this one isn't. So put it on, but first rub off all your lipstick."

"Why?"

"Because oxygen ignites on contact with grease, and I want a pair of lips I can kiss tonight, okay?"

Wiping her lips clean with a sheet of tissue, she says, "Why don't you let me wear the one with hole in the mouth, then?"

"Because I'll do the talking while you do the praying!"

"I should know better than to ask!"

The engine's drone is the only noise they hear until the Cuban controller's voice comes in weakly over the earphones. "Nectar Charlie, triple one, Cienfuegos."

"Go, Cienfuegos."

"This is the 19:45 Zulu special report. The hurricane's eye was last reported eighty miles north of Cape Haitien, Haiti. In the past two hours it altered its course and is now moving west-southwest at forty knots. Its trajectory threatens eastern Cuba and it's expected to hit with maximum intensity in five hours. Its effects will be felt within two hours. There's a *SIGMET* alert for the eastern portion of Cuba, Haiti, the Dominican Republic, and Jamaica. All aerial and maritime navigation must be avoided in those areas. Acknowledge and advise of your intentions. Over."

"Copy your report, please stand by, Cienfuegos. Triple ace," Bob replies, then asks Maureen, "Please hold the wheel a moment, darling. I've got to do some numbers."

"Hey, I've only flown in good weather!" she objects, but holds the wheel. She has had a few hours of experience flying single-engine planes, but even for an experienced pilot, trying to keep the Cessna straight and level in that turbulence isn't easy. Bob quickly draws lines on his navigation chart while plotting a new course, and uses his flight computer to estimate the time of arrival.

Satisfied with his figures, he places the chart and rulers on top of the instrument panel. "No hurricane will make us change our plans. We'll beat it to Jamaica."

"Are you sure?"

"Are you afraid?"

"Only of being alone with you," she smiles fondly.

"Just think how exciting it'll be to feel a one hundred and eighty mile-an-hour gale blowing over our heads. We'll lock ourselves in a bungalow and nobody will bother us for the next three days."

"Nobody will wait on us, you mean."

"Would you want anyone else pampering you?"

"You dirty-minded old man!"

Laughing, Bob takes the microphone. "Cienfuegos radio, Cessna triple ace."

"Go ahead, triple ace!"

Please be advised triple ace will proceed on his original flight plan, estimating one hour plus fifty minutes from present position to Kingston. I'll have *Rancho Boyeros* Airport in Havana as my alternate airport. Over."

"Copied, triple ace. But be aware your route lies within the SIGMET Alert report and you will be navigating at your own risk. We strongly advise you to return to your departure point, or to go to your alternate airport at this time. Cienfuegos radio, over."

"Optimists!" Bob exclaims, and then speaks into the mike, "Roger, Cienfuegos. Triple ace, over and out!"

"What did they say?" Maureen asks.

"That they will stand by in case we need a life preserver. Don't remove your mask unless you have something important to say!"

Smiling, she removes the mask again to say, "I love you!"

Bob adjusts the gyro compass setting to 150 degrees to match it with the rough reading given by the magnetic compass in its incessant twirl. He leans the fuel mixture further to squeeze the most power from the engine.

During the last twenty minutes, they have been flying slowly at 16,500 feet of altitude, parrying the tops of the cumulus clouds. Affected by rapid temperature changes, the dynamic energy in the air creates currents that push the tiny aircraft upward, only to pull it down swiftly seconds later.

Bob's fingers, laced tight around the control wheel, feel numb. He pushes the rudder pedals so hard his back hurts. Even so, the single-engine Cessna performs like a bronco. Struggling to keep it from flipping over, Bob noses it into the top of the cloud ahead of them. Within the mist, the plane shakes so badly its fuselage makes a cracking sound.

Steering that small aircraft with only a basic set of flying instruments is not at all like handling the Stratoliner, which has special indicators for every function. Bob has to make use of all his skills to fly it in some semblance of normalcy. They stay in the cloud for no more than three minutes, but when they break out into the clear, it is as though they have emerged into a different day.

Bob checks the wing roots and the struts for breakage, but none is visible. The aircraft has undergone negative stresses far superior to its structure's design and has passed the test with flying colors.

Astounded, Maureen removes her mask and exclaims, "Hey, look at that!"

Bob emits a long whistle. They are flying within a wide oblong area devoid of clouds, about sixty miles long and ten miles wide. The space is bordered by cumulonimbus clouds, rising taller than 40,000 feet and containing severe storms. The air is ominously calm.

"We're not going to go through there, are we, Bob?"

"I'm sorry, babes, but it looks like the damned hurricane beat us after all. Damn it!" He is edgy, but his immediate reaction is to adopt an air of calm.

"Okay, forget about the calypso and close your eyes," he tells Maureen. "Now listen. Can you hear *maracas*, *bongoes*, and *claves*? It's the *rumba* and the *huaracha*. Now take a whiff of this: legit white rum, Moro crab, lobster, *paella*, and mangoes for desert. All of this and more in the *Pearl of the Antilles*! Wanna spend your honeymoon in Havana?"

"Isn't Havana a men's paradise?"

"Well, it maybe; but this time I'll be taking a very special dish to the formal dinner!"

"All right! For such a gourmet, I'll gladly be the main course!" She laughs, smoothing her hair. "But don't take me again across the earthquake we just came through."

"That was nothing compared to what we have in front of us. Anyway, we won't bounce this time – we'll just get a little wet. I'm gonna go down and we'll go back under the layer of clouds."

While he throttles back to start a steep descending spiral, he tries the radio again: "Cienfuegos radio, Cessna triple ace, over!"

He keeps calling for ten minutes.

"Hell! No use wearing my throat thin. We must be out of reach. I'll try again in ten minutes. You're not scared, are you?"

"Are you...?"

"It's obvious that the wind drifted us to the west, but how far west?" Bob thinks to himself.

Bob doesn't trust the readings he gets from the magnetic compass. The electric disturbances caused by the storms have undoubtedly rendered the radio compass useless. Is he lost? The small airplane, unusually slow, crawls across solid sheets of rain that block forward visibility. Bob can only see downward at the ocean's angry surface. According to his estimate, he should have seen the southern Cuba's shoreline fifteen minutes before. It had to come into view at any moment now. The island is too big and they should be too close to miss it, even if he tried to.

"Camagüey radio, Cienfuegos radio, Havana radio, Nectar Charlie triple one, anyone on this frequency, over!" Impatient, he looks at his watch. "Damned radio operators! They take day-long coffee breaks!"

"Just like some pilots I know!" Maureen kids, trying to appear calm. Having worked as stewardess for over a year, she is familiar with a pilot's demeanor when he faces a critical situation. Bob's keen eyes have that aloof expression and she sees the same alertness in his every move. Furthermore, the needle spinning around on the face of the ADF tells her that they are not following a consistent heading. She realizes that Bob has been navigating by dead reckoning for a long time, relying only on the erratic magnetic compass readings. Flying five hundred feet above the fierce waves is not altogether comforting, so although she does not want to speak lest her voice gives away her fear, she asks, "How much longer to Havana, darling?"

"Don't worry, baby. You'll be under the National Hotel's bed sheets in less than one hour!"

"The National? Oh, boy! I really got me a splendid hubby!" She tries to joke, but she actually feels like crying.

Bob has never lost his self-assurance before. He has flown hundreds of thousands of passenger-hours across oceans safely. Why, then, is he so fearful now? He finds the answer in the right seat. She is not only his wife, but also a young breath of life that depends solely on him.

The Cessna drags on with irritating slowness. "This is madness!" he growls. "We have to be over Cuba! Don't take your eyes off the altimeter, babe. If it shows less than one hundred feet, holler!"

Grabbing the control wheel firmly, he pushes it forward while his gaze pierces the windshield, trying to see something else besides the furiously beating rain.

"One hundred feet!" she yells, startling him.

"*Goddamnit!*" he swears to himself. "*I don't see a thing! Where the hell is Cuba?*"

Something has gone awry. Has the magnetic compass failed, its erroneous readings deviating them toward the Yucatan Channel? If that is the case, maybe he can pick up the Cozumel low-frequency radio beacon.

Checking his navigation chart, he turns the radio compass knob to the 200-kilocycle frequency and positions his earphones just ahead of his ears so he can tolerate full volume over the blare caused by static. Mixed in with the crackling, he hears a faint radio signal in the form of a Morse code: Dah-dit-dah-dit, dah-dah-dit-dit, dah-dah.

"C... Z... M. That's Cozumel's ID!" he cries happily, while the needle indicates, with some oscillations, a bearing of 145 degrees. "Yes, it's Cozumel! Look at that needle!"

He quickly turns the knob to the 280-kilocycle frequency and listens intently. Dit-dah-dit, dit, dah-dah! The dashes and dots are heard slightly louder.

"R... E... M. Merida! Look at that bearing, baby! Eighty degrees to our left. That's just impossible, however...." He jerks the wheel and the Cessna jumps to five hundred feet. "Hold it there, doll," he says, to her.

Taking his plotter, he draws two lines on the chart: one from the Cozumel beacon and the other from the Mérida radio range. Both lines converge to intersect each other in the middle of the Yucatan Channel.

Bob whistles long and low, "Just look at that, babes! If we had continued on this heading, we'd have run out of fuel right in the middle of the Gulf of México! The damned magnetic compass went crazy with all that turbulence."

"What happens now?"

Bob thinks it over in silence. From their present position, the closest airports are *San Julian* in Cuba and *Cozumel* in the island, but to steer toward either of them means flying against a headwind and facing the weather again. Going toward Merida, although some sixty miles farther, is a much better option. They will have a strong tailwind to help them, and improved weather conditions.

Pointing at the chart, Bob explains, "See where these two lines cross each other? That's where we are. It's exactly the same distance to *Cape San Antonio*, in Cuba, or to Cozumel Island. Pumpkin, you're going to enjoy the most romantic honeymoon at the foot of an old Mayan pyramid, listening to sentimental serenades, and having succulent dishes of pheasant and venison."

"Bob, please, what I want is to see land. Any land!"

"You'll see it pretty soon, sugar. I promise!" Taking his computer, he traces a course and calculates the distance and time to Merida. Their indicated speed is 130 mph., but he knows that their ground speed is thirty to forty miles faster. The fuel remaining in the tanks is barely enough to cover the distance, but he relies on his ability and good luck. The risk is worth taking if he can give Maureen an unforgettable two weeks.

The rain dwindles to intermittent showers and the radio signal from the Merida radio range grows louder by the minute. To the west, visibility has improved and the base of the clouds is clearly defined. A dark line appears in the nearby horizon.

"Land ahoy!" Bob cries. "Now I know how Columbus felt when he finally saw land. There's the Yucatan peninsula, baby!"

"Where, where?"

"Right there! See the dark line?"

"Oh, Bob. Now I can breathe again!"

"I kept my promise, didn't I? Get ready, little fairy, you're gonna have the best honeymoon you could've wished!"

"Oh, yeah? Then, here goes your prize," she says, kissing him noisily on the cheek.

"Merida control tower, this is Cessna C-37 Nectar Charlie one, one, one, over."

"Cessna C-37 Nectar Charlie, triple one, over." The yucatecan controller's voice comes through loud and clear through the earphones.

"Merida tower, triple ace, on a VFR flight plan from Miami to Kingston, Jamaica, deviated due to weather conditions. At this time about twenty-five miles east-northeast of Progreso Port, flying along the shore. I estimate your airport in the next fifteen minutes, landing. Request customs and immigration authorities to clear arrival. On board, Robert Calver and wife Maureen Calver. Over."

"Triple ace, copied your request. Will advise authorities. Runway in use 18, altimeter 30.35, wind 350 at 16 knots. Call when you have the airport in sight. Over."

"Tower, triple ace. Be advised that I am in a low fuel condition. Please facilitate arrival and landing, over."

"Triple ace, Mérida tower. We are aware of your condition. Disregard traffic procedure and fly directly to base leg for Runway 18. Standing by."

They fly along a dirt road that lies along the shore. The rooftops of the Merida distant skyline are already in sight. They had flown along the shoreline even though this stretch was longer, because he had not dared to cut across the mainland with the needles on both fuel tanks close to the red line.

Suddenly, Bob feels the first engine power surge. It was a very slight quiver, but it gives him a clear signal that fuel starvation is imminent. He switches the fuel valve to the left tank, but that gauge also reads zero fuel. It's time to land.

"Brace yourself, Maureen. This time it's no joke. You're gonna spend your honeymoon on a beautiful beach. There's a good road to set the plane down, don't worry. It'll be just like any other landing. Just in case, when I tell to you, assume the emergency position, head between the knees, covering it with both hands, you know the routine."

"You're kidding, aren't you?"

The engine coughs twice and runs smooth again.

"There's your answer," and grabs the microphone. "Merida tower, triple ace. Listen up, no time to repeat. I'm making an emergency landing on a dirt road along the shore about ten miles from Progreso. Out!"

Turning to Maureen, he warns, "Here we go, doll! Do what I said and don't worry, we'll be on the ground in a minute."

Before bending down, Maureen kisses him hastily on the cheek. Bob tousles her hair and steers the airplane along the narrow road, which, although lined by tall trees, offers a sensible margin of safety. There should be two or three quarts of gasoline left in the tank, enough to correct his glide if necessary.

He throttles back to idle and sets a point of flaps, and then he realizes he is landing downwind and he doesn't have the time or altitude to do a 180-degree turn.

It's very hot. He perspires profusely. His lack of familiarity in handling such a small aircraft is shaking his confidence. As he approaches the tree tops, the plane goes on gliding, propelled by the tailwind, and overshoots his intended landing site. The road widens considerably about sixty yards ahead, but to get there he has to extend the glide to avoid the top of a tall mango tree. It's worth a try, the safer the better; he knows he can do it. He opens the throttle. The engine responds for five seconds but then quits altogether. An appalling silence descends on them.

The extreme heat and humidity take their toll. The wings lose lift and the airplane stalls clumsily. Bob sees the top of the mango tree grow, its branches reaching up to grab the plane in its foliage. He hears a loud thud and the world topples.

Maureen's scream pierces his eardrums.

Bob recovers consciousness and realizes he's lying on the sandy ground. He is unscathed, except for a lump on his forehead, but his right shirtsleeve is bloodstained. He shakes his head again to clear his vision and finds the wrinkled face of a Mayan native over his face, staring at him with sorrowful eyes.

"Maureen!" he yells, trying to sit up, but the old Maya places a hand on his bloodied shoulder to stop him. Removing his straw hat, he looks toward the overturned airplane, shaking his head sadly. "Maureen...! Maureen...! Maureen!" Bob's cry echoes in the dense brush, through the hollows and gaps that open between one tree and the next, toward the forest the Mayan people call Xibalbá...

Flying in Xibalbá

PART IV – The Mayan Gods' Creation

Chapter 15 – The Human Race

Before the Creation, man did not exist nor did the face of the earth. The oceans were suspended in the air and there was nothing in order, nothing was alive. Thus, there were no feelings, passions, nor instincts. All was kept in silence, wrapped in the obscurity of night.

From within this blackness, Divine Gucumatz, Heart of Heaven, Mother and Father of All That Is, spoke to the Ahau Tepeu, Lord to Be of the Earth.

"It will be good that there be life."

The Ahauab of Xibalbá, Lords of Hell, had been defeated by the warriors Hunahupu and Ixbalanque, whom Gucumatz rewarded by placing them in the sky as sun and moon. Thus light came to be, ending the confusion. The earth was made. The Creator drew the lines and parallels above in the sky and down on the earth. He divided the world into climates. He parted the waterways and they became dammed so that the mountains, the ravines, and the jungle could appear.

Gucumatz then created the animals and appointed them as owners and keepers of the jungle, where they were to dwell therein. The deer, the lion, the bird, the toad, the buzzard, the tiger, the snake; all of them took the forest for their habitat, and theirs was all of the creation.

At long last, Gucumatz created men, but erred in molding them from clay. They spoke, but did not comprehend. They were heavy, feeble, and slow, and they dissolved in water. The men made of clay were Gucumatz's abortion.

After destroying the clay men with a flood, Gucumatz consulted the venerable soothsayers Ixpiyacoc and Ixmucane.

The old diviners drew lots with *tzite* grains, the red beans, and at once advised, "Wood will speak, if you carve men out of it. Do it thus, and it will be good."

Gucumatz made men out of wood and they reproduced. They had sons and daughters but they were foolish, heartless, and petty. They became haughty and forgot about their Creator. The animals punished their stupid arrogance. Xecotcovach, the bird, plucked out their eyes; Camaztotz, the bat, severed their heads; Cotsbalam, the tiger, ate their entrails, and the one called Tucumbalam shattered their bones.

The wooden men tried to escape the rain of fire and resin that Gucumatz poured to destroy them, but in the end, they perished. Only a few remained alive, but they were transformed into the monkeys that roam the forest. That is why monkeys resemble men.

The Divine Gucumatz sat to reflect. "Our creation is perfect, except for men. We have failed in making them fit for life on earth."

"Perhaps we should consult with the animals," Tepeu replied. "They are wise!"

And thus, *Uitu*, the coyote; *Yak*, the wild cat; *Quel*, the turtle; and Hoh, the raven revealed the existence of white maize, yellow maize, red maize, and black maize, which old grandmother Xmucane ground into flour and kneaded into dough.

With the dough, Gucumatz and Tepeu molded the flesh and the fat of men, their arms, their legs and their feet, their heads and the rest, making men of different colors.

Gratified, Gucumatz, Heart of Heaven, tells Tepeu, Lord of the Earth, "Men are made. Now let us place them in Xibalbá, the jungle, and mind them to see if their behavior is right and proper...."

PART V – Yucatan Peninsula – August 1941

Chapter 16 – The Xkanták Central

Ricardo Quel grasps the power plant starter cable handle in his right hand, perches his left foot on the gasoline tank, and snaps back the cord. A bleary explosion occurs inside the combustion chamber, only to die away immediately.

"Open the throttle when it fires, you dumb ox," Ricardo shouts at *Neto*, his scrawny assistant, but his order comes too late and the motor chokes out.

The mechanic yanks a dirty handkerchief from his hip pocket to wipe the perspiration bathing his face and chubby bare chest. "Just look at all this, *hah*? You need to be a real stupid *guariscol* to think that these sorts of luxuries can be had in the middle of the forest! What does this beauty of a new owner we are getting think, hah? If he wants comforts, he should stay in Mérida, or at the beach in Progreso."

Panting, Ricardo fastens his small keen eyes on Neto's half-witted smile and shaking his pointed head slowly looks around him. Waving his hand, he explains, "This *chicle Central* terminal we are in, Neto, is nothing but a hole dug up in the jungle. This is an abode intended for four-legged animals, and two-legged asses like us – we who are needy enough. And if you do not believe me, just look around! What do we have here? A dirty storehouse made of boards and tin sheets, a cluster of grass huts for the workers, a dirt landing strip, this thatched shed we call a tool shop, and that house just built for the new owner. Everything contained by walls higher than those built around prisons."

Frowning, Neto says, "Walls, I do not see any, *maistro!*"

"¡*Caballo*! That you are dumb, Neto! That was just a metaphor, a figure of speech! Do you not see all those trees forming a wall around us? Tell me, could you get away from here on foot? ¡*Máre*! You would not last one day striding through the jungle. It is bad enough over here with the heat, the mosquitoes, and the gadflies sucking our blood day and night. I do not know why the new owner wants a house with so many comforts, as if he were going to live here!" He pauses, and then bends over the motor again. "¡*Andale*! Let us try again. If the motor fires, open the throttle right away. Here I go!"

Ricardo winds the cable around the spring spool and pulls. Responding to his effort, the motor starts with a loud bang, letting out a stream of gas and noise through its exhaust pipe.

"¡*Vaya!* It started at last!" Ricardo exclaims relieved.

"Well, looks like it finally works, *huh, chico*?" a rough voice breaks in.

Startled, Ricardo turns around to find Gumersindo Pallares, the *Tuxpeño,* behind him. His skin crawls, as it does whenever he unexpectedly meets with Xkanták's Central foreman.

"Yes... it works now..." he stammers.

Ricardo fears Gumersindo Pallares because he is as repulsive on the outside as he is despicable in the inside. He is lanky and leathery, built with long legs and arms made solely of bone, lean muscle and skin. On his narrow shoulders sits a chunky head topped by a mat of black hair as twisted as the thoughts that boil under it. His beady black eyes never smile, even if his lips do. A wide flat nose, bony cheekbones and jutting jaws give him the look of a living skull. His scars, frightful grooves of black flesh running along his chest, throat, and left cheek, label him a "man among men." Hanging from his belt, as an undetachable part of him, is his *buruna*, a razor-sharp machete ready to become an extension of his arm, either to clear a path in the forest or, just as easily, to take away a human life. His character is simply evil.

"Look then, like in dealing with mechanical things, there is no one stepping ahead of you, huh, *chico*? Should I try it to see if there is electricity in the house?" Gumersindo asks.

"Yes, but first connect the main switch."

"Of course, *chico*! If I am not that stupid. Let us see...."

Gumersindo goes toward the newly-built house, whose size and prominence strike a harsh contrast with its puny surroundings.

Looking at Neto, Ricardo whispers, "You know what, Neto? To me, Gumersindo fled from Xibalbá, the green hell. He is the true incarnation of Lucifer, hah?" He follows him to the house, as the foreman stomps hard on the steps that lead to the porch to test the strength of the boards carved only the day before. He then walks to the end of the veranda to set the master switch on.

Waiting by the main door, Ricardo watches Gumersindo return with a big smile on his thick lips. He always smirks to air his many frontal gold teeth that are his pride.

"*All the gold in the world would never be enough to erase your ugliness,*" Ricardo muses, as the foreman walks by his side to enter the house.

Once inside, they stand in the middle of the living area to watch two carpenters assemble the dining table. Gumersindo inspects the walls made of logs and entwined twigs plastered with dry clay. The grooved tin roof has a layer of palm leaves on top to insulate it from direct sun rays. Framed mesh protects the windows, draped with expensive fabrics that don't match the rustic building. He jumps repeatedly to try the floor.

Finally easing himself into one of the wicker chairs, he asks Ricardo, "How do you see it, *chico*? Do you like the barn?"

Ricardo frowns, "Why the barn, *bosh*?"

"Does not the new owner come from Switzerland? And what is there in Switzerland other than Swiss cows?" Gumersindo explains with a guffaw. "And for a cow, a barn!"

Gumersindo's conclusion does not amuse Ricardo, but he feigns a smile and goes to the door to look into the adjacent room.

Getting up, Gumersindo shoves Ricardo inside. "Do not be shy, chico. Go in and look at the bedroom. See that dresser? It is the most expensive you can find in Mérida. The mirror is French. And look at the wardrobe and the chest of drawers. I have never seen larger in my life. But best of all is the bed. Nothing is as soft," he sighs, reclining on it. "The mattress is like a feather. Come on, *chico*. Lie down a while. I will leave you some space."

The mechanic's big head shakes in silence. Stalking the room, conscious of his intrusion, he goes to the chest of drawers where an electric fan stands. He turns it on and its blades come alive, sending a fresh breeze toward Gumersindo.

"*Ah, pariente*! What a thing! Like this, you can live in hell itself. Go in the kitchen, Rico, and check if the icebox is also working. Me, I am going to take the nap of my life." Folding his arms under the head, he shuts the eyes.

Looking at Gumersindo with reproof, Ricardo goes into the living and dining area, where the carpenters are placing the dining table in front of the cabinet.

Adjoining the living area, to the west, are two smaller rooms: the bathroom and the kitchen. The kitchen is equipped with a sink, a brand-new electric range, and a large refrigerator. Isolated by a wall, the bathroom has luxuries never before seen in the jungle: a toilet, a wash basin, and a tub with a shower fixture.

Ricardo is awestruck. A soft purring sound catches his attention. It comes from the refrigerator. Opening it carefully, he feels a fresh breath of air caress his gaping face. In ecstasy, he admires the stainless steel trays shining immaculately under the light of a small bulb. He closes the door deferentially and takes two steps backward to appreciate the unit at leisure.

Leaving the house, Ricardo tells his assistant, "Would you know one thing, *bosh*? What you see over there is not just a large shack but a real palace!"

A familiar sound makes him turn to the north. An old Curtiss Robin airplane, painted a gleaming red, appears from the north, flying higher than usual. "¡*Máre*! That must be Cayetano with another load of dumb-wonderful things. Come on! Get a gasoline drum ready because he will want to turn around immediately."

Stretching and yawning, Gumersindo walks out of the main house. "¡*Epa, Galicio*!" he shouts at his assistant working inside the warehouse. "Get two men to unload the airplane!" Then he walks to the shed where Neto and Ricardo are prying open a 200-liter gasoline container.

"Would that be *capitán* Cayetano, what bug bit him that he is flying so high?"

"Who knows?" Ricardo shrugs.

Both watch the airplane that, for a moment, looks as if it is going to fly on. However, it circles around the grounds and then dives to buzz very low over the landing strip.

"¡*Ah, cabrón*! Gumersindo exclaims. "That is capitán Cayetano, always frisky!"

Smiling, they watch the old single-engine plane move in tight to align itself with the landing strip. Seconds later, it grazes the ground in the softest touch down.

Chapter 17 – The Swiss

As soon as the propeller arrests its twirl, Gumersindo approaches the Robin to open its door. His perpetual smile vanishes when, instead of Cayetano, he sees that the pilot is a stranger with an arrogant and disparaging expression.

The man jumps out of the airplane and, with a German accent, says in Spanish, "I am Max Wolff, the new owner of this place. Who is foreman?"

"Gumersindo Pallares, at your orders, *patrón!*" Gumersindo smiles, putting forth his right hand.

The foreigner scans the calloused hand and chooses to ignore it. Regarding the new building, he asks, "The dwelling, is it finished?"

"Finished it is *patrón.*" Gumersindo says, taking back his disdained hand to rub it against the sheath of his *buruna.* "So much so that even the electricity works."

"I will inspect it now," Max says, walking toward the rustic building. After a few steps, he halts abruptly to look around. Addressing no one in particular he asks, pointing at the warehouse, "Why is that pigsty still up?"

"That is where we keep the provisions, the airplane parts, the gum bales, and anything else we might need, *patrón.*"

Max looks at the man with contempt. "For you and everybody else, I will be *señor* Wolff, not *patrón!* When I was here last week, I asked *señor* Pedraza to tear down that warehouse and build two new ones, one for gum bales only, the other for wares."

"I am sorry, *señó Worf.* I was not here then." Gumersindo explains.

"What about those huts?"

"Some of the workers live in them with their women, and that is the corral for the mule trains, *señó Worf.*"

"Everything is as filthy as first day I saw it! I want all that misery cleared far away, behind those trees!"

"But, *patrón...* I mean, *señó Worf....*"

"Pallares, I do not stand for talk back, do you understand? I give orders, you obey them." Max says with a stern gaze.

"Si, *señó Worf!* I understand readily." Gumersindo says, knowing there will be no other way.

"Now, what is a good place for the pilots dormitory?"

"Here? They do not stay here, *señó Worf.* They have bases in Peto, Escarcega, Hopelchen, and others. From there they fly here, and from here there."

"My pilots will live here! I want a dormitory built." He looks around, and then points to the north side of the site. "There, adjacent to new warehouse. Big enough for ten or more pilots."

"Ten? But there are only four airplanes, *señó Worf*."

"I will have ten, twenty. Here, we shall work. I see dwelling now!" Max says abruptly, walking toward the veranda with Gumersindo following him sheepishly.

Ricardo wipes his belly with an oily rag and his gaze travels from the big house to his assistant's face. "Know something, Neto? It looks like the Swiss is not so much of a cow as Gumersindo thought."

Another airplane approaches from the north.

"*¡Andale, Neto!* That must be really Cayetano arriving now!"

A blue 1930 Bellanca Skyrocket glides toward the landing strip. Close to the ground, the high wing monoplane flares hastily and floats for a few seconds before it stalls for a hard three-point landing, raising a cloud of fine sand behind it.

"Yes, that really is Cayetano!" Ricardo snickers.

"*¡Quiubo, Rico!*" Cayetano greets him, coming out of the Bellanca. "I did not see you when I came yesterday, where were you?"

"Down by the river, Cayito, shooting some doves."

"Well, it is good to see you again. Have you locked horns with the new *patrón*?"

"*¡Máre!* May all the gods that dwell in the jungle not permit that! He is a dog that not only barks, but also bites!" Ricardo replies, making the sign of the cross. Regarding the pilot, he adds, "My, Cayito, but you look pretty today!"

"It is because I am wearing a clean shirt, new trousers, and my cheeks look like the butt of a baby!" he retorts, smiling. "Which is just to humor this boss, who, I am afraid, will irk us more than hemorrhoids in the brownie."

"So, will you be staying here as chief pilot then?"

"Yes. The Swiss made me an offer I could not refuse; besides, who can I trust better than you to take care of the plane I fly? I am sure glad we are teamed up again!" And turning to the workers standing by, he hollers, "*¡Orale!* Do not just stand there scratching your balls! Get all the junk off the airplane and take it in the house, before the *patrón* comes out and starts yelling at everybody!"

Cayetano Rodríguez isn't all that old. However, flying thousands of hours in all kinds of decrepit airplanes, and years of squandering, give him an older appearance. His rugged features, the husky physique he carries with ease and his usual good mood win him friends and women wherever he goes.

His habits and traits identify him as a Northern Mexican, but he would just as soon say he is from *Monterrey*, as he'll swear he was born in Chihuahua, or Torreón. He doesn't want his origins known because, somewhere in the North, he has a family he deserted years before.

Feeling weary, he stretches, yawns noisily, and pats his ribs.

"You ran it last night Cayito, hah?" Ricardo asks.

"I ran it, chased it, and never caught it, *vale*. I went to bed around five in the morning and just as I was closing my eyelids, that white elephant came banging on my hotel door to drag me to the airport."

"White elephant? Ah, Cayito. You are funny!"

They both turn when they hear Max's bellowing voice as he comes out of the house, followed by Gumersindo.

"Nothing is like I ordered! I want changes made by tomorrow! That house is to be lived in, not just for spending the night! You understand, Pallares?"

"I did what I could, *señó Worf*," Gumersindo apologizes. "*Señó* Pedraza advised he wanted the house built only a week ago."

"With me, everything will be done quickly, and done well. We are going to work hard! *Capitán Rodríguez*!"

"Tell me, *señor* Wolff," answers Cayetano.

"Today we will make two more flights and we will sleep in Mérida. Tomorrow, I want two more pilots working for me."

"Well, the gum harvesting season is about to start, so most of the pilots are already hired. Unless...."

"Say what you think."

"Well, maybe if I offered them a little more salary than what they get in other gum concessions...."

Max glares. "I will not pay more! I pay the same, but I provide good lodging, good food, and well-maintained airplanes."

"Well, I will see if I can get them."

"'Will see' is not good enough. You get the best, *Capitán*. What about a mechanic?"

"He is right here. This is Ricardo Quel," Cayetano says, beckoning him to approach.

Astounded, Max exclaims, "This is a mechanic?"

"The very best in the Southeast, *señor* Wolff."

Max regards the humble mechanic with obvious distrust. "He takes care of the airplane I am flying?"

"Yes, sir."

"*Verdammung*! Has he gone to a school? What qualifies him as a mechanic?"

With his pride hurt, Ricardo begins to say something, but Cayetano cuts him short. "He learned his trade from me years ago, sir, and ever since, he has been the best aircraft mechanic around."

Annoyed, Max strides to the Robin, shaking his head. "Let us go back to Mérida now."

"*Señor* Wolff, do you want two or three pilots? Remember we have four airplanes," Cayetano shouts after him.

Still walking, Max yells back: "And you remember, I am a pilot!"

The Robin's door slams shut behind Max and the engine starts when Neto spins the propeller.

Gumersindo, Ricardo, and Cayetano trade glances. "What was it you said about a cow?" sneers Ricardo.

Scratching the scar on his chest, Gumersindo murmurs, "The bigger the bull, the worse he chokes when he has a rope around his neck."

Cayetano laughs, but Gumersindo doesn't know why, or at whom the pilot laughs.

Chapter 18 – The Pilots

Flying the blue Bellanca by himself, Cayetano looks around the Campeche airport for aerial traffic. Erected in the seventeenth century to fend off pirates and buccaneers, the San Miguel Fort surrounds the port city of Campeche that lays to the east, with its red-tiled rooftops ablaze in the light of the rising sun. The dark blue open waters of the Gulf of Mexico spread out to the north, and, to the south and west, solid green woodlands mark the periphery of deep forest.

Craning his neck, Cayetano looks toward the airport situated in a shallow valley surrounded by hills. It is the sole level stretch close to town suitable to set up a landing strip. The 900 meter- long dirt strip is short by regular standards, but adequate because it sits at sea level, where airplane engines run at its optimum power. However, because it starts at the rocky shoreline and ends at the foot of a sharp ridge rising 150 meters over the terrain, it isn't an airport suited for novices. Once committed to land, there can be no second thoughts about it, since the prevailing wind is a tail sea breeze blowing onto the glide path. Thus, there is no 'go around' unless the pilot wants to squander the supply of good luck he has brought into the world.

Cayetano is an excellent pilot, but constant drinking and other excessesive indulgences curtail his ability to some extent. Nevertheless, his vast experience usually pulls him out of critical or adverse stuations.

Max Wolff did not allow him to stay up the night before, so right now he feels in top shape. Flying south, he disregards the established traffic pattern and dives the Skyrocket over the Mexicana Airlines' small terminal building. He pulls up, cutting power, and turns tightly to align the airplane with the landing strip.

Whisking the roof of a bus traveling west along the road, which runs parallel to the coastline between the beach and the head of the landing strip, he flares out to let the Skyrocket's wheels roll smoothly onto the sandy ground.

Two minutes later he parks alongside the shabby hangar of the Servicio Aereo Nevarez. Grinning, Tomasito, the mechanic nicknamed *El Chicharrín*, approaches the airplane and shouts, "¡*Ese, mi Tano!*"

"*¿Que hay pues, Chicharrín?*" Cayetano greets him, stepping out of his airplane.

"Nothing, except what the Aeronautical Inspector said about suspending your pilot's license for buzzing the airport."

"*¿Ah, si*? Go tell the old ox that, like Napoleon Bonaparte told Pope Pius Seven: 'His farts may be loud, but its stink doesn't reach me!'"

Both of them share a hard laugh.

Chicharrín asks, "Were you not going to move North to start a passenger route with Panini? How come you are still flying the Bellanca of the widow?"

"Because Estelita sold the concession, flying wrecks and all."

"I bet you had something to do with it."

Cayetano lights a cigarette under Chicharrín's watchful eye. He knows how cagey the pilot is, especially when the dealings involve women.

"Well," Cayetano goes on, "the thing is, she does not have the money to work the concession and was about to see if your boss or Silveira wanted to buy it, when the opportunity fell into my lap, out of the blue. I was talking about the deal with Herculito in the restaurant of the airport of Mérida, when this guy overheard our conversation and butted in. He is a Swiss investor who was looking for just this kind of business, so I took him to Estelita."

"That is funny! Why would an advanced European want to set up a business venture in the middle of a wild jungle?"

"Well, Europeans are hard working people who do not mind getting involved in hardships, if there is a possibility of making a lot of money; and this guy looks to me like he is got a fine nose to find gold any where it may be concealed."

"He may be right about that, natural gum, once processed is nothing but solid gold; just look at how wealthy are Silveira all the rest of the gum concessionaries. So you took him to the widow, and then what?

"Well, Estelita had the Xkanták Central cleaned up, the airplanes scrubbed, and drew a hard bargain selling the Swiss everything at the price of gold."

"You must have made a good commission!"

"The best!"

"The very best, because it tastes like salty sardines, I bet!"

They laugh, celebrating the inveterate *Casanova's* latest conquest.

"And what is the name of the new owner, Tano?"

"*Max Wolff Suppository.*"

"Suppository?"

"Yes, because he is a constant pain in the ass."

They laugh again.

"And what? Did you bring me the Skyrocket for some repair?"

"Say what? You think I do not appreciate my life any longer?"

"*¡Orale, Tano!* What are people going to think if they hear you saying that?"

"Okay. So nobody says anything, sandblast my spark plugs. I felt the RPMs dropping a bit. Where is all the brave tribe?"

"Everybody left already. Who were you looking for?"

"Anyone. I need two pilots. Know of someone available?"

"No. Did you check in Mérida?"

"There are a couple of them there, but the kind you know will be using the plane for a coffin in no time."

"Well, there is this guy, a *gringo,* who used to be a pilot. He may want to fly."

"A gringo?"

"Yes. Don Carlitros Topes, the Aeronautical Inspector, says he is the guy who wrecked a small Cessna close to Progreso, when the hurricane hit last year. The girl who was with him got killed, so he is been roaming around since then. I do not know if this guy is a jack off or not, but the other day a *Mexicana* pilot told me he saw this guy once in Havana wearing the uniform of a captain. He could not remember if it was from Pan American or from Braniff."

"Are you kidding me? Chicharrín. Why do you think this gringo would be looking for a job here?"

"He talks to no one, but I have seen how he slobbers whenever he sees an airplane in flight."

"But why would he be interested in being a *chiclero* pilot?"

"Why not? Could you not be flying for an airline?"

"That is a different story!" Cayetano retorts, somewhat annoyed. "What kind of monkey is he, anyway?"

"He seems to be okay, except maybe he hits the Xxtabentun bottle pretty hard."

"*¡Ujule!* One wino in my family is more than enough. I will look him up nonetheless. Where does he hang out?"

"Day before yesterday I saw him at La Campechana, that eatery by the main plaza where Doña Fortina has a rooming house upstairs. Maybe he lives there."

"*Gracias,* Chicharrín. Step on it, I will not be long."

The *fonda* smells of freshly fried fish and nicely cooked beans. Although the place doesn't look like much — five metal bar tables with their respective chairs, a well-worn wooden counter, and old picture calendars hanging from the walls of a room too big and too hot – the prospect of a full belly whets Cayetano's appetite.

A handsome chunky woman appears by the kitchen door wiping her hands on the apron. Her lively black eyes take in Cayetano with special interest. "Come in, young man! Get the weight off your feet and place it on your butt."

Cayetano turns to look behind him to make sure she is addressing him, and grins. "You flatter me, *señora.* Thank you!"

"Young and beautiful!" The chubby cook complements him again. "What will you have?"

"Is the *pan de cazón* ready?"

The woman grins, amazed. "Son of my soul, you do have a good sense of smell! It is almost ready."

"With an ice-cold Carta Clara beer, please. And listen, I am looking for a gringo who hangs around here."

"*¿Un gringo?*" She disapproves. "My son, do not take the wrong path! *Gringa* is what you should be looking for!"

"No, no, no! The woman that ties me down has to be a portly *campechana* for two reasons: First, because that will mean she is a good cook; and secondly, because she will have plenty of muscle to grab and pinch!"

They both laugh hard and long. Then, the woman says, "My son, you I would gladly support for life!" Suddenly, she glances up at the door. "Look! Talk about the devil! Is that not the gringo you are looking for?"

Bob Calver enters the *fonda*, a much different Bob Calver from the confident captain he used to be. A weeklong beard, worn-out shoes, wrinkled dirty trousers, and old sweat staining his shirt clearly proclaim his moral defeat. With the sparkle gone from his blue eyes, he looks older than Cayetano, although he is several years younger.

Taking the table in the back, he lets himself drop onto the chair and beckons the woman for a beer.

"He eats very little," she whispers to Cayetano. "He asks mostly for beer."

Cayetano nods, gets up and walks to Bob's table. "May I join you?" he asks, in pretty good English.

Bob looks up. Apathetic, he indicates the chair next to his. "You wanna a beer?"

"Thanks, I already asked for one. Is it true you fly?"

The straightforward question startles Bob. "Why do you ask?"

"I have a job for a good pilot."

Bob stares at Cayetano. A sudden flash of interest shines in his eyes, but it immediately fizzles out. His gaze drops to his shaky hands. "I used to do that."

"How long has it been since you flew last?"

"Almost two years."

"Flying can't be forgotten that soon. Who did you fly for?"

"I didn't say I needed a job, so quit bugging me!"

Cayetano stares at him, gets up, and goes back to his table.

The cook enters with the beers, places one in front of Bob and gives one to Cayetano. "Is the romance over so soon?"

"You were right. Next time I will look for a *gringa*."

She grins. "I will get you the fish," she says, then walks back into the kitchen.

Bob raises his eyes, takes a good look at Cayetano and, abashed, gets up and goes over to apologize. "Forgive me, pal. I didn't mean to be rude. Okay if I sit?"

When the cook returns from the kitchen she sees them together again. Placing the dish before Cayetano, she chides him. "Son of my soul, are you taking the wrong path again?"

"What kind of a job do you have?" Bob asks.

"Aaahhh!" Cayetano sighs after taking a long swig of beer. "I needed this cold beer! Well, I'd say it's the toughest kind of flying there can be. We're called *chiclero pilots*. We fly *chicle*, natural gum, the kind used to make chewing gum, out of the forest."

"That doesn't sound so tough."

"Listen first, and then decide. We fly from sunrise to sunset in airplanes that, by your standards, should've been scrapped years ago: Skyrockets, Curtiss Robins, Vegas, Travelaires, and the like. The pride of the fleet is a 1931 tri-motor Ford. We usually haul 1,400 pounds of gum bales in crates designed to lift about half that much, and maintenance is done mostly with used or rebuilt parts. Now, that's the soft part. Then, we make time in the jungle for the best part of seven months, isolated from civilization, women, and booze; eating shit when we get a square meal. We're exposed to malaria, poisonous snakes, and tarantulas. Mosquitoes, gadflies, and gum flies are also part of the fun. As well, we hobnob with thieves, known killers, and fugitives of the worst kind. You can call it hell, the Mayan call it *Xibalbá*. The pay isn't all that bad, but it could be better: six hundred pesos a month, plus room, board, and laundry."

"You sure make it sound attractive!" Bob grins ruefully. "Do you have many applicants for this sort of job?"

"Mostly young guys building up their flying time to take a crack at the airlines, or old hands like me, that get our kicks out of defying the odds." Cayetano takes another swig from his beer, and warns: "By the way, booze is out on working days."

"Don't worry. To die is not one of my priorities."

Flies hover insistently over the remains of the *cazón* fish left by Cayetano. Bob waves them away unconsciously. The cook comes back to remove the plate, and he asks for another beer.

"It's been almost two years already! God! Maureen isn't going to come back to life. What am I doing here?" Bob thinks to himself.

After the accident, he had Maureen interred temporarily in Mérida's quaint Florido cemetery, while he made arrangements with her parents to have her body transferred to New York City. However, using his recovery as an excuse, he deferred his departure day after day, binding himself with a chain of time to the Yucatán Peninsula.

He judged and found himself guilty of Maureen's death. He had destroyed the essence of youth that could have given him vitality and happiness to his waning years. The guilt just kept growing in him. One day, dead drunk to hide from himself the fact that he was sneaking away, he traveled as far as Campeche. He never went back to Mérida, but he couldn't flee any farther either.

He reflects on Cayetano's offer. If he keeps drinking away the money he receives from leasing his Palm Beach apartment, he'll end up a drunkard. That is some sort of punishment, but he doesn't want to debase himself that way.

"Maybe that jungle, that hell as Cayetano called it, is the penance I require."

The taxicab parks by the Bellanca. Cayetano gets off and pays the driver, while Bob climbs down. Looking at the airplane, he drops his suitcase on the ground. "A Bellanca Pacemaker! It must be at least thirteen years old!"

"Nope; it's a Skyrocket, and it's only ten years old," Cayetano says. "However, its engine does have over twelve major overhauls. A little over thirteen thousand hours in the air."

Bob whistles. He looks much better after a bath, a shave, and a change of clothes.

Chicharrín comes out of the hangar, all smiles. "Your plane is ready, Tano."

"Look, Chicharrín. This is Captain Calver. He is going to fly with me in Xkanták, but hush it up because he does not have a Mexican license to fly here."

"¡*Mucho gusto, Capitán* Calver," Tomasito smiles. Bob nods. "The plugs were clean enough, but two of them were leaking. Here they are. I put in two new ones."

"Thank you, Chicharrín. May God repay you!"

"Why do you not repay me? I do not see God too often. Drop yourself with fifty mangoes, Tano!"

"Fifty pesos just to blast the plugs? Did you forget I am from Monterrey, land of the tightwads? Here, take twenty and say you did great."

"Twenty is not even the cost of the plugs I installed in you!"

"To begin with, Chicharrín, you did not install in me any spark plugs, because I fire myself out eating beans and *chile*. Moreover, if you were this smart, you would have noticed that all the plugs in my airplane have a file mark, so nobody messes with them. These ones you gave me have no mark!"

Tomasito grins apologetically. "I know that! I was just trying to kid you."

"Trying to swindle me, you mean!"

Chicharrín smiles, and then turns to look at an approaching airplane. "Hey, look! *Tocho Pérez* is coming in from Chetumal. Maybe he has heard of some other pilot."

A battered Bellanca Skyrocket glides on final approach to land, its engine revving constantly.

"Do you hear that?" Tomasito says, grinning big. "Sounds like its engine is failing!"

"I pity him; he is dropping right into your web!"

The Skyrocket lands heavily on its three wheels, rolls out, and stops in front of the terminal building, its engine coughing and rasping until the propeller stops twirling. With wavering steps, six passengers deplane and, behind them, the pilot and then an assistant who hastens to place chocks against the airplane's wheels.

Tocho, short and chubby, approaches. "Cayito! Happy are the eyes that see you!" the pilot yells, opening his chunky arms to embrace Cayetano.

"Long time no see, *Tocho*! *Oye*, and how did you make out with that Tehuana woman you told me about day before yesterday."

"The witch! She cast a spell on me. Let us have some cold juices of barley, and I will tell you all about her."

"*Gracias*, Tocho, but I am leaving."

"Do not sabotage the fun! Where are you going in such haste?"

"Back to work. By the way, I need a pilot. Do you know of anyone available?"

Hearing Cayetano's question, the young assistant joins them.

"*No, manito*. Not right now," he answers.

Cayetano takes Bob by an arm to introduce him. "Look, Tocho. This is *Capitán* Calver. Bob, he is *Tocho Pérez*."

The two pilots shake hands.

"If I hear of anyone, I will send him over."

"*Capitán* Pérez! Please remember!" the young assistant says urgently, pulling Tocho's shirtsleeve.

"What a dumb ox I am!" Tocho snaps his fingers. "Look, Cayito. This boy flies real well, and he is also an excellent mechanic. We do not have any positions open; otherwise, he would be a pilot already. Give him a chance. I recommend him amply."

Cayetano gives the lad his full attention. "What is your flying time, son?"

"A little over three hundred hours, *Capitán*."

"Have you flown solo?"

"No, *Capitán*. All my time is in the right seat."

"Do you think you could handle a Curtiss Robin?"

The young man's eyes question Tocho.

"I am sure he can, with just a little training." Tocho says.

"Well, then it is settled! When can you start, son?"

The young man questions Tocho again.

"Okay by me," Tocho says. "Be on your way. I am going to cancel the rest of the flight because my aerobanana is failing and, while Tomasito checks it out, I can ask for another assistant from *Villahermosa*."

"¡*Gracias, Capitán Pérez*!" the young man says cheerfully.

"Well, got any luggage?" Cayetano asks.

"Just my overnight bag."

"Go get it then, and let us go... ah.... What is your name, son?"

"José María Ortegón, *Capitán*. But please call me Chema."

Chapter 19 – Xkanták Opens

"Easy, easy, do not jerk the stick; just apply a little backward pressure. Close the throttle slowly, steadily. That is it! Now, start your flare by bringing the stick back smoothly, wings level with the ailerons. Keep the nose straight with the rudder pedals. That is it! That is it, *chingao!*"

The Curtis Robin breaks its glide gently, flaring out with its nose pointed high as it approaches the ground. When the wheels touch the ground there are no jolts, only the rumble of its battered fuselage as it shakes on Xkanták's uneven landing strip.

"Fantastic landing, Chema!" Cayetano cheers happily, slapping the boy's shoulder. "Pull up by the gasoline drums."

Chema applies the brake lever to slow the plane down and stops the Robin by the shed where Ricardo, Neto, and Bob take cover from the glaring sun.

Cayetano whacks Chema's shoulder again. "Well, my son, from now on you make your own decisions. Commend yourself to the Eleven Thousand Virgins, catch one if you can, do three or four good landings, and get back here in one piece!"

Stunned, Chema asks, "Me? Alone? So soon?"

"No way will I babysit you forever! ¡*Orale, cuélele, güerco mondao*! Go fly this kite!" Cayetano shouts over the drone of the engine and walks away, leaving him alone – alone to fly a machine that he's barely familiar with.

The hand he has on the brake lever shakes, while his begging gaze hangs onto Cayetano's sturdy figure. Cayetano, meanwhile, jokes with the others, pointing at the airplane and making threatening gestures. The moment has come – the moment every pilot eagerly awaits and dreads when it arrives.

His previous self-possession vanishes, but he has to give it a try before he loses his nerve completely. His left hand cracks the throttle open and the Robin springs to life. Looking outside to steer the airplane along the center of the strip, he feels crowded in the small cockpit. The heat is unbearable and his forehead, already moist before, now drips. His mind, however, feels cool.

He halts the Robin at the end of the strip and revs up the engine to test the magnetos. He watches the RPM indicator closely, hoping to see its needle drop, but it reads normal.

"Do it!" he exclaims aloud, and points the Robin northeast.

From then on, everything happens as if in a dream. Once the throttle is wide open, the ground slides under the wings. The new

95

storehouse, the main house, and the shouting pilots are left behind. As the speed and the noise increase, what was solid before now becomes a green blotch shooting back from the Robin's nose toward the tail. Suddenly, there is only the deep bass sound of the pistons booming within the cylinders. Chema snaps out of the ecstatic trance he had fallen into and realizes he is suspended in mid-air.

Underneath, the landscape is solid dark green, composed of a terrifying assortment of treetops. *Zaramullos, caimitos, caobos* and *framboyanes* ignite the jungle with the blazing red of their flowers. Mangoes, wild plums, slender gum trees, and, standing proud above all, the gigantic *ceibas*, all of them shaking their limbs menacingly as they threaten to swallow and bring down the mechanical birds to enclose them forever in their emerald underbrush.

Chema cringes. However, looking upward, he finds an ally in the sky's unreachable zenith that invites him to sail in its blue for an eternity, endorsing him in his daring yearning to fly.

A blast of air rushes from his lungs, a cry of savage joy. Now he rules space. He has undergone the coveted mutation from earthbound worm to birdman.

He completes his third successful landing. As soon as he steps down from the Robin, Cayetano and the others rush to his side to grab his arms and legs and drag him to the shed, where they have everything ready to perform his initiation ceremony.

"¡*Orale, montoneros*! Let me go!" he yells, struggling to free himself.

"¡*No, mi cuate*! You are not escaping this one!"

"Do not be mules, please!"

"You have to pay your dues! Take a good hold of his feet, Ricky, and I will hold his arms! ¡*Orale, Neto*! Saddle up and give him the spurs all the way!"

They all shout and laugh, including Chema, on whose belly Neto rides, spurring his back rudely.

"...Eight, nine, and ten!" Cayetano adds up, pulling Chema's arms one last time to make Neto bounce higher. "Now let go of him, Rico!"

Both release Chema at the same time and he flies high in the air to land on his rear with Neto on top.

"Now let us bathe him!"

Bob smiles. This initiation ritual is quite different from his own. When he flew solo for the first time, he only had his shirttail sheared off and paid for a round of beers.

While Cayetano holds Chema by the arms, Ricardo dumps a bucket full of burnt oil on his head, showering him down to his toes.

"May you be blessed by Gucumatz," Ricardo consecrates.

Feeling the oil drip down his lips, Chema instinctively licks it and spits. Then he shakes all over trying to spatter oil on his captors, who run away laughing.

"You will see when I catch you!"

"Who told you to fly solo!" Cayetano yells. "Thank God we are here. Elsewhere you would have had to pay for drinks and girls!"

Gumersindo watches them from the warehouse door, sneering. "They are like children!" he grumbles, unable to understand their joy. Hearing an airplane, he looks to the north. "¡*Epa, tú, Galicio*! The boss is arriving!"

Engrossed in their cavorting, the pilots and mechanics don't hear the airplane until it's already landing.

"¡*Pa'su máre*!" Ricardo exclaims. "Here comes the boss!"

Chema wants to run and hide and Cayetano looks at his oil-stained clothes. "There's no remedy now!"

Upon deplaning, Max looks at them. "¡*Capitán Rodríguez*!" he calls out. "What is the meaning of this rowdiness?"

"Nothing, sir. We were just playing."

"I do not want play during work time. I demand formality. Who are these men?" he asks, indicating Bob and Chema.

"The pilots I got, Bob Calver and Chema Ortegón."

"This one does not look like a pilot," Max says pointing at Chema. Is he an apprentice?"

"No, sir. He is a pilot, and a very good mechanic. A truly useful man."

Max ignores the young man and faces Bob, whom he regards with approval. "You are an American, are you not?" he says, in heavily accented English.

"Yes."

"Excellent! I am glad to have you with me. You will be chief pilot. Latin Americans require a heavy hand, but you will be able to handle them with no problem."

Bob remains distant. His first impression of Max is a sour one and he makes no attempt to disguise it.

"I'm sorry, but I'm not a foreman, and I'll be lucky if I can handle myself. Besides, you already have a chief pilot who speaks English as well as I do."

Max's blood boils instantly, but he restrains himself. "I suppose that at least you are a competent pilot."

"That'll have to remain a supposition," Bob says, holding Max's gaze.

"Pallares!" Max shouts, striding away.

"Ready for what you have to order, *señó Worf.*" Gumersindo replies.

"Does the shower work now?"

"*¡Si, señó Worf!*"

"We will talk after I bathe. I want you to hire workers."

Bob turns and meets Cayetano's sympathetic gaze. He grins morosely and then goes to sit on a rough bench under the shed, his head bowed, feeling abashed.

Cayetano picks up a rag, dips it in gasoline, and removes the oil from his hands.

Observing Cayetano's sullen look, Ricardo sends Chema away, telling him, "*Bosh*, take that bucket with gasoline and go bathe. The river runs behind those trees."

"*Gracias, mano.*" Chema walks off.

Approaching Cayetano, Ricardo says, "I did not understand everything the boss said in English, but it bothered you, hah?"

"*Si, Ricardo.*"

"*¡Máre, Cayito!* For you to call me by my true name, it is because he really blew your good mood. But you are still in command, are you not?"

"In command of what? Command this to shit is what I should do!"

Gently, Ricardo says, "What need do you have to bear assholes like that man, bosh? Why do you not go back home?"

"Because it is not that easy."

"*¡Máre, Cayetano!* Do not be such a *guariscol*! You are stuck here because you want to. As bad as it may be what you did to Idalia, women always forgive. Moreover, she is your wife, the only one who has rights over you, and she loves you! And what about your children? Do you not think they need you?"

"I wrote her once, but she never answered."

"You wrote her? For things like that, you do not write, *caballo*! You go in person, stand before her, ask for forgiveness and work things out. Then you go to Mexicana Airlines, become a DC-3 captain in the wink of an eye, and take your rightful place in aviation!"

"There are other things, Rico. Things even you, my closest friend, do not know about. Come on, go gas my airplane."

"What I am going to do is to offer four tallow candles to the Wandering Head of the witch Xulub, so that Pujuy, the owl, pierces the skull of the Swiss, and that Tamazul the bull toad pisses in his eyes, and his guts entwine in a triple knot!"

Despite his sulking, Cayetano grins saying, "Looks to me like you fell in love with the boss on first sight!"

Chapter 20 – The Chicleros

Sitting inside the Ricardo Nevarez's hangar, Bob enjoys a cold Negra Leon beer while chatting with Chicharrín, who actually does all the talking, using an atrocious mixture of English and Spanish to spell out the *chicleros* farmer's life.

The *chicleros* working for the gum concessions spend seven months out of the year in Xibalbá, the depths of hell; seven months in which they die a little every day, only to flourish suddenly for a short term of five or six weeks.

They endure seven months of slavery in the forest to make, depending on their health and their arm's dexterity to carve the gum or *chicle* trees' trunks with their *burunas*, anywhere from fifteen to twenty-five thousand pesos – a huge sum of money for those derelicts.

They come back to civilization in April laden with riches, infested with vermin, and debilitated by maladies. Spent, almost dead, the first ones to arrive are like a bugle call alerting the towns and villages situated on the periphery of the jungle. General stores take on extra help, the cantinas are stocked with all kinds of liquor, the brothels get ready for around the clock trade, and the price of everything soars.

They arrive in hordes, like human rivers flowing from every path leading out of the forest. The small trains are crammed to the roofs and there are many *chicleros* who, in their haste to arrive ahead, charter airplanes.

Only a few go back to their hometowns to make good use of their money because, for most of them, there are only three choices: life in the jungle, or prison, or death elsewhere.

Dirty from seven months of work, they crowd the stores to buy brightly-colored rayon shirts, white cotton trousers, strong boots, palm hats, underwear, and *paliacates*, multicolored bandanas to tie around their necks. Then, in rivers and public bathhouses, they remove the seven-month layer of grime and sweat from their bodies.

Later, clad in their new gaudy shirts, they invade the gun shops looking for the cherished Super .38-caliber Smith & Wesson or Colt handguns, buying out the stock in two or three days. Those missing out on the sale of these guns buy any other brand or caliber just to show that they are as much of a man as the next.

From the gun shops they splurge on the best dinner ever, and then they head to the cantinas and whorehouses to make up for their seven-month abstinence and to pick a fight so they can fire their new revolvers for the first time.

They ride in taxis all over town, followed by bands of musicians, and end up sleeping in jail only to be released the next day after paying stiff fines. This cycle repeats itself night after night until their wallets are empty.

The aftermath: three or four months of poverty, selling cheaply what they paid for dearly, living on their meager reserves until, once their pride is defeated by hunger, they part with their precious .38 pistol.

For nights afterward, they sleep under the stars in parks, or the outskirts of towns, and many days they sweep the streets guarded by local policemen, until the gum concession owners begin hiring for the new season in September.

The employment line runs under the shadow of the hangar. Over one hundred men wait to go by the table where a bookkeeper enters their names in the Xkanták's concession ledger.

Without a *buruna* hanging from his belt, Gumersindo Pallares feels naked. Fidgety, he shifts the revolver he carries under his shirt so it rides more comfortably on his hip. It's not that he doesn't like guns, but he always feels safer having along the sharp *buruna* that has never failed him. Likewise, he knows that he might need it on occasions such as this. Among the workers being hired, he has seen familiar faces, men who are his cronies and others he has once fired. None of them intimidate him because he is certain that, whether friends or foes, all of them fear him more than they fear the devil. He's more worried about the ones he doesn't know. Among the new arrivals, there could be someone man enough to challenge his leadership, or someone else looking to avenge a relative's life cut short by the sharp edge of his dearly missed *buruna*.

"How many more do you want me to register, Don Gumersindo?" Melchor, the bookkeeper, asks him.

"How many do we have so far?"

"The usual one hundred."

"This time we will take two hundred like the boss wants, and enroll two dozen extra to replace those who shed their skin right away. Looks to me that many of these guys will not pull through twenty bales, many of them look too fucked up."

Actually, there is no set method to select the workers. Those who look weaker are sometimes the ones who have the best chance at survival. Weak or strong, young or old, anyone can die in the forest at any time.

"Name?" the bookkeeper asks the stalwart young man standing in front of him.

"Ramón de la Torre!" he replies with a strong and defiant voice.

Gumersindo almost jumps on hearing the name, and turns to find Ramón's fiery eyes fixed on him.

"Wait!" he tells Melchor, and then asks Ramón, "Where are you from?"

"From *Alamo, Veracruz*. What of it?"

Although it is midday and it's hot, a cold chill runs down Gumersindo's spine. "What is your trade?"

"Trade?"

"*¡Si, pues!* Are you a *picador*, gum cook, mule driver, what?"

Ramón opens his wide strong hands to show his calloused palms, "See these? They can do anything with a *buruna*!"

"*¡Esta bueno, pues!* Sign him up, Don Melchor."

"Sign up my wife too. She will also work. Her name is Rosenda," Ramón says, and walks away with the small salary advance received.

Gumersindo's gaze follows him to the tree where he meets with a young girl.

"*¡Eh, compadre!*"

Gumersindo turns when he hears the voice coming from a group of workers who are keeping away from other *chicleros*.

"*¿Qué pasa, pues?*"

"Nothing much happening, *compadre*," Faustino tells him. "Just that myself and the relatives here want to remind you to place us in the *jato* closest to the Central, given that we would like to be near the provisions as usual. Are we, *compadre*?"

"We are." Gumersindo accedes to his hometown folks' request, but he warns them, "Only this time, Faustino, there will not be nearly as much liquor as before."

"And why may that be, *compadre*?"

"Because the new owner is a demanding man, and you will have me in deep shit with the first brawl you start!"

"*¡Vaya, pariente!* And how come you are you afraid of this boss?"

"I am not afraid of anyone, *pendejo*! I respect him because he knows how to be boss. Have you all you need?"

"*Si, pues.*"

"Then gather your rags and go near the airplanes, to send you out first."

"When the group starts to move away, Gumersindo calls over the oldest *Tuxpeño*. "¡*Parate, Faustino*! Look over there," he says, nodding over to where Ramón stands with his wife. What do you see in that lad, the one talking to the pretty girl?"

"Like he takes after somebody familiar," the old man says after regarding Ramón carefully.

"His name is Ramón de la Torre."

Faustino gapes. "He cannot be! He was just a child six or seven years ago, when his father died!"

"It was nine years ago, and his father did not just die. We gave him a pass for his funeral near Cerro Azul, remember?"

"Do you think the lad is coming after us?"

"Who knows? Lauriano Ortíz saw us kill him, but now Lauriano is also dead. Maybe he is here just for the job, but one thing I tell you: bringing that fine mare to the jungle with him, he is not going to be a concern to us for long."

"Yes, she is in her whole cream." Faustino says, licking his fat black lips.

Bob Calver watches the hiring routine from under the wing of the Travelaire he has been assigned to fly. He feels someone approaching from behind him and turns.

"Hi!" Cayetano says, wiping the perspiration from his brow with his forefinger, to spatter it away. "Some difference, huh?"

Calver doesn't catch on.

"I mean the category of passengers you'll be flying now."

"Oh, yeah! Listen, there's something I don't quite understand. The men on the line are being hired, right?"

"Aha."

"But what about those women? Are they with the men?"

Cayetano looks at the group of trollops waiting near the hiring table. Slovenly and raggedly, their ugliness is out of proportion even in that wretched setting. "No. Those poor women are scum: jail birds, washed out whores, beggars, females who have lost all their worth."

"Yeah, that I can see, but why is it that some of the workers call them over? Will they be taking them along?"

Cayetano nods.

"But why? Or rather, what for?"

"You've never been in the jungle, man. After a few weeks of drought, even a drink of vinegar is welcome."

Bob stares at Cayetano.

"Yes, man. After a month in the jungle anything is better than the bare hand. Besides, they cook, wash clothes, or tend the gum caldrons. Most of those men have families but they leave them behind. See that young guy with the pretty girl? If he takes her along, he'll never make it back."

"What about the girl?"

"She'll belong to whoever kills him and soon after that, to someone else, until she ends up like those women. By the way, don't befriend the workers, especially those talking to Pallares now. They're from Tuxpan, Veracruz. That's why they're called *Tuxpeños*. They're the ones that maintain law and order, or wreak havoc, depending on the situation. Never take them liquor, even if they offer you a sister in return. That's strictly forbidden! If you use booze, hide it the best you can. Understand?"

Bob nods, but a question lingers on his expression.

"What is it?" Cayetano asks, noticing his look.

"There is another thing I don't quite comprehend... All I see around here is... destitution. Where does the profit come from for an investor? How come these wretched workers make so much money? Doing what...?"

"Okay, let me start at the beginning. You chewed gum as a kid, or have chewed gum when you flew to unplug your ears; at any rate, in the States and worldwide, people chew gum, so, that makes it a multimillion business, right?" Bob nods. "Okay, all of that gum originates here, Bob."

"But how, or where does it come from?

"From the *chicozapote* trees that grow all over the jungle. Most of these workers you see are *picadores,* slashers, who climb those tall slender trees and, with their machetes they call *burunas,* slash diagonal incisions in the trunk all the way to the top, to drain its resin, or latex, which is collected in canvas bags placed underneath the slash. These bags are emptied into a large one called a *chivo*, and taken to the cook house to be boiled in copper caldrons for an hour and a half; when it cools down, the resin is emptied in *maquetas,* molds to fashion them into bricks that make up the bales we fly out to the depots to be exported. Presently, each kilogram extracted is worth four pesos and twenty cents, or one dollar, and we are talking thousands of kilograms, or hundreds of thousands of dollars, which are divided among all the people involved in the process, from these workers to the concessionaries, who take the shark's share. Got the picture?"

Smiling, bob says, "Yeah, now I do, and I respect these peoples' purpose in being here."

"Fine, then let's fly them in." Cayetano slaps Bob's shoulder. "It'll take us a couple of days to move all them to Xkanták. Pallares!" he shouts. "Start sending the men over, and as soon as Chema Ortegón gets here, tell him to fly back another group."

"It will be done so, *Capitán*!" Gumersindo yells back, herding his fellow *Tuxpeños* toward the airplanes...

Chapter 21 – Fraü Ingrid Wolff

Rosenda de la Torre sprinkles another pinch of rock salt on the duck *mole* she is seasoning, and reduces the heat on the range. She suddenly feels a burning sensation on her nape and turns around to find Gumersindo leaning on the doorframe of the main house kitchen, staring at her, lusting for her. He is the man of whom she had heard so much about at her husband's home in Alamo, Veracruz.

"What do you want?" she asks, with obvious misgiving.

The foreman can hardly restrain his desire to attack her, but he decides to go easy on her. "Nothing, *chica,* nothing. Just came to see if you are in need of anything."

"I need nothing from you that I know of."

"I see you understood how to work the electric range," he says, approaching her.

"*Si, pues.*"

"Vaya, chica; you are very smart," he commends her, trying to caress her chin, but she backs away. "Smart but unfriendly, when you should be nice to me."

"And just why should I be?" She snaps, turning her back on him.

"You see, it was my idea that you serve the owner of the concession here, instead of going to waste yourself in the jungle. To me, also, you owe that your husband will be working in the closest *jato*, so that he may sneak out here at least over the weekend."

"All of that is appreciated," she replies haughtily, "but do not even think for a moment that helping me is going to give you any rights over me."

"Ponder over this, *chica,*" he mellows. "There is not one single man in the camp who would not want to stuff your tight little cove. If you went with your Ramón to a *jato*, I promise you he would not live past the first night, and then there would be such bloodshed over you, that no *chicleros* would be left to do the gum task the next day. Instead, if you remain here quietly, I will be the only one who enjoys the spicy things you hide under that dress, or maybe even the boss too, because you are pretty enough even for him."

"Get your hands off me, or I will tell Ramón!" she shouts, trying to slap him.

"He is only one man, with no friends. We are many. You tell him, and he is a dead man!"

An engine roars outside, followed by Galicio's voice calling, "¡*Señó* Gumersindo! The boss has arrived!"

"Give it a good thinking, *chica*," Gumersindo repeats, departing hastily.

As the blue Skyrocket's propeller stops spinning, Gumersindo steps forward to open the door. Max lets himself out, and then turns to courteously extend his hand to help *Fraü* Ingrid Wolff step down.

Gumersindo's smile breaks off as he gapes. Never in his earthbound worm's life has he seen such a magnificent woman.

Ingrid Wolff, actually Baroness Olga Scheuermann, jumps nimbly out of the plane, ignoring Max's hand. Shaking her golden curls she takes in her surroundings with one displeased glance. Obviously, she had a negative opinion of her destination, but when her violet eyes gaze upon the actual misery that will surround her, a flash of anger distorts her features.

The workers approaching with their black, sweaty bare torsos and their lusty stares send goose pimples prickling up her arms. Feeling the envy she awakens in the sorry-looking women watching her from the warehouse, she realizes she affronts them with her radiant beauty and her revealing summer garments.

With affected courtesy, Max leads her by the arm toward the house, saying, "Pallares, bring the luggage in."

"¡Si, *señó Worf, de inmediato!*" Gumersindo stutters, trying to tear away his eyes from *Fraü* Wolff's figure.

"¡*Pa'su máre*! Ricardo exclaims, following the woman's walk as she passes where he and Neto pump fuel from twenty-liter cans into a drum. "If that female is going to live here, Xtab will receive many offerings!"

Neto's expression remains blank.

"Xtab, bosh, is the goddess of crime and the gallows," Ricardo explains.

"I still do not understand what you mean, *maistro!*"

"¡*Pa'su mecha, Neto*! You are dumb! Never mind, it is enough that I understand myself!"

"You and your tales of witches and ancient gods, *maistro!*"

"It is mythology, *caballo*! What do you know!" When the blonde enters the house, he crosses himself.

The meaning of Xkanták Central hits Olga abruptly and wakes her up to the reality in which she finds herself. She blinks, trying to erase the images still imprinted on her eyes, wishing she is just having a bad dream. It's impossible that such a place exists in the world she dwells in. The only trace of civilization is the old airplane sitting under the fierce sun. Everything is primitive. The houses are straw huts, the people repulsive, and the surrounding jungle must be populated by insects, vermin, and wild beasts.

Snapping out of her stupor, she looks around. The living area is ample, relatively cool, and furnished with an eye for pragmatism rather than taste. It's the gilded cage that will keep her captive for only God knows how long.

Ambling to the large window she looks outside for a few seconds, and then turns to Max, who waits for her reaction.

"I'll never forgive you for bringing me here," she says slowly, in a throaty voice. "I swear I'll find a way to make you pay for this!"

The afternoon rainfall has charged the air with humidity. A heavy lethargy hangs over the dense brush, turning Xkanták Central into a huge steam bath.

Chema saunters out of the unfinished pilots' dormitory, seeking a breath of the night breeze. Inhaling deeply, he looks around. Not a single leaf stirs. The thick forest's wild noises heighten his sense of suffocation. He unbuttons the collar of his shirt and loosens his tie. Unexpectedly, his ears play a trick on him. He cocks his head to listen. The sound of a languid trumpet, accompanied by a piano, glides through the brush playing a slow, sensuous blues tune. Looking for its source, he walks to the end of the veranda and discovers that the music comes from the main house.

Above, the stars glitter furiously trying to illuminate the pitch-black darkness that shrouds the forest. Below, like a defiant beacon, the main house is a castle of light mocking the firm determination of the shadows to hide everything.

Chema hears footsteps behind him.

"*¡Chichis trais!* Sounds like Herr Suppository wants to inaugurate his business formally!" Cayetano says.

"Yes, with music and everything!"

"But no broads to dance with. However, who knows? Maybe he already has them stashed in the house."

"You really think so, *Capitán*?" Chema gawks.

"Not so far-fetched. If not, why did he ask us to wear ties?"

"*¡Ah, jijo!*" the lad exclaims, looking toward the house. "No wonder that music sounds so horny!"

Cayetano guffaws himself into a coughing fit. "Chema, you really are naive! *No, mano.* What happens is that all Europeans are snobs and, if they invite you to dinner, you have to dress up even in the middle of the jungle. I accepted tonight because this is a special occasion, but if he thinks I am going to spend every night here just to humor him, he is crazy!"

Bob comes out, combing his hair and calling, "Hey, Cayetano!"

"Over here, Bob. Are you ready?"

"Shall we go?"

"Come on, Chema. Let us go partying. As long as the Swiss does not feed us milk, everything will be fine!"

"For the last time, Olga! Are you coming out, or not?" Max calls angrily into the bedroom.

Seconds later, Olga appears at the doorway. "Do you want me to come out like this?" she asks, displaying her alluring figure scantily clad in lacy panties and a brassiere.

"Get dressed!"

Smiling, she stands still.

"By God, don't exasperate me!"

"Exasperate yourself as you will. It is so hot in this damned inferno, I cannot put anything on. Anyway, I will not share a table with your half broken-in apes."

"They are my pilots! Maybe they are not our equals, but they are not savages either."

"Do you fancy yourself still in the *Luftwaffe, liebe* Max?" she sneers, closing the curtain.

Max starts to reply, but a knock on the door holds him short.

"*¡Buenas noches, señor* Wolff!"

"Ah, *Capitán* Rodríguez! Please come in, gentlemen. Have a seat. What will you drink? There is Scotch, cognac, vodka, gin...."

Cayetano's eyes sparkle. "Scotch for me."

"Captain Calver."

"The same, please."

Max cannot grant Chema any standing. "And you?"

"Anything, *señor* Wolff. Whatever is easier."

Max goes to the liquor cabinet, pours Scotch in four tall glasses, adds ice cubes and soda and hands them around. He says, "Because Captain Calver speaks very little Spanish and mine is defective, we'll use English to chat. Captain Rodríguez, you will translate what you deem interesting to your friend, but later." He raises his glass slightly. "To your very good health, gentlemen."

The foreigner's words are like bile in Cayetano's glass. He feels compelled to reply with an insult, but he refrains.

Max takes a drink, regards each one of the guests, and begins speaking his mind. "Gentlemen, I have good news for you. I already signed an exclusive direct, no intermediaries, open contract with an American chewing gum company to sell our entire output. I have started by doubling the number of workers in order to increase the production. Initially I am not interested in making a profit, so, as soon as I receive the first payment, I will buy bigger and better airplanes. I am counting on you to fly out the increase I seek. We will fly from the first light of dawn to the last glimmer of dusk, thus I shall demand that you keep yourselves fit at all times. I forbid you to drink or abuse yourselves in any way."

Cayetano's lips crack in a wide grin.

"I do not think I said anything amusing, Captain Rodríguez!"

"Frankly, Mr. Wolff, what you just said about flying all day long amused me. That may be innovative to you, but for any *chiclero* pilot that has been the norm ever since this exploitation began some five years ago. And," he adds with scorn, "I mean the exploitation of gum, not of the pilots who fly it out."

Cayetano provokes him openly. In other circumstances he would have not allowed that from a subordinate, but right then he cannot afford to lose the only experienced pilot he has. Although his hands are tied, he doesn't yield, so he pours more Scotch in his glass and replies, "I didn't like your innuendo, Captain. I may be difficult to deal with, but I will never go down in history as an oppressor. At the end of the season you all will receive a bonus for each metric ton you fly out."

There is an embarrassing pause while Max takes a long drink.

Considering that, however small, he has won a victory over Max, Cayetano says, "There's a rumor we'd like to touch on, Mr. Wolff. Is it true that you want us to live here?"

Max stares at Cayetano, measuring his insolence. "It is a condition I shall impose on any pilot who wants to work for me. Do you have any objection?"

Feeling that his collar chokes him, Cayetano contends, "If living conditions are bad in villages such as Escarcega or Peto, just think what they'll be here in the jungle!"

"I will live here. If this place is good enough for me, it will be good enough for you!"

Looking about appreciatively, Cayetano replies, "A place like this would also be good enough for me!"

"Once your dormitory is finished, you will have pretty much the same features. Now, going back to our business, how many flights were you able to do in your busiest day last season?"

"Six, to Peto."

"From tomorrow on, six flights will be the minimum. You must fly out an average of three metric tons per day."

"How many tons did you say?" Cayetano gasps.

"Three metric tons!"

"Just how much do you think these airplanes can carry?"

"Both Bellancas and the Travelaire, between five hundred and six hundred kilograms. The Robin, three to four hundred."

Cayetano shakes his head. "Excuse me for saying so, Mr. Wolff, but you're miscalculating. These airplanes may be overloaded once in a while during the wintertime when the temperature is cool, but that cannot be done everyday unless you want to lose them."

"Are you through saying nonsense? I have studied the way you operate and I have eliminated costly transportation blunders." Carried away by his vehemence, Max is shouting now. "What's more, I don't give a damn about the airplanes! In a short while I will be able to buy as many as I need."

Cayetano leaves his glass on a side table and stands up to shout back, "And what about the pilots' lives? Do you also give a damn about them?"

"Good evening, gentlemen!"

A mellow voice caresses their ears and soothes away their anger. With her enticing figure wrapped in sheer fabric and her gorgeous face framed in golden curls cascading down her shoulders, she can only be a goddess who has emerged from the forest's timeless mystery.

Smiling, she says in English, "I am Ingrid Wolff, your hostess. Would any of you gentlemen offer me a drink?"

Cayetano is the first one to react. Going directly to the liquor cabinet, he asks, "Scotch and soda, Madam?"

"I would rather have gin and soda, Mr...."

"Cayetano Rodríguez, your humble servant, Madam Wolff!" He smiles back at her, taking a crystal glass.

Baffled by Olga's sudden and most opportune appearance, Max says, "Thank you for joining us, dear."

With a perfect smile that reveals nothing, she says, "Fortunately my headache has vanished. It was the heat, I suppose." Taking the glass Cayetano offers her, she asks him, "Would you introduce me to your friends, please?"

"My pleasure, Madam." He turns and gestures. "Bob Calver and Chema Ortegón."

Bob and Chema stand up when Olga approaches them with her hand forward, saying charmingly, "Delighted to meet you!"

Chema feels in his hand a velvety touch, soft and mild, just like the warmth he remembers from raising fine pigeons in their hacienda. His mind reels, overpowered by the totality of her beauty.

Bob, who had thought his grief had deprived him of lustful feelings, concludes that his seclusion is a fabrication. He has never lost his flair to appreciate beauty, and neither has he lost his carnal desire. He is reacting like any ordinary, healthy man in the presence of a luscious woman. Discovering this truth makes him withdraw like a snail into his shell.

"If you agree, gentlemen, I will order dinner," Ingrid says.

Max deems it's best to make use of the favorable atmosphere created by his wife's appearance and calls toward the kitchen. "Rosenda!"

The young woman enters timidly, *"Digame, señor."*

"Sirva la cena."

"Si, señor."

Max pulls out the chair at the head of the table for his wife, saying, "You will have to add Spanish to the languages you already speak, darling."

Sitting down, she says, "Spanish sounds lovely. It's a language that sings."

"Like most languages of Latin origin. Do you speak any of them?" Cayetano asks.

"French, although it is not quite a Romance language. Saxon languages are more accessible to me."

"Naturally. But if you speak French, Spanish won't be all that difficult to learn."

"Will you teach me, Captain?" she says, smiling enticingly.

The experienced *Don Juan*, accustomed to courting both easy and challenging women, understands the lure. "My calling in teaching relates to aviation only, Madam; but I will certainly try my best." He feels Max's glare on him. Grinning, he adds, "That is, if Mr. Wolff doesn't mind."

"My husband has always encouraged me to improve my intellect," she replies, and looks at Bob. He was staring at her, but when their eyes meet, he looks away. She is used to drawing all kinds of stares. Lusty ones like Cayetano's and furtive ones like those of the shy young man whose name she did not catch. But she doesn't understand why Bob's are fleeting. Being a mature and vigorous man, with a twist of cynicism in his lips, his smile must be fascinating. Maybe her stay in that hideous place won't be so tedious after all.

When Rosenda comes in with a china bowl, Olga says, "Hmmm! Let's see what kind of exotic soup the regional cuisine has to offer."

"By the scent, I would say it's *chanchak*," Cayetano guesses.

"Shan...?"

"Chanchak, Madam, chanchak! A fish broth of Mayan origin."

"Chanchak! Did I say it right?"

"Perfectly!"

"Are there fish in the forest?"

"Not of this kind, Madam. I flew it in from Campeche. Had I anticipated your presence, I'd have brought something better."

"Captain, you personify the legendary chivalry of Latin men!"

Cayetano grins, flattered. As beautiful as she is, it would not be the first time that that kind of flea jumped under his covers. Several indelible memories of his life's journey are filed in his mind: a dancer who later became internationally famous; an oil tycoon's bored wife; an American missionary gone astray. All of them lovely, worthy of the best man, but not desirable enough to deprive him of his cherished freedom, nor to replace his wife waiting for him up North.

However, this flea is much prettier than the others. Looking around the table, he smiles. Chema is but an adolescent, Bob has God knows what kind of problems, and Max Wolff, although being her husband, is probably a zero to the left.

Chapter 22 – The Passions

Many are the punishments that the *Ahauab*,
Lords of Hell, have in Xibalbá.
First is the *Abode of Darkness*,
Where there is only dejection.
Second is the *Hall of Shivering*, with its glacial walls.
Third is the *Den of Tigers*,
Where the beasts roam in hunger.
Fourth is the *Cave of Bats*,
Wherein a throng of them fly and scream.
Fifth is the *House of Chay*,
Obsidian knives, so piercing
They grate against each other.

"Where is Xibalbá?" the men cry in fear.
The Lords of Xibalbá grin wickedly." They do not realize they
are in it!"
"Let us leave them there, so they can be punished."
"Yes, for they are lewd and stupid!"
"Let them suffer and wail."
"Yes, yes!"
"Hah, hah, hah!" Mock the Lords of Hell.

Following a shrill screech, a grotesque creature appears flying a zigzag pattern, to graze Chema's head. The bat's fetid stink nauseates him, pulling him out of his reverie.

Seated in the dark veranda of the pilots' dormitory, he stares at the main house bedroom window, still lit. Closing his eyes, he pictures Mrs. Wolff's lovely face, and caresses the palm of his right hand with his left fingers, trying to recreate the soft sensation he felt in it earlier. Besides finding her stunning, Chema experiences an unknown fascination for that woman.

Another thought glides across his mind: he has been with few women since the night he spent with Magdalena. For twenty-three long weeks he has worked hard, struggling to learn and to improve his skills, saving money to the brink of going hungry. But the thought that he is a man and that willing women surround him, haunts him all the time. He is particularly reminded of this thought when his friends mock him for not joining them in their binges. He has held fast to a memory and a purpose, which has turned into an obsession. Now that he has finally been able to move his family from Peralvillo to a better neighborhood, he aims to go to Mexico City once the gum harvest season is over, to bring Magdalena back with him to Mérida, or to Campeche, where he can visit her frequently.

"But, why don't I chase women like all other men do, even if they are married? Am I not as much a man as the rest of them?"

Looking at the lighted window again, he observes Olga's shadow on the curtain, obviously naked and toweling her hair. He feels the growth in his crotch, touches it, and finds he has an erection. His face flushes when, in his conscience, he clearly hears the arcane commandment: 'Thou shall not covet thy neighbor's wife!'

Max slips on his pajama shirt and looks up at Olga. She has just taken a shower and wears only a gauzy robe.

Toweling her hair, she asks, "Won't you take a shower?"

"What for?" he replies, annoyed. "I sweat even after taking a shower. But if you'd rather I did...."

Olga looks at him from under the towel. "Why should I make you do it?"

"We haven't made love since the night we spent in *Chichen Itza*"

"True! That night, the romanticism of that magic place and the music under a full moon predisposed me. But cherish its memory, *lieber*. From now on, that bed will be mine alone. If you want to stay in this room, you can use the sleeper."

"What the devil are you saying?"

"Simply that, as long as we live here, you must forget I am your wife," she says casually. Then with deliberate leisure, she unties her robe to display the arrogant perfection of her nude body. "All of this – which, by the way you have never truly possessed – is now solely mine to do with it whatever I please. Maybe nobody will ever touch it, but that I cannot promise!"

Max stares at her in disbelief.

"Don't be shocked. You have never known me really. You were always too busy doing business or playing politics to grant me the attention a wife deserves."

"Now I understand why you decided to show up for dinner. You horny bitch!"

"Max, please! No insults. You're too civilized to debase yourself to the level of those who sleep outside."

Coming in from the warehouse, Rosenda enters the darkened living area. Upon seeing the light filtering through the bedroom curtained doorway, she stops and gazes inside. In the middle of the room, her mistress brazenly exposes her naked beauty. Flustered, her first reaction is to walk on to the kitchen to her cot, but the sight of Olga's body holds her entranced.

Olga keeps her torso thrust forward, luring Max, defying the male in him. She tantalizes him with the firmness of her breasts. Her trim waist challenges him and her smooth thighs demand to be caressed.

He cannot restrain himself any longer. Approaching her, he wraps her in a violent embrace, searching for her mouth.

She turns her head away and says in her deepest voice, "I am going to scream, Max. I am going to call for help until someone comes in. Can you imagine the ridicule you will face?"

Her words scorch him and he pushes her away viciously. She falls by the foot of the bed. Smiling, she gets up and goes to the dresser to direct the electric fan toward the bed. Then she parts the mosquito netting and reclines on the bed to watch him rage helplessly, held back only by his fear of ridicule.

"However," she adds, "I won't be all that mean to you. I promise I'll never ask where you were, or what you did, or if you decided to have an affair. Did you notice the maid? She's very young and pretty. Tell me, did the conquerors of this land have children with the natives?"

Max hurls himself out of the room, grabs a bottle of gin from the cabinet, and takes a long swig, almost choking. When he stops for breath, he finds Rosenda standing in front of him.

"What do you want here? Go to your bed!"

When Rosenda turns her back on him, he drinks again.

Squatting behind a *chaya* bush, Ramón de la Torre shifts his weight from one leg to the other. The waiting period has been too long and uncomfortable. To distract himself from his idleness, he thinks of his wife. Rosenda was the prettiest girl in their village. Not even in Alamo or in larger towns like Poza Rica, was there a more desirable woman than her. She was the perfect bait!

He had been looking for a way to avenge his father's assassination. He needed to take revenge in order to publicly attest his manhood, but going openly after the the murderers was stupid – he could be killed on sight. Thus, he needed something to distract their attention, and that diversion could easily be Rosenda.

Winning her over had been easy. He was good looking, intelligent and had some property, so neither Rosenda nor her parents rejected him. When he asked for her hand, they never imagined he had other plans for Rosenda besides marrying her.

As a small boy, he had listened in awe to the stories his father recounted about the jungle. Daring accounts about rough life and futile death; bold feats, friendship and treachery; about hard work, drunkenness, and other pleasures. During campfire chats in the mountains, or while roaming pastures looking after their cattle, he had learned about life in the *jatos*, the parcels of jungle worked by a team of *chicleros*. He knew Gumersindo Pallares to the core. He was familiar with all of his lies. His father had befriended Gumersindo only to be killed by him during a drinking bout over the price of a pack of cigarettes. So said Laureano Ortiz, who confessed it all before dying.

To kill Gumersindo would not be difficult, but he does not want to become a lawless fugitive. If he kills in self-defense, however, he will never set foot in jail. Now, thanks to Rosenda, things are working as planned.

A tiny glint of light catches his attention. His muscles tense, but he relaxes them. He will need of all his keen attention and his physique nimbleness.

"How many are they?"

He really did not expect an attempt on his life to be made so soon. He thought Gumersndo would wait a while but, obviously, he was anxious to get rid of him. The same light that warned him before, shining on the blade of a machete, now casts two faint shadows.

"Start praying, Gumersindo Pallares, because tonight you die!"

The shadows move forward, closing in on the figure resting on the ground by the trunk of a wild banana tree, covered by a blanket. With criminal stealth, they raise their arms and the sharp blades of *burunas* slash the air, whistling their tune of death once and then again as they gleam in the light of the small fire, followed by hollow thuds. There are no cries of pain; the inert figure does not even stir while the assassins hack it.

"¡*Ya, chico*! He has had enough," a rasping voice hisses.

Ramón smiles behind their backs. He cannot attack them from the rear because that would be incriminating. He has to have them face-to-face, so he jumps out into the clearing.

"Here I am, you sons of your whorish mother!"

The man closer to Ramón turns around, startled to see, only for an instant, the whistling blade that beheads him on the first blow. The other one is Faustino, an old toothless *Tuxpeño*, who wails,

"Wait, boy! For the sake of our blessed Virgin, do not do it! I did not kill your father; you know very well who did!"

Faustino's frightened cries wake up some of the workers sleeping in the *jato*, and in a few seconds Ramón finds himself surrounded by *Tuxpeños*.

Pointing his bloodied *buruna* at Faustino, he says, "These guys tried to kill me in my sleep. I swear this son of a whore will die in a minute. I just want to know if somebody is willing to join him!"

The *Tuxpeño* workers exchange glances. There are eight of them, many of them Faustino's close friends and Gumersindo's cohorts, but to fight that big gutsy young man face-to-face was not an easy task. No one answers the challenge.

"Then do not go saying later that I did not kill him in self-defense, because I will also take on whoever tells that lie!"

"Help me, you sons of your whorish mothers! He is going to do me in!" Faustino whimpers, but no one stirs.

"On that, you are telling the truth! Now try and stop me, *viejo cabrón*!"

Faustino tries, but he knew he was a dead man from the moment when he saw Ramón in front of him. Although he raises his machete to stop the blow, the *buruna* comes down on him with such might that it hits him squarely on the forehead. Blood pours from his head and blinds him as he screams, "Kill me, boy! For the sake of your blessed mother, I beg you, finish me off!"

Looking at the faces around him, Ramón says, "He is begging me! It would be inhuman of me to deny him!" And with a swift motion he takes the old man's life on the edge of his *buruna*.

When Ramón bends down over the body of the other man and looks at his severed head, he swears under his breath. That head is not Gumersindo Pallares'...

Chapter 23 – Multuntzek Rules

Ricardo Quel makes the sign of the cross and kisses his twisted fingers when four workers pass by, carrying two corpses on rough handmade stretchers.

"What is the matter, *chico*? You look as shaken as if you had never seen dead people before," Gumersindo sneers: "Go on; tell them how to place the stiffs in the airplane."

Superstitious fear carves at Ricardo's bowels as he walks ahead of the workers to unlock the Skyrocket's door.

Gumersindo beckons his assistant to his side, asking, "What did you find out, Galicio?"

"According to Romulo, the said Ramón had been forewarned. He covered a banana tree trunk with his blanket to pretend it was him, so Faustino and Tolocho thought they were catching him asleep, but he was hiding behind them."

"But they were killed face-to-face. How did that happen?"

"Because he fought them face-to-face!"

Gumersindo muses for a few seconds, then murmurs, "Hmm, we will have to be very cautious with the said Ramón!"

Discreetly, Ricardo watches Gumersindo's secretive conversation with his assistant. Appalled, he shakes his head and whispers to Chema, "*¡Pa'su máre!* How badly the flights are starting. We may be doing this all season!"

Draining the Bellanca's fuel tanks, Chema asks him, "What do you mean?"

"What is the matter, *ninio*? Have you not ever heard Alab-olal mentioned?"

"How do you eat that, with bread or *tortillas*?"

"Quit being funny, bosh! Alab-olal is the "Future Hope," what you expect will be forthcoming. When you begin some activity, that day becomes Alab-olal and a certain god rules that period. Watch, today we are starting work and the first flight goes out with two corpses. What does that tell you?"

Chema looks at the bodies and shrugs.

"But it is clear as water, bosh! It speaks of fear, terror, and panic! If Multuntzek, God of Terror, is around to rule this harvest season, we are going to reap more corpses than bales of gum!"

Chema looks at Ricardo with an incredulous sneer.

"*Ah, no*? You will believe me when you see it happening!"

121

In the main house, Ramón stands still and calm before Max, Cayetano, and Gumersindo.

"To bring the law in here, *señor* Wolff, is not common practice," Cayetano explains. "The authorities are called in only when it is to the advantage of the concessionary. In cases like this, the owner must resolve the matter within the family, as we could say."

"And let this man go without punishment? He is a murderer!"

Somewhat impatient, Cayetano insists, "No, sir! Over here, not everyone who kills is an assassin. Sometimes it is necessary to do it for a good reason. In this instance, according to the testimony of the witnesses, those two men tried to kill Ramón in his sleep. He just defended himself!"

Indecisive, Max asks Ramón, "Why did they want to kill you?"

For a brief second Ramón glances at Gumersindo, who avoids his gaze. Then he glances at Rosenda peeking through the kitchen door, and shrugs.

"You do not know why?"

"*No, patrón.*"

"Incredible!"

"These things happen here all the time," Cayetano contends.

"But why? Tell me what 'here' means. Everybody uses that word to justify all that happens. Does not anyone respect life? What is 'here'? A mad house? The Stone Age? What?"

"It is something worse, *señor* Wolff. This is the jungle, and we have to live by its code. Anyway, maybe those men wanted to rob Ramón."

"But what can this man own that somebody might want bad enough to kill him?"

Cayetano looks at Max, and then deliberately at Rosenda. Max follows his gaze and there is a pause of understanding.

"*¡Dumpkoff!* Tell me, are we also at risk?"

Cayetano nods slowly while his right hand pulls his shirt tail out of his waist to display a .38 Bulldog revolver, a short but powerful weapon so easy to conceal nobody would have thought he had it on him.

Frustrated, Max shakes his head and asks, "What do we do about the authorities?"

"There will be no problem, *señor*. All we know is that those two men fought among themselves and killed each other. With that explanation and a few pesos, everything will be in order," Gumersindo suggests.

Reluctantly, but persuaded that it was the best solution, Max ends the matter. "All right! Take the bodies to town. We have lost the work of a half day. And you," he turns to Ramón. "Go to work, but do not give me any more problems!"

Ramón nods, glances at Rosenda and walks out. The girl sighs, relieved.

Once outside, Cayetano sees Ramón departing on the path that leads to Jato One. He sniggers, "Dumpkoff!" and goes on to the gray Bellanca that waits with its macabre load.

By the thatched shed, now being expanded and built to look like a regular maintenance shop, he meets with Bob and Chema.

"Did you see them?" he asks, referring to the corpses. "That's how easily people die around here, and that's why you must not mess with the *chicleros*. Flying these old spiders is a lot safer."

"Do you want me to go with you, *Capitán*, in case you need something?" Chema asks him.

"No, thanks: I do not think those passengers I am taking will give me any trouble."

"I hope it does not happen as Ricardo says it will…"

"Is he predicting something?"

"Well, he says that since the season is just starting, and we begin it taking dead people instead of *chicle*, some Mayan god or other may take over and something or other may happen. Why does he say that, *Capitán*? Has he not always been a mechanic?"

"No. You see, his father was a famous *shaman*, a Mayan healer, regarded as a wise man. Naturally, Rico followed on his dad's footsteps and began his "medical" instruction under his guidance; but, during the bloody native revolt against the Dictator Porfirio Díaz, which was called the Caste War, his father, who was also a native leader, was killed. So, when Rico was about 12 years old, he attended an experimental program established by the government to incorporate the natives into the civilized way of living, but the dumb naturals did not accept the seclusion or the food they were fed; so, they all went back to the forest, except for Rico; who was later on adopted by some Baptist missionaries. With them he learned enough English, and went to work for a gringo archeologist for several years; this guy taught him all he knows about the Mayan lore. If you want to learn anything about Mayan history, archeology, or mythology, just asks him."

"Ah, no wonder then!" Chema grins.

"I see he has already told you some of his stories."

"Yes, he does all the time, and some of them are really interesting. But I do not know how true they are."

"I like him better as a mechanic. He started with me as an apprentice about ten years ago, and there you have him, faithful to his gunstock. Well, see you later. Get to do some flying, but be careful!"...

Bob wiggles the broomstick sideways, and grins. *"It's ludicrous".*

After so many years of holding a polished control yoke in his hands to ferry choice travelers at hundreds of miles per hour over the Caribbean Sea, or across the Atlantic Ocean, now he uses a broomstick to steer a battered Travelaire slowly above the jungle, loaded with gum bales. The base of the metal control stick broke at Xkanták, and Ricardo has temporarily replaced it with a sawed-off broomstick.

He looks out the windshield to verify his route visually but, after a week of routinely flying the same leg from Xkanták to Peto, five or six times a day, he still can't recognize any landmarks. Everything is identical – trees and more trees. Once in a while he sees a narrow river or a cornfield, but these are all so similar there is no way to tell them apart. He has to use the magnetic compass to maintain his course to the terminal. He verifies he is on a heading of 356 degrees, the correct magnetic bearing. The idea of drifting in a strong crosswind makes him shudder.

Almost two years have elapsed since it happened; however, the accident is still fresh in his memory, the only blemish on his otherwise perfect professional record. Trying to allay his conscience, he still searches for explanations to validate the accident, but he finds none. It was simply the consequence of his recklessness, of an absolute lack of respect for life. He recalls making a long-distance call to New York and listening to Sergeant O'Leary's silence, followed by a groan so pitiful it still resounds in the convolutions of his brain.

He looks down and perceives marshland through one of the few openings between trees. How often has he thought of dying? If the engine failed, he would enter that green dungeon. His left hand moves over to the throttle to pull it backward slowly. The engine becomes a whisper and the airplane's nose dips. It won't take but a few seconds to reach the mesh of trees... he will hear tree limbs and metallic parts breaking, then perhaps the crackle of fire, and then the perennial darkness of the dense brush would descend over him; heat, hunger, thirst, fever and death... suitable punishment.

When the left wheel strikes the top of a tall ebony tree, Bob instinctively guns the engine and pulls the stick back sharply.

Once back at a safe altitude, he takes a deep breath. He had almost buried himself alive. Still in shock, he climbs further to 3,000 feet, where the temperature is less suffocating. He levels off and looks at the wooded horizon. The iridescence of the clouds suggests it hadn't been the wheel striking the tree that yanked him out of his suicidal trance minutes before. Something foreign to himself had blocked his death wish. He doesn't want to be deceived. What had it been?

He looks at the sky, searching for the mysterious motivation and suddenly finds it. The slanting sunlight hits a cloud, dyeing it a pale violet. It's the color of misses Wolff's eyes, those smiling eyes fixed on him, revealing more than social interest.

To have discovered that unwelcome, but undeniable truth, irks him. He is reluctant to accept the fact that he has avoided death only because he feels attracted to a woman he hardly knows...

Flying in Xibalbá

Chapter 24 – Xzuhuykaak Compels

The yellowish light flickers with each voltage surge and the flutter of dozens of gadflies and mosquitoes swirling around the bare bulbs.

The airplanes fly all day long, so routine maintenance has to be done at night. Nothing is postponed for the next day except major repairs. This schedule is truly exhausting for Ricardo and his four assistants. They start their evening refueling the airplanes, greasing the engine points, and checking magnetos, and then they work on repairs until dawn. Their eyes are bleary and their arms, chests, and backs are swollen by insect bites. Nevertheless, Ricardo and his grease monkeys pull through their grind every night.

"¡*Pa'su máre*! I am getting pissed off!"

"Why now, *maistro*?" Neto asks.

"My hapless hide has so many bites, I do not know if I want to scrape this spark plug, or just simply scratch myself! Would you know something, Neto? I am going to leave for *la chingada*!"

Neto regards him indulgently.

"You may say that I complain out of habit, bosh; but it is not so. We have always worked nights, but not this much. Does this damned *chele* suppose that we are made of iron? Instead, just look at him! He spends two or three nights in Mérida every week, and we have to stay here working our asses off! ¡*Pela nah*!" He swears in Mayan and angrily looks toward the pilots' dormitory. "Then, look over there! The pilots just play cards, or scratch their fat balls!"

"And where are we leaving to, *maistro*?"

"'We' sounds to me like a herd! I am leaving alone! I will grab my tools and go to work in Mérida for Sarabia at Aerovías Del Sureste, hah?"

Neto scratches at his most recent bug bite and reminds Ricardo, "But your wife is in Mérida, is she not, *maistro*?"

"¡*Pa'su máre*! You are right! I had forgotten about that *xish*! Look, Neto, if I stay here, it is just because I will not desert my friend Cayetano. Otherwise...."

Neto sniggers while Ricardo goes on scraping the spark plug and swatting mosquitoes.

On the pilots' dormitory veranda, now protected against insects by a fine metallic screen, Cayetano shuffles the cards. Who opens?"

"*Manda dos*," Bob says, trying his Spanish.

Cayetano looks up at Bob. "*Manda*," he mocks. "Manda is what you promise a saint when you want him to grant you a miracle, and a *manda* is what you'll need to beat my hand, gringo *güey*! You must say '*mando*'. Mando cuatro!"

"No, yo *manda dos*."

"You may bet two, but I'm betting four. Your two, and two more. What about you, Chema?"

"No, *Capitán. Yo no voy.*"

"I will not go! I will not go! ¡*Chingao*! Do you not know any other song? You look after your money worse than a tightwad from Monterrey does! You should learn from me! Will you pay, or not, Bob?"

"*Pago. ¿Que tengo?*"

"Darn you, Bob! You sound like somebody from Tabasco, always speaking backwards! You must ask, '¿*Que tienes?*' There!" Cayetano throws downs his cards happily. "Three kings and two queens!"

Bob lowers his hand slowly, revealing four fours and a ten.

"You lucky sonafabitch!" Cayetano laughs, slapping Bob's back. "Lucky in gambling, loser in love!"

Bob's hurt look makes Cayetano realize he has poked a sore spot. Chagrined, he says quickly, "Shall we play another hand?"

"Whatever you say, *Capitán*," answers Chema.

"What do you say, Bob?"

"*Paramos. Yo quiero... morder?*"

"If you were a dog, maybe!" Cayetano guffaws. "No, *morder* means to bite. What you want to do is *dormir*, to sleep."

"Oh, yeah! *Dormir, dormir, dormir*!"

"Crow the roosters of Saint Agustin! ¡*Orale pues*! Last one in bed turns the lights out!" Cayetano shouts, running inside to tuck the mosquito net under his mattress. "And take a good look under your sheets. Last night a tarantula that found my tight little ass enjoyable, almost got me!"

Bob walks to the farthest end of the dormitory where he has his bunk and his chest of drawers. After the first night he moved away from Cayetano's snoring, which was so loud it could keep a regiment awake.

Wearily, he sits on the bed and remains quiet for a moment, his mind a blank. He notices that Chema waits by the switch to shut it off, and tells him, "That's all right, Chema. I'll do it."

"Good night," Chema replies, walking to his bed.

When Chema turns in, Bob discreetly lifts the corner of his mattress to pull out a flask. He slips it in his back pocket and steps outside after turning out the lights. Unaware of the night's wild voices, he walks to the edge of camp and sits on a fallen tree trunk. He takes a swig from the flask to isolate himself from the world around him, and to protect his mind momentarily from his thoughts' whirlwind. However, an onslaught of memories pierces through his alcoholic armor.

"Maureen..."

Her name is all it takes to create a howling distress in his mind – a cry of fear. Fear of facing the possibility that he no longer wants to live. Can he go on existing like this? He is changing into an asexual vegetable that doesn't care anymore for the exciting things that life has to offer.

Another long swig cuts his thread of somber thoughts. He gets up to walk around, feeling the first faint effects of alcohol in his brain. He stops in front of a darkened hut and hears familiar human sounds – moans, excited groans, the heavy breathing of two creatures climbing the slope of lewd satiety. He can't bear it. Chased by that ugly sensuality, he flees, groping in the darkness.

The main house blocks his blind rush. He stands by the rear wall of the bedroom, so close he can look inside through the tiny holes in the clay stucco. By the light of a small lamp on the night table, he can see Ingrid Wolff, reclining on the bed almost nude, just as he has seen her for the last two weeks in his tormented dreams. He takes another drink from the flask and peers inside again. She sleeps fitfully. A surge of yearn stirs Bob's loins.

Xkanták is quiet. Men and women sleep. Max is away. Only Ricardo and Neto work on the Curtiss Robin, at the far end of the clearing. He could easily sneak through the front door and into the bedroom. She would be surprised and maybe would resist at first, but he knows she will most certainly give in. He drinks the last of the whiskey, throws the flask away into the brush, and walks around to the front of the house.

He climbs the veranda steps cautiously and pushes the outer door open. All the lights are out except for those in the maintenance shop, but the mechanics are busy. He goes past the front door and stalks toward the bedroom, but wavers before stepping inside. His mouth is dry. He can see the dim outline of the liquor cabinet. He reaches for a bottle, any bottle, and takes a drink. Replacing it, he parts the curtain and sees Olga again in her stunning nudity.

"This is madness!" he realizes, and whirls around. Almost running, he heads for the pilots' dormitory...

The annoying buzz vanishes for a few seconds, and then comes back. It's only one mosquito, but one mosquito within the net is enough to keep her awake. However, that isn't really what keeps her in vigil. It's the squealing of nocturnal birds, the distant laughter of workers mocking everything, the chilling cries of bats in their blind flying, footsteps roaming behind the house, and other noises that permeate the unbearably humid air. She turns off the lamp, hoping that darkness will make the heat less oppressive.

The transfer from gilded Europe to a primitive outpost is too drastic. When the Gestapo chased them all over South America, she did not experience such aggravation because in Rio de Janeiro, Buenos Aires, Montevideo, Lima, or Santiago, she met friends who recreated the splendor of her Viennese court for her. She didn't, as Max did, conceal her presence in the Latin American capital cities.

She abhorred anonymity, and although her passport identified her as Ingrid Wolff, her true personality surfaced with the slightest pretext. Thus, it was easy for the Gestapo agents to find them. The Nazis had just been waiting for the right moment to capture them and ship them back to Germany.

Because of her exhibitionism, Max planned their last trip covertly. No one, not even she, had known their final destination would be México. Their arrival in Mérida went completely unnoticed. The immigration authorities saw them as a couple of European tourists stopping over to visit the Mayan archeological region. Suddenly they moved from Mérida to Xkanták, from a blissful life to the agony of a prison without walls.

Although she suffocates in that house, her fear of everything on the outside stops her from leaving. She dreads the men and their obscene gazes, the horrendous women grudging her, the malarial insects and the wild beasts of that cursed jungle. The house is actually a safe harbor with the comforts provided by modern living, except she has no one to share them with. She has no friends to gossip with, or lovers with whom to release the lust that wears her out.

Her only company is provided by Rosenda or Max, when he is there, but she will not yield to his sexual demands in hopes that he will take her out of there. However, he is not being held captive like she is. In Campeche or Mérida, there are many women to satisfy his cravings.

She hears a noise. It's well past midnight. Someone is walking in the living area. Moments before, she heard steps behind the house. Everybody knows her husband is away. Who would dare?

"*Rosenda?*"

Her fear increases as seconds tick by. Then, a soft voice answers, "*¿Me habla, señora?*"

"*¡Gott sei dank!*" She sighs relieved, and calls her again: "Rosenda!" It's one of the few Spanish words she speaks.

The girl's figure appears at the doorway: "*Mande, señora....*"

"*What can I tell her?*" Not knowing the language, how could she explain she needs company? "*Here, in!*" she says, beckoning her to enter. "*Kommen Sei here in*, Rosenda!"

Shyly, the young woman approaches. Olga points at the lamp on the night table and says, "*Bitte, machen Sie die lampe on.*"

Hesitant, the girl asks: "*¿Quiere que prenda la lampara?*"

"*Ja, die lampe, anmachen,*" Olga nods.

It's a small crystal lamp, but it's bright enough to illuminate the bed area. Through the sheer mosquito net, Rosenda beholds Olga, scantily clad in a transparent nightgown. The sight of the luscious body flusters her.

Aware of Rosenda's recoil, Olga smiles to herself and points at the windows. "*Bitte, machen Sie die Vörhange zu!*"

Going to the nearest window, Rosenda touches the curtain and looks at Olga, who nods. She opens all the curtains and, keeping her eyes low, asks, "*¿Se le ofrece otra cosa, señora?*"

Olga points at the corner where an insecticide sprayer rests on the floor, and then gestures vaguely to the interior of the mosquito net, saying, "*Holen Sie bitte den fliegenzerstäuber. Es ist ein Moskito in dem moskitonetz.*"

Rosenda picks up the sprayer and applies insecticide around the room. Meanwhile, Olga observes her. She is truly a very pretty brunette. A fine figure can be appreciated beneath her coarse clothes. Her ample cotton blouse reveals a firm bust.

"*She looks so clean!*" she says to herself. "*Her hair is so shiny, as if she had just taken a bath. Where does she bathe?*"

When Rosenda stoops to place the sprayer on the floor by the night table, her blouse opens wide in the front. Unbound, her well-developed breasts remain exposed to Olga, bringing back memories of her adolescence spent in *Neuchatel's Finishing School*. She recollects the games played by girls who, becoming women in seclusion, substituted parental love for the affection of friends, which in turn awakened their libidos.

She can still taste on her lips the sweet breath of *Astrid*, the petite *Neuradstadt* countess. She can feel on her skin the softness of *Annette Lesage's* hands. *Ula Fornäs'* passionate hugs were so brazen it was rumored she had been expelled from Sweden because her ardor threatened to melt the fjords in *Stora Sjöfallets National Park*. And how could she forget *Tina Benso*, the exquisite Neapolitan, whose friendship was disputed over by all the school residents.

Nine years had gone by since she enjoyed that fondly remembered stage of her life. Although at nineteen she traded girlish games for a heterosexual reality, she couldn't erase the memory of those maiden frolics. Maybe her failed union with Max had much to do with it. But before and after Max there had been other men in her life. What is wrong with her? Is she sick? That could be it. At least now she certainly feels ill.

"Rosenda...."

The girl stops by the door. Her name has sounded like a rueful call, a cry for help. Apprehensive, she turns around.

"Rosenda!"

The pleading voice draws her to the foot of the bed.

"*Ich bin krank!*" Olga whispers. Rubbing her stomach, she adds, "*Ich habe Schmerzen in meinem Mahen....*"

"*¿Se siente mal, señora?*" she asks anxiously.

"Rosenda, *Ich fühle mich nitchwohl,*" Olga repeats in a doleful tone.

"*¡Vírgen Santa! ¿Qué hago señora? ¡Voy a llamar a alguien!*"

When she starts to leave Olga nearly yells, "Nein, Rosenda! *Kommen Sie here!*"

Distressed, Rosenda approaches the bed and Olga points at the water pitcher. "*Bitte, geben mir ein Glas Wasser.*"

Rosenda hastens to fill a glass and pulls the mosquito net aside to offer Olga the water, but her mistress doesn't move.

"*Kommen Sir Näher. Setsen Sie Sich,*" Olga says, patting the bed. "*Helfen Sie mir das Wasser su trinken.*"

Rosenda sees the imploring lips and understands. Sitting on the bed, she timidly places her left arm under Olga's back to raise her head carefully, and brings the glass to her mouth. Olga takes several sips and then smiles like a grateful angel.

"*Why cannot I refrain from sex? So many other women do, for different reasons!*" Her thoughts torment her as she fights her needs, knowing that Rosenda will leave soon. "*Maybe it's better for me to die. Die! Die! Die!*"

Rosenda is getting up. To stop her, Olga places a hand on the girl's thigh, receiving a rousing shock. Her thigh is firm, bursting with vitality. Touching her stomach, she moans, "*Meinen Magen... Ich habe Schmerzen... Schmerzen!*"

Her woeful inflection perturbs Rosenda. *"¿Que le pasa, señora? ¿Tiene alguna medicina que pueda darle?"*

"Geben Sie mir Irhe Hand."

Rosenda feels a warm softness envelop her hand as it is placed on Olga's abdomen. Embarrassed, she feels the smooth flesh under the nightgown. Olga presses on Rosenda's hand, hinting that a massage might alleviate her ailment.

Not long after, Olga's lips curve upward in a thankful smile. Rosenda sees Olga's large violet eyes fixed on hers, and feels herself tumble into their depth. Their brilliancy and luminosity fascinate her. All she can see is the hypnotic color of those alluring eyes, numbing her mind. Smiling, sweet, loving eyes, and the contact of that soft but firm belly.

Rosenda never notices how or when she began to feel the smooth skin in the palm of her hand, but realizes that the nightgown doesn't get in the way anymore. Those enslaving eyes have enfolded her in a violet-colored web.

"How is it possible that her husband does not want her, if she is so pretty?" Rosenda wonders. *"He must be a fool!"*

Stroking the velvety skin, her hand has descended of its own will. Her fingers now rake a tangle of ringlets, so silky that she could go on fondling them forever. She is suspended, poised at the rim of a bottomless pit from which an uncanny melody emerges to drag her down. Slowly, joyously, she plunges into the opalescent abyss. A subtle flutter of butterflies' wings grace her lips, inflaming her. A kiss arouses her, its gentleness inspiring a deep craving and a tenderness that immediately commands devotion.

Rosenda can't understand the nature of these unusual feelings. Maybe they are evil, but they are delightful. The spell has been cast, rendering her helpless, unwilling to reject the burning wedge that parts her lips, forcing its way into her mouth to intoxicate her. Neither can she brush aside the soft hand that cups her left breast, a frantically demanding caress that threatens to shove her over into madness.

Suddenly, the spell is broken. Olga brusquely turns her back on Rosenda. Her eyes redden and her face takes on an expression of fright mixed with self-repudiation that is quickly washed away by a surge of silent tears. Her body shakes, giving way to her bitterness and desperation.

Frightened, Rosenda gets up from the bed and backs away toward the door, where she stands for several seconds trying to understand Olga's outlandish behavior. Then she runs into the kitchen to spend long hours striving to understand the mystification of feelings that have stirred up her soul.

Ricardo lowers the pliers slowly and cocks his head above the Robin's cowling to listen intently.

"What do you think that wail was, *maistro*?" Neto asks him.

"I do not know, bosh! It sounded like the scream of a woman!"

The rest of Xkanták Central is quiet, its fountains of light shut off. The moonlight gives the jungle a pale eerie glow.

After an expectant pause, Neto points at the main house with a screwdriver. "To me, it seems that it came from the house. Could it have been the mistress?"

"Who knows? Maybe it was an animal. If the mistress had been in trouble, Rosenda would ask for help. She sleeps in the kitchen. I am sure it was the wail of an animal."

"And what finally happened to the bridal maid, *maistro*?" the apprentice asks, wanting to hear the rest of the Mayan legend Ricardo had been recounting before.

"Ah, yes. Well, when the goddess *Xzuhuykaak*, who looked after preserving the virginity of the maid *Ahlaak*, realized she was using her maids to satisfy her sexual urges, lest she sinned with men, the goddess expelled her from the temple and condemned her to live isolated in the jungle. As you can see, the poor bridal maid could not resist the temptations laid out by Xzuhuykaak and she burned in the fire of her carnal desires. No one can resist the enticements of Xzuhuykaak."

Fascinated by the story, Neto inquires, "And that maid, Ahlaak, do you think she still haunts the jungle?"

"That is what the legend says, *ninio*. But be careful not to bump into her because she will copulate you, or your woman, to death."

"With the need we have for a pretty woman around here, I would not mind meeting her," Neto says eagerly.

"Yes, bosh, but if she catches you unawares, she will steal your soul as soon as you enter her."

The warning freezes Neto's enthusiasm. He knows that Ricardo never jokes when dealing with Mayan legends. And he has always proven to be right…

Chapter 25 – Jato Number One

Clack, clack! Clack! Clack! Clack, clack! Multiplied by echoes that reverberate in the dense brush, an incessant din drifts across the forest. *Clack! Clack, clack*! *Burunas* slash the *chicozapote* trunks, opening slits that bleed the precious sap in a descending spiral, dripping into canvas bags regularly spaced along the lean trunks.

Ramón de la Torre stoops down to check his spurs, the sharp steel nails strapped to his boots, making sure they are tightly fastened. He wipes his sweaty neck and picks up his leather-and-rope climbing gear, fitting it to his waist. Before climbing, he takes his *caramuela* to his lips. The hardened squash-shell container gives water a sweetish taste.

Nimble as a monkey, Ramón climbs the trunk of the tree in a few seconds. *"Not at all bad!"* He says to himself. *"I have slashed ten trees this morning. At ten pesos each tree, that amounts to one hundred pesos. It happens that I came to avenge the death of my father, and I will go back a rich man! That is, if Gumersindo does not get up earlier than me to try to slay me!"*

Slashing a uniform gash in the soft bark, he sneers as he remembers how Rosenda described her strange experience with Ingrid Wolff on Friday night. *"I set a trap for the rooster, and who falls in it but the hen!"*

He gashes the trunk with machine-like precision while a smile lingers on his lips. The wanton episode between the mistress and Rosenda amused him immensely. *"Ah, how I would have enjoyed seeing that!"* He had laughed without regard for his wife's embarrassment, adding, *"The poor woman must be roasting in her own heat!"*

Rosenda recounted the episode to him the next day, which was Saturday, when he went to stock his weekly provisions and spend the night with her. She had also told him that every man in the Central coveted her and had propositioned her. The only reason she hadn't been raped so far was because she lives in the main house.

However, what he wants to take place is not happening. Gumersindo hasn't bothered Rosenda since his *compadre* Faustino's death.

"Is he scared, or maybe he is just waiting for someone else to kill me in the jato? I have to be very careful!"

"Speaking of the devil!" Ramón exclaims aloud as he sees several horsemen ride into the next clearing to stop by the gum cookhouse, a thatched shed sheltering a crude stone stove where the sap is being cooked in large copper caldrons. "Like one has to show up, in order to be kept in mind," he murmurs.

The horsemen are Max, Gumersindo and three workers that stop by the cookhouse. From his saddle, Max looks around in disgust. He is already vexed by the long horseback ride through the forest in the extreme heat, and he is aggravated at finding that the stove is placed amongst so much rubble and trash. That place could very well be a dump. He dismounts and walks toward the shed, where he suddenly feels nauseated.

Using long wooden staffs, two women stir the gum in the caldrons. They are clad in rags that hardly cover their emaciated bodies. Appalling as they are, at least they retain some human semblance. The man tending the third caldron, however, is an unburied corpse, partially disintegrated but still moving. His face, or what remains of it, resembles a living skull. The decayed flesh around his left cheek exposes his jaws and yellow teeth. His nose is missing, leaving his orbital bones uncovered. His ears have crumbled and he has a large festering blister on his right cheek.

Aghast, Max raises a shaky finger, exclaiming, "That man...!"

Gumersindo comes to Max's side and, forcing a smile, says, "Do not fear him, *señó Worf*! *Nicolás Antonio* does not have leprosy or anything like that."

Max looks at Gumersindo for an explanation.

"He is just bitten," he says.

"Bitten? What do you mean?"

"Have you not heard of the gummer fly? It is a golden fly this big," he holds up two fingers, "and when it bites, that is what happens to people." He gestures toward Nicolas.

"That is not possible! Why?"

"Well, people say," Gumersindo replies, wiping his face with his bandana, "that there is a black serpent big as a boa, called *zaquicaz*, that has a blister on its back just like the one Nicolas has on his cheek. These flies stand on the big blister of the snake and suck on it, then, when they bite people, the person becomes infected and ends up like Nicolás. The worst part is that there is no cure for it."

Max regards the *pailero* and shudders. Mercilessly, he points at the forest. "Pallares, send this man away from here right away!"

Bewildered, the foreman looks at Max.

"Did you not you hear me? Get rid of him!"

"But, *señó Worf*...." Gumersindo objects, meekly.

"All this filth! If someone from the American Chewing Gum Company came here, they would never buy my gum again! I want it all very clean, immediately! Clear away the brush, this trash, and these people. Just look at them!" Max yells, indicating the women who blend the gum. "Their filth goes into the gum!"

Nicolás Antonio, the *pailero*, has ceased stirring the gum in the caldron to stare at the hollering foreigner. His eyes, almost shut by his swollen lids, are clouded over and his bony hands claw the wooden staff. He moves his jaws, rehearsing how to speak clearly. Then in his shrill voice he shouts, mispronouncing the words through his toothless gums, "*Señó amo, yo soy Nicolás Antonio!*"

Max stops yelling and stares at the specter.

"*¡Yo soy Nicolás Antonio!*" the man repeats, anxiously.

"What is he saying?"

"What he means, *señó Worf*, is that he is Nicolas Antonio, the famous "Man of the Jungle." He opened up the trails from *Chiapas* to *Campeche* on the edge of his machete. Now he is old and cannot climb the trees anymore, but in his time he was the best of all *chicleros*. There has never been a more courageous man or a better worker in this forest."

Regarding the disfigured face with revulsion, Max replies, "The story of his life does not interest me. He is not to be near the gum any more. Give him money and chase him away!"

The wooden staff balances itself in the boiling gum for a few seconds and then slides to the rim of the caldron to sink in the gum bubbles. Having heard Max's words and seen his scornful gestures, Nicolás has let go of the staff and now unsheathes his *buruna*, whose edge shines in the sunlight.

Gumersindo jumps aside, leaving Max exposed to the lethal blow swooping down from high above Nicolás' head.

The other workers wince, waiting to hear the mashing sound and the cry of pain. The women open their mouths to scream, and the jungle grows silent to listen at the deadly shriek of the blade as it slashes the air.

Receiving a full impact at the waist, Max reels to the ground avoiding by a fraction of an inch the steely edge aimed at his neck.

Ramón de la Torre also rolls on the floor and jumps up like a tiger, leaving a battered Max behind him. Seeing that Nicolás Antonio is raising his arm again, Ramón pounces and rams into him unarmed, burying his shoulder into the sick man's abdomen to sweep him backward against the caldrons. Both men fall among the melted gum and burning logs, locked in a deadly embrace.

Max gets up, still shaken, to look toward the thatched shed. From behind the stove, amidst smoke and dust, four legs thrash about. He hears the shrill wail of death, and then two of the legs convulse and lay still.

Ramón appears from behind the stove, smeared with melted gum and coal embers that the two women hasten to remove from his back. He stands up and looks down. Nicolás Antonio's glassy eyes are fixed on him. His own *buruna* is buried in his chest just below the left nipple.

"Rest in peace, Nicolás Antonio, man among men!" Ramón says, makes the sign of the cross, and walks out of the shed. He swipes away chunks of burning, melted gum stuck to his arms.

Speechless, Max stares at him. Ramón stares back.

Gumersindo approaches the sturdy young man and says, "If it had not been for you, he would have killed the both of us!"

Ramón glares at him. "That would not have been any great loss!"

"Well, maybe not with me, but with the *patrón*...."

Ramón keeps quiet, but his glance at Max is eloquent.

Looking at Nicolás Antonio's motionless legs, Gumersindo says, "It was better this way. For him everything was finished anyway, and at least he died like a man of dignity."

Recovering from the shock, Max tells Ramón, "You saved my life. What can I do for you? Ask me whatever you want!"

Mockery flashes in Ramón's eyes as he answers, "That easy and big, you should never express yourself, *patrón*! I might ask you for something you would not be willing to give me."

Max frowns, but considers that it's better not to pursue his meaning further. However, he insists, "If you prefer I can find work for you at the Central. You would be better off there."

"And I would be with Rosenda, my wife, but I would not be making as much money as I am making here. I already told you, *patrón*. Forget it."

Max nods, pretending he understands. He turns to Gumersindo and says, "Let us go back."

Max mounts his horse and waves good-bye to Ramón.

Gumersindo taps Ramón's shoulder as he walks toward his horse, and says with a phony friendly tone, "And you, Ramón de la Torre, better be on the alert now because it is for certain that you will be in trouble. Nicolás had many friends."

Ramón wipes his shoulder where Gumersindo touched him, answering, "From friends you should not expect much, Gumersindo Pallares. What has to be done, must be done in person." Posing with his hand on his *buruna's* handle, he adds, "Around here, there is no other or better friend than this one. It is the only friend you can trust!"

Climbing on his horse, Gumersindo says, "You said it, Ramón, and well said it was!"

Chapter 26 – Thy Neighbor's Wife

"*No, yo no quiero, gracias.*" Cayetano covers his cup with his hand to stop Rosenda from pouring coffee in it. Then, in English, he explains, "I've never been able to drink coffee. It shatters my nerves."

From the other side of the table, Max pours brandy in a goblet, saying, "I am sure this will settle your nerves. So, tell me. How many tons do you think we will move today?"

"Well, let me see.... This next will be my fourth flight, so... I guess it'll be a little over three tons."

"Didn't I tell you?" Max exults. Turning to Olga, who sits by his side eating quietly, he says in German, "Do you realize what this means? When the war is over we shall be able to go back to the *Vaterland* wealthier than ever, to reclaim our position."

Annoyed by his boast, she asks acidly, "Are you so anxious to go to a Nazi prison?"

"The Nazis will be defeated!" he sneers.

"Oh, yes? And who will defeat them? According to the news on the radio, they defeat everybody, every day. Holland, Belgium, and France have surrendered, and England is about to fall. Have you not heard?"

"Bah! England is indomitable!"

Olga stares at him, contemplating how to hurt him. "The Luftwaffe you deserted, *lieber* Max, is tearing England apart."

"That is stupid! Göring is an imbecile; a blown-up peacock that does not know what can and cannot be done with the aerial arm. If the Führer does not invade England, he will never conquer her! The Small Corporal respects that island so much; he will never set foot on it!"

Max notices Cayetano is watching them with interest and apologizes, "Oh, excuse us. I forgot you do not speak German."

"German?" Cayetano repeats surprised.

Max realizes he has blundered, and quickly explains, "Yes. We are from a northern canton in Switzerland where German is spoken. You see, in the West people speak French, and in the South and East, they speak Italian, so our telephone operators in Bern must speak the three languages."

"It must be quite a job," Cayetano agrees. However, his references to Göring, the Führer, and the Nazis have been too obvious. "By the way, Madam, when will we begin your Spanish lessons?"

Olga grins. His question confirms that he has a distinct interest in her. Although his self-assurance annoys her, she recognizes that in spite of his age he is a very attractive man. She assumes he is a philanderer, but his experience as a lover must make him even more enticing.

"You are so busy flying all the time, Captain," she says, looking him in the eyes.

"Well, the flights are over when the sun goes down, Madam. Maybe, if Mr. Wolff doesn't object, I could come over for a while before or after dinner."

"Like I said before, my husband does not object," she flirts openly. "Even if he is not present."

Angrily, Max bites on the tip of the cigar he is about to light up. When Rosenda places the ashtray in front of him, he looks for retaliation. "Ah, Rosenda, wait! Do not go. I want to tell you something," he says in Spanish.

The girl waits, her eyes lowered.

"But let me see those pretty eyes, girl. You must feel proud!"

Rosenda looks up in surprise.

"This morning your husband behaved bravely. A man tried to kill me, but your husband saved my life. He killed the other man with his bare hands." Reaching out, he caresses her arm blatantly, adding, "You and your husband will have a good reward by the end of the harvest season. You tell him I said so."

The news trouble Rosenda. That's the third time Ramón has killed in less than two weeks. Shaken, she withdraws to the kitchen without responding to Max's phony praise.

Olga remains puzzled until Max explains, "I was praising her husband, darling. I was totally wrong about him. He has won my appreciation." Squashing his cigar in the ashtray he says, "Captain, let's get back to flying!"

Cayetano gets up and brazenly looks at Olga saying politely: "Thank you very much for lunch, Madam. If you like, I'll come tonight to give you your first class."

An enticing smile lingers on her lips as she replies, "I will be expecting you, Captain."

When Cayetano turns around, he meets Max's frowning gaze, but instead of cringing, he asks him directly, "And you, sir, where did you learn your flawless Spanish?"

"I was a flight instructor in Spain," Max says tartly, unaware that for the second time that day, he has given himself away.

Her merry laughter freshens up the ambience like a cool breeze. From the dormitory veranda, Bob looks toward the main house, exclaiming, "Damned fool! You're in for a lot of trouble!"

Chema looks at him inquiringly.

"Cayetano," Bob explains when he notices Chema's stare. "*Mucho* look for women. *¿Entiendes?*"

"¡Ah, si! He waited eagerly for the day to be over, to go and give Mrs. Wolff her Spanish lesson."

Chema hears the jovial laughter again. Irked, he looks toward the house. If he didn't know Max was there too, he could have sworn Cayetano was teaching Mrs. Wolff something else other than Spanish. He throws his cigarette on the floor, smashes it with his boot, and inhales deeply until he feels his lungs are about to burst. Then he lets the air out slowly.

Bob regards him discreetly. It's true that he has known Chema for only a month and the language barrier prevents a better understanding between them, but he can tell that something is bothering him. He appreciates that Chema is a quiet, introspective young man who is so lacking in deviousness, that his feelings are crystal clear. Following his gaze, Bob sees that his eyes are fixed on the main house and that every time the feminine laughter is heard, he looks crossed. It's definitely the response of a jealous man.

"*And what about me?*" Bob thinks. "*I don't feel that much at ease either. Dammit!*"

Unaware of Bob's scrutiny, Chema stands up from his chair, goes down the veranda steps, and walks toward the landing strip, engrossed in his thoughts.

But what the hell do I care! If he fucks her, her stupid cuckold husband is to be blamed!

Slowing his pace, he saunters to the opposite end of the strip, where no human voices are heard and all is jungle silence. He stands there, looking at the darkened brush, and makes a conscious effort to think of Magdalena.

What color are her eyes? In his his confusion, a face flashes in his mind. He is blinded by the bright violet color of two striking eyes. "*No! That's not Magdalena!*"

In desperation, he rubs his face and whispers, "Magdalena!"

Bob uncaps the flask slowly and brings it to his lips. The whiskey makes his bile rise, and he spits into the dark jungle. His gaze wanders to his left, toward the lights in the maintenance shop and at the warehouse. To his right, far away and half-hidden by the trees, he makes out the yellow lights of the oil lamps illuminating the workers' huts. Above, the stars appear briefly through a broken layer of clouds, and in front of him is the main house with its bright windows, its endless music, and, on top of it all, that alluring laughter.

Was the loneliness of the jungle getting to them? Or is it that Ingrid Wolff's beauty fascinates all of them? Cayetano is seeking to win her over, no doubt about that. Chema is in love with her. But what about him?

He pushes the question to the back of his mind, but the answer bounces right back: he also wants her. He is aggrieved to discover this truth. If he yields to his desire, he'll be betraying Maureen's memory. Suddenly he feels emptier than before. What is he doing there, anyway? He never answered Nick Harper's letter asking him to come back to his job, or at least to return to the States. But go back to what? To his plush, desolate apartment? To the flashy chrome of his sports car?

He goes inside the dormitory to look for a fresh bottle of whiskey in his mattress, and then tosses back several drinks.

"Just look at this!" Cayetano exclaims, picking up the empty bottle from the wooden floor. "What a waste of good whiskey! Come on Chema, help me undress this ox. He gets plastered and then we have to wrestle him to bed. You had better keep a closer eye on him. If Mr. Brush catches him like this, I don't want to smell the barrage of farts he'll fire at him!"

"When I walked out earlier, he did not have a bottle."

"All right, all right! Come on, pull his pants off!"

"And now, who is Mr. Brush, *Capitán*?"

"Who wears a haircut like a brush and is always singing the same song: 'I want this clean! I want the other clean'?"

"Ah!" Chema smiles. "The boss!"

"The boss, right! Who should first clean his own eyes so he can see the peachy wife he has!"

Chema raises his eyes and Cayetano sees fire in them.

"Why are you looking at me with those dagger eyes?"

Embarrassed, the boy shakes his right hand, "¡No, *Capitán*! Not at you. I mashed my finger with the gringo's big shoe!"

"¡*Ah, vaya*! I was beginning to wonder. Now just pull the mosquito net over him. Some hangover he's going to have tomorrow!"

Chapter 27 – Frustration

The gray Skyrocket accelerates for its takeoff roll. When it swishes past the maintenance shop, Chema, Bob, and Ricardo see Cayetano wave goodbye from the right seat with a jesting expression meaning "until never." In the pilot's seat, Max does the flying.

"*¡Pa'su máre!*" Ricardo exclaims, "I think this is the first time ever I see Cayetano flying as a sack of potatoes!"

"You know the boss; he does not trust any of us." Chema says.

"*¡Caballo!* As if he were such a big *pirish!*"

"What is *'pirish'*, Rico?"

"You know, bosh. Pirish means ass, the browny, the posterior!"

"Lend me your attention!" Chema starts an exchange of double entendres.

"I shall lend you a doll, the one hanging between my right and left ball!"

"Be careful and do not eat it all!"

"You want it wide, or you want it tall?"

"Take your choice: long and pointed, or thick and dull."

They laugh heartily, celebrating their exchange of *albures*. Eventually Ricardo says, "I hope Cayetano gets those metal rings for your airplane, or you will be burning oil all week, Chema."

"You mean the Robin, not me!"

"The Robin in its cylinders, and you in the afterburner like when you feast on beans."

"Careful you don't soil your jeans!"

"Jeans... jeans... You win, bosh! I cannot find a rhyme for jeans."

"Well, anyway. Were they going to Mérida?"

"*Si, bosh.*"

"I hope Cayetano has a chance to wire the money to my mother, and does not forget to buy Bob's 'prescription.'"

"What? Is he still hitting the *tianguarnis* bottle badly?"

"Badly and daily! As you see, right now he must be thirsting for a drink!"

Scratching his large head, Ricardo comments, "As long as he does not start drinking in flight, it will not be so bad." Suddenly, he jokes. "Listen, bosh. Now that Cayetano is not here, why do you not give the *chele* her Spanish lesson?"

Chema doesn't take the suggestion as a jibe. "That is not a bad idea!" he replies. He feels a burst of excitement at the remote chance that this could happen.

"Let's drink to a next and more fruitful transaction," Max proposes, raising his glass full of gin.

"To a more gainful one!" Lysander Wynn toasts, sipping his drink.

Max's guest, a gum purchasing agent from America, constantly looks with watery eyes toward the door that opens into an arched corridor.

"What's the matter, Lysander?" Max asks. "Are you nervous, or you just can't curb your anticipation?"

Embarrassed, the executive clears his throat to control his voice. "There is something troubling me. As you know, I must go back to New Orleans tomorrow. I'll be home the following evening and my wife, you know... well, she's very demanding in some aspects. Do you follow me?"

"Not exactly," Max lies, concealing his amusement. "What does your return home have to do with your being so edgy?"

"The young ladies that are coming, are they prostitutes?"

"Prostitutes?" Max laughs snidely. "Of course not! If that was your concern, stop worrying. I have always been very cautious in that respect. They are decent but poor girls, who must work to help support their families. Naturally, an extra income of this sort always helps. Relax! They are perfectly healthy and pretty as they can be."

Wynn sighs, relieved. Then he hears footsteps in the outer corridor.

"That must be them!" Max says, getting up to walk across the spacious parlor of the old mansion that preserves the splendor of the *henequen* era. These days, with the prime of the fiber industry gone, and the exploitation of the workers ended, he leases the property cheaply so that he has a place to spend his leisure nights in Mérida, or to entertain American purchasing agents, as he does now.

In the corridor, cool with giant ferns and azaleas, Max greets the women. Three of them pretty and lively, the fourth beautiful but abashed.

Enedina, the shortest one, extends her hand warmly. "¡*Hola, lindo*! I am so glad you called me. Look, I brought along a new friend of mine. Her name is Ligia Cu."

Max is surprised to see that Ligia is tall, compared to the average Yucatecan, and that her features are rather Caucasian than Mayan. She smiles at him warmly, but her eyes betray her shyness.

"Very pleased to meet you, Ligia. What does Cu mean?"

"It is Mayan, for dove's nest, sir," she replies, trying to calm her apprehension.

"Very pretty, like you. But you are not Mayan, are you?"

"No, sir. But my father liked everything Maya."

"You will have to tell me all about yourself later, and please, call me Max. Let us go inside to meet a friend of mine." He gestures toward the door.

In the parlor, Wynn is at a loss before the three women. However, after introductions and three stiff drinks, the satyr hidden behind his repressed personality emerges to chase Teresa and Otilia, who run around the parlor teasing him.

Seated on a sofa, Enedina grins, satisfied, as she regards Max and Ligia. The girl, aroused by the liquor and Max's caresses, loses her inhibitions. Max, who usually takes purchased satisfaction with minimal fervor, seems to be enthusiastic.

Max pours himself a fresh drink and looks at his shivering hands. He is frightened. The young woman he has before him is a challenge, and he questions his adequacy to confront it. He wants to get from liquor the endurance he lacks.

Aware of Max's weaknesses from personal experience, Enedina goes to his side to whisper in his ear, "The dove is on fire. Why do you not take her to your bedroom now?"

Max nods, and taking Ligia by the hand, stands up. "Come with me, precious. You and I have to talk in private."

"Do you want me to help you?" Enedina offers.

"Did I ask for your help?" Max snaps. Annoyed, he sways across the parlor, dragging Ligia behind him.

Enedina shakes her head and sits on a chair in the corner of the room to amuse herself with Lysander's ridiculous antics. Now that he has finally caught Otilia, and has her on a sofa, he doesn't know what to do with her.

At the height of her arousal, Ligia becomes impatient and demanding, which further deflates Max's already declining self-assurance. As he tries to tear open the door that blocks his way to such a trifling conquest, he realizes he is about to have an ejaculation. He can't hold back. The moment to admit another defeat looms inexorably before him, reminding him of another occasion, another place, and another time...

From the small second-floor window, the stillness of the placid lake at Bad Aussee reflects the Austrian Mountains in the first light of dawn. He smokes, gazing at the distant Tyrol Alps to the west, while uncertainty gnaws at his entrails. Behind him, apparently exhausted, Olga sleeps on a feather mattress. A brisk thrust had been enough to take the arrogant Baroness' virginity and claim her as his possession. It had been so easy, he feels skeptical. Were all her moans and groans a well-rehearsed farce? There hadn't been a drop of blood to authenticate his conquest. Suspicion destroys the pride and the satisfaction he was supposed to experience at this moment.

Defeated, he rolls to the opposite side of the bed and shuts his eyes to sleep off his shame. By his side, Ligia still moans, unsatisfied.

Minutes later, Enedina comes into the room to find Ligia holding her belly, aching and crying sadly, thinking she has lost the money she was to be paid.

"Why are you crying? What happened?" Enedina whispers.

"Nothing! Nothing at all!"

"Do not worry, baby! This imbecile pays anyway, I know. It is better this way."

Olga touches the tip of her cigarette with the match flame, inhales deeply and drops the match into an empty cup of coffee, listening to it hiss as it extinguishes. Avoiding Olga's eyes, Rosenda rolls a table holding several liqueurs into the room. From that strange night on, she hasn't looked Olga in the eye, and whenever possible she evades her.

Olga envies the girl. She must live a sexually satisfied life. On Saturdays and Sundays she has her husband, that hunk of a man who kills so easily. Most certainly he leaves her sore for the rest of the week.

How odd she isn't pregnant. Maybe she can't conceive, like me. How could I ask her?

"Rosenda..."

"*Mande, señora.*"

"Rosenda, you... no children?"

Puzzled, Rosenda looks up. "*¿Que si tengo hijos, dice?*"

Olga nods.

"No, señora."

"*Wieso?* Ah... why?"

Instinctively, Rosenda touches her stomach as she explains slowly, "*Una vaca me golpeó.*"

"*Schlag?*" Olga asks, hitting her stomach lightly.

The girl nods sadly. Olga takes her hand in a comforting hold and Rosenda smiles happily, but her beaming face awakens Olga's resentment. "*Why does she smile like an idiot? The other night, instead of rejecting me, she responded. I wonder if it's instinctual in her, or it's just that she simply couldn't resist me?"*

The memory of her seductive powers makes her relapse into one of her frequent moments of narcissism. Her beauty hasn't ebbed in the least and if she can subjugate a woman, she can still have the world at her feet. Or couldn't she?

Olga releases Rosenda's hand and slides her fingers up the shapely brown arm, wrapping it in a caress that sends a tingle through the young woman's body. Olga notices how, where seconds before only the firmness of her breasts was visible, now two hard nipples poke through her blouse. She stands up to face her, and their eyes meet.

Once again Rosenda faces those violet eyes drilling into her soul, arousing contradictory and baffling sentiments. *"Nothing of what Ramón says is true! What evil can there be in those eyes that look like the eyes of a child begging for a little affection? They are so beautiful! And her golden hair, so fine! Her skin, so soft! Holy Virgin, is this wrong?"* Rosenda closes her eyes. Her body trembles in her excitement.

Proud of her deft touch, Olga pats Rosenda's cheek lightly to bring her out of her reverie, then walks toward the window oblivious of the agony she inflicts on the maid's simple soul. Her triumphant smile fades, however, when she looks outside and realizes that she is nothing but a woman chained to a gilded prison by the stupid whims of a maniac.

Rosenda opens her eyes to see Olga standing by the window. Although she cannot see her face, she knows Olga is crying silently and she feels distressed to see her mistress' anguish. Clasping her hands together to stop their trembling, she walks quietly into the kitchen.

Olga's tears flow freely while her blurry gaze sweeps the grounds of the Central, stopping at the lights sparkling against darkness. The men around each of those lights are only slightly better than apes. The idea of being intimate with any of them makes her shudder.

But she immediately recognizes a figure emerging from the pilots' dormitory. It's the American. During the past five weeks, she has thought about him frequently.

"He's peculiar. Maybe he's also in some kind of trouble. Why else would a civilized man be in this stupid jungle? He's the only one I would get involved with, but then he seems to be the only one who's not interested in me. Or isn't he?"

149

Wiping her eyes, Olga walks outside to the veranda and calls, "Captain Calver, is that you?"

The figure halts in the middle of the clearing. "Yes, Mrs. Wolff. Anything I can do for you?"

"Could you come here for a minute?"

"Err, yes, ma'am. Right away!" However, he wavers before walking to the steps where he stops, looking like he's hiding something behind his back.

"Am I bothering you, Captain?"

"No, ma'am. No way!"

"Would you like to come in for some conversation?

"It'll be my pleasure!"

The object Bob hides glints in the light, and Olga guesses what it is. "Is that such a good liquor that you don't want to share it with me?"

Holding up the bottle, Bob grins. "You caught me, so I guess I'll have to."

"Then come inside, I'll provide soda and ice."

He bows and walks in behind her.

Olga goes to the record player. "I suppose you like jazz."

"That Armstrong's you have is my favorite."

"Feel at home, Captain. I'll have some gin."

The music hovers over them, filling the air with the sensuality flowing from the captivating trumpet. Cooled by ice cubes, the whiskey has a different, pleasant taste. The breeze created by the electric fan revives him and the bright lights, the fine perfume, and the lively color of the vaporous robe Olga wears, attacks his senses arousing his sexual desire.

It's so easy to wrap her in his arms and move together, following the seductive rhythm. Her warmth, her closeness, her femininity captured in her perfume, and the spell cast by her total beauty overpower him. He yields to the sexual siren call unleashed by the bewitching woman.

A rigid figure stands in the middle of the clearing, a statue cold on the outside and throbbing and boiling inside. Chema stares at the dancing couple through the open window. His fists open and close repeatedly while a burning sensation pierces his stomach. Angrily, he strides toward the dormitory and stops by the steps looking for a weapon; anything, a rock, a club, his own hands. He wants to kill, to destroy everything around him.

"Why? Why? Why?" He seethes. Enraged, he turns toward the window. He can still see them. Through clenched teeth he curses, "¡*Me lleva la chingada*! *Why the hell do I feel like this*?" Beset and susceptible because his jealousy has no justification, he sits on the veranda steps.

Embracing, pretending they dance, Olga and Bob move toward the bedroom doorway. His lips look hungrily for her mouth, for her neck, while his hands explore her warm flesh, caressing and undressing her.

Locked in his arms, she drags him to the bed and slides onto it, falling with him on top of her. She is going to fulfill herself as a woman at last, enjoying carnal pleasure until all her sexual energy is spent.

Outside in the clearing, Ricardo Quel tightens the last nut on the Travelaire's number three cylinder and says wearily, "Go on, Neto. Crank the propeller. Let us test it."

Ricardo walks around the airplane to get in the cockpit and shouts, "Switch is off. Spin it only two or three turns."

Neto pulls the propeller counterclockwise, feels the cylinders loaded, and yells, "Switch on!"

"On!" Ricardo replies, flipping the magnetos switch on.

Neto pulls the propeller's blade tip, jumping back to clear away from it. The propeller spins and the engine coughs intermittently until the pistons fire with a loud snarl.

Immersed in a violet-tinted stupor, Bob feels whole again. Life begins to have meaning as he is about to reach the ecstasy he had been denying himself. Olga pours endearing words and sensual moans into his ear; however, the sound of the engine roaring outside bores into his mind, awakening in him a mournful memory that he had momentarily overcome.

A scene he has dreamed of many times emerges from the dense haze enveloping his senses: a huge tree reaches up to entangle his small airplane in its limbs, pulls it down, and smashes it against a sandy road, where he finds a beautiful rag doll with her chest pierced by an aluminum tube.

A hoarse, urgent voice calls him back to reality. "Please, darling, please! I am dying! Give it to me now, now. Enter me, please!"

Instead of heeding to Olga's urgent demands, Bob rises bewildered, and his confusion turns to shame. Burning with desire seconds before, now he sees his masculinity flaccid and lifeless, a reflection of his inner feelings. Abashed, he gets up and backs toward the door.

Lost in a sensual frenzy, Olga bucks on the bed, moaning, "Don't make me wait, darling! I'm dying!"

When nothing happens, she opens her eyes and finds Bob at the door. Jumping up to stand in his way, she yells at him, "What's wrong? Why are you leaving?"

Bob avoids her eyes. "Forgive me! I – I just can't do it!"

"What do you mean?" Astounded, she notices his manhood's limpness. "No, not you too! Now I understand why you hide in this place!"

He doesn't want to argue, to apologize, or to offer explanations. He just wants out of there.

"No! You are not leaving me like this!" she yells, slapping him once and again. "You're going to stay here and fuck me, if I have to make you do it!"

He tries to push her aside, but she doesn't budge.

"You want to leave?" She spits at his face. "All right! Get out! I have no use for impotents! Get out of here!"

Bob staggers out of the bedroom, dragging his humiliation and shame with him. Olga follows him into the living area and stands trembling and panting. When he walks outside, she notices a motionless shadow watching her.

"Rosenda!" she sobs.

Slowly, bewitched and unresisting, Rosenda moves toward the outstretched arms that close around her.

Outside, two men confront very different emotions. One wants to kill out of jealousy. The other wants to die because of his failure.

Chema climbs down the steps, yelling his hatred at the American, but his shouts are drowned by the Travelaire's engine noise. Unaware, Bob trudges along the landing strip toward the darkness of night.

Regarding Bob's attitude, Chema becomes aware of the American's intense grieving, and his anger dissipates. He doesn't know what took place in the house, but whatever has happened, it is not what he had anticipated…

Chapter 28 – At the Gate of Hell

"How low do you figure the ceiling is, *Capitán?*"

"*¡Sepa Dios!*" Cayetano grumbles, squinting at the white mass of stratiform clouds. "Less than one hundred feet, I would say!"

It's the third consecutive day that a dense overcast hangs low over Xkanták Central, from dawn until the sun burns it off.

"How do you see it? Should I go now?"

Frowning, Cayetano looks at Chema. "What is it? You want to show off in front of my friends here, or you want to break your neck? What is your rush?"

"None. It is just that in a little while Mr. Brush will come out yelling because we are not working yet!"

"Bah! Let him risk his own neck!"

"I told you!" Chema warns. "Here he comes."

"Oh, shit!" Cayetano turns to the two young men standing by his side at the maintenance shop. "Go on. Put on your intelligent faces, here comes the boss!"

Max reaches the group and says, "Good morning, gentlemen. Are we ready to fly?"

"The airplanes are ready, *señor,*" Cayetano chuckles. "If you deem it is safe, we can leave anytime!"

Max studies the overcast. "There is some ceiling now, and at Peto it should be even higher."

"For everybody's sake, *señor* Wolff, I suggest we pull a bale out of every airplane to load in a little more fuel. Just in case we have to hold somewhere."

"We didn't have any problem yesterday, *Capitán*, or the day before. Within an hour, Peto will be completely clear. You know that better than I do!"

"That is why I would like to be cautious. Yesterday and the day before there was some wind," Cayetano rebuts, holding Max's stare. "Today, it is absolutely calm. These clouds can hang over here for hours."

Max looks again at the sky. "Let's go, we're losing time! The sun is hot and will soon burn these clouds away." Suddenly aware of the presence of two new men, he asks, "Who are these men?"

"*Calixto Gomez* and *Manuel Torruco.* I brought them yesterday from Peto on the last flight. They are pilots."

"They look like everything except pilots. Any experience?"

"As copilots, they...."

"Let them answer for themselves. You, what have you flown?"

Feeling abashed, Calixto replies, "Bellancas and the Vaq trimotor, as copilot. Solo I have only flown the Stinson Junior, and very little, *señor* Wolff."

"How little?"

"About fifteen hours."

"And you?"

Manuel swallows hard and answers, "I have only flown copilot, for about a year."

"Neither of you qualify. But there is no better here. I will pay you assistant mechanics wages and you will fly whenever possible. Soon now, I will have three new airplanes to be flown by *Capitanes* Cayetano, Calver, and him," he says, indicating Chema. "The Travelaire and the Robin will be yours to fly if you qualify. When you think you are ready, I will check you out myself. Now, get to work!"

Max strides to the Skyrocket. Before climbing in, he turns around to Cayetano and asks, "And where is *Capitán* Calver?"

Cayetano looks around. "He was having breakfast. He will be here right away!"

"I have insisted too often that everyone must be ready on the flight line at the same time. No one has special privileges! Call him! I want him to take off right after us!"

"¡Si, *Señor*!"

Chema runs to the Robin and Cayetano goes to the shack where they take their meals. "Where is the gringo?" he asks Doña Ticha, the cook.

The small woman, clapping tortillas by the fire, shrinks even smaller with displeasure. "¡*Guá*! Can you not hear his retching back there?"

Cayetano takes a cup from the table. He looks in it and discovers the remains of heavily salted coffee. He shakes his head.

"I guess he woke up the worst today," says the cook. "He had two cups of that stuff before it had any effect on him. It would be good if you did not let him get so *xkis pol*, because later on I get all the flies that the stink of his puke attracts!"

Bob comes in holding his stomach and wiping his mouth with the back of his hand. Self-consciously he says, "Sorry, Cayetano!"

"How do you feel?"

Bob blows his nose. "Worse than a pig!"

"Will you be able to fly?"

"Yeah, I guess so. Just let me get some food down to settle my stomach."

"Let me see your hands."

Bob raises his hands slowly.

Worried, Cayetano shakes his head. "They jiggle more than a hula dancer's hips. Look, I'm gonna have a bale removed from your airplane so you take Calixto along. Let him lend you a hand, Okay?"

"Yeah, Okay. Was that Wolff taking off?"

"Yeah, but don't worry about him. I'll cover for you."

"Thanks, Cayetano." His words are short, but not so his gratitude.

Bob shuts his eyes and shakes his head to clear his brain. He then cranes his neck to look up and estimates the cloud ceiling to be even lower now. It hovers almost at treetop level. The opposite end of the landing strip vanishes in the haze.

He steals a glance at Calixto's angular features. The boy rides copilot, seated on a gum bale. He is twenty years old and very nervous. Bob smiles, trying to instill in Calixto some of his own faltering confidence, and ask in Spanish, "How many bales on board?"

"Twelve, *Capitán*."

"You how many kilos?"

"Sixty-two."

"Twelve bales, plus sixty-two kilos are...."

"Six hundred and sixty-two kilos total, *Capitán*," the kid adds quickly.

"Oh, Okay. Not much weight. ¡*Vámonos!*"

Bob pushes the throttle open. At 1,800 r.p.m., he tries the magnetos. Stepping on the brake pedals, he accelerates until the engine develops full power and then releases the brakes to let the Travelaire roll along the center of the strip.

Ricardo and his assistants watch the long wavering takeoff until the plane disappears in the overcast. "Well, my little dirty belly-wipers," Ricardo yawns, stretching lazily. "Let us have breakfast so we can sit nicely and hatch our balls while they come back, hah?"

The engine's drone permeates Bob's head making him feel as though his brain is about to burst. He can barely make out the turn-and-slip indicator, the airspeed, and the altimeter readings that help him determine how to keep the plane in a climbing attitude within the haziness that blocks his external visibility. He doesn't feel the sun's warmth yet, nor does he see that the cloudiness will become any clearer. His indicated airspeed is 80 mph. If he tried to climb at a steeper angle, the Travelaire would lose lift and stall out of the sky. He has to maintain that climbing speed.

"How high can the top be at a thousand feet? Dammit! Yesterday I popped out at seven hundred!"

The altimeter indicates an altitude of three hundred and eighty feet.

Have we been flying for only three minutes? Jesus! Why doesn't this fucking wreck have an artificial horizon? It'd be so easy to fly it with full instruments... Shit, the course! I'm more than 40 degrees off course. Dammit! I'm flying worse than a stupid beginner!

At eight hundred feet, the heavily-burdened plane lumbers up at a slow 120 feet per minute. The layer of nimbostratus clouds becomes lighter and the upper air already feels hotter. At last, he sees blue sky and the blinding sun.

Bob dons his Raybans and looks at Calixto. He is pale. The pilot grins, beckons the kid to take over the controls and points at the compass, "Heading *tres, cinco, cero.*" Calixto holds the command stick clumsily while trying to maintain the plane on course. *"¿Subimos más, Capitán?"*

Bob doesn't hear the question. His effort to concentrate left him exhausted and he stares ahead emptily.

"¿Subimos mas, Capitán?" the kid repeats, insistently.

"What? Oh, no! Level out. *Ah, ¡nivela!*" Bob signals.

"Am I this wasted? How could I have flown so clumsily? Even this guy must've noticed! This isn't the first time I've flown with a hangover. What's wrong with me? If I can't do even this anymore, I'm finished!"

Out of the corner of his eye, Calixto looks at the pilot and notices he's mumbling to himself. He can see Bob's lips quivering, while a deep groove of concern creases his forehead. Is he crazy, or is he always like that?

The engine coughs and Calixto jumps on the gum bale. He looks at Bob, who is so absorbed in his thoughts he doesn't respond to the warning sound. He is calming down when the aircraft shakes so hard it feels as if the engine is tearing off its frame. The fuselage rattles. Instinctively, Calixto scans the engine instruments. The oil pressure is dropping and the temperature of the cylinders is increasing dangerously. He is about to call Bob's attention to the situation when he realizes that the pilot is already at the controls, turning slowly to return to Xkanták.

"¿Que pasa, Capitán?" he asks fearfully.

The vibration worsens, followed by a deafening explosion. A section of the cowling breaks loose, letting out a big chunk of metal that flies back and strikes the upper part of the windshield, smashing it, while a flood of oil stains it black.

Calixto screams in fright, but Bob's strong hand clutches his left shoulder. "Don't panic, son," he says reassuringly. "Let old Bob sweat this one out. We'll make it, don't worry. Bad weed never dies."

Bob's fearless face is altogether different from the one he saw moments before. His serenity in handling the old airplane restores his confidence. Calixto grins while watching Bob turn off the fuel shutoff valve and the magneto key. The propeller stops, the vibration ceases, and the monoplane dips nose downward, descending in a steep angle toward the mantle of clouds that hides the ground beneath them.

The Travelaire enters the clouds that engulf them in a white blindfold, and deadly silence ensues. The seconds tick by endlessly. Bob's left hand holds the stick with commanding prowess maintaining the aircraft in an almost normal descent, except for the excessive vertical speed. He watches the unwinding altimeter needle as it goes past 400, 350, 300 and 250 feet above sea level.

Standing by the freight train's caboose in Peto, Cayetano raises his beer bottle high and empties it quickly. He wipes his mouth, grimacing, and gives the bottle back to the train conductor.

"This warm beer tastes like horse's piss!" he grouches.

Inside the blue Bellanca, Pepe, the stevedore, thrusts his tanned back hard against the last gum bale on board, while two other men unload it from the ground.

"*¡Listo, Cayito!* You may leave now," Pepe yells, jumping off the aircraft.

"*¡Gracias, Pepe!* Remember...," Cayetano says softly, taking care that the other men do not hear. "Out of this load, skim one fourth and put it in my storehouse. With this much, the total hoarded will add up to five tons this week, which will be twenty-two thousand five hundred pesos. The buyer will be here tomorrow. Collect cash, take your cut, and deposit the rest in my checking account, not in savings. Got it?"

"*Si, pues!*" the man says.

"*¡Orale!* Be seeing you!"

Walking back to the Skyrocket, Cayetano thinks of Bob. The clouds have burned off and the sky is clear, but there's no other plane in sight.

"¡*Gringo atarantao*! Wolff is going to shit all over him!"

When they break out under the cloud layer at 200 feet, Bob immediately looks through the oil-stained windshield for a clearing in the forest, but there is none. Everything is a lush mass of treetops.

Speed 100 mph. His left fist clutches the stick and pulls it backward just enough to level off. The plane soars over the trees while its lift lasts, then it begins to lose forward speed, to 95 miles. He brings the stick further back and still there is no clearing in sight,

Now he's at 85 miles. The old Travelaire sinks forward. Its wheels graze the upper limbs of trees, hitting them harder every time the plane bounces down. At 70 miles, the aircraft shudders, announcing a stall. Everything is green. Finally, gravity takes its toll pulling the heavy plane down. Calixto's fingers curl and he quickly draws the sign of the cross over his forehead.

The impact severs the top of a huge *ceiba* tree and its nose stabs a dark hole between two ebony trees. The crash rumbles through the forest frightening away flocks of birds and *saraguato* monkeys that jump from branch to branch, screaming angrily. Seconds later, in the silence that ensues, the jungle becomes alive again with its own sounds.

Cayetano breaks under the thin layer of low stratus clouds still covering Xkanták, spots the river, and then, two miles to the south, the landing strip. He steers to align the Bellanca and reduces power to begin his glide. On the final leg of the landing pattern, he sees only two airplanes parked by the maintenance shop.

"¡*Újule*! We will not meet the mark today!" he remarks, assuming that the other aircraft have broken down. Taxiing down the landing strip, he sees Ricardo signaling him to pull up by the shop.

"¿*Quiubo*? What bug bit you now?" he shouts at Ricardo, jumping off the Bellanca.

"¡*Máre*! That it looks like the gringo crashed!" Ricardo replies. "He has not come back from his first flight."

Max approaches, quickly. "Did you see Calver?"

"No, *Señor*. When I left Peto, he had not arrived yet."

"With the fuel he had, could he have gone somewhere else?" Max presses.

"Rico, was Calixto with him?" Cayetano asks.

"¡Si, bosh!"

"He had a copilot with him? Why?"

"He wasn't feeling well, sir."

"Well, what do you think?"

"If he had an engine failure, maybe he diverted to Los Lirios or to Chunhuas. But I doubt it. It was still too foggy to find those small landing fields. We had better start searching for him. In ten minutes the whole route will be clear."

Max snaps to action and starts giving orders. "Ricardo, fill up my airplane too. I will go by Hopelchen; you, José María, go by Boloyuc and you, *Capitán*, look for him along the route. He may be in some clearing."

"*¡Si, Señor!* I would also suggest that we take several men in each airplane so we have more eyes searching."

"Approved! We'll meet in Peto."

"*¡Diantre de Gringo tan pendejo!*" Cayetano broods, searching the jungle for the faintest sign of the downed Travelaire. He urges the others on board, "*¡Orale, cabrones!* Open your eyes big and look hard in every hole! I did not bring you along just for the ride!"

Manuel, Ricardo, and Galicio strain their eyes through the Skyrocket's windows and windshield as it flies at a thousand feet over the thick woods.

"This high, we might not even see him!" Ricardo says, scanning the jungle below them.

"And lower than this, we would see even less, *¡pendejo!*" Cayetano growls edgily. "Do you not see that this way we cover more ground? Besides, I am flying this kite at minimum speed. Look hard and shut up, but if you see something, holler!"

"*¡Allá! ¡Allá!*" Galicio yells.

"What, you ox? Speak up!"

"I do not know! I saw something!"

Cayetano makes a tight 180-degree turn, increasing power to avert a stall.

"Where was it?"

"There, straight ahead!"

Cayetano searches anxiously. They are approaching a small clearing in the forest when a glint of light starts a happy clamor among everyone aboard.

It doesn't last long. "*¡Bola de pendejos!* It is just a water pond reflecting the sunlight!"

"You said we should holler if we saw anything!"

"Of course you must! Even if it is just your imagination!"

A spark of consciousness activates his brain enough for him to recognize a profound exhaustion that keeps his eyes shut. Then a deep pain stabs his chest, and finally his eyelids open to reveal – in the scanty light sifting through the foliage – that his vision is blurred. He tries to keep his head raised up, but this movement causes him shocking agony. Whenever he can raise his head, he can discern through the broken windshield dozens of tree trunks rising tall through the undergrowth.

He can also see capering butterflies and birds flying past him to vanish in the brush. Monkeys hang momentarily from fiber strands to watch this alien entity with curiosity. He hears cries, trills, and chirps. Everything veiled by a ghostly penumbra and the sweat flowing down his forehead. It is so hot!

Images and memories break into his mind, and a sudden premonition shoots a squirt of acid into his bowels. Fearfully, he cranes his neck around and finds what he had anticipated: half of Calixto's motionless body hangs outside the broken windshield. His chest is nearly divided in two halves and his right arm has disappeared, sheared by the window's Plexiglas. A gory cavity reveals mashed bone, bloody muscles, and ripped tendons. Mercifully, he cannot see his face.

Bob tries to call him, but a lump blocks his throat. To clear it, he spits up a bloody clot and doesn't try to speak again. The roof is bent over his head, blocking the space above him. He stirs in his seat and his blood chills despite the unnerving heat. He can't budge. He's caught by the weight of the load of gum bales.

Pushing hard with his back he tries to free himself, but it's useless. Craning his neck as far as it will go, he finds that the full load of bales, about 600 kilograms, has him pinned against the instrument panel. Enduring excruciating pain, he extricates his left arm from under his chest and shakes it to verify he can move it. Then he props his hand against the panel and pushes back again, but the strain depletes what little strength he has left.

Then he yells in desperation, "*Calixtoooo...!*"

His shout travels through the jungle, returning in echoes. Calixto is dead. He is trapped alongside a corpse.

He welcomes the solid darkness of unconsciousness.

They dine in silence. Max is upset and thoughtful. Cayetano eats without appetite. Olga looks at both of them out of the corner of her eye and smiles at Rosenda when she comes to the table. The girl smiles back, tenderly.

Cayetano raises his head and catches one of those exchanges, but thinks nothing of it. "¡Ah, que Bob!" he murmurs to himself.

"Did you say something, Captain?"

"Nothing, Mr. Wolff. I was thinking about Bob. Where could he have fallen?"

Max shrugs. "Maybe we'll find him tomorrow. We'll organize the workers to search by *jatos*, and comb the route by flying in an open formation. We have to see broken trees or some sign of the crash."

Cayetano shakes his head heavily. "No, sir. Don't rely on that. I've looked for fallen airplanes before. If the pilot doesn't survive, there's no way we can find him. The jungle opens up, swallows the airplane, and shuts up again. That's it!"

Gumersindo appears at the door, hat in hand. "*Buenas noches, señó Worf*," he says. "May I have your permission to enter?"

"Ah, Pallares! Come in! What is it you want?"

"Just to tell you that out here I have two *picadores* who claim they heard an airplane that sounded like it was failing."

Max rises immediately. "Tell them to come in."

Cayetano remains seated, engrossed in Olga's astonishing beauty. The tragedy that disturbs everyone doesn't seem to affect her. On the contrary, she looks different these last few days, almost happy. *Is she giving in to this confinement? Or maybe her relationship with Max is back to normal? No, I don't think that's it. What is it then?*

The workers' voices break into Cayetano's thoughts. He stands up and goes to the group gathered outside the door.

"Look, *patrón*," says an emaciated man, obviously affected by malaria. "We hear the airplanes every day as they come and go, so we know very well how they sound like. Early this morning we heard this one and it did not sound right. *Aurelio* and I even looked up because we heard an explosion."

Impatient, Max cuts the man short. "Where were you when you heard this?"

"In *Jato* Three, where we have our task."

"How far, in what direction?"

"We heard it close by, like going that way."

"To the east?"

Cayetano frowns. "That's not right. *Jato* Three is to the north of here. He had to be deviated from the route."

"Some other pilot maybe, but not him," Max disputes.

"Who knows?" Cayetano declares. "Anyone can make a mistake. His compass could have been off. He was flying above, or within the cloud layer."

"That's possible. Pallares!..."

"At your orders, *señó Worf.*"

"Tomorrow send ten men to look around *Jato* Three, and let these two men guide them."

"*Si, señó.* Come along, Ramiro."

"*Buenas noches, patrón.*"

Max waves them good night and goes back to sit in a rocking chair to meditate.

Cayetano stays by the door. Hesitantly, he looks at Olga, who is stirring her coffee. He moves toward the small table where the Spanish books are.

"Go on and rest, Captain," Max tells him. "We'll start searching for Calver at first light."

"Very well, sir. Good night, Madam."

Olga looks at him, grins, and then graciously bows her head.

He licks his dry lips and finds that the bittersweet taste of blood has disappeared. Despite the pitch-black darkness, the high humidity makes the heat unbearable.

What time is it?

Long before nightfall, the impenetrable pit of foliage had obscured the cockpit obstructing his view of the cadaver by his side, which alleviates some of his agony. He searches in his memories for a similar situation for comparison, so he can try to figure out how much physical and mental adversity he can endure. Going back as far as his youth, all he can vaguely remember are some childhood illnesses. No painful accidents, no fractures, no surgical interventions. He has no way of measuring his fortitude. He has always been a pampered person.

"*What time is it?*" he wonders again.

His right arm, still caught between his chest and the instrument panel, hurts terribly. Every time he tries to remove it, he feels it rasp against a sharp edge protruding from the panel. He needs to unbind his arm in order to free himself.

Arching his chest again, he props his left hand on the panel and gathers his strength. He pushes with his hips, and yanks his trapped arm outside his chest, crying out when the metal tears the muscles and scrapes his radius bone. Despairing, he pushes on his right fist with his left hand and his arm suddenly snaps free.

The phosphorescence of some lichen plants, the only thing he can see outside the broken windshield, fades away as he blacks out again.

Through the window, Olga watches the Robin taking off to join the other two airplanes already circling above the Central. It's the third time they've flown together that day searching for Bob.

I hope they never find him. The imbecile! I would like to see all of them go down and get lost and never come back!

She walks back toward the stream of air coming from the fan and sits on the rattan rocking chair.

Why did he suddenly go limp, when he was hard as a rock? And then why did he run away like a frightened child? Hatred rushes from her when she looks outside again. *Verdammung! How I hate this place!*

She feels a disquieting sensation and turns to her right, finding Gumersindo by the door, gaping like an idiot and dribbling lust.

"*Was Sie mange?*" she demands.

Raising his arm, he shows a string of small fish. "I allowed myself to bring the lady some little *mojarras* I pulled out of the river, in case you wanted them. They are very tasty!" He smiles, shrewdly.

Pointing to the kitchen she orders him, "*Legen Sie jene fischen in den küche.* Rosenda!"

The girl appears from the kitchen.

"Rosenda, take that!"

"*Si, señora.*"

"No, do not bother, *chica*," Gumersindo says to Rosenda. Just tell me where to put them."

"Over here, in the sink," she says, walking into the kitchen followed closely by him.

"And how goes it, *chica*? Look, I have not had a chance to talk to you for some time."

"It is not needed, anyway!"

"Maybe not for you, but for me and for your man...."

Rosenda looks at him disdainfully. "Leave the fish there, and get out!"

"No way, *chica*. I will scale them for you, so you can rest your little hands, which were made for other more pleasant chores," he replies, taking a knife to start cleaning the fish at his leisure.

"I do not need your help. Get out of here!"

"Shut up and listen to me, you silly girl! If you knew how hard it has been for me to restrain the friends of Nicolás Antonio's from killing your Ramón, you would not be so rude to me."

"Ramón does not need floaters to swim!"

"As long as one or two try to kill him, maybe not, *chica*; but the day a dozen or more pounce on him, there will not be anything left of him big enough to feed a buzzard, and that will not take long if I do not prevent it. What do you say if tonight you come by my hut just for a little while? I do not want you for the entire evening because you would suck the marrow out of my poor bones."

"Go fuck your mother!"

Forgetting where he is, Gumersindo pins her to the sink, trying to kiss her.

"Pallares!"

The shout startles him.

"*Scheren Sie Sich Raus!*"

He doesn't understand Olga's words, but her firm attitude and her extended arm pointing outside say it all.

"Please forgive me, *señora Worf*," he mumbles meekly as he slinks away.

Olga takes the string of fish and dumps it in the trash can. Then she turns to the girl and their eyes meet, forgetting the gross incident. Using soap, Olga scrubs her hands thoroughly. While wiping herself with a kitchen cloth, she looks at the trash can.

"Fischen in river?"

"*Si, señora.*"

"River, pretty?"

"*Si, muy bonito.*"

"Far?"

"No, it is close by. There is a covered pond where I bathe. Would you like to come with me some day to see it?"

"Me? Go?"

"Yes, with me. The place is cool and the water is clean and clear. Maybe you would like to swim in it."

Olga shakes her head, "*Nein. Ich habe angst... miedo?*"

"Are you afraid?"

"Aha!" She smiles, embarrassed.

"There is nothing to be afraid of, *señora*. There are no animals and nobody would see you either. Men are not allowed to go there. Would you like to go?"

Olga thinks it over, and smiles. "Yes, I go. You and I!"

One on top of the other, both watch needles point at number twelve.

"Twelve o'clock...? Noon...? Must be, there is light." Bob thinks.

He looks at the small thermometer hanging from the shattered windshield. Its dual-degree scale reads 42 degrees Celsius, 107 Fahrenheit. He has already survived twenty-seven hours and a half, notwithstanding his certainty that he would die the first night. A full day in that agonizing posture, pressed on by only God knew how many kilos of gum.

The blood has coagulated on his wounded arm, plugging the hemorrhage. But when is that pain going to stop?

How much longer before I die, God? Please! How long would it take for death to obliterate his consciousness? Every time he faints, he senses it coming closer. During his last spell, he had detected its cold presence. Now it had arrived to remain seated by his side.

Calixto, or what had been Calixto, continues to swell as its corpse decomposes. At dawn, Bob perceived the first whiffs of the sweetish smell that, with every passing hour, is becoming more pungent and nauseating.

"There they are again! Flying right on top of me!" He reacts to the sound of several engines passing overhead. "I'm here! I'm down here!" he hollers. "Are you blind? I'm down here! Right under your noses!"

The engines' drone diminishes and finally fades away.

He looks up. Nothing! Not even the blue of the sky. Only the green maze of limbs, leaves, and shrubbery that encloses him. Ferns and flowers – pink flowers, white flowers, red flowers, and blue flowers, flowers of all shapes and sizes. More than enough flowers for his funeral.

His head drops onto the instrument panel and he remains panting for a moment, his mouth open, swallowing with each gulp of air the stench of rotting flesh.

His eyes, staring at the panel, are actually looking into his soul. *"You don't deserve any better!"* he tells himself. *"Death would be a blessing. Enjoy your own private hell while you can, because there will be a moment when you won't know what's happening anymore. Have the guts to endure it."*

He suddenly bursts out, "No! Godammit! I don't want to die! I don't want to go crazy either. God! God! Please help me! Get me out of here!"

His shouts deplete his breath and the effort weakens him further. Every shape before his eyes undulates and melts away...

Chema banks the Robin to turn on final approach. Xkanták is straight ahead, to his left is the luxuriant jungle, and to his right the river meandering through the thicket, looking fresh and inviting. He closes the throttle and begins to pull the stick backward. The wind is calm and the humidity is dropping, helping the Robin to glide smoothly until the three wheels touch ground evenly. It's so simple to shoot a good landing.

"Flying is great!" he muses. *"It's a shame that accidents have to happen. I wonder why Bob went down. Maybe his hangover had something to do with it."*

He taxis the plane, following Ricardo's instructions to park. He closes the throttle, switches the magnetos off and the propeller whirls down to stop.

"*¡Quiubo, que jains*?" he greets the mechanic.

"Nothing, bosh! Not even signs of the *Gringo*."

"*¡Hijole*! Tough luck! What about Cayetano and the boss?"

"The boss stayed in Mérida, and Cayito went to Campeche to get some more airplanes from Sarabia, Don Ricardo, or Don Pedro to assist in the search. But what's the use?" Ricardo sniffs. "Last night the fireflies kept coming into my hut."

"Did their landing lights keep you awake?"

"*¡Máre*! You know what that means – they announce the death of someone you care for. They are the messengers of the jungle. By now, both of them must be being eaten by worms!"

"Do you really believe they are dead?"

"Look, *ninio*. You are new here and do not know enough. If at least one of them were alive, we would know already. They would have set the airplane on fire, so we knew they were alive."

"What if they are hurt?"

"Hurt is the same as dead. There is no one who can survive over thirty hours in the jungle if he is injured. Either the heat, or a snake, or some wild beast will get you." He slaps his arm. "Just the mosquitoes or gadflies give you more than enough agony!"

Chema nods, wiping the perspiration from his neck.

Neto approaches. "Listen, *maistro*! Doña Ticha says not to forget about dinner."

Ricardo shakes his head and exclaims, "*¡Oh, que joder*!"

"What is it, Rico?"

"I promised the cook to hunt something for dinner, but you came in early!"

"So what?"

"How so what? ¡*Caballo*! Now I have to lubricate the Robin!"

Chema's eyes sparkle. "I will go! Lend me your shotgun!"

"No, bosh, lest you get lost."

"¡*Achis*! You think I am that dumb?"

"Okay. Neto, fetch my shotgun." Turning to Chema he instructs, "Look, you do not need to go too far. See that *zaramullo* tree on the north side of the strip, about half way down? There is a trail there that will take you to the river. Walk about 200 meters on the north bank and hide under any leafy tree to wait. In a little while the white-wing doves will arrive to settle for the night. Let us see how good a hunter you are."

"We always have doves for dinner," Chema complains. "Is there not anything else?"

"¡*Claro*, bosh! There is deer and everything you want, but not close by, and I am not going to send you out to get lost, or to be eaten by a jaguar."

Neto comes back holding an ancient flintlock gun, which he hands to Chema.

"¡*Ah, caray*! How many dinosaurs did your great-great-great-great-grandfather kill with this fire stick?" Chema kids, looking at the antique.

"Dinosaurs maybe not, but my father did kill his share of deers, jaguars, and also a few pale faces during the *Caste War*. However, I would not trust you with it. This is heavy artillery. Neto, bring him my Browning shotgun."

Wringing out his sock, Chema shakes it and places it on a berry bush branch to dry. He crouches to sneak under a canopy of *virgin's mantle* and looks up through the flowers toward an ebony tree above him. It's the perfect hiding place to watch for the arrival of the doves. He feels like smoking and, propping the 12-gauge semiautomatic Browning against a branch, he pulls out a cigarette.

"But what if the doves can smell the smoke? Just in case, I had better not. How could I be so dumb?"

Earlier, he had crossed a ford by stepping on the rocks protruding out of the water, but he slipped and his left foot plunged into the water up to the knee. It would take a long time for his sock to dry, so he decided to put it back on wet as it is.

Amidst the sounds of the jungle, he hears a different sound, like the laughter of small children. "A bird, maybe?" he wonders. "And what about the doves?" Sunlight is dwindling. With their bellies full, the doves should start looking for their resting place.

"What was that?"

He had seen something moving in the growth, going toward the river. "¡*Ah, chingáo*! It is a deer!"

He grabs the gun and crawls out from under the mantle of flowers to spring up to his feet, while the grayish shade jumps from an opening into the thick shrubbery. Staggering, falling, dodging bushes and thorns, he runs toward the river and stops at a clearing to look around. He spots the shadow moving onto a sandy beach bound by a clump of reeds. Taking two steps aside to clear his field of vision he raises the shotgun to his shoulder, centering the prey in its sights: a famished dog, that, unruffled, ambles toward the river for a drink.

Disappointed, Chema lowers the gun and turns around to go back to his hiding place, but the sound of laughter holds him still. It's very close now and it isn't children laughing. It's distinctly feminine.

"Women from the Central, doing their laundry," he guesses.

He starts to walk back to his observation post, but an idea holds him. "What if they're bathing naked? Nah! They're too ugly to look at!"

He walks on, listening to the laughter.

"That is funny! The women from Xkanták do not laugh like that! It sounds like the laughter of.... No, it cannot be!"

Thoroughly curious now, he backtracks to the reed field, stealthily reaches the sandy beach, drops on his stomach, and crawls to the edge of the stream, leaving the shotgun behind. Pushing some reeds aside slowly, he finds a curved riverbank that makes up a deep pond screened by tall *madroño* trees and abundant underbrush. He can see water being splashed up and then raining down. Someone is frolicking in the water. Crawling farther, he looks to his left and then gapes.

In the stream, immersed to the waist in the gentle current, are two naiads emerged from the Mayan lore recounted by Ricardo. One blonde, stunning; the other brunette, splendid. They splash water at each other playfully.

Thinking that heat deludes him, he shuts his eyes but continues hearing water splashing and playful women giggling. Slowly, fearfully, he opens his eyes. The alluring, unreal vision persists, a feast for his eyes: Mrs. Wolff and Rosenda, their laughter, the splashing water, their admirable beauty. Astounded, he watches their breasts bounce, an incredible sensual sight that sends a bolt of yearning shivering all over his body.

The women go on playing. Round flexible breasts jiggling, limbs in bloom, round curves of tantalizing delicacy. Chasing each other, they wrestle and finally fall into each other's arms, lest they slip in the stream. They embrace for a long time; their bodies tightly bound together, their arms locked around each others' backs. Even though their laughter has subsided, their happy spasms continue.

From his hiding place in the dim twilight, Chema watches them kissing mouth to mouth, the ivory arms sliding up and down the hazel back in an ardent caress, but he still considers the whole idea as an absurd notion arising from his imagination.

Releasing their embrace, the women help each other wade the river to the opposite side and climb the embankment, where they have their clothes.

Chema absorbs their beauty as they towel off and dress. Maybe they both possess similarly beautiful attributes, but he has eyes only for the blonde goddess. His gaze caresses the golden hair that falls in ringlets on her mother-of-pearl shoulders, her breasts topped by two rosebud nipples. Her taut belly ends in a triangle of old gold from which tiny droplets of water trickle down to her quivering thighs. He surveys her amazing back from her neck down to the lusty cleft dividing her magnificent rump.

Their clothes hide these treasures all too soon and Chema cherishes his last stolen glimpses. When they part the *chaya* leaves to disappear behind them, each beat of his irregular pulse is an explosion in his temples.

He is exhausted. With his belly pressed against the sand, he feels that his already wet manhood is boring the earth to its core.

"I.... I'm sure I laughed!" On four or five occasions, big bubbles of laughter gushed from his throat. It was silly, or rather stupid; to laugh under such circumstances, but the incident had been amusing after all. *"Did the dumb broad think that, just by swaying her tight ass at me, she could get a prize stud? Besides being conceited, she is dumb... and beautiful!"*

Bob inhales deeply to relieve the pain piercing his chest, but the pungent stench nearby makes him retch once more.

"God! There's nothing left in my stomach but bile!"

Reluctantly he looks to his right. Through a rip in a trouser leg, he discovers a new blister on Calixto's black-and-blue leg. It's the third one growing on him that day. The other two are bigger and have already burst, attracting a cloud of dark-green flies that suck on the foul pus and the watery blood oozing from the decayed flesh.

"If I could light a cigarette, maybe the smoke would chase them off my face...."

The hundreds of flies hovering above him make a dull, hypnotic, buzzing sound. *"How long before nightfall, so they quiet down!"*

How long before the smashed windshield cools down enough for condensation to occur so he can pick up the dew with the palm of his hand, to quench his suffocating thirst?

"How long before I die?" Bob verbalizes aloud. "Jimmy, Jimmy! Get Maureen in the intercom. Tell her to fetch some deodorant spray. The whole plane stinks of puke! Are you deaf, Jimmy...? Answer me, Godammit!"

Bob grabs Calixto's shirttail and yanks it off his back.

"Are you trying to be funny...? Hey, Vince! Gimme a position fix. It's so dark outside I can't see where we are...! Relax, Baby! Everything will be okay. We'll shack up in Havana.... Pretty soon we'll be making love in clean, sweet-smelling sheets."

Cayetano casts his eyes down. "You are right, *señor* Wolff. There is no point in searching anymore. Even if one of them were alive, three days in the jungle without survival equipment kills even the sturdiest, healthiest man."

"Pallares! Load the airplanes. We go on working!"

"*¡Enseguía, señó Worf!*"

When Gumersindo exits the living room, Max scrutinizes his pilots' faces. Cayetano scratches his right ear thoughtfully, Manuel looks at the floor, and only Chema holds his stare defiantly, annoying him. "What is wrong, José María? Do you not agree, or are you reluctant to go back to work?"

"Do you want the answer of a man?" the young man replies, taking offense. "I have never feared work. What bothers me is that we give up the search. We should go on looking at least until we found the wreck!"

"Calm down, Chema!" Cayetano intervenes soothingly. "It is useless!"

"More than twelve airplanes searched yesterday and found nothing! Do you want to go on looking? Do it on your own time with your own means! I am not willing to waste any more time or money. I cannot be blamed for the stupidity of a man who flies drunk!"

Sitting in a corner, pretending she's listening to the radio, Olga watches them discreetly. Although she understands little Spanish, she observes their voices and gestures and concludes that Max and

José María are arguing, which is definitely interesting since she has never before seen anyone defy her husband.

Chema glares at Max. "Who said he was drunk?

"I know he was an irresponsible drunkard!"

Chema pounces toward Max, swinging his large fists, but Cayetano, with unsuspected agility, blocks his way and holds him off.

"Let go of me! Let me bust the face of this bastard!"

"Shut up!" Cayetano slaps him twice. "Do not be an idiot!" Shoving him toward the door, he adds, "Bob is dead! Get that through your thick skull!" Turning back to Max, he says, "Please don't mind him. This is his first experience, and he's upset!"

"All right!" Max concedes. "Loyalty is a worthy attribute. There's no problem. Let's get back to work."

Everything in Olga is shut off except for her admiration for Chema and his splendid fury. His sparkling green eyes make him positively handsome. Now she notices his admirably cut features, enhanced by small scars that render his features so virile. In one glance, she has recognized that he is a brave man embodied in a powerful frame of marvelous proportions. How was it that she had not noticed him before, those muscular arms ending in big, strong, manly hands? Yes, he is a real man in spite of his youth. He is what she needs to come back to life and, perhaps, to find freedom outside that hideous prison.

At the southwest end of the strip, Chema applies the hand brake and runs the engine to check magnetos. Then once again looks at Olga, who watches him from the house window.

"She is looking at me again, like she did when I tried to hit her husband this morning. Was she glad, or is it just my imagination?"

He applies full throttle, releases the brake and starts his takeoff roll. When he goes past the house, he shoots a glance at her and sees her hand wave a discreet goodbye at him. Dazzled, he rolls off the strip and has to jerk the control stick for an early and lumbering takeoff.

After his initial fright wears off, he thinks of her again. *"Maybe she does not love her husband. Cayetano must know how things are between them. I ought to ask him. The problem is he also likes her and, in dealing with women, he is a bastard!"*

Minutes later he notices that he has diverted from his route. "You see, you ox!" He slaps his face playfully. *"You got distracted watching the blonde and almost wrecked the airplane. Now, you are off course.... Ah, but she is so lovely!"*

He veers left to correct his course and looks down out of the corner of his eye. When he breaks out of the turn, he realizes he has seen something odd in the trees over which he has just flown. He immediately banks the Robin 60 degrees and flies in the opposite direction for two minutes.

There it is! The very top of a huge *ceiba* tree is missing as if it had been sawed off with a gigantic chainsaw. He also notices that several limbs of the neighboring ebony are broken. Throttling back, he circles around the site at a dangerously slow speed to peer into the forest.

About forty meters below the upper foliage he makes out a gray mass. It is the Travelaire. He has found it! Spiraling upward, trying not to lose sight of the *ceiba*, he climbs high enough to see Xkanták Central's clearing in the distance. He flies directly toward it while writing down the heading, speed, and time flown.

Back at Xkanták Central, Cayetano quickly makes calculations. "Indicated airspeed 112 mph, flying at 2,000 feet, temperature 33 degrees Centigrade, equals 119 mph. There is no wind, so that is also the ground speed... in six minutes and thirty seconds, the distance is exactly 13 miles!" he concludes, putting down the computer he was using. "What course were you flying?"

Chema answers, "My heading was 208 degrees, so the reciprocal is...."

"Twenty-eight degrees! Cayetano shouts excitedly. "Are you sure, Chema? That is quite a ways off the route!"

Blushing, Chema admits, "I was distracted, *Capitán!*"

"Fortunately! Then those two workers from *Jato* Three were right! He is north of here! Did you see anything, Chema? Something that indicates they are alive?"

"I am telling you I could barely see the airplane!"

"And how does it look? Is it badly wrecked?"

"I do not know, *Capitán*! I do not know!"

"Well, what are we waiting for? Let us go look for him!" He calls out, "Pallares... Pallares!"

"Should we not we wait for the boss?"

"Forget the boss! Come on, Rico! Get hacksaws, cutting pliers, you know what we need. Bring two assistants and a compass!"

Gumersindo arrives at a run. "What is it, *Capitán*?"

"We found the Travelaire." He starts to give orders. "Get the best ten *macheteros* you have to open up a trail. Take enough supplies for two days. The large emergency kit and a couple of mules, right now! Let us see, what else? Chema, go as fast as you can to Campeche and fetch Dr. Lanz. Tell him it is an emergency, but do not tell him we are going to go into the jungle. Just get him over here, whether he likes it or not. I will have a guide and two horses waiting so you catch up with us. Come on, hit the air! Rico, are you ready?"

The workers of Xkanták Central, usually lethargic, come alive. The news of the Travelaire's discovery spreads rapidly and even those not taking part in the rescue run around helping with the preparations.

"... that they already found the airplane, *señora*! They found the *gringo*!"

Olga takes the news impassively, wondering why Rosenda is so excited. She knows what had happened in her bedroom, so why is she so glad?

"Get me clean clothes," she says, walking into the bathroom.

Baffled by Olga's aloofness, Rosenda goes to the bedroom to look for the clothes.

Thirteen miles, twenty kilometers, and nine hundred and twenty eight meters. Only six minutes by air, but on foot the experience is totally different.

Cayetano halts to wipe the sweat that runs down his forehead and neck, drenching his chest. "¡*Pa'su mecha*! It is hotter than hell!"

"How much ground you figure we have covered, Cayito?" Ricardo asks him.

"Not more than ten kilometers."

"And it is already past noon."

"Give me a little water."

"We left at eight thirty, so we are doing something like...."

"Two and a half kilometers per hour," Cayetano replies, spitting out the warm and salty water. "We will be lucky if we reach the site before sundown."

Looking ahead, Ricardo agrees. "You are right. And so far we have just strolled in the park, in a manner of speaking. From here on it will get harder!"

"Hard my prick, and harder what we will find!"

"What do you mean, bosh?"

"What do you think I mean, dumb ox?"

"Well," Ricardo pouts. "At least we will be able to give them a Christian burial."

"That is, if we find anything to bury. Pallares!"

"What is it, *Capitán*?" Gumersindo answers from far ahead.

"Let us get going with balls, or we will never get there!"

"We are tackling it, *Capitán*, but the underbrush is getting thicker!"

Cayetano strides ahead. "Then let us use the *burunas* as if we were men! Hand me that!" He snatches the machete from Gumersindo's hand and shoves aside another man clearing a path. "Move over, here I go!"

It's man versus nature. The steely blade slashes thick underbrush, the core of fiber strands, thorny bushes and shrubs, cutting and slicing tender stems and hardened trunks with the strength and dexterity of a powerful arm. "Just follow the trail of my sweat!"

"¡*Gua, pariente*!" Gumersindo exclaims, impressed. "And I always thought the machete was not used in northern México!"

"Maybe not in the north, but what about in the hot lands where I come from: Coyuca de Catalán, in the state of Guerrero, no more, no less!"

"¡*Máre*! Now you are from Guerrero!" Ricardo jeers.

Gesturing as if he really recognized Cayetano's superiority, Gumersindo urges his men. "Now you have an example! Let us see if you start learning from it."

One glance around Xkanták is enough for Chema to conclude that the rescue party has not yet returned.

"Hand me my bag," the old lanky doctor says, getting off the airplane. "Where are these wounded men?"

"I guess they have not arrived yet, Doctor."

"Have not arrived from where?" he asks, irritated. He is an impatient man.

"From the forest."

"But you said they were here!"

"Well, here, yes, but not here in Xkanták."

The doctor starts objecting as Max approaches hastily.

"What is happening, José María? Is it true you found the wreck?"

Defiant and this time vindicated, he almost shouts, "Yes! And very close by!"

"How close?"

"Thirteen miles, on a heading of 028 degrees!"

"To the northeast? That is incredible! Are you sure?"

"Yes, sir. I saw the airplane!"

"And what were you doing so far to the north of the route? You were looking for him, were you not?"

The question bewilders Chema, who momentarily wavers but immediately regains his confidence. "Yes, sir! And I found him!"

"We shall discuss that later. Now, if the wreck is so close, why have they not returned yet? It is one o'clock! Why are things done without my permission? All this nonsense has already cost me too much money!"

A worker approaches Chema and says, "*El Capitán* Rodríguez said to tell you we were to leave right away. The horses are ready."

"Leave? Where to?" Max shouts, furious.

"I warn you, I am not going to go into the forest!" Dr. Lanz objects, propping his gold-rimmed lenses up his nose.

"We are going to meet them in case they need your care, Doctor."

"You are not going anywhere without my permission! Do you understand, José María?"

The young man is not listening. Shoving Max aside, he takes Dr. Lanz by an arm to lead him toward the horses. "Come on, Doctor. Let us go!"

"This is final, you hear? You disobeyed me by searching instead of working. If you defy me now, you do not work here anymore!"

Chema is heaving the doctor up on the saddle. "Go on, get on the saddle and stop whining!"

Max stands in front of the small horse. "I am telling you! You do not work here anymore! Get off that horse!"

"Clear the way!"

Max holds his ground. "All this is on your own. You will have to repay me from your salary!"

Chema digs his heels into the horse's ribs, bumping Max aside and shouts, "Take my salary and stick it up your ass!"

From her window, Olga smiles and waves his hand at Chema. Abashed, he spurs the horse and urges, "Hurry up, Doctor!"

The *burunas* dig a tunnel in the forest, leaving behind mashed pulp and severed branches bleeding green sap all around them. In the depth of that primal jungle human voices grow muffled, while the screams of the *saraguatos* and the cries of the *chachalacas* steal away through the treetops, high above the rescue party.

Cayetano's arm feels so heavy he cannot raise it any longer. Pausing, he takes a compass out of his shirt pocket to verify their heading, looks at his clock, and shakes his head. "Four-thirty and it is already getting dark! Within one hour we will not be able to see a damned thing down here, while up there the sun will still be shining! Dammed jungle! If Chema made the slightest mistake in reading the course, we may pass by the wreck and not even see it!"

"You think we are still far from it, bosh?"

"Who the hell knows? Let me hasten those oxen up ahead."

Cayetano reaches the lead workers as Gumersindo is putting away his *buruna*.

"*Quiubo, pues*?"

"Nothing, *Capitán*. There we go, fast as we can!"

"Not fast enough for me. Come on, hurry it up!"

"That is not possible, *Capitán*! Just see how tough this brush is." He yells at the workers. ¡*Orale, cabroncitos! ¡Métanle duro!*"

Five, six, seven slashes and the men in the lead halt. A thick *ceiba* tree trunk blocks their way.

"*¿Qué pasa, chico?*"

"Nothing, we hit hard stuff!"

"Go around it, then!"

"Just let us catch our breath."

When the sound of their voices dies down, everyone hears a droning, buzzing sound.

"What the hell is that?" Cayetano asks, looking around.

"God knows. Sounds like... I do not know, like wasps!"

"It would have to be a giant hive. You hear that, Rico?"

"*¡Pa'su máre*! Sounds like an electric motor!"

Aghast, Galicio whispers, "*Capitán*, I think I know what that is!"

"What?"

"Flies!"

Cayetano's voice falters as he asks, "Gummer flies?"

"Not gum flies. Just as big, but the other kind. The green ones that look for rotten flesh!"

"Good Lord!" Cayetano cries, horrified, and looks up to the top of the tree. He cries out, "Hey! Look up there!"

The higher *ceiba's* limbs hang broken and lifeless.

"Quick, let us get around this trunk!"

The machetes strike up a furious tune of hisses and thuds as the brush recedes unevenly. When they finally flank the trunk, they see the sign they were looking for: the hole made in the foliage by the airplane as it fell.

"Over there! It has to be in that direction!"

The buzzing grows louder and a few meters ahead the stench of rotting flesh hits their nostrils.

"*¡Hijue'puta!* We do not have to hurry anymore."

Cayetano pours water on his handkerchief, uses it to cover his nose, and walks ahead. With three swift slashes, his machete opens a path that brings the wreck in sight. There is a clearing in the brush made by the aircraft as it slid sideways.

"Almighty God!"

A green cloud of flies hovering over it, covers the Travelaire's right side. The insects' wings make a scary buzzing sound that heralds death and putrefaction.

"*¡Pa'su máre!*" Ricardo exclaims, crossing himself.

Cayetano stares at a wheel lying by the tip of his right boot. "We have to pick up what is left of them, Pallares. Get the tarpaulin and the first-aid kit."

"Getting them, *Capitán!*"

Their previous haste vanishes. Nobody feels like taking the first step toward the wreck. Gumersindo brings a large tin box forward. "Here is the kit."

"Find in there two bottles of formaldehyde. Spray it over the bodies and put them in the bags. And hurry, please!"

Gumersindo finds the bottles and calls two of his assistants to follow him. Shielding their faces with their bandanas, they approach the wrecked Travelaire.

Looking around, Ricardo asks, "You want me to pick up whatever we can salvage?"

"No. Leave everything as is. We will come back another day. Let us go back. I have never been able to stomach that stench!"

"*¡Capitán!*" Gumersindo suddenly yells from the twisted cockpit. "Come and see this!"

Cayetano halts and turns around, wavering.

Gumersindo's voice urges him again. "Come on, hurry up!"

Forgetting the stench and his fear of facing a picture of death, Cayetano strides toward the cloud of flies that hides the smashed cockpit and sees what Gumersindo is pointing at: Bob's head, hanging sideways. His half-closed eyes are dull and glassy, but there is still life in them.

Swallowing the knot that clogs his throat, Cayetano whispers warmly, "You lucky sonafabitch!"

Chapter 29 – Back to Life

With the tip of a syringe needle, Dr. Lanz's steady hand locates an emaciated vein, pierces it and tapes the needle down, connecting the line that feeds revitalizing plasma into Bob's arm. After verifying the flow, he looks at Chema, who holds the plasma container, and says, "Find something to suspend the bottle above the level of his arm."

Cayetano taps the doctor's shoulder, and asks, "How is he, Doctor?"

Folding down his shirt sleeves slowly, the physician looks down at Bob, who rests quietly in his bed in the pilots' dormitory. Staring at his pale features, he says, "He will live. Fortunately, the wound in his arm did not become infected and it should heal properly, but...."

"But what, Doctor?"

"I cannot ascertain that his mental health will ever go back to normal."

"Is he going to remain an idiot?" Chema asks, dismayed.

"Well, not exactly," Lanz says softly, "but the traumatic shock of being beside a corpse for so long may have affected his mental balance."

Standing at the foot of the bed, Max asks, "Do you think he will be able to fly again, Doctor?"

"Probably, but he has to recover physically first."

"How long will that take?"

"I cannot say precisely. Anywhere from three to six weeks."

"He is a strong man. He will get well in less time." Max's stern gaze cuts short the reproach beginning to show in the pilots' faces. Turning his back on them, he strides outside.

The group assembled around Bob falls silent for a moment, as if waiting for the last vestige of their boss' presence to vanish.

"We will fix you a bed in here, Doctor. In the meantime, come with me. Let us get some well-deserved dinner."

"Thank you, *Capitán* Rodríguez."

"Ricardo, stay with Bob for a while, will you?"

"Go tranquil, Cayito. I will look after him." When they leave, Ricardo sits on the floor beside Bob, and starts chanting a prayer in Mayan.

It is a night of lights and joy in Xkanták. It's Saturday night, when the workers come out of the holes dug in the vastness of the forest to crowd into the storehouse, joking and laughing, some shouting their orders for coffee, dry meat, cigarettes and basic supplies, while others protest in jest the restriction on liquor.

Walking toward the diner, Dr. Lanz looks around, remarking, "Is this place always so lively, *Capitán*?"

"No, my good doctor. Today is the end of the week, so the *chicleros* come from the *jatos* looking for provisions, clean clothes, and new gossip. But do not worry; you will be able to sleep in peace. Pretty soon the laughter and the singing will quiet down. *El señor* Wolff does not allow any disturbances or brawls, and of this," he gestures to indicate drinking, "nothing! Too dangerous!"

"Well, that is a relief. You may think I am a spineless man, but the truth is I fear these people, especially when they drink."

"You have every reason to be concerned, Doctor. But over here, we keep them more or less on a tight leash. So far this season we have only had three deaths, and I believe that is a record."

They reach the door of the diner. "Here we are, Doctor, this is our new dining room, and do not let its looks deceive you. We have an excellent cook!"

By the light of a lamp filled with engine oil, Ramón stuffs his clean clothes into a small *henequen* fiber bag in such a way that, if he thrusts his hand inside, he can grab his revolver and fire it without having to pull it out.

Sitting by his side, inside the straw and palm hut where they spend the weekend nights, Rosenda regards him in silence. There is a look of reproach in her eyes that, however slight, does not go unnoticed.

"Why are you so hushed tonight? What is it?"

"Nothing."

"Do you not feel well?"

She shakes her head.

"Are you angry at me, or what?"

"No."

"Then?"

The question goes unanswered. What can she say? Although there is no guilt in her conscience, she cannot explain an unfaithfulness that is not really an infidelity and that, if it is sinful, is possibly excusable. Is there not a feeling of compassion at the core of her relationship with Mrs. Wolff? Moreover, what is happening to her now? Why is she experiencing a feeling of aloofness, maybe even aversion, toward Ramón?

Her silence makes him turn his attention to her. "Has someone done something to you?"

She shakes her head, but her evasive eyes give her away. His hand claws brutally at the front of her dress. "Do not deny it! Someone did something to you! Who was he?"

Turning her head away, she retorts, "You are crazy!"

"Tell me! It was Pallares, was he not? Tell me, so I can go after him right now!"

Suddenly she finds the reason for her detachment and mixed feelings. Taking a firm grip of that conviction, she yells back at him, as she has never before dared to do. "That is what you want! That is why you brought me out here!"

Ramón immediately lets go of her. Befuddled, he goes on poking in his *morral*. He had thought she was naive enough not to find out his true purpose. Now he realizes how wrong he has been. Taking stock of himself as a man, he admits her accusation. "Well, now you know!"

In the exterior there is laughter and festive shouting, while inside reticence permeates the hut. Rosenda stares at her hands, her mind empty of thoughts, while Ramón looks hard for an explanation. Finally he tells her, "I wanted to tell it to you before we left Alamo, but I thought you might chicken out. I have to avenge the death of my father, you know that. But if I killed Pallares just like that, I would be locked away for twenty or thirty years... Now, as you saw, I killed three men already and nobody said anything because I did it in self-defense. Pallares is a coward; that much he has already proven. He will never meet me face to face. How am I going to kill him then?" He moves closer to her and lifts her chin. "You do not want me to rot in jail, do you?"

Rosenda shakes her head slightly, evading his eyes.

"You see? Then I have to provoke him!"

"Using me as bait!"

"Well, I do not want him to harm you, I just want to know when he tries to, and then I will be avenging your honor, and mine. Do you understand that?"

Rosenda's eyes still avoid him.

"Well, whether you like it or not, it will be so!" he says, throwing his *morral* by the head of a bed made of reeds and covered with a straw mat. "Now, lay down!"

She reclines on the cot, vanquished by disillusionment.

"Now what? Are you not even going to undress?"

She pulls her dress by the hem up to her waist, exposing only that part of her body needed to satisfy her husband's lust.

When the waning moon hides behind the tree-lined horizon, Ramón rolls to his side of the cot to reach for a cigarette. "I could have had more fun with a corpse!"

He blows out the match. In the darkness, he doesn't see Rosenda's revulsion as she wipes her mouth with the back of her hand.

Chema inspects an undershirt in the morning sunlight that bathes the dormitory, finds it full of holes, and tosses it aside. He picks up another one from the bed, inspects it, and places it in his cardboard suitcase. Then he looks up to see Dr. Lanz place a new bottle of plasma on the improvised rack.

Cayetano comes into the dormitory. Seeing Chema's suitcase, he asks him, "Are you going somewhere, or what?"

"Yes, I will ride with you when you take Dr. Lanz back to Campeche."

"Why is that?"

"The boss fired me yesterday because I did not obey him."

"Obey him about what? Make sense, man!"

"Yesterday he got angry because nobody asked his permission to do the rescue. He said that if I went to meet you, I would not work here anymore!"

"Oh, yeah? Come with me!"

"Where to, *Capitán*?"

"Just follow me!" he barks, already striding toward the main house.

When he reaches the door, he calls, "Rosenda, please tell *señor* Wolff I want to talk to him!"

Seconds later, Max comes out of the shower room, splashing lotion on his freshly shaved face. "What is it, *Capitán*?"

"Chema tells me you fired him yesterday. Is such a thing true?"

Max doesn't answer immediately. He waves his hand to admit them inside the house and goes to sit down at the table. Taking a banana from the fruit tray, he peels it slowly and chooses his words carefully. "Discipline is an important factor in man's every endeavor, *Capitán*. In aviation it is of outmost importance. A pilot must obey orders, even if the orders seem to be absurd. He did not obey my orders."

Cayetano takes a deep breath and releases the words he would rather hold back. "If he leaves, I shall also leave, and the mechanics will go with me!"

Max slices a bit of banana. Before taking it to his mouth, he asks calmly, "And where will you go, *Capitán*?"

Cayetano is caught by surprise. "Me? I... anywhere! Job offers abound."

"Will it be that easy? I want to know who will trust you due to your... strange dealings. I have there," he points at his desk, "some figures I was about to discuss with you. They are the tonnage of gum that has left Xkanták in your airplane, which does not match those delivered by you in Peto. I want to know where the difference landed, *Capitán* Rodríguez!"

Cayetano is confused.

"That shortage, translated into pesos, amounts to a great deal of money. Fortunately, I have receipts signed by you, for every kilogram of gum you have flown out of here!"

"Receipts?"

"Yes. Those yellow weight-and-balance sheets you don't pay any attention to."

Cayetano's eyebrows rise, expressing helplessness.

Olga comes out of the bedroom, smiles at them and takes a seat at the table.

"*Bitte!*" Max says to her. "We are busy. Could you wait in the bedroom for a few minutes?"

"Affairs of state, *lieber* Max? Please continue. If I hear anything classified, I swear I will take it to my grave."

Max's neck reddens, but he tries to appear calm. He looks back at Cayetano. "You have not answered me, *Capitán*. Where will you go? I need to know so I can send you a bill for those shortages."

Frustrated, Cayetano casts his eyes down.

Max knows he has the pilot in a dead-end alley, but his satisfaction turns to aggravation when he notices how Chema stares at Olga and how she seems to be responding with a subtle smile.

There is contempt in his voice when he says, "Get out! The two of you! This time I will overlook your cheating, but be sure I won't forget it!"

Cayetano jerks his head toward the door, indicating Chema to follow him.

Looking at his wife, Max slices the banana and says, "If it pleases you, I will tolerate your flirting, but if I ever suspect any real infidelity on your part, you will end up in the jungle to serve as a piece of well-deserved sexual relief for the workers. Maybe you would enjoy that. You could satisfy your lust at all hours."

Blood drains from Olga's features but her voice, cold and harsh, hits him where it hurts the most. "Yes, maybe I would enjoy that more than living with someone who doesn't know how to be a man."

Back at the dormitory, Cayetano stops on the steps to look back at the main house. "Just how stupid can I be?"

"Is what the boss said true, *Capitán*?"

"Of course it is! Otherwise, where the hell was I going to get enough money to feed as many mouths as I have scattered around?"

Dr. Lanz comes out of the dormitory. "*Capitán*, my patient is resting now. I would like to leave, if that is possible."

"Do you think he will be all right?"

"Yes. I will come back on Wednesday. Maybe by then he will have reacted favorably to the treatment. In Campeche, I will give you the vitamins and medications he needs. When he regains consciousness, he may take chicken or beef broth and *atoles*. No irritants, a lot of fruit, vegetables, and fluids."

"Well, then we can leave at any time, Doc." Cayetano says, walking with the doctor toward the airplanes.

Later, watching the Skyrocket take off, Chema asks Ricardo, "*Oye, Rico*. Is Cayetano married?"

Ricardo looks up from the magneto he is cleaning. "*¡Pa'su mecha!* What a question!"

"What do you mean?"

"He is five times married, and I have always been his best man!"

"*¡Ah, jijo!* Listen, and is he a widower, divorced, or what?"

"Neither, bosh. All his five wives are alive and well, and he has more kids than you can count with your fingers and your toes!"

"No wonder, then! Listen, and how come they do not catch him?"

"*¡Caballo!* He has them in different towns. Why do you think he never says where he is from, really?"

"Do you know where he is from?"

"*¡Claro,* bosh! But I am not telling. He is my friend."

Chema wants to find out more about Cayetano, but the way Ricardo busies himself scraping the magneto, tells him he will offer no further information. Grinning, he goes to the dormitory.

Bob is unconscious. His even breathing reveals the relaxation he attains when deep slumber quiets his mind. He needs that rest, because his waking hours wear him out. Staring at him, Chema is awed by his pallor. It seems that death has left its imprint on his features after being by his side for so many days. A shudder runs along the young man's spine and he feels the need to get away from Bob.

He goes to his own bed and sits down, resting his chin on his hands. From that distance he can watch Bob, undisturbed. He hears the noise of an engine accelerating and sees the Skyrocket race by on takeoff through the window. Aboard are Max, Gumersindo, and his assistant Galicio.

He looks at his watch. Only ten in the morning and the heat is already unbearable. It's Sunday, and there is nothing to do. His gaze wanders around inside the dormitory, and for a second he wished he were Bob, who sleeps under the breeze of an electric fan. How long is he going to be unconscious? When he wakes up, his eyes open onto a nightmare. His crazy babbling reveals how he continually relives the horrors he experienced.

Upset, Chema stares at the floorboards. "*Magdalena...,*" he says to himself. "*Why does her name pop up when I'm trying to forget her? But why should I forget her? I have a responsibility toward her and someday I'll have to live up to it. She is a docile, sweet, and pretty girl. Is she really pretty? What color are her eyes? Almond! That at least I remember!*"

He covers his face with both hands, trying to remember exactly how she looks, but her features are a picture faded by time.

"*How long has it been? One year and a half! Nineteen months. Five hundred and seventy days. How many hours is that? Why do I have to figure all that out? It's dumb!*"

That morning, when he closed the gray door of his Peralvillo home, is long gone from his memory. However, he still remembers some details, like the four sad chimes coming from the Saint – "*I forget the name of the church!*" He also recalls the chilly walk, block after block in the stillness of dawn, to the depot from where a battered second-class bus took him along endless roads to inhospitable tropical lands. There, honeyed promises were exchanged for hard work, hunger, and deprivation worse than any he had known before. From being a competent automotive mechanic, he had been demoted to "belly wiper," cleaning oil from the underside of old airplanes, until he learned his new trade, and after that he had begun flying.

"*¡What a difference!*" After all, the struggle had been worth his effort! Now, when somebody addresses him as "*Capitán,*" he feels proud and conscious that he is starting a professional career. He is only starting it, however, because he has a long way to go to gain the knowledge and category of a true captain, like Bob is; which may endorse his desire to fly for an airline.

"*But, do I really want to leave Xkanták?*" The question flutters in his mind. Yes, provided Olga goes with him!

"*I'm a perfect idiot! Just because she smiled at me twice, I'm assuming she would leave with me. All you have to do is look at her to know she is used to a lavish lifestyle. She is Swiss, and I don't even know where the fuck Switzerland is!*"

He sweeps these thoughts away from his mind. "*¡Chirrion! It is so hot!*"

He gets up, walks to the door, and sees Ricardo and Neto in the shop, working on the Curtiss Robin.

"*My airplane! Although it is so old, it is a beauty,*" he admits to himself.

How can those poor grease-monkeys work in that hateful heat? And on Sunday! Reluctantly, he walks toward them.

"*¿Quiubo, Rico?* You almost finished?"

"*¡Máre!* Am I cooking *panuchos,* or what? If you are lucky, maybe you will be able to test fly it this afternoon. And you were fortunate that your problem was only charred valves. This engine could have ended up like that one." Ricardo gestures toward the Travelaire's engine, salvaged from the wreck, which rests by the twisted wings and fuselage that lay outside under the sun.

Chema walks toward it, but stops when he detects the smell of death still rising from the wrecked fuselage.

"Then what, are you going to repair that piece of junk?"

"Do you think airplanes are given away, bosh? Of course I am going to repair it. Just now the boss left for Mérida to get some parts to fix the engine."

"Has he said anything about the new airplanes?"

"He was also going to check on that."

"*¡Uchale!* What damned heat!"

"You suffer because you want, *ninio*! Go take a swim in the river. Just do not let an alligator bite your ass off!"

"My ass is too tough, even for alligators!" Chema laughs heartily, but the memory of the scene he witnessed at the river bend quickens his pulse.

"Ah, do you not believe me?"

"I have never seen alligators."

"Just wait for the rainy season. Anyway, when you reach the crossing where the women wash their rags, stay on the south bank, and two hundred meters beyond that, you will find a deep pond where you can swim."

"With the women?"

"Yes, but just leave your pants on."

"What if I take them off?"

"¡*Pa'su máre*! If those women get a glimpse of your boyish tender dangling banana, they will assemble a pyramid on top of you!"

When their laughter subsides, Chema says, "How about if I borrow your shotgun? Maybe I will get lucky and hunt something."

"Go get it – it is by my cot. But please do not bring back Galicio's dog for dinner," Ricardo snickers.

Chema sets the butt of the shotgun on the sand and slowly moves the screen of reeds that conceals him. He is reliving the moment that has robbed him many hours of sleep during the past few nights. The intimate pool formed by the river bend is there, but no one disturbs its calm surface.

It couldn't be otherwise. Now he has corroborated that his recurring dream had been just a hallucination caused by the extreme heat – the same heat that now makes him perspire from every pore. The stream looks inviting. He leaves the shotgun on the sandbar, undresses, and leaps over the reeds, plunging feet-first into the current.

"Aarrrgh!" The cool water makes him shiver. He rubs his chest and arms vigorously, and then crouches to propel himself underwater to the opposite bank. Surfacing, he shakes the water off his head and is astounded at the sight before him.

Inches away from his eyes, two small feet stand on the edge of the bank. The round, well-proportioned toes end in manicured nails. Those feet can only belong to one person.

Fearing that this sight is another illusion, he slowly lifts his gaze, following the line of the ankles, the slender calves, the knees with their smiling dimples, and, under a gauzy skirt blown by a mild breeze, the beginnings of two pearl-colored limbs.

"¡*Hola*!" says a caressing voice.

Chema gapes. It is she! His blonde goddess, grinning at him with a mixture of naiveté and enticement that confuses him all the more. He blushes when she notices he is furtively glancing under her skirt.

"*Du bist Gut aussenhend, so wiemein furchtsamer lowë jedoch bereit dein offer zu verschligen,*" she whispers, comparing him to a young lion that, although tame, is ready to devour her.

Dreading that someone might see him there alone with Mrs. Wolff, Chema glances around. Understanding his apprehension, she squats down, her knees almost touching his face, to say, "You and I, alone!"

It is his wildest dream come through. However, he's convinced that the apparition will disappear if he touches it. Timidly, his fingers brush the knee before him lightly. The incredible vision remains tangible, so much so that he feels her hand cover his gently. Then, she takes his face and turns it around away from her.

"*Warten!*" She says. "Wait!"

"He waits impatiently. A few long seconds later, he sees a nude figure fly over his head. It is *Aphrodite*, plunging into her native element to reappear in the jungle as *Nicte-Ha*, the Mayan *Water Flower* Princess.

Chema expects her to emerge midstream, but she surfaces by his side. No words are needed. The only possible communication has been established long before. She is a woman, he is a man.

The first contact between two human beings that desire each other fiercely is a jolt, a product of the energy long stored in their young bodies. Exhilarated, he takes her in his arms, intent on keeping her forever. His lips crush her mouth while her lips hungrily search for his, and their kiss melts their bodies to re-cast them into one.

They take cover under the shadow of the *madroños*, to be lulled by the buzzing of bees searching for nectar and the flight of electric blue butterflies, caressed by the faint breeze and anointed by sweet herbs. Under their bodies they feel the softness of moss and the gentleness of the meadow.

At this moment, the jungle trades hostility for embraces. Strong, rough hands touch smoothly. Kisses run down the delicate line of her neck, across the curved shoulders and along the languidly stretched arms. When those kisses reach her, she shudders. When they feel that their burning lust cannot be contained any longer, the carnal union of the strong young man and the insatiable woman is consummated once and again, between breaks filled with fondling and tender kisses.

The luxuriant foliage that serves as a natural cove that shelters their physical love traps the sun's last rays while she comes back to life, resurrected for the fourth time.

She takes his face in her hands, the face she now appreciates. She looks deeply into his eyes and says, "*Du bist mein Mann!*" and then translates for him, "You are my man!"

Fulfilled, his inhibitions forgotten, and so happy he feels like crying, he can do nothing but look into her violet eyes. They go on looking at each other, saying with their eyes what they cannot express with words, as if the whole world had disappeared and only they were left behind.

However, the world is present behind the bushes. Through sparkling tears, Rosenda watches them, experiencing a strange anguish. She wipes her tears to steal away, taking the trail that leads back to Xkanták...

Flying in Xibalbá

Chapter 30 – The Chances

Standing by the door of the train's second-class car, Chema avidly drinks the last of a beer. Putting down the bottle, he sees the gray Skyrocket taxiing to park at Peto's freight terminal ramp. Giving the bottle back to the railway conductor, he says, "Come on, *Don Nabor*. Get the coldest one you can find. Here comes *Capitán* Rodríguez!"

Don Nabor steps inside the only passenger coach of the small train carrying both freight and passengers. He reappears in seconds, holding a cold, dripping, pot-bellied bottle. The rheumatic old man hollers to Cayetano as he gets out of his airplane, "¡*Orale, Capitán*! Hurry up before it gets warm!"

The pilot jogs to his side, snatches the beer from the knotty hand, and empties it without pausing to breathe.

"That is some throat gargling!" Chema cheers. "Get another one, Don Nabor!"

"Are you buying, or what?"

"Of course!"

Cayetano scrutinizes the young man, and then asks, "What is happening with you?"

"Nothing, why?"

"Do not give me that 'nothing'. It has been several days now that you have been acting funny! You are always cheerful, and you have become a big spender. Why? Are you in love, or what?"

Disconcerted, Chema replies, "Me? With who? Doña Ticha the cook, maybe?"

Cayetano stares hard and long at Chema, then says slowly, "No, not with Doña Ticha, of course...!"

Blushing, Chema changes the subject. "Did you see Captain Calver this morning?"

"Yes, he looks a lot better."

"What did the doctor say?"

"That maybe he will get well sooner that he expected, and...." Cayetano trails off as he looks up, searching the sky at the sound of an unfamiliar engine.

"¡*Ah, jijo*! What is that?" Chema exclaims, pointing at a large single-engine monoplane approaching the field.

"It is what I would like to be flying – a Bellanca Aircruiser!" Cayetano replies, shading his eyes to admire the airplane as it turns on final to land.

"Who do you think it belongs to, *Capitán*?"

"Aeronautica del Sur, I suppose."

Their curiosity piqued, both men walk from the side of the train to the cargo ramp to wait for the Aircruiser. When it parks and the door opens, Max jumps to the ground.

"¡*Capitán* Rodríguez!" Max shouts. "Come see your new airplane!"

Cayetano is pleasantly surprised. "You're kidding me, *señor* Wolff!"

"Of course not!"

Cayetano hurries to peek into the Bellanca's cabin. "Hey," he shouts excitedly, "you can stuff more bales of gum in here than in a railroad car!"

"That's the idea – to fill her up. You'll be able to move two tons in it!"

Cayetano's joy goes sour. "That's a bit too much!"

"No. With minimum fuel, you shouldn't have any problem. Come on, José María, you're wasting time!"

"I was already leaving, *señor* Wolff."

"But not to Xkanták. We will go in your plane back to Mérida, to pick up another Aircruiser as soon as I teach *Capitán* Rodríguez how to handle this ship."

"Don't waste time on my behalf, *señor* Wolff. I have ample experience flying these airplanes," Cayetano bristles, resentful.

"Are you sure?"

"I'm telling you!" Cayetano growls, holding Max's gaze.

"Anyway, you won't fly today." Max declares. "Your breath smells of alcohol!"

"Alcohol? Ah, yes! I just had a beer. I mean, that's just a refreshment. Nobody gets drunk on a beer!"

"I have given orders not to drink during working hours, *Capitán*. Simply obey them!" Max strides directly toward the Curtiss Robin and sits in the pilot's seat. "I will fly! I do not trust pilots who drink while they work!"

Cayetano forgets the incident. His only thought is getting into a new airplane he has never flown before. He climbs in and sits at the controls. Elated, he looks at the instrument panel and finds it complete. It has altitude, roll and yaw, airspeed and climb indicators, an artificial horizon, radio compass, and even an H.F. radio – everything needed to fly solely by reference to the instruments.

A red button calls his attention. On it, in white letters, is engraved the word Starter. On top of all the other refinements, this airplane is equipped with an electric-start motor. No more cranking the propeller by hand.

Forgetting he is leaving the Skyrocket behind, he flips on the battery switch, connects the magneto key, pushes the mixture lever open and hits the starter. As if by magic, the propeller spins and its 575-horsepower engine fires with a mighty roar. After the Robin takes off, he releases the hand brake to let the Aircruiser roll toward the head of the strip. Lining up on the airstrip, he opens the throttle, feeling the machine pick up speed on the uneven surface like a nervous mustang. In less than 500 feet it reaches 79 mph. and lifts its tail from the ground.

Cayetano pulls back on the control wheel lightly and the plane takes to the air. When it hits 105 mph. he turns tightly to fly back to the field, over the airplanes parked by the ramp and the old locomotive. On his second pass, he sees his pal Chato Juanes crossing the landing strip on foot and he dives to chase him. Poor Chato lands belly-first to avoid the Bellanca's propeller.

Getting up, Chato dusts himself off with one hand, while with the other he gives Cayetano the finger.

During dinner, Olga constantly seeks to hold Rosenda's eyes with her own. When she comes to the table to serve or to take away the dishes, Olga tries to start a conversation, but the maid replies with monosyllables. Her aggrieved attitude has now lasted several days.

"*Why, how did I offend her?*" Olga wonders.

Relishing the aroma of the Cuban cigar he has just lit, Max says, "Excellent tobacco! The best money can buy!" Regarding Olga, he asks her, "Are you worried, or annoyed?"

Olga replies with a distant look.

"Your pretty head is so unaccustomed to think that, when you do, it's too obvious. What are you thinking about?"

Olga smiles and says, "About how adorable you are *lieber* Max."

He swallows the bile behind her sweet words and tries to follow suit. "I cannot change what I am, but I give what I can. In your case, everything possible. I am presenting you with an empire. You already have subjects, all the servants you need, and if you are missing any luxuries, you'll have them shortly. Money buys everything. With money I bought you, and soon I'll be able to give you more than you ever have imagined."

"*Danke Schön, lieber,*" she answers slowly. "Could I have a small advance? Tomorrow I'd like to visit a famous local seamstress to order a gown. It's for the reception I'm planning to celebrate your birthday. We'll have as guests the most distinguished families in

Xkanták, Count Pallares and the flying knights included. It will be an unforgettable soirée!"

"I'm glad to see that you preserve your sense of humor."

"Why shouldn't I? I'm so thrilled being here, and I love you so much, that if I had some arsenic I would use it to sweeten your coffee!"

Max merely sneers and sucks on his cigar, enjoying it. Irritated, she throws her napkin on the table and stands up to go to the liquor cabinet to pour herself some gin. Raising her glass, she toasts, "Heil Hitler! May his victories be many and glorious. *Prost,* you despicable traitor!"

Only Rosenda's presence precludes him from getting up to slap Olga. He warns her through clenched teeth, "If you ever say that again, I will give you a beastly beating!"

"Well, I'm glad you finally admit you are a beast!"

Rosenda senses the hostility between them and furtively looks at them both. Feeling that her presence restrains Max, she takes her time in picking up the dishes and then saunters slowly back toward the kitchen.

A few seconds are enough for Max to realize his violent outburst only places him at disadvantage. "I apologize, Olga," he offers. "This isolation must be as unbearable to you as it is exacting for me. There are many obstacles I must overcome to make this business succeed. The people, to begin with. They're all worthless and dishonest. But this situation won't last forever. Whether the war is won or lost, in the end we'll be so wealthy that the Nazis will have to respect our prominent position. Your social standing will be higher than it was before. I promise you!"

Going to the window, she replies, "Only I will be too old to enjoy it. I won't wait that long, Max. There are other rich men out there in the world."

Olga's retort angers him again. "Yes, you said it, 'out in the world'!"

"Then I'll have to go out and look for them!"

"You won't get out of here unless I say so!"

Olga sees Chema sitting on the dormitory veranda. "You shouldn't be so certain!"

"If you think one of the pilots will take you out of here, forget it! They have orders not to do so. As well, remember the Gestapo is still looking for us."

"I doubt they will be interested in me, except to find you!"

Max stands up and walks to her side. Caressing her chin, he says, "Remember what I promised I would do it if I find out you are unfaithful to me? I will do the same if you try to leave me!"

Aware that Chema is watching them, she slaps his hand away from her face.

Her purposeful gesture conveys a clear message to Chema. His dismal mood changes to elation. "¡*Ah, chirrion*! It really looks as if she does not care for her husband. My luck sure is changing!"

He sees her withdraw from the window. Seconds later, the light in the bedroom comes on.

"I am going to go crazy if I am not with her soon!"

Chapter 31 – The Face of Multunzec

At *Jato* One, bonfires are kindled to allay the chill of dawn, to keep beasts and vermin away, and to track down treacherous shadows. Fires keep the *chicleros* warm and dry while they recount deeds and feats, or to plot in whispers the death of an enemy.

"The night is plenty dark," the *Tuxpeño* with the bushy mustache remarks.

"Aha, a good night to go hunting," murmurs the one with the pointed ears and the hook-like nose.

"Gumersindo gave us until tonight," the one hiding his face under his blanket reminds them.

Three more nod gravely.

"That is right. This could be the night!"

"Before he makes more friends."

"Friends will not do him much good. Nobody is brave enough to challenge us."

"So, what do you all think?"

All six nod in agreement.

"Then we will wait till dawn!"

"Aha, to give him an early rising! Hah, hah, hah!"

Ramón de la Torre possesses a sixth sense, that of a born assassin who mistrusts dark nights. He shuts his eyes and cocks his head, and with his acute hearing scans the obscurity around him. His fire went out a while ago and just a few embers glow amidst the ashes, but his sagacity has always been accurate. He detects a rustling, so faint it could be the crawling of a worm over the leaf of the bush that grows by his side. His left hand creeps inside the *morral* and his fingers slide around his revolver's antler grip. Its contact affords him confidence, since he has courage to spare.

In the same clearing, just a few steps away, sleep Rafael and Miguel, the two *chiapanecos* with whom he has pledged an alliance against the *Tuxpeños*, their traditional foes. He has to wake them up because his instinct warns him they are in jeopardy. There is something in the air, something in the forest's strange stillness that spells danger. His right hand feels the ground for a loose pebble. He estimates where Miguel is laying and throws it. He hears him stir and throws another pebble.

"What the...."

"Shhh!"

"What?"

"Get ready!"

Half a dozen words sail into the air to blend with the breeze. Hands close around the handles of deadly *burunas*. Silence. Subdued creeping noises, like those of snakes slithering on the grass. Where are they? His eyes cannot discern them and his hearing is so sharp he misconstrues the slight sounds. Which sounds are human? How many men are approaching?

Suddenly, a clue! Ramón opens his nostrils to catch the unmistakable smell of marijuana that the breeze blows in from his right side. He is glad to be a trained hunter. The *marijuano* hiding behind the *chaya* bush ignores the rule that hunters must stalk prey by moving upwind.

Ramón has to know how many more are there and where they are, and to do that he has to strike first. He brings his revolver up to eye level and aims it at the center of the *chaya* bush. His forefinger coils gently on the trigger and then tightens around it. The shot is the snap of a bullwhip that rouses the jungle from its placid slumber.

Disconcerted by the unexpected attack and the cacophony of frightened birds, the *Tuxpeños* surrounding Ramón and his friends give away their situation.

"Watch out! They are awake!"

Sprinting up behind the bullet, Ramón pounces on his foe. In his left hand his revolver shouts death, while in his right hand his *buruna* silently searches to take a life. Behind the *chaya*, cursing and painful bellowing are followed by a doleful moan.

A volley of bullets ensues and the *Jato* comes alive. Machetes slash the night, find enemy flesh, and cleave away life. Time drains away to dye the dawn blood-red.

"If you keep on giving me feasts like this for breakfast, Doña Ticha, I am going to need a bigger airplane just to carry my belly!" Cayetano tells the cook, placing his empty jug of coffee on the oilcloth-covered tabletop, to take a crumpled cigarette pack from his pocket. He is about to light up when he hears shouts outside the dining shack.

"¡*Señó Worf*...! ¡*Señó Worf*...!" It is Gumersindo's voice and he sounds frantic.

Cayetano gets up quickly and walks out of the diner, followed by Chema, to see Gumersindo arriving at the steps of the main house.

"¡*Señó Worf*...!"

Max appears at the door, buttoning his shirt.

"There is fighting, *señó Worf*! The men from *Jatos* One and Two are killing each other!"

"What is happening?"

The women from the Central approach timidly to listen in.

"A *picador* that just arrived, wounded, says that Ramón de la Torre started a squabble last night!"

Rosenda, listening behind Max's back, feels her heart falter. Despite their quarreling, Ramón is still her husband. Biting her fist she runs inside and bumps into Olga, who throws her arms around her to collect her tears.

"Are they still fighting now?"

"*¡Si, pues*! We must go and stop them!"

"We?"

"And who else? We will also have to take the airplanes, because besides the dead there are many wounded men who must be taken to Campeche for treatment."

"I do not know," says Max, doubtfully. He turns to Cayetano. "What do you think, *Capitán*?"

Cayetano clears his throat. It isn't an attractive prospect at all. "Maybe, if we go well-armed, our mere presence will placate them. About the airplanes, beyond *Jato* One there is a clearing by the lagoon we could use to land. So, it's up to you, *Señor*."

Considering the situation, Max takes a decision. "All right, get the Aircruisers and one Skyrocket ready. Pallares, arm all the available men with the rifles we have in the storehouse."

"Right away, *señó Worf*!"

Max goes into the house while Cayetano shouts at the mechanics. "Come on, you bunch of bulky balls. Did you not you hear? Get the airplanes and yourselves ready!" Looking at Ricardo's twisted face, he asks, "What is the matter, Rico? Afraid to risk your head?"

"Would you know one thing, bosh? I think this time we are going to meet Multuntzec, God of Terror, face-to-face."

Olga watches Max buckle on his holster, and smiles. "I think this time that gun will not be a simple ornament, *lieber*."

Ignoring her, he draws his 9-mm Parabellum pistol from its holster to check it.

"What should I do if you don't come back from this caper? Who should I sell all this garbage to? No, don't tell me. I'll give it away to the women gawking outside."

Max looks at her. "Have you considered that if I die, you would be at the mercy of these savages? Hold that thought in your mind, *liebling*, while you wait for me to come back."

One after the other, the three airplanes fly around the lagoon and land in the clearing. Max gets out of his Aircruiser, looks around, and observes that Cayetano has already lined up his men.

"I'll take over from here, unless you know something about military tactics."

"I don't know about military tactics, *Señor*. Do you?"

Max ignores the pilot's pointed inquiry and merely replies, "What matters is strategy. Where is that man, Chinto?"

"Here I am *patrón*!"

"Where are the *chicleros* fighting?"

"Look, *patrón*. When I left, the men from *Jato* Two were by that banana field close to the lagoon. The men from *Jato* One were right in front of them."

"Pallares, who do we take on first?"

Gumersindo shrugs. "The truth is, I do not even know why they are fighting."

"What happened was," Chinto explains, "a man came by yesterday selling guarumo, and – "

"What is this guarumo?" Max interrupts.

"Marijuana, *señó* Wolff."

"The men from *Jato* One got stoned and began fighting among themselves," Chinto continues. "Then, the *chiapanecos* from *Jato* Two, stoned also, joined in the brawl, wanting to finish the *Tuxpeños*."

"I do not understand anything!" Max exclaims impatiently.

"I do, *señó Worf*," Gumersindo says. "I think we must start by taking on the men from *Jato* Two!"

Max counts the men – thirteen, including him, all carrying rifles or shotguns. "This will be an easy task. They will not dare attack us with machetes only. Let us march along this shore and, when we arrive at the banana field, we will attack them from the rear." Max orders, taking the lead.

Flustered, Cayetano beckons his men to fall back. "Listen up, guys! That dumb ox does not know what the hell he is doing. Even if the *chicleros* are doped or drunk, they heard us arrive. Be ready to shoot our way back if things get rough. If we stick together we will not be sitting ducks."

Max strides forward briskly, convinced that everything is a hoax. "Where are they fighting, Pallares? I do not hear anything!"

"Maybe we arrived too late and they are all dead, *señó Worf*!"

"Look! Look who is in the lead!"

"The very same Gumersindo Pallares! Leave him to me!" says Timoteo Gomárez, from Comitan, Chiapas, as he centers Gumersindo in his gun sights.

"Do not be stupid, Timo!" his companion admonishes. "If you shoot now, they will get away, and just look at all those beautiful weapons they brought for us! Let them get closer. If we get their rifles, we shall finish off the *Tuxpeños* in no time!"

"You are right!" the man from Comitán admits. Lowering his revolver, he gestures to his twenty-six *chiapanecos* to hide in the brush.

"Hurry up, Rafail!" Ramón de la Torre urges his friend, who limps behind him. "If the men from *Jato* Two ambush the boss, we will not walk alive out of here!"

"Do not worry, Moncho. They are *chiapanecos* and will be on our side."

"There are no 'sides' here, *pendejo*! If they get those weapons and, stoned as they are, they shall kill everybody! Hurry up!"

Rafael's leg bleeds profusely. "I cannot walk any faster!"

"Look, I am going to go ahead to warn the boss about the ambush, then I will come back to help you."

"No, *Moncho*! Please do not leave me alone here!"

Paying no heed, Ramón runs ahead to intercept Max's group.

"*¡Chingáo*! I do not like this one bit!" Cayetano growls. Looking about, he tells his men, "Everything is too quiet. Take the safety lock off your rifles!"

"Get ready!" Timo orders his *chiapanecos*. "As soon as they all are in front of us, we jump on them!"

"*¡Patrón*! Stop right there!" Ramón yells from afar.

Max raises an arm to halt his group. "Who is that?"

"Ramón de la Torre!" Gumersindo exclaims, bewildered.

"Go back, *patrón*! The *chiapanecos* are hidden in the brush waiting for you!"

"*¡Sobre ellos, compañeros*!" Timoteo hollers, and his men, turned into blood-thirsty beasts by alcohol and marijuana, leap out of the tall brush with their machetes held high above their heads and firing the half-dozen guns they have.

Following Cayetano's example, the pilots and mechanics fire back a volley of bullets that hardly holds back the horde of frenzied *chiapanecos*.

Max fires point-blank at a one man, blowing up his intestines and splattering his face with blood, alcohol, and half-digested food.

"Back to the airplanes!" Cayetano shouts, firing rounds until he runs out of bullets. "All together! Do not disband."

Still nauseated, Max obeys Cayetano retreating toward the airplanes.

Noticing that he is losing the opportunity to seize the coveted weapons, Timo shouts, "Call in the rest of the men to cut them off!"

One *chiapaneco* runs away carrying the order to another band hidden in the banana field.

Not far away, nine surviving *Tuxpeños* are ensconced in a thicket, some of them wounded.

"Look at that, *compáres*, the *chiapanecos* are about to get to the *patrón*! Maybe we should help him out...!"

"Not now. Let us wait."

"But, Gumersindo is with him..."

"So what? Let them kill a few more *chiapanecos*, and then we come out and save the *patrón*, winning us a big reward!"

Cayetano's party is about to reach the airplanes when another twenty *chiapanecos*, armed with machetes and a few guns, appear from behind the banana trees to intercept them.

"Run toward that thicket, and keep firing!" Cayetano yells.

The blast of rifles and shotguns, more than the poorly aimed bullets, compel the *chicleros* to hit the ground, allowing Cayetano's group to reach the bushes safely. However, Gumersindo's assistant stumbles, wounded.

"They shot Galicio!" Chema cries. "We must go get him!"

Cayetano pounces on Chema to hold him. "Let it go! We cannot help him!"

Horrified, Max sees two *chiapanecos* crawling toward Galicio to raise their machetes over the grass and swish them down on the wounded man. His agonizing cry reaches Max. Once they have Galicio's rifle, both men slither away like serpents. Distressed, the German looks at Cayetano.

"They are not soldiers, *señor* Wolff. We have to play it by ear!"

"What will happen now?"

"One of two things: either they sober up and flee, or they hold us here until we die of thirst. It will depend on how much marijuana they have left."

"I still do not understand why this is happening!"

"This son of a whore is to be blamed," Gumersindo says, pointing his revolver at Ramón.

"Is this true?" Max asks Ramón.

"If I am to be blamed, so be it!" Ramón retorts evenly, adding, "But first ask your foreman here, why I was attacked."

Max stares at Gumersindo.

"Me, what? I was not even here, I was at Xkanták!"

"This is the second time he orders his men to kill me, because he wants to keep my wife!"

"He is lying! If I wanted his woman, I would kill him myself!"

"Your paltry courage would not be enough for that!"

Gumersindo raises his revolver, but Cayetano grabs his arm. "No fighting among us now!" Then he turns to Ramón and asks, "Why did the men from *Jato* Two get involved?"

"Because two of the *chiapanecos* are my friends, *Capitán*. When Miguel was wounded, he ran to *Jato* Two to ask for help. Near the pailas are some twelve men dead and no less than twenty wounded."

"God helps us!" Max exclaims.

Cayetano, keeping an eye on the *chicleros*, warns, "It looks like they are closing in on us. Come on, guys! Take cover behind the trees and form a circle so we can shoot in every direction!"

"Are we going to wait here to be killed?" Max objects.

"No, *Señor*. Chinto! Where are the *Tuxpeños*?"

"If there are any left, they must be behind that thicket, on the other side of the banana field."

"Do they have any firearms?"

"Ten pistols, at least."

"That will do! Look, one of us can go through this forest to the creek, to tell the *Tuxpeños* to approach the *chiapanecos* from the rear so we can have them on crossfire. That will give us time to bring men from *Jatos* Three and Four to help us. Who goes?"

"I will go!" Both Ramón and Gumersindo exclaim.

"You go, Pallares. They are your people and they will listen to you. When you are ready to attack, fire twice and we will attack at the same time."

"Very well, *Capitán*. Later, you and I, Ramón, will finish our pending business!" Gumersindo says, and disappears into the brush.

"Now, pay attention! We have to keep them at bay. Do not waste any bullets, understand?" Cayetano instructs his men.

They all nod.

Cayetano looks at Max, who watches the brush intently. "Don't worry, *Señor*. In less than an hour we will have these monkeys on a leash. And I mean all of them. We'll let the authorities deal with them!"

Olga stops in the middle of the room and looks at the clock on the central wall. Time goes by without news about the brawl, and she grows restless. Rambling through the house, she goes to the window and looks outside.

In the clearing she sees that the women of the Central have gathered at the diner and by the storehouse's door. They also wait. Famished, raggedy, dirty, their empty gazes frighten Olga. They look like birds of prey expecting a signal to swoop in on her. She moves away from the window and sees Rosenda leaning against the kitchen sink, her head bowed.

"Rosenda..."

She turns, startled.

"Rosenda, I... am afraid!"

Propelled by their fears, they fall into each other's arms, seeking mutual comfort.

"What's happening?"

"If we don't get help pretty soon, I think we are doomed, *señor* Wolff. Watch that prickly pear plant, see?"

"Yes.... Someone is running!"

"Exactly! Now look, to the right of the plant, nobody moves. They're waiting for a signal to jump on us. *¡Escuchen todos!* This time cut them in half. Make sure each bullet counts – it is either them or us!"

A shot is fired on the opposite side.

"That must be the signal! Do not let them get here!"

Cayetano proves to be right. The *chiapanecos* advance, crouching. It's hard to aim at them. Given that the only effective shots are only those fired by Cayetano, Max, and Ricardo, in less than two minutes the *chicleros* have them surrounded.

A metallic sound slashes the air and the hard dull noise of a blow is heard. Neto falls with his head sliced in two halves. Like hyenas, two men jump on the orphaned rifle and struggle over it. From the tree where he takes cover, Cayetano rapidly fires his last two bullets and the scuffle over the rifle ends.

Although he remembers the massacres he witnessed in Spain, this experience is becoming a nightmare for Max. The proud Luftwaffe officer, who once covered himself with glory in the fields of *Castile* by utilizing the most modern means of destruction, now fights hand-to-hand for his life against a mob of savages in a remote jungle, realizing he is about to die in the most absurd way. That idea, or fear itself, turns his anxiety into rage and he blindly fires his 9-mm Parabellum.

When its clip empties, a scraggy *chiapaneco* pounces on Max flinging his *buruna* at his head, but he misses and falls within the reach of the German, whose strong hands close on the scrawny neck, tightening on it like a vise. Strangling the worker, Max stares at his malaria-yellowed features while the man wriggles to escape his lethal grip. The dark eyes, seemingly floating in a swamp, bulge until they are about to burst out of their sockets. Max hears choking sounds spurting out of the man's throat and smells his alcoholic breath. Implacably, he blocks out the worker's breathing until his fingers meet at his nape. He is ending the man's life with inhuman aplomb when, suddenly, a colored explosion blinds him into unconsciousness. As he skids to the ground, his hands loosen their grip and he slides down on top of the other man's lax body.

Cayetano picks up a machete to fend off a blow aimed at Max's torso. His next swipe severs the attacker's arm.

Cornered against a wide tree trunk, Chema, Ricardo, and Manuel fire their last rifles' rounds as Cayetano bellows, "Here come the *Tuxpeños!*"

The assailant *chiapanecos* can see that the *Tuxpeños* are arriving reinforced by many men from *Jatos* Three and Four. They attempt to flee but are soon enclosed. Dropping their weapons, they surrender.

Cayetano bends over Max, who is coming around. "Don't worry, Mr. Wolff. You were hit with a rifle stock, but it doesn't look so bad. Everything is under control now, and we'll be outta here in no time. Chema!..." he calls. "Come over here and take care of the boss. Pallares!... Pallares!... Where is Pallares?"

"Do not look for him right now, *Capitán*." Chinto says. "He and Ramón just left for the thicket to settle things among them."

Cayetano shakes the head heavily. "¡*Ni modo!* We will have to spare one of them. Foremen of Jatos Three and Four, over here...! Search everybody and take charge of all the weapons you find. I do not want anyone armed, except you!"

"What about us?" the *Tuxpeños* object.

"You much less than anybody! ¡*Órale*! Tie down all those wranglers. *Tuxpeños* and *chiapanecos* elbow to elbow. You answer to me if any of them runs away. Search the entire area for wounded men. And move it!"

Bitching, but without alternative, all the *chicleros* involved in the brawl capitulate.

"You know why I came here; do you not, Gumersindo Pallares?" Ramón asks as they walk through the thicket.

"I guess I do, *chico*," answers Gumersindo.

"Well, you look very collected!"

"And I am, *chico*. I am!"

You know, maybe I misjudged you in thinking you were a coward. I must apologize."

"That is all right, *chico*."

"Anyway, you must start saying your last prayers. This is not the same thing as stabbing someone in the back, like you did my father. This is measuring of yourself against a man, face-to-face."

"See here, I have never backed away, *chico*. This one," Gumersindo says, patting his machete, "will testify to that better than me!"

When they arrive at a clearing in the forest, Gumersindo stops. "I guess we have gone far enough. I do not want to walk back from farther away."

"Then, you think you are going to go back?"

"I will, *chico*. I will, and to be very happy with that pretty mare you are bequeathing me."

"You son of your whorish mother! Defend yourself!"

"Defend yourself, *chico*, that I am laughing at you. ¡*Órale, Josefo*!"

Startled, Ramón looks around and gapes. From behind the mahogany trees six *Tuxpeños* headed by Josefo Martínez, appear wielding their *buruna*s above their shoulders…

Chapter 32 – Emancipation

Dr. Lanz conscientiously scrutinizes the depth of his patient's pupils and, satisfied, nods. Sighing, he removes the lamp from his forehead and pats Bob's arm softly. "A few more days, and he will be completely recovered."

"Do you really think he is all right, Doctor?" Cayetano asks, standing at the foot of the bed.

"Physically, he has recovered."

"Then, why does he not speak?" Chema asks, concerned.

"Maybe a psychiatrist could answer that better than I can. Tell me, does he react to anything, at any time?"

"Well," Chema offers, "when he is awake and an airplane takes off, he looks for the noise as if he recognizes it."

"See? That is a good sign. He may snap out of his shock any day now. Well, I must go redress the wound of *señor* Wolff."

"I will go with you, Doctor." Cayetano says. Chema and Manuel stay behind watching Bob.

"It must be awful to be like that, right?" Manuel remarks.

"Like a flower pot in the corridor!"

"Did you collect your wages?"

Chema nods in silence.

"Will you go to Campeche then?"

"No. What for?"

"What for? At least to go visit the loving dolls, otherwise the calluses on the palm of your hand will grow out of proportion!"

Engrossed in his own thoughts, Chema shakes the head.

"Well, it is you who will miss a trip to heaven!" Manuel says, leaving.

Chema walks slowly to his bed, sits on it and takes an envelope from under the pillow. Opening it, he takes out a wad of bills to count them.

"*Three hundred pesos. What a pittance!*"

Choosing a ten-peso bill, he crumples it and puts it in his pocket. Before wetting the glue on the envelope, he reads the address written on it: *Doña Laura O. Vda. De Ortegón. Jojutla 95 bis, Dpto. 12. Colonia Roma, México, D.F.*

"*It has been over six months since I moved them out of Peralvillo,*" he muses. "*If I stopped sending them money, maybe I would be doing them a favor. My sisters would be compelled to look for a job. Perhaps then they could meet a nice man to marry.*

Magdalena could go on helping my mother in the store. They really do not need anymore the money I send them."

To alleviate the remorse of his decision, he looks in his cardboard suitcase for the last letter he received from his sister Margarita, the only one who writes him because — regardless of time and distance – Doña Laura's resentment has not abated. Slowly, his sight moves over the small, even handwriting.

"...Mother gave us twenty pesos from your last wire to buy cretonne to sew the prettiest drapes. Now our apartment looks really nice. When will you come? We miss you very much, even Mother, I know. I was offered a job in a large department store, but Mother did not let me take it because too many men work there. Carmen finished her beautician course, but most likely Mother will not let her work either. Listen, about the radio we bought, we only gave the down payment, so you know... You must think we are always asking you for gifts, but Mother keeps all the money you send to buy merchandise for the store. You should see how well-stocked she has it. She does not tell us how much money she makes every month, but it must be plenty because it is the only notions store in the neighborhood. But then you also earn good money, which makes us happy because...."

Chema breaks off reading the letter, thinking, "*She never mentions Magdalena, except that time about a year after I left when she got sick and they needed more money for her medical attention. Was it a year after I left...?*"

Intrigued, he takes a stack of envelopes and looks for one in particular. He opens it, reads the date on the sheet of paper and counts with his fingers.

"*Nine months... Nine months...? ¡Ah, chirrión! Could it be that she was pregnant? No, it has to be a coincidence. They would have told me. They are not so mean. My mother maybe, but not Margarita.*"

He opens the new envelope again and looks at the bills. He takes the crumpled ten-peso note from his pocket and stares at it, musing. Suddenly, with a hard frown, he takes the sheaf of bills, puts it in his pocket and tears the envelope in pieces, throwing them out the window. Experiencing an unusual sensation of achievement, he walks out of the dormitory.

Cayetano watches Ricardo fuel the Aircruiser, drawing gasoline with a suction pump from a 200-liter drum.

"*¡Máre!* My arm is getting tired. Now you try, Cayito. It will help you reduce your paunch."

"What paunch? This you see here," he says patting his gut, "is nothing but abdominal muscle. ¡*Ora pues*! Let me do it! ¿*Que hay, Chema*? Are you going to Campeche with me?"

"No, *Capitán. Gracias.*"

"Do you want me to wire your allowance to your folks?"

"Well," Chema hesitates, "I do not think I am going to send them anything this month. I need to buy some things."

"What things do you need, you?"

"Well, many things, no? I do not have even a pair of shorts that is not torn. I always send them all the money I make. Am I not entitled to some of it too?" He walks away moodily to sit on one of the rocking chairs of the dormitory's veranda.

"And now, what flea bit him?" Cayetano says with a suspicious look.

"To me, it seems he is changing. Like his naiveté is wearing off, bosh."

"That is one thing I do not like," Cayetano murmurs, loading his words with mistrust. "If he does not want to wear torn underwear, it means he is baring his ass before somebody he cares for!"

Dr. Lanz ties the bandage, remarking, "There will be no need for a new dressing, *señor* Wolff. Your wound has healed properly."

"You see? Flying did not affect me in the least!" Max boasts.

"Flying was not prudent. There was the possibility that a clot could have gone into your bloodstream, causing an embolism. By the way, many of your men have been released from the Civil Hospital in Campeche. In view of the fact that they are in custody, the Public Prosecutor wants you to file a complaint against those guilty of the massacre."

"This business with the Public Prosecutor has already cost me a fortune!" Max grumbles. "Imagine, he wanted me to assume responsibility for the death of twenty-six workers! I could not afford the indemnification even if I sold the concession!"

"It was a deplorable affair, it is true."

Max has risen from the table to go to the door. "You!" he calls to a passing worker. "Tell Pallares to come over here right away!" Then he asks the doctor, "What about the pilot, how is he?"

"He is doing pretty well."

"It is better that way! That matter has also cost me too much money! *Verdammung*! I work to pay for stupidities. The *chicleros* do not take quinine until they are sick and cannot work anymore.

Everything is fevers, snakebites, and festering sores. All calamities for me!"

Gumersindo appears at the door. "Did you send for me, *señó Worf*?"

"Yes. See here, go with Dr. Lanz to Campeche and tell the Public Prosecutor there are no charges against anyone. Tell him to release all the men so they can come back to work."

"All of them, *patrón* – I mean, *señó Worf*?"

"Yes, all of them!"

"But, most of them are *chiapanecos*!"

"I do not care! Your duty is to maintain order amongst the workers. You do that, or I find another foreman!"

"¡No, señó! There is no need for that!"

Rosenda enters from the kitchen carrying freshly ironed linen in her arms, her pallor contrasting sharply with her black mourning dress. She pauses for a second to look at Gumersindo with hatred, and goes into the bedroom. Gumersindo's gaze follows her greedily.

"It was good to see that you are doing fine, *señor* Wolff," Dr. Lanz says, offering his hand.

"Goodbye, Doctor. Go with him, Pallares!"

The recollection raps on his mind, insistently. He feels it knocking, trying to tear open a veil of solid haze. It persists, unrelenting, demanding to break loose until, with gale's force it finally cracks its way into his consciousness. The recall is a phrase spoken by Maureen in an outburst of irresponsible happiness: *"No, sir! I won't defy fate! If it said Jamaica, we'll go to Jamaica, hurricane or not!"*

An indefinable sense of well-being appeases Bob. He closes his eyes feeling his lips curl into a grin. Sleep arrives and with it, tranquility and peace.

"Well, let's drink to these young pilots and to Capitan Calver's health," Max says, raising his glass. "May you fly well and without mishap, for the welfare of everybody."

Cayetano, Chema, Manuel, and Alfonso Teja, nicknamed *"El Pato,"* hired just two days before, raise their glasses toward Bob, who sits at the head of the table in the main house.

The whiskey slides down Bob's throat, doing a better job at healing him than all the vitamins he ingested during the last weeks. It was what he needed to feel completely well. It's not a crutch anymore – that is over and done with – but its tang takes him back to the time when he didn't have any hang-ups. It also makes him forget momentarily the place he is in, and the people he is with. He's living a moment free of obsessions and bitter memories.

While he drinks, Cayetano stares intently at Chema and Ingrid Wolff. He has come to suspect that a secret relationship exists between them and he has applied himself during the last two weeks to find out exactly what it is. Max may be blind, but not him, and right there, with all of them gathered around the table, he perceives an amorous language in their eyes. This discovery hurts his pride deeply. He can't admit that, with youth and good looks, Chema might be able to outbid his experience.

"Madam," Cayetano says in English, "I hope you don't take it as an imposition that we use your house to offer Mr. Wolff this dinner to celebrate his birthday."

"I'm glad you did, Captain. It's been a long time since I had the opportunity to attend a party."

"And I'm happy that you consider this a party. And by the way, how's your Spanish doing, Madam?"

"Oh, very but very well," she replies in Spanish. "Now I can speak very much."

"Amazing!" Cayetano exclaims, truly surprised. "From what I can see, you've been practicing it a lot!"

Olga senses the sarcasm, but replies casually, "Yes, with Rosenda. I speak to her all day, and she with me. But I want more classes, to learn more."

"Splendid! We'll start right after dinner, if you wish."

Chema betrays himself. The spark of anger in his eyes is too hot to go unnoticed. Cayetano smiles.

Olga continues in Spanish, "No, no, no! After dinner we have party, we take many drinks and have music and I dance with men... very... How do you say?"

"Gallant?"

"No, that, no! Big and... pretty? Yes! I dance with pretty men and tire. I dance with husband also, if he remembers how!"

"Well, your Spanish has really improved, Madam!" Cayetano admits. He stares at Chema who, confused, casts his eyes down.

Max is not as blind as Cayetano assumes. The exchange warns him that something peculiar is happening.

Slightly drunk, Olga walks onto the veranda. She finds Chema in a dark corner sitting on the floor, leaning his head against the wall. "José María?"

He turns, startled. In her lips, his name sounds different, sweet and manly, but right now he is sore.

"What do you want?"

"Why outside? No dance with me?"

"I don't know how. Besides, in there you have many pretty men to dance with."

Smiling playfully, she kneels by his side. "*Eifersüchtig*? Angry because other men?"

"You mean jealous. Yes, I am jealous, and very much angry!"

She takes his face in her hands to kiss him tenderly. "You only man mine! But we have secret, understand?"

Chema's face beams. "Forgive me. You are right!"

"Come inside, but wait. Dance with me."

Olga stands up and goes in. Chema jumps up nimbly, determined to join the party, but suddenly freezes. Through the window, Cayetano watches him. Sneering, he winks an eye. He has found out his secret.

Chapter 33 – Reprisal

Now there is no way around it.

The night before, he had been able to avoid a confrontation by keeping himself away from the other pilots. This morning he had risen earlier to take off before Cayetano so they wouldn't meet in Peto or Xkanták, but now they are face-to-face in the dormitory, and Cayetano's sarcastic smile says it all.

"¡*Quiubo, Chema*! Are you not going to confide in me your little secret?"

"What little secret?"

"Come on! Do not play the role of a duck when you are a shotgun! Last night you really astonished me. Such a quiet little mouse!"

Chema doesn't dare to look at him in the eye. He wants to garner enough courage to ask him not to meddle in his affairs.

"We are buddies, are we not, Chema? I only want you to tell me how you did it. One can learn something new every day, regardless of the age attained. Just look at that! I was using my best lines to get to her a little at a time, and you suddenly did away with the whole cake!"

"*Capitán*, to me this is not like – like the things you do."

"What things, I do?"

"Well, I do not know how to explain it! For you it is easy to win women over, and you go for all of them. I cannot do that!"

"¡*Uchale, mi cuate*! What would it be like if you could?"

"Look, *Capitán*, honestly, I mean... what is going on between Olga and I is something serious, and...."

"¡*Oye, párale, párale*! To begin with, which Olga are you talking about?"

"Well, you know, the misses."

"Mrs. Wolff?"

"Which other one?"

"You are making her, and you do not even know her name?"

"Her name is Olga!"

"You are all fucked up! Her name is Ingrid!"

Chema smacks his lips in irritation.

"Oh, come on, do not get mad! This is no joke. Who told you her name is Olga?"

"She did!"

Cayetano muses, "That is odd!"

"What is odd?"

"Never mind. Well, are you fucking her, or not?"

Chema lowers his eyes.

"Or are you telling me your 'thing' with her is just platonic love?"

"I do not know what that means."

"That you just hold hands and that is all, you dumb ox!"

The boy wrings his hands and stares at them. Aware that Cayetano will not relent, he says, "I already told you, *Capitán*. Our relationship is serious. I love her, and she...." His voice breaks. "I – well, as soon as I can, I am going to take her away from here!"

"¡*Si, Chucha*! And what about her husband?"

"Like he does not exist!"

"¡*Ándale*! So I was not all that wrong! Well, if you do not want to tell me how you did it, that is all right! Everyone squashes fleas his own way!" he says, moving away to take from his battered chest of drawers some Spanish texts.

"Where are you going?" Chema asks sulkily.

"Me? To enjoy the pleasure of exercising the tongue of Cervantes with... Olga!" he says, piling sarcasm on his words. "Maybe she might feel like practicing it with me also!"

Compelled by jealousy, Chema jumps up from his bed. His fists, like in Peralvillo, are like hammers, ready to strike.

"Relax, *chiquito*!" Cayetano warns him, raising his left arm to stall Chema. "I am doing this for your own sake. If she goes for me too, she is not worth risking your neck over her. Wolff may not realize you are crowning him with the biggest set of antlers, but I promise you one thing: if you try to take her away, he will kill you! He does not kid around, so we better make sure. Do you not think so?"

To avoid a confrontation, Cayetano leaves the dormitory. Once outside the dormitory, he sighs, relieved. He is not afraid of Chema, but trying to bullfight him in his jealous disposition, with those fists he has, is not at all healthy.

Sitting on the ground behind a *chaya* bush, Chema hits the soil with his right fist once more. His predicament has him bewildered.

A dim light in the sky increases, and he looks up. Through a veil of cirrostratus clouds that curves over the horizon, a crescent moon becomes visible. Pushing aside a limb of the *zaramullo* that hides his presence, he looks toward the Central and perceives a white figure running in his direction. He gets up quickly to go around the bush to receive his blonde goddess in his arms.

"¡José María!"

In her lips his name sounds like an alluring call.

"¡José María!" she repeats, clinging avidly to his lips.

When they unclench momentarily, he glances at the path that leads to the Central.

"No fear, Max drink much. He asleep."

Under a *zaramullo's* foliage, their bodies harmonize in a way known to man from eternity, its song casting a spell that holds time and existence still.

Looking into the violet depth of her eyes, he asks her, "Do you love me?"

"Love?"

"Do you feel something for me...? Love?" he insists, angry at his inability to explain what he means.

"Love, for you?"

He nods timidly.

Olga smiles tenderly caressing his forehead. "Love I have much, for you. *Ich liebe dich!*" she whispers in his ear, looking again for his kisses and his caresses.

"Olga," he calls her softly, bringing her out of her ecstasy. "I want to know one thing."

When she turns, her golden curls unfurl on his arms.

"Would you go away with me?"

"Go away, you and me?"

He nods.

"Where?"

"I do not know. I am poor. I have nothing to offer you."

She pouts pensively, then smiles. "Go to México City?"

"Yes."

"You have work in México City?"

Chema considers the question, then answers, "Yes. I can work for an airline making more money than here. Would you go with me, then?"

"*Mein kliner löwe!*"

"Yes?"

"Yes. You and I go!"

"What is a 'clainer loui'?"

"*Kliner löwe*? Oh, a lion, like this," she says, indicating with her fingers something small.

"Ah, your small lion!" He grins, amused. "When do we leave?"

"We wait," she says. "Max has much money in house. I want...."

"No! I do not want anything from him!"

"No, *lieber*. No Max money. Money mine. Max take from me! Understand?"

"He took it from you, and he has it?"

"Yes, yes! He has it in... *tresser*, ah?

"In a strong box?"

"Yes. I do not know how to open it. When I know, I take money. Then we go. Yes...?"

"Well, if it is yours, I guess so. We could use it to get started and then, when I...."

She doesn't let him continue. Her mouth sucks his breath and her closeness sweeps away all his thoughts.

He is too heavy to prevent the floorboards from creaking under his weight. Hesitant, Max pauses at the dormitory's entrance. What explanation can he offer if he is found there? Regardless, anger makes him enter resolutely.

On the first bed he recognizes Cayetano, snoring under the mosquito net. In front of him sleeps Manuel. The next bed is empty. Whose is it? Quietly, he walks to the next bunk and sees Alfonso Teja. Bob is in the last bed.

"*So it is with José María that she is wallowing with in the mud!*"

Blinded by rage, Max storms out of the dormitory, stamping his boots on the boards, unconcerned about the noise. Alfonso wakes up and looks around but, not seeing any one, he merely stirs and goes back to sleep.

Max stops in the clearing, looking in all directions, wielding his 9-mm pistol with a murderous grip.

"*Where can they be?*" he rages. "*I'll kill them together! First, the filthy bitch...! Where can they be?*"

His head spins. He sees everything through a red haze. He is groping in the shadows of the Central for the adulterers when he suddenly notices the blue Bellanca Skyrocket.

"*No, she is going to char in her own heat until she drops on her knees to ask for mercy! Then I will throw her to the beasts in one of the Jatos. He shall go first!*"

He strides into his house, goes directly to the chest of drawers in the dining room to fetch the sugar bowl, and walks back to Chema's Skyrocket. Making sure nobody sees him, he climbs on the right wheel and reaches for the fuel cap to remove it.

"*If I pour too much sugar, he may fall close by and be found. It has to be the right amount!*"

216

Two thirds of the sugar in the bowl go into the tank to mix with the fuel. His merciless reprisal is set.

Olga walks quietly into the bedroom and instantly becomes aware of the reigning silence. Apprehensively she peeks toward the sleeper where Max should be asleep, and sees a red dot glow in the darkness. The aroma of a recently-lit cigar permeates the bedroom.

"I hope the dawn's dew has cooled down your heat, because that was your last escapade," his voice says in the dark.

Immobile, she waits for a burst of retaliation, but only the red dot glows silently. She reclines on the bed and waits, and waits until daylight starts to creep through the window...

Chapter 34 – Calpachkeban Chhatohil

"*¡Auat!... ¡Auat!*" *Ahau Multuntzek*, God and Lord of Terror, cries like a raven.

"I have seen it...! I have seen it!" replies Xtab, the Goddess that Punishes Crime. "*¡Calpachkeban Chhatohil!* Reprisal for adultery!"

"What will you do, Xtab? What will you do?"

"I will do something about it! I shall do something about it!"

"¡Alab-olal! ¡Alab-olal!" reminds them Xkanleox, the Mother of Gods, the Loving One of the Yellow Leaf. "Remember that Alab-olal is the day to forgive in hope of future happiness, my children."

Although Multuntzek and Xtab feel daunted, they regard the matriarch embittered.

The earth shakes. The walls dance wildly, the bulb hanging from the electric cord swings around and the furniture jiggles. Cabracán, the God with Two Feet, jerks about in the forest shaking it, and someone approaches rapidly, shouting incoherent phrases.

"*Órale, Chema!* Wake up! Are you not going to work today, or what?"

Chema wakes up, driving out the last traces of his nightmare. He finds Cayetano moving the bed with his foot.

"*¡Ándale!* Get up!"

"*¡ 'ta güeno, ai voy!*" Chema says thickly, trying to keep his eyelids open. When he sits up, he feels his muscles go limp; his body weighs a ton. Placing his feet on the floor, a dizzy spell sends the walls of the dormitory swirling around him.

While showering he bends to pick up the soap and, when he stands up again, all the stars in heaven appear before his eyes. At the breakfast table he devours four scrambled eggs with half a dozen tortillas, and still feels hungry.

"Doña Ticha, please give me some more beans," he asks the cook, passing over his plate as he stretches and yawns.

"I wonder how many times the bellows blew last night... that it ran out of air!" Cayetano banters, adding: "By the way, Chema, whenever you get up during the night to do your... necessities, do not make so much noise. Last night you startled *El Pato*."

Chema looks at him inquiringly.

"He says last night someone made a hell of a racket walking around the dormitory. Now that I see you so sleepy, I suppose it was you. Was your stomach upset, or what?"

Chema nods silently.

Going by Chema's side, Cayetano pats his back. "That is because you eat too much, boy. Come on, leave the beans alone and let us do some flying."

Chema gets up to follow the pilot. Once outside, Cayetano stops to look at him. "You are searching for the cat's fifth leg, knowing he only has four! Better be cautious, boy!" he says earnestly, and walks toward his airplane.

Chema inspects the Skyrocket's load, verifying that the bales are properly stowed and tied down. He goes through the external inspection routine: control cables, control surfaces, empennage, wings, drain valves, wheels and tires, then he measures the engine oil level and verifies that the fuel cap is on tight. Everything is in good order. At the controls, he wiggles the joystick to verify its freedom of movement and checks that the magneto key is off.

"Off!" he shouts outside. While Ricardo turns the propeller, he buckles on the safety belt.

"On!" Ricardo calls.

"On!" Chema responds, switching the magnetos on.

The engine fires at the first pull and Chema opens the throttle. The Skyrocket moves forward. At the head of the strip, he reads the engine instruments: the oil pressure is normal and the temperatures are already in the green level, which is premature but not unusual. The cylinder heads normally reach that temperature after a few minutes in flight.

"*Maybe the mechanics warmed up the engine longer than usual,*" he thinks.

The magnetos work fine. Aligning the plane with the strip, he takes off.

During the climb, the Bellanca feels heavier than usual, but Chema assumes that the high heat and humidity are the reason.

Fifteen minutes later, the needle of the cylinders' temperature indicator is past the green range. Chema grows restless, but seeing that the oil pressure and temperature read normally, he disregards the possibility of a problem.

"*Problem is the one I have with Olga. I barely have enough money to pay for the airplane fare to México City. Then, no way I would stay at the apartment of my mother. Just imagine: – Mother, see this beautiful woman? Well, she is my lover! ¡Híjole! The fit she would throw! No, we would have to lease an apartment. And what about furniture? A soapbox for a table and a petate for a bed? Well, she's done it with me on the grass... If she loves me, she'll have to get used to what I can provide. Oh, yeah! ¡Pendejo! If she were Magdalena, maybe, but... Magdalena! And what about that poor girl? Is she going to remain waiting for me to make good on my obligation? I deflowered her, so she is my responsibility. Sure, sure! Am I to be blamed for her hot panties? ¡Híjole! How mean can I get? But, what else is there to do...?"*

He glances through the side window to check his progress. He is flying above a densely wooded area. Watching the compass, he notices a slight deviation and corrects it, turning 10 degrees to the northeast. According to the time flown, he is halfway to Peto. A drop of perspiration trickles from his forehead, reminding him of the cylinders' temperature. He looks at the gauge and his heart skips a beat. The needle leans against the end of the red mark. *"No wonder the cockpit is so hot!"*

His gaze leaps to the rest of the instruments. The oil temperature is excessive and its pressure, instead of low, is too high. The engine seems to be working fine, but it's obvious he's in a critical situation.

Panic hinders his reactions. His hands don't obey his brain's commands, which stumble over the clutter of his confusion. His training hasn't included emergency situations. However, his chaotic state of mind lasts only a few seconds, but the emotional impact received has been so intense it leaves a violent tremor in his hands.

The initial panic gives way to a reasoned fear that allows him to adopt the applicable emergency procedures. Reduce power first. He pulls back the throttle. The engine noise diminishes and the speed drops to 105 mph.

"Now what, should I go to Chunhuas? ¡Carajo! I did not even notice if I already flew past Los Lirios!"

He scans the horizon to the west, trying to locate any of the nearby fields.

"But if I deviated to the north, I must be closer to Boloyuc. Where is the lagoon?"

There are no lagoons, nor roads, not even trails in sight that provide him a clue to his whereabouts. All of a sudden he feels something odd. The engine's beat has changed. He looks at the tachometer anxiously: the revolutions per minute are rapidly dropping. He holds the stick with the left hand while with the right he crosses himself. Abruptly the Bellanca rocks and he cannot believe what he sees. The propeller has stopped. Such a thing cannot happen in flight while the airplane is still moving at a hundred miles per hour. Nevertheless, the propeller is static, one blade pointed at the sky, the other at the ground. What is wrong? At 100 mph., the propeller should spin by itself! The wings flutter slightly, and the Skyrocket's nose dips across the wooded horizon, starting to descend.

"The fuel valve is open. There is fuel in the tank. What is happening, then?"

He looks through the windshield. In front of him is the feared jungle, lying like an open mouth ready to swallow him. A terrifying vision unnerves him: Bob's airplane stuck in the trees, with the gum bales crushing him against the instrument panel. Instinctively, he changes the airplane's glide by placing it in a sideslip applying full left rudder and full right aileron. The plane skids on its starboard side and hits the treetops, tearing branches violently.

The maneuver is effective. The increased drag reduced the forward speed considerably, and he crashes sideways. The impact is dampened by a large number of tree limbs as the airplane slides to the ground.

Seconds later, still dazed, Chema realizes he is alive and unscathed. Unbuckling the safety belt, he gets out of the seat. Wriggling his body, he pushes aside two gum bales that block the door and kicks it open.

He stands outside the airplane silently taking stock of the wreckage. The fuselage is badly bent and its fabric is torn all along the right side. The wings are fractured in two sections. The engine is intact, but it's so hot it still smokes. Fuel drips through the tank cap, but that is due to the airplane's position.

"What the hell happened? Why did the engine quit? It had fuel and oil. The oil pump was delivering pressure; it does not have any leaks... Then, what...?"

Pondering on the situation, he walks to the front of the engine and pushes the propeller to make it turn.

"¡Ah, carajo!..."

Puzzled, he stoops to place his shoulder under the blade to push it up. Nothing! The propeller does not turn.

"Why? That's not normal. Let us see." His toolbox is in the cockpit.

The wrench slips and hits his left thumb. *"¡Me lleva la tiznada!"* he swears angrily, placing the wrench on the nut again to loosen it. Burning his fingers, he removes the nuts that were already unfastened and pries open the lid to the cylinder with the tip of a screwdriver. Looking inside the combustion chamber, he finds the cause of the failure.

"What kind of shit is this?"

The piston and its rings are welded to the cylinder's wall by a dark, rock-hard taffy smeared all over the combustion chamber. Using the screwdriver, he chips off a piece of that black foreign substance and tastes it.

"*Sugar...! Someone tried to kill me...! But who? Cayetano...? It had to be him. Who else?*"

Cayetano jumps out of the Aircruiser and looks around. Two workers are loading bales in *El Pato's* plane while he watches the operation. Max's Bellanca is turning away from the Central, and while en route he had seen Manuel and Bob.

Ricardo approaches with two assistants, rolling a drum of gasoline. Placing a chamois-covered funnel in the Aircruiser's tank filler, he asks Cayetano, "Did you see Chema?"

In response, Cayetano asks, "Did he already leave on his second flight?"

"*¡Caballo!* He has not even come back from his first. Was he not been in Peto?"

"No."

"He is delayed then. I thought he might be in Peto fixing something on his airplane. *¡Máre!* Do you think he might have crashed?"

"No. If he is not here, maybe something else happened!"

Almost running, Cayetano goes to the main house. Inside, he finds Rosenda.

"Listen, is the mistress here?"

"Si, *Capitán*. You want me to call her?"

"No." Baffled, he goes back to his airplane.

"What happened, bosh?"

"Nothing. I thought...."

"What is it, Cayito? Could he have had an accident?"

"Maybe! *¡Muchacho pendejo!*"

"We should start looking for him, hah?"

"Of course! Fill up my tanks. Pato, come over here..."

"*¡Ándale, Chebo!* Run and fetch another drum!"

"Tell me, *Capitán*," Alfonso says.

Cayetano is about to instruct him, when he sees Olga on the veranda. Suddenly, an idea makes him change his mind. "Look, *Pato*. On this trip, go by Los Lirios and Chunhuas. If you see Chema landed there, go down and see if he needs anything. If he is not there, go to Peto, unload quickly, and get back here right away!"

"*¡Si, Capitán!*"

"¡*Órale, pues*! He says, and turns to Ricardo. "Do not fill it up. Just put in an extra twenty liters."

"Are you not going to look for him, bosh?"

"He could not have crashed in the jungle. He is not that dumb! I will go by Boloyuc and Xiatil. ¡*Órale, muchachos*! Load me quickly!"

Puzzled, Ricardo scratches his big belly while he regards Cayetano's strange unruffled attitude. "And what do I tell the boss when he gets back?"

"Well... do not tell him anything yet. We have to be sure first. You know how he does not go for Chema that much."

"What about Manuel, or Capitan Calver?"

"Tell them to check the route carefully on their next trip," he says with his eyes fixed on Olga.

Chema is looking at the top of the trees. The ceiba's foliage is so dense and high it makes it impossible to be spotted from above, even if the search party flies right over him. He has to do something to let them know he is there when they come looking for him. Turning to regard the wrecked Skyrocket, he considers the idea of setting fire to it, if he hears an airplane engine close by. That solution, however, involves the risk of being fired by Max. Although damaged, the Bellanca can be repaired.

His gaze goes back to the trees. He could cut down some branches to build a fire, but with what? The hacksaw in his toolbox is broken. He wipes the sweat from his neck and stares at the aircraft. There must be some gasoline left in the tank. If he picks up wood, he can start a fire that throws lots of smoke.

He is walking away from the wreck when he hears the familiar sound of a Skyrocket engine.

"*That's Bob's airplane! They are looking for me already!*"

The noise increases, crossing over the forest from northeast to southwest, then it decreases until it fades away.

"*No, not yet. That was Bob returning from Peto. It will not be long, though.*"

Fearing he may remain trapped in the inhospitable jungle, he hastens to look for fallen branches. Picking up the first one, he realizes the futility of his idea, the high humidity rots the wood before it dries. Discouraged, he looks around - grass, ferns, elephant's ears, banana trees, everything green and tender. Nothing dry, nothing to burn except the airplane. Looking at it again, he finds the solution, *"The fabric! Yes, the fabric that covers the fuselage is old and now it is torn all over. It will have to be replaced anyway."*

In a frenzy of haste he runs to the aircraft, takes hold of a hanging strip of fabric and pulls at it, ripping off a long patch.

Cayetano's eagle eyes, used to probing the forest's thickness, explore every clearing, hole, and nook, hoping to find the fallen Skyrocket. However, his hope, which arises from an unwritten code of loyalty, is somewhat commingled with an urge to betray, a feeling kindled by his hurt pride.

He has already covered half the route and his mind isn't made up yet. He wipes the perspiration dripping from his forehead and shakes his head in despair.

"Damned gnawing conscience. It could be so easy to cross him!"

Dipping the Aircruiser's left wing, he surveys a small clearing in the jungle.

Chema hastens to wet a piece of burlap with the last drops of gasoline flowing from the drain valve of the airplane's central tank and runs to wring it on the fabric he has piled up several meters away from the wreck. Moments before, he had heard an airplane circling nearby, which means the search was on. Maybe another aircraft will come soon. He must be prepared. Holding a matchbox in his hand, he squats to wait.

"How long will it be before another one comes by?"

Right then, the unmistakable drone of an Aircruiser is heard approaching.

"That's Cayetano!"

The excitement makes him break the first match's head. The second one blows out, but with the third he lights a piece of burlap and throws it on the pile of fabric, which blazes explosively. Hardened by several coats of old paint, the fabric burns quickly, generating a cloud of black smoke that rises toward the tree limbs.

The rumble increases and Chema cavorts happily, watching the smoke grow thicker. It won't be long before he is found and by the next day, at the latest, he will be rescued.

Suddenly, his joy turns to amazement. Before reaching the top of the *ceiba*, instead of going up and out into the open, the smoke column stoops and travels horizontally among the branches. Due to the damp air trapped below the branches and the dry hotter air above them, the foliage creates a pressure differential that thwarts the ascent of the smoke. Fate plays him a tragic joke, just when the Aircruiser is exactly above him.

Cayetano growls to himself, "*¡Me lleva la tiznada*! Even if I wanted to, I can't bring myself to betray him. Foolish kid, I wonder where the hell he is?"

As far as he can see, everything is untrodden forest. His sense of smell suddenly warns him something is burning, and his gaze takes in the engine instruments in one quick scan, finding nothing abnormal. Regardless, the odor persists.

"*Something is burning*!... *A short circuit maybe*?"

Stooping from the waist, he tries to take a look at the electrical wiring running under the instrument panel. Nothing is burning there either. As suddenly as it had arisen, the odor vanishes.

"Was it the smell of rubber burning, or... something like paint?"

"*Burning paint*?" He finally reacts. "*A wreck*!"

He steers the airplane around to fly a reciprocal heading. Nothing in sight for miles around, except the faint haze caused by heat and humidity. Now he isn't even sure if there had been an odor or not.

Precisely below, Chema listens to the Aircruiser's engine circling the site at low altitude. Has he been found already? Is that Cayetano's or Max's Aircruiser?

Sitting at the head of the table in his house, Max grumbles, "If this keeps on happening, I'll never be able to make a profit here!" Biting angrily at the tip of his cigar, he asks Cayetano, "What must we do to prevent more accidents from happening?"

Cayetano's manner reveals he has something to say.

"Come on, *Capitán*! Say what is on your mind!"

"The problem is obvious, *señor* Wolff. Our planes are old and they're not given preventive maintenance. We fly them until they fail. In addition, the loads we carry far exceed any sensible safety procedure. I don't think it's reasonable...."

"Reasonable?" Max blows his top. "If we fly out less gum, then this business cannot be profitable. You know I'm not holding any of you. You can leave whenever you feel like it. That's the way we fly here and I will not change the system. What I want is that you all mind what you do!"

"If we did that, we wouldn't fly anymore!" Cayetano asserts, irked, looking at his comrades. Bob tinkers with his glass, while Manuel and Alfonso don't even dare to look at Max in the eye.

Lighting his cigar, Max murmurs disdainfully, "¡*Verdammte Mexicaner*! *Alle Sind Sie feiglinge und träge!*"

Cayetano doesn't understand what Max says, but he perceives his derogatory tone. His gaze questions Olga, who, seated on a chair, pretends to read a book.

Smiling sadly, she breaks the silence. "Since you teach me Spanish, Captain, it's only fair that I teach you some German."

Max glares at her, but she goes on casually, "*Verdammte* means damned; *Mexicaner*, Mexicans; *Alle Sind Sie*, all are; *feigling und träge*, cowards and lazy."

A vein throbs in Cayetano's temple as he turns to look at Max's reddening face. They stare at each other in silence, expressing the mutual hostility they conceal less every day. Bob watches them both. Expecting a clash, his mind is already made up if he has to take sides.

"Everything has a limit, *señor* Wolff!" Cayetano warns, pushing his words through his teeth.

"I am glad you understand that. Let's try not to over step it, for the benefit of everyone involved!" Max says, undaunted, and walks to the door. "I am going see how Ricardo is doing with my airplane. You all may leave."

His solid steps resound on the veranda and become lost outside, leaving behind an embarrassing silence. Olga drops her gaze to the book in her hands, while Bob, Manuel, and Alfonso get up and walk out.

Watching Olga, Cayetano remarks, "I've seen you very quiet, Madam, as if you were sad or worried."

"Why should I be worried?" she asks with a faint smile.

"I know our affairs are of little interest to you, but we have a downed pilot. I thought that might have distressed you."

"Oh, that!" Her features cloud over. "Do you think he is dead?"

He scrutinizes her every gesture and reaction. The tone of her voice, so devoid of emotion, sounds phony. However, her eyes moisten. "I don't know, Madam. Maybe."

The Baroness remains silent, her eyes fixed on the book.

"Don't you ever cry?"

She looks up, feigning surprise. "Should I cry for that boy?"

Cayetano, the old fox, can see that the question is but a mere affectation of aloofness. He decides to speak frankly. "That young man was madly in love with you, Madam. In fact, he was your lover!"

Her features grow pale. "Did he tell you he was my lover?"

"No. To watch his happiness was enough tale tell. Didn't you love him too?"

Standing up, she walks slowly to the window. Looking at the sky, she says softly, "I've been showered with riches, nice people, and flattery all my life. My parents taught me that feelings must be disguised, or disposed of, in order to get the best out of life."

She continues, "My father had nobility titles, but he lacked the fortune Max represented. I was the eldest of my sisters, so our marriage was arranged between our parents, without my assent or Max's. We had been married for five years when war interfered with Max's businesses and... here we are!"

A thousand questions race through Cayetano's mind, but he keeps quiet, waiting for her to go on.

"If I loved Max, maybe I'd endure this confinement, but I despise him and that makes my situation harsher. Amidst this ordeal, the only beautiful thing I had found in this place," she says as she turns to look at him directly, "was José María's soul, his love, his child-like innocence, and his manly chivalry. Also, he had promised to take me away from this here."

Cayetano walks over to her, and stands outside of the window frame to avoid being seen by Max. "I lack all the virtues the boy had, Madam, plus I'm not young anymore. I'm base in many ways and even despicable in others, but experience has taught me that, being as I am, one can win many advantages in life. We are alike in several ways," he says, looking at Max, who is busy talking to Ricardo in the shop. "What I can offer to console you isn't much, but I'd do anything for you, including getting you out of here whenever you ask me to."

Taking her by surprise, he pulls her from the window to embrace her, looking for her mouth. Olga resists at first, but the experienced lover's caresses inflame her lascivious nature and she begins to respond with a craving satisfied only twice in the last six months.

Moments later, Max returns to find them engaged in the monotonous repetition of the Spanish phrases. He notices that she has lost the melancholic look she displayed before dinner.

Doña Ticha fills the ladle with *relleno negro* and pours it into Cayetano's bowl. Tearing a tortilla in two halves, he uses one as a huge spoon to attack the dish.

"¡*Máre*! Nothing spoils your appetite, hah?" Ricardo remarks, watching the pilot with displeasure.

Looking at the mechanic out of the corner of his eye with his mouth full, he inquires, "Are you blaming me because Chema fell only God knows where?"

"No, bosh. But in my case, I do not even feel hungry!"

"Even better. Maybe that way you will reduce that big pot belly!"

It's past noon and Cayetano eats while his airplane is being loaded. His sole companion is Ricardo, who dabbles his spoon in the dish, making no pretense at hiding his dissatisfaction. "Tell me, bosh. Are some people more valuable than others?"

Puzzled, Cayetano frowns. "What is it with you? Since this morning you are throwing hints at me, like you want to say something. What is biting you?"

"It bites me that you and the rest of the guys are so tranquil, as if nothing had happened, while poor Chema is maybe on his way to hell!"

"Is that what is bugging you? Are you stupid, or blind, or what? Have you not you seen that on each flight we are covering several routes to look for him?"

"Yes, but when the gringo fell, we even brought planes from other concessions to look for him, and we stopped working."

"It is no wonder that your last name is 'turtle'. What you want is a pretext to hatch your balls. Look, stick to your job and do not meddle in things that do not concern you. The boss knows what he orders and why he does it," he concludes.

Shoving away his unfinished dish, he walks out of the diner, leaving a lump in Ricardo's throat. He not only has to grieve the possible loss of a friend, but also the strange aloofness, almost hostility, that Cayetano exhibits.

Eager to mitigate his sorrow, he murmurs, "Maybe he is right. Maybe Chema is already dead. Tucur, the owl, sang mournfully close by last night!"

"That is true, *lindo*! I also heard it, but I thought it was my imagination," Doña Ticha remarks, distressed.

"True it is, Doña Ticha. You know that whenever Tucur sings, someone you care for dies!"

"I better go make an offering to the gods." Ricardo thinks to himself.

The last vestiges of burnt paint stench have vanished, being substituted by the wild blue bells' fragrance that cuts through the humid air.

Chema stares at a red flower blooming on the *framboyan* bush growing close by his feet. Lying on his back under the Skyrocket's bent wing, he is quiet. No thoughts disturb his mind. The heat dulls his senses, keeping him physically and mentally exhausted.

Blinking, he comes back to the world of ideas and looks about. The thick twisted trunk of the tall ceiba branches up endlessly, hosting lichens and ramblers in its nooks and wrinkles. The gray patina is garnished with new, green, perennial ornaments of moss, lianas, and climbing plants. At its foot, the soil is covered by a profuse mantle of ferns, tall grass, palms, *zaramullos, caimitos*, and a thousand different species of bushes, blocking the way in every direction like zealous guardians of the jungle's virginity.

Once more he holds the magnetic compass he removed from the windshield and observes its movement. Suspended within an oily fluid, the horizontal card swings slowly from left to right until it stops, then reverses its motion until, slanted forward, it halts. The pointer indicates a heading of 275 degrees. He has repeated the same operation twenty times and only on three occasions has the magnetic reading been the same. The crash has affected it adjustment. He can't trust its erratic indications to follow a course through the forest.

"Should I stay here? If I go south, I will go deeper into the jungle, if I go west or east, it would take me weeks to get out. I have to go directly north, but what if I walk in circles? I do not have any water, unless I come across a lagoon or a river. ¡Carajo, with so much water around here!"

There are muddy embankments and rotten stinking marshes, but no drinking water anywhere. He scratches at the many mosquito bites on his arms and realizes that without quinine he may catch malaria, and then the fever will consume him in a few days. He looks up again. He has heard airplanes searching for him several times, but he hasn't been able to do anything to let them know he is there. The red *framboyan* flower near him is a souvenir he took that morning when he climbed the tree trying to make himself visible. But from that point to the top, the foliage was several meters high. His effort had been useless. He could only hope for a miracle.

Except that, for Chema, miracles didn't happen very often. Olga is the only miracle in his life, but now fate conspires to rob him out of that happiness. A tear trickles down his cheek. He cries in rage.

"If I ever get back, Cayetano, you are going to regret betraying me!"

Chapter 35 – Sunday, December 7, 1941

"Ho-hum!" Craig J. Newton yawns and, stretching his short chubby arms, lowers his feet from the hammock to the marble floor. "There's nothing like the lazy life of these Latin countries to truly relax one. Doesn't it affect you, Herr Wolff?"

Max puts his highball glass down, and regards the haughty chewing gum company executive. He really does seem to be enjoying the Sunday afternoon stillness, reclining on a tan-colored flax hammock hung in the cool arched corridor of the aristocratic residence.

Sitting back in an ample wicker chair, Max says, "If I allowed myself to be affected, I wouldn't be able to deliver the volume of gum my concession is producing. By the way, will my quota be increased as I requested?"

"Again?" the American asks, feigning surprise.

"I can do it, if you guarantee purchase."

"There will be no objection. Things don't look too good in Europe. If we get involved in war, the armed forces will buy out our production. We'll need all the gum we can lay our hands on."

The grin that spreads over Max's face puzzles Newton. "Does your smile have any special meaning, Herr Wolff?"

"Just egotistical satisfaction. And please, call me Max."

"Then you think we'll get involved in this war, Max?"

"You participated in the last one, didn't you?"

"Well, yes. President Wilson had treaties with England and France."

"And this time, President Roosevelt is seriously committed to the Jewish people Hitler is trying to wipe out."

"Now, honestly Max, as a neutral observer, who do you think would win?"

"For the time being, the Nazis appear invincible, and with Japan and Italy as their allies, they could overpower the Old World. It'd take all of America's financial and military resources to defeat them."

"But the question is: Can the Nazis be defeated?"

Max nods, expressing absolute confidence.

"Well then, we have nothing to worry about. While the rest of the world makes war, we'll make money!" Newton laughs heartily, his sides shaking. "And speaking about more gratifying matters, Lysander Wynn, my zone manager, told me about your superb private collection of local dolls...."

"Maybe Wynn exaggerated a little...."

"Lysander is a very conservative man. If he was impressed, there had to be a reason. Now, if your collection is strictly private, I wouldn't have mentioned it!"

"I have arranged a small intimate reunion for tonight."

"How small and how intimate?" Craig delights in the idea.

"Yourself, your assistant, myself and six selected young ladies!"

"Two for each one? Splendid!"

"Mr. Newton...! Mr. Newton!" Craig's assistant frantically yells, startling them, as he appears from the interior of the residence.

"What is it, Hill?" Newton asks, standing up.

"Pearl Harbor, Mr. Newton! Pearl Harbor has been attacked by the Japanese!"

"Pearl Harbor? What the hell is Pearl Harbor? What are you babbling about?"

"Our naval base in Hawaii, where the Pacific Fleet is moored, has been attacked by Japanese aircraft. I just heard it on the radio. President Roosevelt has convened Congress for an emergency session tomorrow!"

"Good Heavens!" Newton says, looking at Max's smiling face.

"It was unavoidable! I know Hitler. The imbecile just signed his death warrant!"

"We're at war, Hill!" he shouts, and turns back to Max. "Do you really believe we can win?"

"It won't be easy, but it's certain. Now what do you think, will you increase my quota?"

Newton smiles. "No matter how much gum your forest yields, it will never be enough!"

"Excellent! Now we do have a real reason to celebrate. I'll make sure it's an unforgettable party!"

"With confidence in our armed forces – and the unbending determination of our people – we will gain the inevitable triumph, so help us God...." President Roosevelt's last words are drowned by applause. Bob turns off the transoceanic radio.

"¡*Caray*!" Cayetano exclaims. "That's gonna be tough!"

Bob nods, feeling he needs a drink. "Tens of thousands men died in the last world war, including my father. This time it'll be worse. Who'd have thought the Japanese would side with the Nazis!"

Cayetano frowns. He has suddenly found the connection with Max and his wife he had been hinting at. "I – I've got something to do. See you later," he quickly says to Bob, leaving the dormitory to go to the main house.

He meets Rosenda in the living room and inquires, "*¿La señora?*"

"She is in the shower. I will call you when she is finished."

"I am finished!" Olga says, walking out of the bathroom, barely covered with a transparent robe. "Good morning, Captain!"

"Good morning," he answers, stressing the word 'good' as he delights in her provocative figure, revealed by the thin fabric that clings to her wet body.

Aware of his avid stare, Olga turns to Rosenda. "Take clothes to river. Wash with care."

"*Si, señora.* As soon as I pick up the table."

"No, Rosenda. Go now!" she says firmly, fixing her gaze on the pilot.

Rosenda quickly picks up Olga's clothes from the bathroom and leaves the house. Olga goes to the bedroom doorway and, parting aside the curtain, invites him in with a gesture. A slight pull is enough to open her robe and let it slide from her shoulders to the floor.

"Incredible!" he says. "You're incredible!"

"Do I daunt the intrepid aviator?"

"No, it's that I... have never seen such perfection!" he falters, trembling like a schoolboy.

"Isn't this what you came looking for?"

"Not exactly, but that can wait!" he replies, recovering his aplomb. His greedy hands run along her trembling, magnificent body that anticipates pleasure.

Ricardo enters the dormitory and looks around. Manuel is reclining in his bed reading a mystery novel. Alfonso is putting his laundry away, and Bob appears to be asleep.

"What is it, Rico?" Manuel asks him.

"Nothing, bosh. I was looking for Cayetano."

"He's in the main house. What did you want?"

Looking toward the main house, Ricardo hesitates. "No, it's just that I have saved two drums of gasoline, and I...."

"And you want to sell it to Cayetano?" Manuel quips.

Well, today being Sunday, I thought he might want to look for Chema."

"Explain slowly," Bob says, rising on an elbow.

"Although *señor* Wolff said we should not look for Chema anymore, if any of you wanted to fly, I have four hundred liters of gasoline we could use to look for him."

Bob considers the proposition. He owes Chema his life, his regained confidence, and being a whole man again. Standing up, he goes to the door. "I'll talk to Cayetano, Rico. Put gas in my plane." He says, already walking toward the main house. If he finds Chema he'll pay the balance of his debt. Once that's done, he can leave Xkanták. His time is up. His wrongdoing has been purged. He's free to go back to Miami with a clear conscience.

He enters the living area and stops abruptly. Rosenda stands by the bedroom doorway, spying in through the parted curtain. Startled, she turns and runs into the kitchen. Perplexed, Bob walks toward the bedroom and stops again. He doesn't have to go in to realize what's happening inside. The heightened moans and the noise of the bedsprings disclose a wife's infidelity and a friend's treason.

His astonishment turns to rage and his fingers clutch the curtain, but they remain griping the fabric while his conscience debates between indignation and the gratitude he owes Cayetano. If he nabs them in the act, he will certainly get on his bad side, which is something he doesn't need. Nauseated, he walks away.

Pumping the gasoline into the gray Skyrocket, Ricardo turns to look at Bob. Shrewd as he is, he immediately perceives his consternation. "What happened, bosh? Did Cayetano say no?"

"Is plane full?"

"Almost. Is Cayetano coming?"

"No. I'll fly. Finish quickly!"

"Can we go with you, Capitan? More eyes can cover more terrain, hah?"

Bob nods, climbing into the Bellanca.

They spend one hundred and ten minutes in a useless search, flying back and forth across the invisible skyways. However, Bob doesn't give up hope. He's going to keep on flying until the fuel that Ricardo saved runs out. He exchanges a sad glance with him.

All the eyes aboard the Skyrocket search earnestly, surveying the trees and searching the clearings, the few rivers, and the apparently clear lagoons, trying to find a trace of their fallen friend.

Despite the circumstances, not everything is sadness for Bob. Inwardly, he enjoys feeling born again. He is in the air, finding pleasure in flying. He is in absolute command of an airplane, regardless of its size or condition, and is handling it with his usual confidence and skill.

He remembers a happy Maureen, flirty and in love. He finds in the jungle's emerald the color of her bright eyes, reflecting the green of the Irish meadows. Then, saddened, he sees the mortal pallor in her serene face, framed in a small window of a white casket. That vision causes him intense pain, but no remorse.

"I didn't kill her. We acted on a burst of irresponsible joy that defied fate!"

He closes his eyes for a moment. When he opens them, he feels a serenity that amazes him. The crisis is over, and now he can again face the world, his world.

The jungle scurrying beneath the airplane's shadow loses the fascination it had previously exerted over him. Seeing it in the light of his regained identity, he finds it repulsive. He has to get out of there as soon as possible. War duty waits for him back home; maybe in the military he can find the meaning he has been looking for his life.

Ricardo's sudden yell brings him out of his reflection.

"Over there, Capitan!"

"What is it?"

"I saw some broken branches! Turn around!"

Bob reduces power and begins a slow descending turn.

"Everybody! Watch when we go over that *ceiba*!"

The seconds it takes to reach the site are filled with expectancy. The four men center their gazes on the trees, trying to pierce a path through the foliage.

"There's something blue down there!" Manuel shouts.

"It's the Bellanca. I saw the tip of a wing!" confirms Alfonso.

"Are you sure?"

"Positive! Go around once more, Capitan!"

The second time around Bob flies at minimum speed over the top of the *ceiba*.

The sight of the Skyrocket's cabin makes the men explode with a roar of savage happiness, celebrating their find.

"Did you see Chema?" Bob's question quiets their joy.

"Not me!"

"Neither did I!"

"¡*Máre*! I hope he is not hurt, or... something!"

"I fly more. You all look!"

Below, the drone of the airplane mixes with the monkeys' cries and the birds' unconcerned chirping.

"Do we go back to Xkanták?" Ricardo asks.

"No!" Bob veers the plane away quickly, its engine roaring. "I saw clearing, not far. There!"

"We go down there?" Ricardo's voice falters.

The glade is a small square that someone had cleared years before to grow corn. Lengthwise, it's no more than 500 meters long. To put down an airplane there is insane, but Bob doesn't doubt he can do it. He over flies the open space twice. Except for its short length, it offers no other risks. On the third approach he reduces speed, faces the aircraft into the wind, raises the nose high and slowly applies just enough power to hang the craft from its engine. As soon as it clears the tree boundary, he pulls up the flaps and the Skyrocket plummets, falling on its three wheels within the first five meters of clear terrain. The plane rolls, tumbling on the washed-out and hardened furrows and stops long before reaching the opposite hedge.

Ricardo opens his eyes. "Blessed Holy Wise Men of Tizimin, we are alive!"

"Let's find Chema!" Bob urges them.

They were right. The blue patch they had seen from the air is the top of a wing, still covered with fabric.

"Chema...! Chema...!" They call out.

The air is loaded with wild noises, but devoid of human response. The four men halt at the edge of the brush cut down by the weight of the airplane as it fell.

"Look! The fuselage is stripped of its fabric!"

"You think Chema tore it off?"

"Of course, you dummy. Who else?"

The four men run to look inside the cockpit.

"He's not here!"

"There is no blood, either!"

"No! Not a drop anywhere!"

"Chema...! Chema, we're here, by the airplane...!"

"¡Eitale! Come look over here! There are ashes and bits of burned fabric!"

"He must have wanted to make smoke!"

"But where is he?"

"Maybe he started on foot to Peto!"

Looking into the cockpit, Bob notices, "He removed compass!"

"¡Máre! Just look at this! Chema opened a cylinder. See how it is inside!"

"Looks like the metal melted!"

"¡*No jodas*! What you are looking at is taffy!"

"Taffy?"

"Yes, bosh! Melted sugar. Someone put sugar in his gasoline!" Ricardo asserts.

Bob looks at Ricardo, and says heavily, "Someone tried to kill him and now he knows it!"

"But who could do a thing like that?"

The four men look at each other, trying to guess the answer, but none of them dares to name a suspect.

The fading daylight filters through the thatched roof, throwing shadows on the men's faces already darkened by distress. A deck of Spanish cards rests on the oil-stained workbench. Only one thought fills their minds: Who had tried to kill Chema?

The light in the living area of the main house comes on, catching Bob's attention. Cayetano comes out and crosses the clearing toward the dormitory.

"¿*Quiubo, mis contlapaches*? No card game tonight?"

They all remain silent, expressing their disdain.

"What happened? Looks like somebody died on you!"

Ricardo cannot restrain himself and bursts out, "Cayetano, you have no mother at all!"

"¡*Quiubo, cabrón*! What is it with you?"

When nobody answers, Cayetano looks toward the main house and believes he guesses the reason behind their attitude. "¡*Ujule!* How hallowed can the children of Lucifer be? What I do in the main house is no concern of yours!"

"True! We do not give a damn about that," Ricardo says. "Forget it, hah? That is not what I was talking about!"

"I see, you are sniveling over Chema again, right? Well, do you want me to cry too because he is lost? Was his accident my fault, or what?"

Ricardo looks at him out of the corner of his eye and says, "This is the second time you ask me that, Cayetano!"

"So what?"

"Someone made his accident happen, and we are not going to stop until we find out who it was!"

Their suspicious gazes humble Cayetano. "Now that I remember, who went flying and what for?"

"We found his plane," Bob says.

"You flew?"

Bob nods.

"And you found him...? Where is the boy? Is he – dead?"

"Whoever wanted that, failed!" Ricardo says.

"What's this imbecile trying to say, Bob?"

"Someone put sugar in his fuel tank. The pistons were stuck to the cylinders. Apparently, Chema came out unscathed because he wasn't there, but he knows someone tried to kill him, so, maybe we'll see him here pretty soon."

Cayetano ponders over the news and beckons Bob to follow him outside. "I warned the kid," he says, once they're out of earshot from the others. "I told him Max would kill him if he kept messing with his wife, but he wouldn't listen. If he comes back, things are gonna get nasty." He looks toward the main house, muses for a moment and says, "Maybe I better warn the misses. With Max, you never know...."

Bob nods and Cayetano strides toward the house.

Olga is closing the fridge when she hears steps and turns to look. "Ah, it's the heroic Spartan! I thought you'd be sleeping by now." She smiles cheerily.

"On the contrary, gorgeous! I came back to make sure your exhaustion wasn't fatal!"

"As you can see," she says showing him the chicken thigh she has in her hand, "your ardent efforts only gave me a hearty appetite. Do you think you'd survive if you stayed overnight?"

"Do you want to find out?"

Olga extends her hand toward the bedroom, but he just caresses her chin instead of following her. "Thank you, but the truth is I would die, though not by lovemaking."

"By what, then?" she smiles.

"By your husband's wrath!"

"What?" She laughs.

"He tried to murder José María!"

She stops laughing. "What do you mean?"

"Bob found his plane, and the mechanics discovered that the engine was tampered with."

"Is José María dead?"

"No. He wasn't there anymore, so he must be on his way back. Will that change things between us?"

There was no mockery or cynicism in his voice, but a tone of entreaty that amuses Olga. "I thought Max scared you! I must warn you, he swore he'd kill anyone who courted me, or tried to get me out of here."

"Then it was him!"

"Did you doubt it?"

Cayetano paces the living room, thinking. Then he stares at her and asks, "Do you really want to get out of here, no matter what?"

Olga nods.

"Then tell me the whole truth. You're not Swiss, you're Germans, right?"

Surprise shatters her self-assurance and she remains silent.

"And from what I've been able to infer so far, Max was a military pilot. What happened, did he desert?"

Her lips tremble slightly as she says, "What if that was true?"

"Well, deserters are punished, especially during wartime. A simple notice to the German consulate in Mérida would rid us of Max forever!"

"No! Not that!"

"Then, it's something more serious!"

"No, no! You must understand. I'm his wife; I'd also be deported. You mustn't even think of that!"

"I could hide you. I know of a thousand places where you'd never be found!"

"No! Those damned Nazis would find me anywhere! Besides, I don't want to live in hiding anymore! Please, forget that!"

Cayetano doesn't seem persuaded, so she changes her tactics. "I see! You've lost interest in me!"

"Why do you say that?"

"Because you're selfish, like all men! You wanted to prevail sexually, that's all! You proved experience is superior to youth, and that satisfied your ego, so the rest doesn't matter!" Her last words make her mouth quiver and the wetness in her eyes trickles in silent tears.

Cayetano is an easy prey to her deceit. "That's not true," he objects. "Look, I may be anything but I'm not phony about this. I don't want to lose you. You decide what to do."

Olga smiles, relieved. Taking him by the hand, she leads him into the bedroom. "Max will come in late tomorrow. Come, we'll think about what we must do."

When the light in the living area goes out, Rosenda moves back from the kitchen door. Lost in her confusion, she bumps against the sink, her soul trapped by the passions that have assaulted her simple existence. It doesn't make sense for her to go on living that way. What can she expect from the future? To go on nourishing her strange infatuation? Her fingers fidget with an object lying on the sink. Nothing is normal anymore. Why hadn't she cried over

Ramón's death? She hates Gumersindo, not because he murdered Ramón, but because he constantly torments her. She doesn't want to love anyone except that woman. She finally identifies the object in her fingers: it's a sharp, serrated bread knife. With it, she can put an end to her bewilderment. She pushes the knife against her stomach and feels how its tip tears her cotton blouse. The first pain makes her stop. Frightened, she throws the knife away.

Outside, many eyes watch the main house. Suspicious eyes, eyes saddened by resentment, and eyes bright with desire. The eyes of Gumersindo, Ricardo, and Bob see how the last light in the bedroom goes out while Cayetano remains inside.

In Mérida, within the weathered splendor of the mansions fringing the Paseo de Montejo Boulevard, Maximilian Görzten entertains his clients lavishly, while attempting to rehabilitate his own manly attributes on the shaky base of paid-for female affection…

Chapter 36 – Hunpel Pixan U Metnal

At midnight, leaping from the jungle's intricate maze, the Balamoob Tats roam in the shadows. They are the mischievous and crafty goblins that transform the forest into a purgatory to terrorize travelers' souls with their wizardry.

Searching for unaware victims, the sorcerer animals emerge from the shadows: Uay Uacax the bull, Uay Ttul the rabbit, Uay Taman the ram, Uay Cuuc the squirrel, Uay Tuc the goat, and all the rest of them. They do not attack their prey face-to-face but do it furtively, fearful of confronting Balam, protector of the men who traverse the jungle, guardian of the souls that hike across this purgatory, indefatigable watchman of all the pathways.

"*Baam yohec, hunpel pixan u metnal.*" Balam knows a soul wanders in purgatory.

The leg holding Chema upright finally collapses out of weariness and he falls, kneeling on the wet ground. His back also gives out and he tumbles, hitting the grass face down. He remains that way, dead-like, until, only God knows how long after; a bright light shining close to his eyes compels him to open his eyelids. The blue-white light glows for a few seconds and then fades away mysteriously.

He cannot understand what is happening. Where is the light he has just seen? It appears again, abruptly, moving in every direction. It goes away, comes back, and cavorts about in an exciting dance, a dialogue that conceals some arcane enigma.

"¡*Cucuy*!" Chema recognizes it, his lips dry. "Go away! Shooo!"

Uay Cucuy, the ominous firefly that, according to Ricardo, visits men to announce sickness and fevers, hovers persistently over his head, appalling him. Fearing he might be catching a fever that would prostrate him in the middle of the jungle, he feels his forehead. No, it is cool and wet.

"Shooo! Go away, infernal fly! Go tell Patan and Xic they will not sicken me!"

The luminous insect flies away, only to come back with its annoying and foreboding flight. Finally, it coerces him to stand up. Gathering the rest of his energy, he walks on in a darkness jammed with limbs and branches that hit him, and thistles and thorns that prick him, cut him, and cause painful gashes and sores that poison his blood a little at a time.

Exhausted, his mind and body numbed by exertion, he bumps into a thin trunk, which he grabs for support. Gasping and sucking at the heavy air in big gulps, he remains still for a moment. Suddenly, he clearly hears a shrill and prolonged whistle that startles him. Has it been a bird? He hears it again. Long, vibrant, close. It sounds like the whistle of a muleteer driving a pack of mules on a trail. It cannot be anything else! A mule train carrying a load of gum from a *Jato* to a nearby concession central.

"Help...! Please, help me...!"

His anguished cries resound through the brush, and he anxiously awaits a long while for a reply.

Far away he hears the rumble of hooves pounding on a muddy road, voices of the mule-drivers, a puzzling hubbub, snorts of the beasts and more whistles approaching rapidly.

"Help...! I am here, very close to the trail!"

The strange and rhythmic cacophony continues to draw nearer. Judging from the direction of the noises, the muleteers and beasts should go by in front of him. Although the voices are closer now, none of them respond to his call for help. The trail must be only steps away.

"I have to find it!"

Letting go of the trunk, he pushes some branches out of his way and walks through tall grass, tripping, getting up, and hearing the mule handlers almost at arm's length. However, he stops and listens because the shouts, snorts, and whistles scurry through the dense shadows, avoiding him, going around, and positioning behind him.

"Hey! Listen! Where are you? Where is the trail?"

In agony he retraces his steps, striding hard for a stretch and then stops to listen again. His head snaps right and left. The noises go one way, then another, to the four winds, and then abruptly, the clamor ceases.

After a few silent seconds, he hears a gruesome wail that freezes his blood and makes his hair stand on end. It's the long and sorrowful groan of a dying man going to meet with the Angel of Death. It is *Auyaaz,* the echo of the trails, the repetition of sounds that has previously traveled through the jungle and then lodged in its roots.

"No! It's not true! It's all tales that Ricardo made up. There are no ghosts, no sorcerers or goblins or echoes or nothing...! Listen, friends, do not go! Please do not leave me here...! Heeeelp...!"

His forehead, cool and wet before, boils now. His temples thunder with each heartbeat and a fierce thirst smothers him. His shirt is soaked with a mix of sweat and blood oozing from a dozen minor wounds, poisoned by wild toxins.

He runs out of the brush and then stops, remaining still. Something is happening. Although it is night, the jungle is lighting up. A chalky brightness allows him to see the contours of the trees. Standing in the middle of the trail he looks up and down. There is no doubt. Trees flank both sides of that cleared path. The luminosity grows. He squats and sees, with absolute clarity, tracks of hooves and shoes on the ground.

"Now, which way do I go?"

Falling on his knees he observes the tracks. They all go in the same direction. North...? South...?

No matter. Wherever they go, there will be people... one merciful soul who will give him a drink of water. He gets up, and, feeling that hope restores some of his waning vigor, he treads on.

A few steps ahead something leaps onto his path. He stops. An animal stands in the middle of the trail, its eyes fixed on him. Its breast is white and its back and ears are gray. It's big, too big to be real, and it watches Chema's every move, waiting to catch him unawares to pounce on him.

Raising his arm slowly, Chema points his forefinger at the animal's eyes and shouts, "Let me go by! Do not go thinking you deceive me, animal! I know you are Uay Ttul, the sorcerer. Now get out of my way or I shall kill you! Do you hear?"

Undaunted, the rabbit looks at him, twisting its nose as it chews some fresh grass. Angered, Chema tries to kick him, but the small rabbit jumps into the brush.

Chema takes a step forward but he hears somebody giggle behind a bush. He realizes it is Balam, his benefactor, who is there to chase away his enemies. Balam, the elf that protects lost travelers, is with him. He has nothing to fear; he will find help ahead.

He walks on, following the curves of the trail now lit by a full moon, favoring his march. He walks and walks, striding quickly because a while back he saw the Katoobs hiding behind the bushes that edge the path. He sees them in pairs, in trios, spying on him, whispering among them and picking up pebbles. They are small but can throw rocks with precision and strength. Fortunately there are not many stones in the fertile soil. Nevertheless, they scare him.

He feels the first smack of a pebble on his forehead and it terrifies him.

"Balaaaaam! Where are you, Balam? Look at the Katoobs, they are pelting me!"

He runs. He runs breathlessly, choking. He runs until he feels his lungs are about to burst. He runs as fast as his weak legs can carry him, then stops and looks back for the Katoobs. He doesn't see them anymore. He breathes again, regaining his life, gulping it from the tepid nocturnal air scented by bluebells, drinking the dew that trickles down a ray of moonlight. His legs are invigorated and he feels they will not fail him anymore.

He treads on the path, turns a bend and, at some distance, finds the sign of life he has been looking for, a light! A bright light illuminating the foliage of a huge *ceiba* tree isolated from the rest of the forest. At its foot, emerging from the thorny leaves of a *Tazacam* plant is an alluring native woman with a slender figure. Her face is framed by long and silky black hair. Her brown eyes, serene like the night's still air, look at him bewitchingly while her hands smooth the cotton dress that covers her virginal body in a revealing way. The smile on her lips enraptures him and her crooning voice ensnares him in its sweetness.

"José María...! José María...! Come with me, José María," she calls with a familiar intonation.

Wavering, he stops. Does he know her? She is not speaking any more, but she wraps him in her smile, fascinating him. He is unwilling, however, to heed her call. He digs his heels on the trail's lose ground and tries to lower his eyes. "Leave me alone, woman!" he shouts. "I know who you are and what you want! Leave me alone. Go away!"

"José María, come with me!" she insists in the sweetest tone.

"No! I shall not! You want to waste me, I know you are mean!"

"*Sacred and noble is the ceiba tree, for its womb to give birth to anything evil*!" the jungle murmurs.

"Come with me, José María!"

"No! I shall not go!"

"José María...."

"Leave me alone, I said! I do not want to go with you. You are the Xtabay, you want to bewitch me, drag me to the bottom of a *cenote* and drown me!"

"Look at me, José María. Raise your eyes and look at me."

Chema recognizes her unmistakable voice. He lifts his eyes and, amazed, sees she is not the Xtabay. She is a splendid blonde whose red and longing lips call him, luring him with violet eyes.

"Come, José María. Let us go where I keep love...!"

"Olga...! Olga, wait! Wait for me! I am coming, do not leave me out here!"

Getting away from Balam, the only protection he has, Chema leaves the path to be devoured by the jungle. He gets lost in the fronds that conceal a hole, dark as the mouth of a dreadful cave in which the future blends promises of happiness with threats of misfortune…

Chapter 37 – Settling Accounts

Max's temper flares. He can hardly restrain himself from attacking Bob, who stares back at him. "I hired you to fly, not to do rescue missions. You'll have to repay me with work the flying time you wasted!"

"I warned you I shouldn't be trusted. Anyway, I won't fly until I find Chema. If I owe you anything, I'll repay you later."

"You stupid drunkard!"

Bob's right fist flies up, swift, hitting Max on the mouth, sending him reeling backward against the Aircruiser's fuselage.

Gumersindo's *buruna* whisks out of its sheath, but his arm is held back by Cayetano's firm grip. "This is not your fight!" he tells him.

Max wipes the blood from his lips, looks at it, and then at Bob. He spews out his hatred. "Pallares! This man may leave anytime, but he must take nothing except what he brought in." Then he addresses the other pilots, announcing, "None of you will fly him out unless I say so!" Facing Bob again, he says, "Now do as you please!"

Cayetano can't hate Max more than he already does, but he refrains from taking sides. He knows Max is furious because Bob found Chema's airplane, not because of the waste of flying time. Cayetano has too much at stake and can't risk losing it if he yields to his feelings of loyalty or friendship toward the American.

Bob walks away toward the dormitory and Max beckons the foreman, saying, "Pallares, I will be away for several days, so you are responsible both for my wife and that man. I want him out of here, but on foot. He must not fly out with the other pilots. Do you understand?"

"Understood it is, *señó Worf*. Do not worry about it."

Going to his aircraft, Max orders, "Everybody get back to work!"

Embarrassed, the pilots march to their airplanes while the mechanics assist in starting them. Gumersindo goes to the storehouse and Cayetano stalls, pretending to check a tire on his Aircruiser.

When Max taxies away, Cayetano approaches Bob to tell him, "Screw the boss! You can leave with me anytime."

Bob grins. "I knew I could count on you, but I have to find Chema. Thanks, anyway."

Three very worn sets of clothes and a bottle of Scotch is the sum total of his belongings. Sitting on his bed, Bob regards those garments that symbolize the disadvantaged situation he has allowed himself to arrive at. *"How could this have happened?"* he speculates.

Christmas and New Year's Eve have rolled by once more, the saddest holidays in his life. He has lost not only two years of his life but also of his career, when he was at the top of the airline's seniority list. By now, his fellow pilots are flying newer and larger equipment and those under him on the seniority list have taken his place. There is a possibility that the airline will honor his precedence in taking him back. Although he has influential friends to help him, he relies on the validity of his professional record. Alternatively, a war has started with unprecedented ferocity, and his services could be useful there. However, at 44, maybe he is too old for military duty. Anyhow, he will find something to keep him busy.

Ricardo's presence snaps him out of his assumptions..

"Am I bothering you, Capitan?"

"What you want, Rico?"

"Well, I heard the boss say he will be away for several days, and because you want to look for Chema, well... I came to see if you want to come with us, that way you can take whatever you need and Gumersindo will have no say in it."

"Rico... Let me understand you well. You want you and I go look for Chema?"

"No, Capitan. We are going to disassemble Chema's Skyrocket to bring it back. I will be taking mules, food, and supplies. If you come with us, you can look for Chema and use our supplies."

"Oh, I understand! Very good, I go. When?"

"At noontime. But look, so Gumersindo does not suspect anything, go ahead now and wait for us by the river, hah?"

"Okay, Rico. I go now."

Cheerful, Ricardo goes to hasten the preparations and Bob closes his suitcase. Hanging a canteen from his shoulder, he takes a bottle of quinine from the bedside table and leaves the dormitory.

He stops in the middle of the clearing. Slowly, his eyes scan over the loathed place: the dormitory, the shabby diner, the storehouse where Gumersindo, the reptile, rules; the repair shop with its mechanics working dutifully; the wretched huts behind the trees. He glances one last time over the purgatory where he has atoned for his guilt. It will take time, but those sorry images will be erased from his memory someday.

However, when he takes in the main house, his gut twitches. Inside is the woman that humiliated him. It will take longer to forget that incident, but he will do it, now that he is determined to rise above such pettiness.

Gumersindo sees him and comes out of the storehouse to meet him. "What is happening, *Capitán*? Do not tell me you are leaving!"

There is nothing but hatred in Bob's eyes.

"If you are leaving, you are leaving well, as the *patrón* said, taking only your stuff. Now, with such equipment as you are taking, you shall not go very far. However, since I do not have any bad blood for you, let me wish you good traveling, *Capitán*!"

Bob feels like spitting on the man's face, but he simply turns his back on him and takes the path that leads to the river.

The shadow cast by the Ramónales and the breeze that cools on contact with the river's surface combine to make him drowsy. He is laying on the grass, dozing away, when he hears the caustic laughter that has haunted his dreams during his stay in Xkanták.

"*Am I going crazy?*"

He twists around to look back and finds, among the ferns, Olga's silhouette.

"Is this the way you plan to rescue your friend?" she chides him.

Again, as it happened minutes before in the clearing, a bilious spasm hits his stomach. His pulse rushes as he gets up to confront her. "What are you doing here? What do you want?"

"Don't fancy I came looking for you. Hitting my husband doesn't make a man out of you!" Wickedly, she adds, "It happens that I frequently come here to swim. I hope that doesn't bother you."

"It's your river, I'm leaving!"

Opening her blouse, she asks him, "Does the sight of a nude female body offend you?" She continues unbuttoning until the partition between her breasts is visible.

"Listen, lady," Bob says holding back his anger. "That night there was a reason behind what happened, which I don't have, or want to explain...."

"Are you saying it would be different now? Would you be today, like you Americans say, 'up to par?'" she asks. Deliberately provoking him, she takes off her blouse to leave her beautiful torso exposed. "I don't want to demean you, but I can hardly believe that."

Bob sets eyes on her quivering breasts challenging him.

Olga's fingers grasp the zipper of her skirt and she draws it down, letting it fall on the grass. The splendor of her body is displayed shamelessly. "Now prove to me you're a man and not a pathetic impotent!"

Bob takes on the challenge and shoves her onto the grass, falling on her. Her soft flesh, accustomed to be caressed, feels the sting of the hard surface on her back.

The pain inflicted by the fall changes gradually into a bizarre excitement that inflames her with desire. She becomes hypersensitive as never before and her face flushes, although it hasn't been touched. A fiery, alien vitality overpowers her. She reaches for Bob, who straddles her legs, and tears off his shirt with both hands.

Aroused by Olga's excitement, he rips off the rest of his clothes and swoops down on her. Men of dissimilar natures, enjoying all the refinements of sex, have made love to Olga, but never before has she indulged in the full height of pleasure like she does now.

For Bob, the experience is also unfamiliar. His need to retaliate for his wounded pride adds to the passion accumulated during his long abstinence. That, plus the realization that he has entered the most luscious woman he has ever met, makes their encounter a furious, frenzied clash.

Their copulation is lengthy, violent and painful, and ends only when Olga, half fainted, releases a river of life that smothers her lust as she had never imagined it could happen, even in her wildest, tormented ravings.

When Bob disappears, following Ricardo's group by a path that leads to the remotest forest, she remains on the grass under the shadow of the *Ramonales*. Nude, with her eyes half-closed, her lips murmur a monotonous litany, "*Danke, lieber...! Danke... Danke... Danke...!*"

Reclining in a wicker chair, Max offers Cayetano a cigar, lights his own, and then adjusts a dial on the radio.

The Mexican commentator's voice comes in a bit more clearly, saying, "If we analyze this information, it can be inferred that the situation on the African front is dire. The running of the German blockade around Tobruk was only a respite for the English Army. It's obvious that, once reorganized, the German-Italian troops will prepare a powerful counteroffensive at El Alamein, which will be challenging to stop given the inferiority in numbers and equipment of the British Expeditionary Force.

It was presumed that the replacement of Marshal Braushitsch last December 19th, by which Adolf Hitler assumed supreme command of the German Army, could have been a grave tactical mistake. However, as it looks, such measure was yet another success of the German strategist who has consolidated, with his military alliance between the States of the Tripartite Pact, a pact that might pose a grave threat to the Allied World.

The preparations for a spring offensive on the Russian front are obvious. Thus, the question arises: Will U.S. intervention tilt the scales in favor of the Allies? Thus far, this looks uncertain. The devastating attack that Japan's aero-naval forces inflicted on the Seventh Fleet at Pearl Harbor, and the advance of the Nippon Marines that has cornered General Douglas MacArthur in Manila, reflect the unsuspected power of the Imperial Japanese war machine.

On the other hand, the United States is converting its industries hastily and is recruiting millions of men. But matching the preparedness of the Axis Nations takes time. A soldier cannot be made, much less equipped, overnight. Thus, another distressing question arises: will Hirohito, Mussolini, and Hitler declare themselves rulers of the world? With this ominous thought in mind, we leave our commentaries for...."

Max turns off the radio and remains still and quiet, gazing abstractedly at the floor's woodwork. Cayetano stares at him. His attitude goes beyond that of a defeated man. The aura around him is infectious. There is something else. His eyebrows move independently of the rest of his features and his lips form soundless words, revealing an inner conflict. It is obvious that Hitler's triumphs affect him deeply. He has changed. His character grows more embittered every day. He's no longer the proud martinet but another very different man, consumed by a fire of resentment. Even the greed that had previously driven him seems to be waning.

To find out just how bad Max's condition is, Cayetano places his glass of cognac aside and says with feigned indifference, "Well, a German triumph will not affect us here in America. Don't you agree, Mr. Wolff?"

There's emptiness in Max's gaze, but he considers the question at length and then replies, "Distances don't matter anymore. Maybe the Nazis will not invade the United States, but if they threaten to destroy their huge, defenseless cities and blockade their world trade, they will prevail in the end. Latin America would easily fall prey to those butchers. Don't assume we are that safe!"

"But how could the Nazis attack the United States from so far away."

"With long-range jet aircraft and nuclear submarines!"

"Jet aircraft?"

"Yes! Airplanes capable of flying at subsonic speeds, using turbines instead of piston engines."

"You mean like the rocket ships in fiction tales?"

"Only they are no longer figments of the imagination. Over three years ago, I think it was on August 27th of 1939, a Heinkel He 178 was flown by commander van Chain. That was the first pure jet to fly. Then, the following year, the Italian fighter ace Mario de Bernardi flew a Caproni-Campini jet aircraft. By now, their improved versions must be being built and, maybe soon, the skies over Europe will be swarming with jet fighters. England's Royal Air Force will be crushed. Moreover, Germany has a large fleet of *U-Boats* that can sink the most powerful navy."

"*How is it he remembers these facts, dates and all?*" Cayetano wonders. He then remarks: "A couple of Mexican oil tankers were sunk in the Gulf of Mexico recently. Do you think these U-Boats might have attacked them?"

"It's quite possible."

Max stares through the window into nothingness and remains still, as though his own speculations have inflicted a deadly blow on him. But then a violent surge of emotions erupts in his gut and he smashes his goblet on the floor.

"*Verdammt idiot*! Why didn't I kill him personally? I could have done it!"

When his frenzy abates, he finds himself standing by the liquor cabinet. Taking the cognac decanter, he drinks long swigs from it until he chokes, coughing.

Cayetano smiles imperceptibly at Max's deterioration. Hitler's triumphs and Olga's hatred are clearly smashing his pride.

Max's coughing fit subsides He realizes he has allowed himself to be overwhelmed by anger. Regaining his composure, he slumps in the rocking chair.

"I apologize, Captain. I can't control myself when I remember how Hitler hurt my family with his militaristic schemes. We met him in 1937, when he visited our factories in Munich. He promised he would promote our production line. Instead, he expropriated them and ruined us. Our Swiss government, advocating neutrality, refused to intervene on our behalf, so we left Switzerland in search of a new life."

"*Eine serh traurige geschichte*," Olga says behind Max's back, coming out of the bedroom. "Every time I hear that sad story, a flood of tears flows from my eyes!"

The sarcasm in her voice is acerbic. Smiling, she goes to the liquor cabinet to pour herself a glass full of gin that she drinks like water.

These two people intrigue Cayetano, and he wonders what is there beneath their surface. He can guess the root of Max's problems, but Olga still puzzles him. She has also changed. Although she gives herself to him on every possible occasion, her sexual behavior suggests a lack of arousal. She can't reach the point of excitement necessary to obtain satisfaction, although he makes use of all his sexual talents.

Also, there is something amiss that keeps gnawing at his mind. After Bob's departure, during Max's absence, Olga kept to herself for five days, claiming a sudden ailment. Two weeks have gone by since then and it has been during that interval that she has changed. Furthermore, she hasn't mentioned again her desire to leave Xkanták.

"Is she waiting for Chema's return? I have to find out what's going on!"

"Have you decided anything on the new airplanes, sir?"

"No," Max replies, apathetic. "Newton agreed to increase my production output again, but he hasn't confirmed it yet. We're flying out the required tonnage between the four of us. I don't know what's happening. I heard rumors in New Orleans that an artificial chewing gum is being developed by the industry."

"¡Ah, *caray*! That would certainly ruin us!"

"I know!"

"Ricardo will have the Skyrocket ready to be flown out in a couple of days. Do you want me to look for another pilot?"

"Have you had any news on Calver?"

Cayetano, the sage fox, perceives a spark of interest in Olga's eyes and, intentionally, circumvents. "Well, yes and no. I learned that Ricardo took him with his group as far as the wreck site. Then he went back there two or three times during the first two weeks to replenish his provisions. When Ricardo saw him last, he said he was going to keep looking for Chema until he found him. This week, a mule driver brought news that he had seen a *chele*, a blonde man, close to *Chanchakan*."

Olga fidgets with her glass, obviously affected. Watching her, Cayetano continues, "The puzzle is that both Calver and Chema are blonde and the muleteer could not describe accurately whom he saw."

"We don't need either of them. Get another pilot. In fact, get two. I'm getting tired of flying, and besides I'll have to travel to New Orleans again to pay closer attention to sales," Max says, ending the conversation.

Olga pours herself another drink, ignoring both men.

"Would you like to practice your Spanish, Madam?"

Looking at her glass, she says in a faint voice, "No, thank you."

"Good night, then."

There is no reply. Cayetano leaves.

Olga takes a sip from her glass and takes a seat in front of Max. She stares at him for a moment and then asks, "Have you found somebody in Mérida to make you happy?"

Max is surprised. There has been no sarcasm or rancor in her flat voice. "Do you think you or I could find someone here worthy enough to make us happy?" he asks, sincerely.

Olga stares at him. It's the first time in a long while that they have started a conversation without intending to pick a fight.

"I don't know. These people are so different from us. However, Mérida is a large town, and among so many women...."

"Mérida is nothing but a large village. People there are simple and amiable, but they lack our breeding."

"But you will not deny you have sex with some women."

"True, but nothing meaningful." He looks at her for a long moment and then, lowering his head, says, "What I did to José María was wrong, and I am ashamed of it. I let myself be carried away by rage."

"Because you care for me, or because you think of me as your property?"

"By God, please understand me! I know our marriage never was... I mean, it lacked romance and other things that lead to a congenial relationship. Furthermore, we lived apart for long spells due to various circumstances. If it hadn't been so, maybe our life together might have been different. I've always felt that, had I known how to love a woman, it wouldn't have been anyone other than you. And I... I still feel the same today."

The baroness remains silent. Then she asks in a whisper, "Is that why you killed the boy?"

"Yes, but I didn't – well, he may still be alive."

"That is true!"

The possibility disturbs him. "If he came back, would you go on loving him?" he asks, brokenly.

She looks at him. There is such distress in his expression that she feels sorry for him. She remembers some occasions, at the very beginning of their marriage, when they had been almost happy. Smiling sadly, slightly drunk, she says, "I never loved the boy, Max.

To me he was like a toy, or rather like a pet that endears itself to you because of the devotion it shows toward you, but I never loved him."

Her words work on Max like a balm. Taking her hands, he says, "We have nothing but ourselves, Olga. We're far away from everything that has any meaning for us. If we don't share our lives, what good is all the wealth I can gather? Maybe the day when we can leave this place isn't far off. Together we could again enjoy the lifestyle we're used to, among people of our class, and we could make up for the hardships we're enduring now. In the meantime, if you're willing, I will try to improve our relationship."

He's not the proud despotic man anymore; he is humbling himself, begging her to validate the manhood she has always negated in him. He's the spoiled child seeking acceptance after being punished for misbehaving.

Leaving her glass on the floor, she takes him by a hand, rises, and smiling tenderly, leads him toward the bedroom.

Rain drizzles down on the still hot, sandy ground. The resulting steam envelops Xkanták, creating an illusion that a cloud wraps around it, to lift it toward the dark sky. It rains softly, quietly. The clouds are shedding silent tears to wash away the sins that soil the jungle.

"¡Schweinnnn...!" A piercing scream slices through the sound of the rain.

Standing nude in the middle of the bedroom, Olga screams at Max in rage. "You will never change! You want me to love you, but you think of nothing but yourself. Am I one of your cheap prostitutes to serve you only as a sexual relief?"

"Don't shout, Olga, please!" Max begs, rising from the bed to go to her side.

"Leave me alone! Don't touch me! Don't ever touch me again!"

Taking her by an arm he pleads with her. "Come, I promise you I'll...."

She slaps his face with her free hand again and again, until she is exhausted. "You will not keep me here any longer! One day, when you come back from wallowing in filth with your prostitutes, you will not find me here!"

"Schwein...." Cayetano murmurs, sitting in the dormitory's veranda. "That sounds very much like swine." Pondering on these words, he throws away his cigarette's butt, which falls in the water gushing from the gutter, and floats away toward the murky shadows of night. A smirk dances on his lips as he rises to walk into the dormitory, yawning noisily.

The rain of the previous night has infused the atmosphere with humidity, creating a dense fog that hangs a few feet above Xkanták Central. Over the fog, a compact cloud layer blocks the sunlight that vainly tries to burn off the mist.

Impatient, the pilots wait. Manuel and Alfonso want to build up their flying time. Any delay means a decrease in Max's profits, which makes him edgy. Cayetano paces from the shop to the landing strip. He wants to get a head start on Max so that, at a certain moment, his arrival back in Xkanták will coincide with Max's departure so he can be alone with Olga.

Only the mechanics enjoy the delay. The fewer the flights, the less they work.

"¡*Máre*! It would be nice if we had this weather all day long!" Ricardo sighs, lazily looking at the cloud layer.

"I say it will, because maybe it will rain!" says Nico, an assistant.

"Do you think it will rain, bosh?" Ricardo asks Cayetano, when he comes under the shed. "I sure hope so...."

"You take pleasure in hatching your big balls, eh Turtle?"

"Quel means 'turtle,' and that is my surname!"

"What if you were paid per tonnage flown, like we are?"

"That is why I am not a pilot!"

"Is that it? Or maybe you don't have what it takes?"

"¡*Caballo*! Flight is for the birds. Anyway, if it rains, it cools down and we all work better, hah?"

Irked, Cayetano looks for a way to lash out him. "You are such a good friend! You want it to rain so that Chema drowns in the jungle, right?"

Embarrassed, Ricardo lowers his eyes. "Do not even say that, bosh! Poor Chema, I wonder what happened with him? It's about time he had shown up!"

"Do not worry. Most likely he is spending his honeymoon with his gringo friend, in the jungle."

Cayetano's affected indifference offends Ricardo.

Gumersindo counts the gum bales that arrived that morning by mule train, and goes to the Aircruiser where Max waits under the wing. "They brought in fifty *quintales* from *Jato* Three, *señó Worf*."

"Good!" Max says, turning his back on him. "Tell the foreman he will receive a bonus if he keeps up the good work."

Gumersindo has noticed something unusual in his boss' face and shrewdly positions himself to have a better look. "I will tell him so, *señó Worf*." He notices that there are bruises on Max's cheeks and black-and-blue marks under his eyes.

Gumersindo smiles, wondering if those blemishes are the aftermath of the shouting heard the night before in the main house.

"Do you want me to prod the rest of the foremen to see if they also improve?"

"Yes. That's a good idea. But I do not want any fights!"

"There will not be any, *Señó*. It is not good that people go around slapping each other, right?"

Max becomes angry, feeling that Gumersindo might be mocking him, but then he realizes he couldn't have known what happened in his house last night. He's just an ignorant peasant that can hardly speak Spanish.

"*Could I trust this man? With money, maybe.*" He can't risk leaving Olga alone. If she leaves Xkanták, the Gestapo would spot her, and through her, they would find him. Besides, he doesn't want her to leave. "Pallares!"

"Tell me, *señó Worf*!"

Max makes sure nobody is listening. "Can I confide in you?"

"In body and soul, *señó Worf*!" the demon offers, surprised.

"I am going to give you... a confidential assignment. Secret, you understand?"

"*How can I explain myself?*" Max suddenly thinks to himself. "*Maybe this is a mistake!*"

He decides to plunge ahead anyway. "It is something personal. No one else must know!"

"Just say it, *señó Worf*, and that by me, I swear no one will know!"

"Look, *la señora* Wolff, she – she does not like this place. She wants to go to a city, but I need to be here to look after my business, and she must be here with me. Do you understand that?"

"That is how it must be! The wife with her husband, like the priest says when he ties the knot."

"I am glad you understand. You see, sometimes she does not obey me, and I think she may try to convince one of the pilots to take her away. If she tries to leave, you must not allow it. Say those are my orders and they must be complied."

"Do not worry any more, *Señó*," he answers, his diabolical eyes shining. "I will answer you with my life. The *señora* will not go anywhere, unless you say so!"

"That is all! And remember, no one must know!"

"Nobody will know by me, that I already swore, *señó Worf*!"

Gumersindo walks away toward the storehouse and Max looks at the cloud cover. In the last few minutes it has lifted enough to reveal the treetops.

"Let's go, gentlemen!" Max shouts at the pilots talking under the shed. "Let's take off with a three-minute separation!"

Cayetano runs to his Aircruiser. Moments later, only the airplanes under repair remain on the ground.

The line of stratocumulus and nimbostratus clouds outline the boundary of the cold front as it moves from northwest to southeast. Through the Aircruiser's windshield, Cayetano studies the weather signs, figuring that the frontal system cruises along at about 15 knots. He thinks he can arrive in Xkanták before the rainfall intensifies. He skipped lunch in order to out-fly his boss. If Max departs Xkanták now and gets across the rainy area, he won't be able to return.

However, the wind seems to be increasing and the clouds under his airplane look too dark. He flies on top of the clouds to maintain visual conditions, but in three minutes he will have to start descending before the ceiling drops lower and the rain reduces the visibility. If he can make it to Xkanták he will force Max to fly to Peto. That will be easy, for all he has to do is goad his pride.

The Aircruiser's nose dips into the white mass, and seconds later lunges across the first squalls. Immediately, the aircraft feels heavier than the ton of gasoline and oil it carries on board in cans. Although the sun is up, the day becomes an amorphous grayness. Cayetano feels the drag created by the rain opposing the Bellanca in his rugged hands. He increases power to compensate for the loss of speed but, even so, the vertical speed indicator indicates he is losing 800 feet per minute. Four minutes later, he breaks under the clouds. Flying at treetop level, he finds Xkanták's clearing.

When he is half a mile from the landing strip, he locates the other Aircruiser taking off in his direction and hears the crack of a microphone as it opens.

"Are you listening, Captain Rodríguez?" Max's voice comes through the speaker. "How is the rain?"

"Very refreshing, Mr., Wolff!"

"You know I don't appreciate jokes!"

"Sorry, Sir. I think you can make it through. Although I have a ton of cargo on board, I flew through without losing altitude. The line of squalls isn't very wide. It looks worse than it really is."

"All right, I'll see you later."

"Have a good flight, Sir," Cayetano answers. He's confident Max would rather die than turn around, for fear of being ridiculed by the other men. He has all afternoon to be with Olga.

"¡*Me lleva la chingada*!" Cayetano curses while climbing down out of the airplane. "That frigging rain is going to make me lose the whole afternoon. The boss?"

"Did you not you see him? He just took off," Ricardo says.

"¡*Ah, carajo*! I hope the rain does not force him down. It is really pouring hard. Well, no rush, guys. It will be a while," he says lightly.

He walks slowly toward the main house. At the door, he shouts loud enough to make himself heard by everyone, "Mrs. Wolff, can I come in for a moment?"

Only one person pays attention. His eyes narrowed into slits; Gumersindo has followed Cayetano's movements. Being deceitful himself, he can detect deceit in Cayetano's attitude.

Cayetano walks into the sitting room as Rosenda hurries out of the bedroom. He starts to ask her about her mistress, but the girl's agitation and her elusive attitude baffles him. He takes in her shapely figure scurrying toward the kitchen and notices that her skirt is unbuttoned at the side and she is tucking in her blouse.

He shrugs and continues to the bedroom. Parting the curtain, he looks inside.

"Hi, sweetheart," he says, finding Olga in bed. "My, you're one lazy doll!"

She covers herself with the sheet up to her chin as if she were in the presence of a stranger. Cayetano sits on the bed, regards her lovely face fondly, and notices her blush. When he kisses her, he finds the taste of fine liquor on her lips, which though warm and moist are devoid of response. That's odd, but he doesn't know what to attribute it to.

"Isn't it too hot to be covered?" he asks, pulling the sheet down to enjoy the beauty of her body in broad daylight.

"Don't! Somebody might come in!" she almost shouts, holding on to the sheet.

Her outburst puzzles him further. "Max just left and it'll be a long while before he comes back. The rain...."

"Rosenda is in the house!"

Cayetano tries to take her in his arms to kiss her, but she turns her face away, "No! I can't today!"

"Why?"

"I can't. Don't you understand?"

"No, I don't understand. What's wrong with you?"

"I have my period. I don't feel well!"

Cayetano slaps his forehead. "I'll be an idiot! I'm sorry, darling, I – hey, wait a minute! You had your period two weeks ago!" he remembers.

Olga gets up from the opposite side of the bed covering herself with the sheet to go to her dresser, "I'm different from other women. Please don't look!"

Cayetano faces the window and exclaims, "¡*Caray*! After all my efforts to be alone with you! These things only happen to me!" He gets up. "Well, I guess I'll get back to work."

"No! Don't leave. There's something we must do."

Hopeful, he turns toward her. She is pulling her brief panties in place and, through the sheer fabric; he sees the outline of a sanitary napkin.

"What is it?"

Donning a silky robe, she goes to the door to make sure Rosenda is not in the living room. "Let's try to open that safe," she points at the heavy steel box standing in a corner of the room. "How long will Max be gone?"

"At least three hours, or maybe until tomorrow."

"I have the first six numbers of the combination. If we open it, we'll leave today. Can you fly in this weather?"

"Of course! I'll fill up the airplane and take some extra gasoline cans. This rotten weather must end somewhere!"

Olga takes a piece of paper from her dresser and gives it to him. "Here, only the last two digits are missing. Try all the combinations you can think of."

Cayetano kneels before the strongbox. "Let's see. Five, left to twenty, right to ten, left to thirty, right to five, right to twenty-five. Now, let me think.... Yes, left to fifty and right to ten again."

He tries the doorknob in vain. "Shit! That wasn't it! But never mind, we've got lots of time."

He tries multiple possibilities while Olga looks impatiently over his shoulder, suggesting more combinations.

Meanwhile, through one of the many holes in the rear wall, other eyes follow the scene with particular interest. Spying on them, Gumersindo caresses his revolver's handle. Cayetano is no patsy. He is a very dangerous adversary. His knows that his *buruna* is not any match for the pilot.

Above Peto, the clouds are completely dark and the nimbostratus layer hanging underneath releases a deluge on the jungle.

Manuel Torruco starts to say something, but he shuts his mouth when he notices the fiery blaze in Max's eyes, hot enough to burn off the clouds. He decides to remain silent.

"Rain must end soon; it's been falling for two hours. Are the provisions loaded?" Max asks him.

"¡Si, *Señor*! They are in my airplane."

"Good. We will leave as soon as there is some ceiling, if it lifts. Be ready to depart as soon as I do." His tone is final. He wants to be alone to think.

He is so far away from Germany, so estranged; he ignores the true facts regarding the European situation. With the Americans involved in the conflict, the news are now tainted with propaganda from the Allies, claiming their defeats as triumphs of a newly-born strategy. However, while these sources of information contend Germany will be beaten, the Wermacht's soldiers advance on all fronts. Hitler is proving to be a miracle-working demon. How can the German industry keep its war machine in a constant offensive? Where do so many German soldiers come from? How can a man of such obscure origin manipulate the German people to such extent that everybody, without exception, supports him?

He shakes his head in despair. His peer, Adolf Galland, has been named general of the Fighter Arm, the third-highest post in the Air Ministry, right behind Göring and Jeschonneck, while he, Maximilian Görzten, has been eliminated from Germany's future. This is the answer he is looking for: there is nothing to go back to. His future is here.-

"But why am I so uptight then? What is this fear I'm experiencing? Do I dread that without Olga's challenge I can't survive? No, it's not that. I just don't want to lose her!"

He looks again at the rainfall and notices that the ceiling is higher. Now he can contest for the one thing that will give meaning to his life: his wife. Forgetting to advise Manuel he is leaving, he climbs in his Bellanca to fly toward his haven in the jungle.

The large raindrops slap against his bare head, pursuing him relentlessly. When he stands to rest by a tree, flashes of lightning explode before him in blinding blasts, splitting limbs and setting the wet wood on fire, forcing him to run into the brush. He can't get any wetter. It's the constant pounding of the rain that makes him flee, sliding and slipping in the mud or crawling on all fours, searching for a place to hide.

Bob falls again, this time because the terrain goes uphill. Against the rain, he makes out a knoll. He straightens the pack on his back and, panting, starts up the slippery slope while holding firmly onto the old flintlock gun that Ricardo gave him. While he hikes, he feels his stomach rumble, demanding food. A bolt of lightning lights his path, allowing him to see a dark cleft in the hill – possibly a cave. The idea of escaping the rain hastens his pace.

It isn't a cave, but rather a vertical fissure. He can't estimate its depth in the darkness caused by the cloud cover and the rain. He goes inside just far enough to escape the torrential downpour, wipes the water from his face, and tries to see the end of the recess. His panting and the noise of the raging storm are the only sounds for a few seconds. Then he hears another one that stiffens his muscles and makes him shiver: a low growl. Hidden in the shadows, a beast is ready to secure its lair.

With slow and minimal movements, lest he arouse the beast, he unties the string holding the oilcloth wrapped around the weapon's butt to keep it dry. Amplified by the resonance of the cave – or perhaps because the beast is closer to him – he hears another roar. Now his hands tremble because this time he thinks he might have heard two different snarls simultaneously. If there are two beasts within the den, he stands no chance. The old flintlock mechanism fires only once. He will have to pour powder through its barrel nozzle, drive in a plug, pack it with the steel rod, feed the bullet, insert another plug, and then compress it again. It'd take him at least two minutes to reload.

He listens intently and feels, rather than hears, the beast's tense breathing. Sensing that the animal is about to pounce, he rapidly unwraps the cloth from the gun. Cocking the trigger, he aims into the depths of the pitch-black lair. A sudden glint off the eyes of the beast and its snarl as it springs forward warns him that it is charging. He sees a shadow in the air and fires.

The burrow rocks with the blast and dust cascades from its roof. The wounded creature slams into Bob, slashing his left shoulder with a claw; letting out a terrifying howl, it drives Bob to his knees. As it dies, growling, Bob notices that it is a young cub, lying on its side. Stunned, but conscious of the risk, Bob begins to reload hastily. A second brute, perhaps the mother of the cub, might be crouching in the depths of the den.

He quickly rams the powder with the metallic rod. He knows it isn't rain which dribbles down his face now but cold sweat prompted by fear of imminent death. With his eyes fixed on the back of the cave, Bob pushes the plug inside the gun barrel hoping he has heard wrong, but he hears it again: a ferocious growl, hoarse, adult, and powerful, at his back.

Whirling around, he finds a jaguar a few steps away, standing huge in the rain. Man and beast stare at each other. Ponderously, the jaguar backs up just enough to crouch and pounce.

Terrified, Bob cocks the trigger and fires. The beast lands on his chest, knocking him down like a puppet. He is living his lasts seconds. He can feel teeth gashing his face and lashing at his throat – claws ripping through his back to shred his lungs. Crazed by fear, Bob closes his hands on the jaguar's thick neck and squeezes it with all his might.

Max jumps out of the Aircruiser. His pulse is racing and a bitter taste fills his mouth. However, when he sees Gumersindo waiting, unruffled, he relaxes.

"How's everything going?" he asks.

"Everything is going fine, *señó Worf.* Until now nothing to worry about. I am keeping a sharp eye on... everything!"

Max sighs relieved. The premonition that had disturbed his peace of mind was merely a false alarm. Gumersindo's smiling face, although mocking, provides him with some assurance.

Content, he says, "See that my airplane is loaded quickly. I will spend the night in Mérida." Looking around, he asks, "When did *Capitán* Rodríguez leave?"

"Not more than an hour ago."

"Ah, he will be able to come back safely." Then he addresses Ricardo. "No more flights today. It is still raining. How are the airplanes?"

"Fine, *señor* Wolff. We just have to lubricate them."

"Call me when airplane is loaded," Max says, walking toward his house.

Seated on a rocking chair, Olga listens to a Viennese waltz on the transoceanic radio. Her little finger is on the frequency selector knob, while the rest of her hand holds a highball glass. She doesn't seem to notice Max when he goes toward the liquor cabinet.

He takes the gin decanter and finds it almost empty. With his back to her, he says, "If you go on drinking like this, I'll have to keep the liquor under lock and key."

"Are you adding stinginess to the rest of your virtues?" she replies in a tired voice.

"I don't care what you think. You're drinking too much!"

"Are you going to deprive me of that solace also?"

"I'll do whatever is necessary to keep you from ruining yourself!"

"You can't bear to see your property depreciate, correct?"

Max watches her in silence. Even in that languid mood, she looks magnificent. If only he could make her change her attitude toward him. "It'd be a pity to see you deteriorated."

Olga opens her eyes and looks at him. "You're very considerate, *lieber*. Too bad you're not the same in bed."

Max tightens his grip on the glass, breaking it. His thumb bleeds, but his features remain unaltered. Covering the wound with his handkerchief, he sweeps the glass fragments together with the tip of his boot.

"Violence is always self-defeating," she observes, smiling.

Staring at her, he says, "I'll spend the night in Mérida."

"To sleep with one of your concubines?"

"I'm meeting with Newton. There is a possibility that he may confirm my quota increase, even with the artificial gum debacle."

"The women you share your bed with must be less demanding than your wife!"

"With Newton's approval, by season's end we'll have a net profit of three million pesos."

"There are women who are satisfied with so little."

"Three million plus what I can get from selling the concession and the airplanes."

She shuts up.

"I'm going to sell the business so we can get out of here," he says slowly, still looking at her.

"What's wrong? Are you sick, or have you lost your mind?" She inquires, sipping on her gin deliberately.

"We'll net over four million pesos, an amount large enough to buy authentic immigration documents, even a different face. There will be enough left to start a business in México City. Nobody will doubt we're Dutch. We'll forget Germany."

She can't understand the sudden change. "Are you serious?"

"Isn't that what you want?"

"And you would do it for me?"

She reads the answer in his eyes. It is so unexpected she feels disconcerted. Leaving her glass on the table she gets up and, to hide her bewilderment, walks slowly to the window.

"¡*Señó* Worf! Your airplane is loaded!" Gumersindo shouts from outside.

"Max, is this another one of your ploys?"

"There will be only one condition...."

She turns to look at him, searching for the catch.

"Bear with me while I learn to be your husband."

There is no catch. His gaze is clean and she can see in his eyes a sincerity she hadn't known before. Her heart leaps. The man she faces is altogether different from the usual Max. She can't restrain an emotion that moves her to tears. Pushing them back, she answers, "It'll be... as you wish, Max."

The man indifferent to feelings, who has always deemed love as something meaningless, is dying. He's seized by a yearning to embrace her, but a diffidence born from his hastily adopted resolution to capitulate, holds him back and only allows him to say, "*Danke*. You have made me very happy. I wish I could stay, but – have a pleasant evening. *Bis dann, liebe*."

"*Auf Wiedersehen*, Max!" she replies with a thread of voice while her eyes follow his figure through the door to see him disappear inside the airplane.

Then she walks onto the veranda to watch the airplane take off. When it swishes past her she sees his hand waving goodbye and she raises hers to respond.

Turning to return in the house, she looks down and a shiver runs down her spine. Gumersindo is at the foot of the steps staring at her, his nasty lust shamelessly obvious. Annoyed by his insolence, she turns her back on him.

Bob's fingers tremble while locked tightly around the jaguar's neck. He is nauseated, about to pass out; evidently it's the first stage of dying. However, time passes and only the beast's weight keeps him pinned to the ground. As his panic subsides, he realizes that the jaguar's fetid muzzle rests motionless on his shoulder. He releases the grip on its neck and confirms that it isn't breathing. With an effort, he shoves the huge feline aside and raises himself up on an elbow to look at it. Propelled by the powder blast, the steel rod he used to compress the load bored straight into the jaguar's chest, piercing its heart. The tip protrudes out of its back. His panicky shot saved his life.

He sets a knee on the ground and gets up unsteadily. Still dazed by his lucky break, he walks to the mouth of the den and sits on the ground to look outside. The rain has dwindled to a fine drizzle that filters the daylight into gray tones. The unearthly atmosphere created by the mist and the silent air inspire him into a meditative mood. He seldom thinks of God, but right then he feels an urgent need to thank Him for his life.

"As soon as I find Chema, I'll leave!"

He has wandered in the jungle for four weeks, enduring hunger and thirst, going from trails to paths to tracks through the unexplored forest, exhausting all possibilities. He is about to give up, realizing the futility of trying to find a man in that jungle. Besides, is Chema alive? How many times has he barely escaped a snake or a poisonous spider bite? If he hasn't found Chema by now, maybe he never will. The serenity of the hour, the coolness of the cave, and fatigue make him drowsy.

"I'll spend the night here, and tomorrow I'll walk north to Peto. From Peto I'll ride a train to Mérida, and from Mérida take a plane home... back to life...."

Cayetano drags the last gum bale to the Aircruiser's door and shouts, "Catch it, Pepe. I'm leaving!"

"Are you not you going to take back gasoline today, Tano? There are some cans left."

"*No, mano.* I'll take them tomorrow. Right now I'm in a big hurry to return to Xkanták."

He pushes the bale out of the airplane and hastens to sit at the controls. Setting the mixture lever to the rich position, he cracks the throttle open, switches the magnetos on, and hits the main switch. He looks outside to make sure the propeller area is clear and stabs the starter button. The starting motor clacks, but the propeller doesn't move.

"Now what the hell!"

He punches the starter button several times with the same result. Angrily, he shouts through the storm window, "Chompipe!... Get over here with the ground batteries!"

A mechanic from Aeronaves del Sureste brings over the battery cart to connect the auxiliary power to the external plug. He shouts back, "¡*Listo, Cayito*! Try it now!"

Cayetano tries once more, but it's useless. "¡*Me lleva la chingada*! The damned starter must have broken!" He shouts again, "It is not the battery, it is the starter. Please crank it by hand!"

"Okay! On, then..."

"On!"

Chompipe tries to turn the propeller by hand, but it's so heavy he can barely make it spin half a turn at a time.

Impatiently, Cayetano climbs down and pulls the propeller himself three times to no avail. In the meantime, the last of daylight vanishes in the western horizon.

"It will be night soon, Cayito. Why do you not stay here?" Pepe suggests him.

"I need to get back to Xkanták!"

"What for? Are you already too old to meet the demands of *la prieta* Gloria?"

The question makes Cayetano pause, and his urgency fades away. It wouldn't be difficult to locate Xkanták's lights, but landing on a dark strip isn't easy. What's more, Gumersindo might squeal on him and Max would question his motive to arrive so late. He has to be extremely careful now that he is about to achieve his goal.

"*Anyway, if I stay here, I can make sure my plan works. It's a reckless idea, but it's worth taking the risk!*"

"You are right, Pepe! There is nothing so pressing to go back to, having Gloria here. How is my *prieta linda*?"

"Getting prettier every day and always sighing for you!"

"Then, a visit to her is in order, no?" After all, Olga is indisposed and he doesn't like to play the role of Count Dracula. Instead, here he has *la prieta* Gloria, the sexiest female ever born in Peto, who also happens to be madly in love with him. Furthermore, it is likely that Max would also be gone the following evening. There were a few combinations left to try on the safe, and if he doesn't find it, a stick of dynamite can split open the damned safe any time.

"I have my jalopy ready, Cayito. You want me to drop you by Gloria's bar?"

"Sure, but first take me to the telegraph office."

In the Telegraph Office, Cayetano replaces the pen in the chipped inkwell and rereads the telegram he wrote:

C. General Consul

Consulate of Germany in Mérida

Known address,

Mérida, Yucatán

German colonel Maximilian Görzten, who deserted the Luftwaffe, hides posing as a Swiss citizen in Xkanták Gum

Concession in Quintana Roo Territory, accessible by airplane from Campeche, Campeche.

Cap. Cayetano Rodríguez.

After satisfying himself with his message, he muses, "And just in case this dispatch fails, it won't be a bad idea to put our immigration people on his case."

Dipping the pen in the inkwell, he writes a second telegram.

Her reflection on the polished surface of the French mirror could deceive anyone. It doesn't even remotely reflect her twenty-seven years of age; twenty-two, maybe. Even under close scrutiny she can't find a wrinkle on her forehead, around her eyes or at the corner of her lips. The image she beholds is as exuberant and fresh as that of a flower native to the tropical jungle. After all, she owes the jungle her clear skin; the constant perspiration eliminates all impurities.

Opening her robe, she regards her figure. Its slenderness is also due to the heat that burns away all fat. Her shapely legs still rise in beauty toward her thighs and her hips are a perfect ellipse that opens in a curve toward her chest. Her body preserves the beauty that had captivated men in every European court. Without a doubt, she will become the queen of Mexican society, envied – and perhaps even desired – by all women.

Satisfied, she brushes her long, silky hair, daydreaming about the receptions she will offer as soon as they are settled in Mexico City. Hearing a slight noise in the living room, she calls. "Rosenda... come here. Brush my hair!"

The curtain rustles, soft steps shuffle behind her and she raises her head expecting to see Rosenda's adoring gaze, but instead her skin crawls. Gumersindo's hellish face is in the mirror, drooling from his mouth at the sight of her nearly naked body. The monstrous lust in his beastly black eyes shines with hypnotic brilliance.

With a demon's look in his eyes he opens his mouth, wet with lust, to say: "Rosenda is at the storehouse babbling with the women, but I am here ready to do whatever you need, and to do it even better, because I am a real man, *señora*!"

His croaking voice breaks the spell. Olga gets up, closing her robe.

"Get out of here!"

Gumersindo is trembling inside, desire chewing at his entrails, but he thinks it best not to frighten her. Shrewdness can get him what he wants. His voice softens. "Do not fear, *señora*, please. I am here as a friend. I only want to be of help to you."

"*Scheren Sie Sich Raus*! Get out!"

"*No, señora, no.* First we must talk."

"You have nothing to say here. Get out!"

"We will talk, and a lot," he says moving backward to win her confidence, "as friends, like I already said. It is about your husband...."

"What of my husband?"

"Well, it has to do with something he told me and something I saw."

"I do not understand. Explain!"

"Well, *señora*, you see, I do not know other languages, but I do know what a man and a woman do when they are alone."

Olga thinks she understands. "Of my husband and other women, I do not care!"

"No, no. Do not get me wrong, *señora*. I am talking about you and other men...."

Despite the afternoon's coolness, Olga begins to sweat. "Explain!"

"Well, it is not that I like to spy on people, or mind what they do, but at noon I saw all that happened when *Capitán* Rodríguez was here. See that corner?" he asks, pointing at the wall. "There is a small hole there from where I saw everything that happened here from the moment he came in, till he left, kissing you."

Olga turns her back on him, realizing she is in his hands, and he surely wants to blackmail her. "What do you want?"

"Well, we still have not talked about the most important part."

Intrigued, she turns to him.

Growing confident, the snake goes on. "It so happens that your husband, poor trusting soul, he loves you so much that he ordered me to look after you, so you do not run away with one of the pilots. Knowing that you want to leave, and seeing that you and the *Capitán* tried to open that safe where *señor Worf* must keep his money, I think I know the rest of the story. The good thing is that el *patrón* does not know the whole story, as we do...."

"*The imbecile coward didn't trust me!*" Outraged, she stares at the brute and asks, "Will you tell my husband?"

"Me? No, *señora*! No way! I am not a squealer, nor am I so mean. Cayetano is my friend and you; you are so very good, besides being so pretty...."

Olga's hopes rise slightly. "Is this true, Pallares? You will not tell my husband?"

"Never, *señora*! Gumersindo Pallares swears to that!"

"Thank you, I take that well. We will give you money!"

Gumersindo smirks and moves toward her imperceptibly, saying in a thick voice, "No, I do not want money. I have more money than I need. You see, every worker gives me a little something to hire him or her at the beginning of the season, and, when the season ends, they give me a little something more. Also, not all the gum that leaves the jatos gets here. Some loads get stuck along the way and their worth ends up in my pockets. Also, something more drifts in from the staples that we trade in the storehouse."

He is so close now that the rancidity of his sweat offends her more than his presence. "So you see, I have come to learn many things that the *patrón* does not know. There are eyes that see things and mouths that keep shut, but not to me. You have been good to Chema, to the gringo Calver, now to Cayetano and even to that fine mare that you keep fenced in the kitchen. The only thing I ask is that you be good to me too. Give me what I deserve, and I will show you what a real man feels like inside you."

Olga suffers in her arms the burning touch of the black claws, and sees the frightful scar that crisscrosses Gumersindo's gaunt chest. When his thick revolting lips approach hers, she considers letting him do his will, but repugnance wins over her fear and her hand rises to fall against his cheek. "*Hör doch auf*!" she cries out. Twice again she strikes the offending face before Rosenda appears, knife in hand, forcing him to back away.

Olga moves quickly to the bedside table, takes out Max's 9-mm pistol and aims it at Gumersindo's chest shouting, "Get out of here!"

The sight of the weapon daunts him.

"Rosenda saw you here. If you tell my husband, I will tell him what you did to me!"

Chagrined, his cheeks burning from her slaps and his humiliation, he leaves, already plotting his revenge.

Olga looks at Rosenda and smiles, "*Danke, liebe*! I am all right," she says, caressing her face. Rosenda takes the gun from Olga's hand and looks at it with interest.

"Do not need it more. Put away in night table."

"You should teach me how to use it, *señora*. That wicked man is relentless!"

Chapter 38 – A Debt Repaid

Pushed on by high winds, the low pressure area vanishes leaving a clear blue sky over the Yucatán peninsula. Its recently-bathed greenery shines under the first rays of a brilliant sun rising from the Caribbean Sea.

Bob takes a drink from his canteen, rinses his teeth and spits the water. Smacking his lips, he verifies that only a slight hint of the jaguar's meat flavor remains in his mouth. Now that his hunger is satisfied, he feels like a savage because he used some dried-up offshoots cut from the brush growing by the entrance of the lair, to char-broil a leg of the young jaguar and ate most of it.

"Why should I be concerned? Other survivors have eaten their own dead buddies," he reflects amused. Swinging his backpack over his shoulder, he picks up the flintlock gun and walks out of the den.

The first contact of the warm sun rays on his damp clothes is pleasant. Checking Ricardo's compass, he heads north. Without further delays, he should be in Peto by nightfall.

Restlessly, Gumersindo stands by the storehouse door scanning the horizon for Max's Aircruiser. When he finally spots it, his lips curl in a smile that, strangely enough, also reaches his eyes.

When the aircraft touches ground, Olga sees the foreman hastens to meet Max. She knows he is always ready to greet her husband, but today he has been leaning against the storehouse's doorjamb since early morning. Is he going to tell on her? She feels her stomach tighten. She hasn't had any food because she wanted to have breakfast with Max.

Watching every detail, she sees that as soon as Max gets off the Bellanca, Gumersindo tells him something, pointing toward the storehouse, and then they both walk calmly in that direction. One way or another, her question will soon be answered.

"What's wrong, Pallares?" Max asks, ill at ease

The Tuxpeño looks around, spots the storehouse keeper, and tells him, "See here, Raul. Go outside for a little while."

Once the man is gone, Gumersindo says, "The news I have for you is not very good, *señó Worf!*"

"Speak up!"

"It is something I saw yesterday, at noon. After you flew away and before it rained, *Capitán* Rodríguez arrived and went into your house. Obeying your orders, I spied on him inside the house and saw him talking to your wife in a most familiar way. Then they went into the bedroom and tried to open your strong box, which they could not do. Then, shortly before you arrived, they kissed and he left."

A bolt of lightning wouldn't have struck him more severely. Max is so enraged he can't coordinate his thoughts.

"To be totally honest, *señó Worf*," Gumersindo adds in order to further stoke his anger, "I must say that the *señora* was almost naked. It seems to me that when I withdrew I made some noise and they found me out because, later on, the *señora* sent for me. She told me that, if I told you what I saw, she would tell you that I had tried to have my way with her, and she would use Rosenda as witness to back up her accusation."

Dazed by the revelation, Max leans on the counter. At length, he murmurs, "I will kill that man!"

"And why should you soil your hands, *señó Worf*? Leave that to those who have nothing to lose, but something to gain."

Max stares at him.

"Just give me one thousand pesos to hand out among some men I know, and the said *Capitán* Rodríguez shall never bother the *señora* again."

Max sees this as an obviously pragmatic solution. "I will give you that and more, but nobody must know I ordered it!"

"Not to worry, *Señó*. Whoever does it will ask no questions. What I would suggest is that you say nothing to the *señora*. You just relax knowing that, while I am here, she will be more than secure."

Distrustful by nature, Max finds Gumersindo's suggestion a bit suspicious. "All of this happened at noon, yes?"

"¡*Si, Señó*! That is so!"

"And I came back later in the afternoon. Why did you not tell me then?"

Gumersindo goes pale, but retorts immediately: "Because of the *señora* threat, I had to think it over. Her accusation was a serious one. Who would you believe more, her or me? But you see, I thought it over all night long, and I ended up throwing away my fears to come forward with the truth. You favored me with your confidence, so I could not fail you."

Max weights the foreman's reply for a moment. He realizes he has to give him some credence since he is too stupid to fabricate such a complicated story. "When did Captain Rodríguez leave this morning?"

"He did not come back yesterday."

"And who would you...?"

"You must not even think about that, *señó Worf*. Just start looking for another chief pilot." Gumersindo smiles, and keeps on smiling as Max walks toward his house, deep in thought.

Troubled by conflicting passions, Max looks at his wife with distrust. Carefully made up, she waits on him personally while presenting him with a regal breakfast. Smiling, asking a thousand questions, she seems to be really excited by his proposition. Still doubtful, he tries to discover the truth about the situation. "Did the storm last long after I left yesterday?"

"Oh, yes! It ended after eleven, cooling off the evening."

"Did you have a good rest?"

"Wonderful! Though I didn't sleep all night – I was thinking about the things we'll do, and I waited eagerly for your return. Tell me; is there nobility in Mexico City, *lieber*?"

Lieber! It's the first time in a very long while that she calls him darling, without a hint of mockery…

"There must be some nobles left. The Spanish crown reigned over Mexico for many years and, more recently, they had an Austrian emperor… Maximilian, if I recall correctly."

There had been nothing in her tone of voice, or attitude that seemed insincere.

"Ah, yes, I remember now!" She glows, "Archduke Ferdinand Maximilian of Austria, who married Princess Charlotte, the daughter of king Leopold I, of Belgium. She was my mother's distant cousin."

Olga looks radiant as she connects her thoughts with the memories of her nobility ties. Had Gumersindo lied to him with some fiendish purpose in mind? He is doubtful. It's true that he has noticed the courtesies that Cayetano tenders Olga, but he has to admit they have always been respectful and lavished when he was present. Cayetano is a man to be wary of, but he is useful, almost essential to run the business.

Rosenda takes away the fruit bowl and Olga serves him a dish of ham and eggs.

"Rosenda, she is the key! But will she tell me the truth? No, most likely she will side with Olga. How can I find out the truth?"

Max eats his breakfast but doesn't enjoy it. When he bids her goodbye, she kisses him on the cheek..

"Was that a Judas' kiss...?" He thought.

Cayetano's Aircruiser has just landed. He is stopping by the shop when Max steps out of the house.

"Good morning, Mr. Wolff!" he calls.

"How are you, *Capitán*?"

"Fine, Sir. I couldn't return yesterday because the starter failed on me in Peto, but it's already fixed."

"Good. Let's get to work then," Max says, walking toward his airplane. When he realizes that Cayetano isn't following him, he turns and sees him smiling at Olga, who stands by the window, smiling back. There is a mutual understanding in their smiles. When he goes by the foreman's side, he looks into his eyes and nods once, then he climbs into his Aircruiser.

Gumersindo's gaze follows Cayetano as he crosses the clearing toward the diner, and his eyes smile.

"You are as good as dead, you shitty little Capitán!"

Bob halts, holding in mid-air the branch he was pushing aside. Intrigued, he cocks his head to listen in various directions. Amid cries of parrots and *chachalacas*, the squealing of *saraguatos* and whistles he can't identify, he thinks he has heard a human voice singing.

He shakes his head, dubious. *"Who would feel like singing in this terrible heat?"*

Suffocated, he takes a strangled breath, wipes the sweat from his eyelids and brushes aside a clump of ferns to proceed, but stops again. There is a path in front of him. A path means people. Has he really heard singing? A familiar acrid scent fills his nostrils. Smoke! Toward the end of the trail he makes out a blue veil that confirms his hopes. He hasn't seen a human being in six days.

As he follows the narrow lane, he hears a female voice singing in a strange language, gradually becoming louder. Some eighty meters ahead he comes upon a clearing where two huts stand side by side. They are made of sticks and palms. One lets out smoke through its roof, while the other one is smaller and simpler.

Bob hesitates. He knows the Mayan natives are peaceful and accept foreigners with decided hospitality, but he still feels uneasy. There is no movement outside the huts so he approaches the large one, where the singing comes from, and stops by the door to peek inside.

The singing stops. A young female native, kneeling before her *ca* and holding the *kabtun* with both hands, stops grinding corn dough and looks at him with curiosity, but without surprise. She wears a lively-colored cotton skirt tied at her waist. Her chest is bare, but long jet-black hair hanging loose over her shoulders covers her chest.

Bob notices movement in the hut. There is another woman in the corner, maybe a bit older, dressed in similar fashion except that her hair is braided with colored yarn. Both make a unique picture: two wild maidens with classic Mayan features, keeping in their naiveté the enigma of the jungle.

Since they aren't frightened, Bob walks inside and points at the boa that stands full of water close to the maid grinding on her *ca*, and says, *"Agua, por favor."*

The girl takes the boa and asks, *"¿Ha?"*

Realizing she doesn't understand Spanish, he signs slowly, "Yes, water for me!"

She leaves the boa on the ground and quickly gets up to take a clean *cum* from the *peet*. She dips it in the *buleb*, a large earthen vat that keeps the water clean and cool. Eyes lowered, she offers Bob the clay jug full of water.

He drinks avidly and returns the jug smiling. *"Gracias!"*

She smiles happily and replaces the jug in the *peet*, a small cabinet hanging from the roof held by four henequen strings, where they keep their clean pots, food, and old tortillas. Going back to the *ca*, she waits, not knowing what for. Both women regard him, giggling, as if they shared some secret.

Bob looks about the hut. He is hungry. They have food and he has money in his pocket. Showing them a few peso coins, he touches his stomach, opens his mouth and makes signs of eating. Then he points at the freshly-made tortillas resting by the *comal,* set on four boulders over the fire, and at the pots in which something is cooking.

Amused by his grotesque but effective signs, both girls laugh. The older woman pushes forward a three-legged stool, saying, *"Kache!"*

"Gracias!" he replies, sitting down and propping the flintlock against the wall.

The older looks at the other one and says, *"Hach xanhi u kuchul tumán hach chambel u tal!"*

The younger nods and, approaching Bob, points at his pack, indicating he should remove it from his back, while the elder asks him in a sweet voice, *"¿Baax ca chivic?"*

When Bob shakes his head to imply he doesn't understand, the maid leans over the pots on the fire and picks up two of them to show him what they contain, so he can make his choice. He points at one and is surprised to find it contains a piece of chicken in broth.

Eating with a day's hunger, he enjoys the soft dough drink garnished with salt in grain and green peppers the Mayan call *kayeb.* Then he sees a man's hat hanging on the wall. Pointing at it, he says, "Man's hat. Where is man?"

"*Ppooc*?" she inquires, and runs to fetch the hat and offer it to him.

"No, thank you!" Bob laughs. "I mean, where is the man?"

They look at each other, baffled, and become restless when they see he gets up, ready to leave.

"*¿Kin a zut is cahal*?" the elder woman asks him.

Bob misunderstands and nods. Taking the coins he showed them before, he places those in her hand, saying, "Thank you very much. You have been most kind!"

The girl takes the coins, looks at them, and then throws them on the peet. She inquires earnestly, "*¿Yan tuux a kuchul? Ua mae ppaten uay tiniucnale!*"

Unaware that he is being offered the hospitality of their hut, Bob shakes her hand and steps out, but they run ahead of him to block his way. Realizing they don't want him to leave, he explains, "I have to go. Thank you very much, and goodbye."

When he tries to leave, the elder points at the other hut and takes him by a hand. She leads him to the door, indicating that he must go in.

"No, thank you. I have to leave now," he insists.

Inside the hut, a weak voice calls out, "Who's there?"

Cayetano remains thoughtful for a moment, then looks at Olga and asks, "Are you sure Max behaved normally after he talked to Pallares?"

He has delayed his departure to let Max fly away from Xkanták so he can meet her alone, and now Olga has made known to him the previous evening's events. To avoid suspicion, they chat in the living area, where everybody can see them. They are aware that Gumersindo watches them from the storehouse's door.

"If Pallares told him anything, he didn't show it, but I doubt he was alerted. Max is too impulsive. He'd have beaten me, or he'd have killed you when you arrived."

"True. I didn't notice anything odd about his demeanor either. We better be careful. Pallares is treason itself. Anyway, I think I did the right thing in sending those telegrams."

"What telegrams?"

"Huh? Oh, some messages I forwarded to friends of mine in preparation for our departure," he lies. Looking at her lovingly, he adds, "We'll leave tomorrow, I promise you. Start getting ready to see the world again! If Max spends the night in Mérida, I'll come visit you tonight."

Cayetano turns the key in his wardrobe's lock, opens the door, takes out his .38-caliber, snub-nose revolver, and slides it into his waistband. With Gumersindo involved, a man can lose his life for lesser reasons.

Chema blinks repeatedly and rubs his eyes in disbelief before he exclaims, "¡*Capitán* Calver!"

"Chema! By God, it's you!"

Chema tries to express his happiness, but chokes in his excitement.

"You sick?" Bob asks, noticing that, reclining on a straw mat laid on a cot, Chema looks thin and jaundiced,

"It's the chills, *Capitán*. Malaria. But I feel better now!"

"Can you walk?"

"Yes, but who is with you? Where are the others?"

"No others, just me alone."

"You came by yourself?" Chema is amazed. "Did you come to look for me by yourself?"

Bob nods.

"And the others, why did they not come?"

"All of them think you are dead, but not me."

Chema doesn't know what to say. He could never have imagined that the gringo cared for him. "¡*Gracias, Capitán*!" he murmurs, adding, "Do you think we can get out of here"

"We walk north, Peto very close."

"Ah, now I understand!"

"What?"

"The owner of these huts is a Mayan. He found me unconscious in the jungle, brought me here, and took my money. The next day he gave me herbs, quinine, and a tonic against malaria. I guess he bought all that in Peto."

"Where is he?"

"During the day he and his son go to work a corn field they have nearby. His daughters take care of me. Did you see them?"

"Yes. They gave me food."

"They are good people. I do not know how to repay them...."

Bob looks outside and sees the girls chatting happily among themselves.

"Yes, very good people."

"And Cayetano?" Chema asks, his gaze now alert.

"In Xkanták. He is flying."

"*¡Desgraciado!*"

"You are mad at Cayetano. Why?"

"That low-life tried to kill me!"

"Cayetano? No, no, no! He did not do it!"

Chema keeps quiet.

"Why do you say that?"

"Forgive me if I do not explain my reasons, *Capitán*. It is a personal matter that must be resolved between us!"

"Because of Mrs. Wolff?"

Chema stubbornly keeps silent.

"Chema, Chema. Cayetano likes Mrs. Wolff very much, but he did not try to kill you. Mr. Wolff did. We know."

Bewildered, Chema looks at Bob. "Mr. Wolff?"

"Yes. He is very mad at me because I found your airplane. We fought because of that. He knows that you and Mrs. Wolff had... a relationship."

Confused, Chema fixes his gaze on the ground. "Cayetano was right then! I have to get back to Xkanták. Can we go now?"

"Are you okay?"

"Not so okay, but I will feel the same elsewhere. If you do not mind, I would like to leave now."

Bob helps him up. "*Vamos* Peto is not far. We'll talk on the way."

Chema is weak, but his desire to go back to Xkanták shows in his resolute expression.

Aware that Chema's presence in Xkanták will only bring trouble, Bob tells him, "From Peto, I will take a train to Mérida, and then a plane to Miami. Do you want to come?"

"You are not going back to Xkanták?"

"There is nothing for me to do in Xkanták, and there is nothing for you to do there either. You better go some other place, México City, maybe. Find job in airline. You are a very good pilot."

"Yes, I will do that, but first I need to... I mean, there is something I must do in Xkanták."

"Mrs. Wolff...? She will only bring trouble for you. Bad trouble!"

Chema looks at Bob trying to explain his feelings, but fails to find the right words. At last he says, "I can get a ride from Peto. Please help me get there, *Capitán*!"

The Mayan girls wave good-bye when they see them walking down the path that leads to the cornfield. Chema wants to thank the man who saved his life...

Chapter 39 – The Aftermath

In the storehouse, Gumersindo scrawls large, crooked numbers on a rough piece of wrapping paper, the latest production figures and raises it above his head so that the six foremen sitting around him can read them.

"As you can see, *Jato* Three is ahead of the rest, and already winning a special reward for all its workers – and their foreman, of course. So, the *patrón* told me to tell you that whoever sends in the most gum will be the one that earns the most money. Now, if you all pull together, then we all shall win. What do you say?"

The six men nod their consent, and slap their leader's back, although they can't hide their envy.

"Now, like the *patrón* says, we do not want this to cause any wrangles among you, much less among the workers. The first one who starts something loses his reward, and loses his job. Understood?"

Again the accepting nods, the smiles, and the jabs.

"Well, now, who is the one who wanted to leave a few pesos at the card table?"

"Me!" answers Liborio de la Rosa, a tall, muscular Afro-Mexican who laughs stupidly for no good reason.

"I am also in!" says Josefo Martinez, famed for his ill temper, foreman of *Jato* One, den of the feared *Tuxpeños*. The notches hacked on his *buruna's* handle are not mere ornaments.

"Well then, let us go see if the pilots will let us in their game."

Gumersindo and the foremen leave the storehouse to go to the pilots' dormitory veranda, where Ricardo, Manuel, Alfonso, and Cayetano gamble.

Gumersindo approaches the table and announces: "If the stakes are not too high, here are three poor workers wanting to try their luck."

Cayetano looks at him over his cards. It isn't unusual for the workers to gamble, but that happens mostly on Saturdays when they come to replenish provisions or quinine.

"What saint performed the miracle of unsticking you from the gum, *valedores*?" he asks, not masking his distrust.

"The *patrón*, *Capitán*. He wants more and more gum and asked me to offer the foremen a reward if they send in more *quintales*," Gumersindo hastens to explain.

"If you want to play, I do not mind. Let us see what the *compañeros* have to say."

No one objects. Ricardo fears them and the young pilots are apathetic. The three of them grab chairs, with Josefo Martínez seated across from Cayetano.

As the moon climbs over the horizon, the stakes climb along with it.

Sitting on the windowsill, Olga looks out into the night while listening to dance music on the shortwave radio.

Max looks at her from his rocking chair. He perceives death prowling silently around Xkanták's grounds. As of yet, he cannot come to terms with the idea of utilizing such a lowly scheme to deal with a situation he is uncertain about. To kill a human being isn't alien to his nature; he killed men in Spain as a soldier. He conspired to have a man killed, but plotting Hitler's death had been a patriotic duty. Blinded by rage he had killed a woman, and to save his life he strangled a worker with his own hands. Out of jealously he had tried to kill José María. Those were his deeds, direct and always justified. But what about this matter? Is he becoming a coward?

He looks again at his wife trying to find an answer. Then, in order to hear her voice, he asks her, "What are you looking at?"

"Here? Nothing... I was far away from here."

"In Mexico Ciy?"

"No. Although I could be. I was picturing the interior of the cabaret where that music is being played."

"Where is that?"

"New York City."

"Ah!"

He wants to know if she is deceiving him, simply buying time to flee at the first opportunity. He doesn't want to accept such action of hers as real. He still has misgivings about Gumersindo's report and doesn't have conclusive evidence against Cayetano. What does he have, really? A couple of smiles that very well could be an indication of a simple friendship. He would like to ask her if she has changed her opinion about him somewhat, and if she wants to repair their relationship, but he still doesn't know how to go about it. If he just said it directly.... Yes, maybe that would be the way to do it.

Olga points at the dormitory, and asks: "Isn't it too late for the pilots to be awake?"

"Are they still awake?" He checks his watch. "What are they doing?"

"They are playing cards."

Max gets up and goes to the window to look toward the pilots' dormitory. A shiver crawls over his skin when he sees Cayetano playing with Gumersindo and the foremen. Earlier, Ricardo and the young pilots had quit playing. Only Gumersindo, the foremen, and Cayetano remain at the table.

He suddenly decides that he has to prevent a useless death. "You're right, *liebling.* They should be in bed. I'll go tell them to stop!"

While Max walks outside, Olga sees that Cayetano stands up from the table flinging up his arms, and shouting something.

Enraged, Cayetano yells at Josefo, "That ace fell to the floor from your side!

"Real men do not cheat! No wonder the winnings were going only your way!" Josefo retorts.

"For a motherfucker to call me a cheat, he has to be a better man than I am!" Cayetano retorts, although before the last word escapes his mouth, he realizes he has been set up but he cannot back away, and he's already hearing the reply he anticipated:

"For a man, a man and a half, you son of a whore!"

Max stops in the middle of the clearing to shout, "Stop, Pallares! Stop it!"

But Josefo Martínez is already jumping over the table, wielding his deadly *buruna* while Cayetano steps back, gun in hand.

A shot thunders out, and a voice warns: "Look out! He is armed!"

Laughing like an idiot, Liborio draws a pistol from under his *guayabera* and pulls the trigger.

Five or more shots ring out, overlapping each other. Only God knows how many. Three men jolt like puppets on a string, shaken by the impact of bullets. Then a wake-like silence falls over Xkanták while the night wraps the scene in the darkness of mourning.

Appalled, Max watches the bloodcurdling scene.

Olga holds on to the windowsill, lest she faints.

Frightened eyes peer out through every nook.

Max's mud-covered boots move closer to a dying man who opens his mouth in an effort to speak. His words gush out unintelligibly amidst blobs of blood: "Rico... Idalia... In Cerralvo... Tell her..."

Max's eyes question Ricardo.

Holding Cayetano in his arms, Ricardo whispers, "He means his wife, Idalia Rodríguez. She lives in Cerralvo, Nuevo León."

"I... I was coming to tell him to go to bed."

Gumersindo steps in front of the moribund. Do not grieve *señó Worf*. Nothing has happened here. The three men involved in the brawl did themselves in," he says, indicating the three bodies lying on the floor.

Cayetano utters a hoarse groan and his eyes close slowly.

"Go to your house, *señó Worf*, and do not fret about it. I will take care of this."

Olga watches Max as he approaches. A cluster of qualms and fears race though her mind, becoming firm convictions. One thought that dominates over the others pushes her into hysteria: Max is a soulless murderer, and she is at his mercy. She has no one to turn to. José María, Bob, and Cayetano are gone, and now she is alone among these implacable beasts. When Max comes in, she reads the guilt in his eyes.

"You had him killed!"

Max walks in, dazed, and disappears into the bedroom.

She is lost, without recourse. Shaking all over, she goes to the liquor cabinet to pour herself a glass of gin. Then, defeated, falls into the rocking chair.

"If I remain here, he will have me killed too, or he may let me loose in the jungle, at the mercy of those beasts. I have to leave this place as soon as possible, no matter how!"

Curiosity wanes, and friends' loyalty is subdued by fatigue. In the farthest corner of the storehouse, Gumersindo sits by the three corpses, keeping vigil. He drinks, toasting to his latest knavery. Possessed by a stupid euphoria, he's beginning to feel drunk when he hears a noise at the door. Getting up, he walks to the entrance and stops, amazed. Before him is the woman who has been at the center of his coarse fantasies. He is even more surprised when he realizes that she doesn't look angry. In fact, she smiles. She has to be smiling at him, since there is no other living being in there.

"¡*Señora*! What do you want? If *señó Worf* finds you here...."

"*Señor* Wolff is drunk! I came to look for you, Pallares!"

"For me? What for?"

"I need you," she says in a hoarse, teasing voice. "You are a true man, you said...." While she speaks, she lets her robe open with pretended neglect, allowing him to see part of her breast.

Astounded, Gumersindo can't believe what is happening.

"You are a man, no?" she repeats, moving closer to him.

Gumersindo backs away in awe until he bumps against the counter. Her breasts almost touch his sweaty chest.

"You have money, but not enough for me. I want all the money. All of it! Xkanták, gum, airplanes, I want all mine. I the owner, you my foreman. Understand?"

"You want to keep everything for yourself?" he asks, thinking he has misunderstood.

Olga nods, smiling. "With your help!"

"What about *señó Worf*?"

"I'm tired of him. He is not man enough," she whispers, running her soft fingers over the dark scar crossing his chest. Then she lowers her hand to grab the handle of his *buruna*, pulls it out of its sheath, and places it between his chest and her bosom.

"Ah, I understand now!" he exclaims. He sheathes the sharp machete in its scabbard, and embraces her. "But first...."

The beast in him is unleashed. Clumsily he takes Olga in his arms and his lips look for the alabaster hidden within the silk. She endures this nightmare for a few seconds, leading him on, and then pushes him back. Fixing her violet eyes on his dark and flaming ones, she says firmly, "No! Not now! Later, when you and I are alone!" Then she runs out of the storehouse.

Gumersindo drinks the last of the *Ixtabentun* from his bottle.

The night of dread drags on, endlessly.

The echo of the shooting still rumbles through the forest when the evil intention drifts across the clearing like a death-rendering shadow, wrapped in a mist of alcohol and marijuana smoke and, impelled by consuming lust, rides the demonic breath of Xibalbá, which is being released earth- bound from the depths of hell through the cracks in the ground.

It quietly climbs the steps to the main house and creeps through the door clutching a sharp steel blade, cold one moment, and hot the next dripping blood's warmth after plunging once and again into the river of life.

Max's cry of agony, and Olga's horrified screams, drive sleep away from recently closed eyes, emptying all beds.

Gumersindo looks at Olga with crazed eyes, "Our time has come..."

Olga screams, but the sound is drowned out by several thunderclaps. Lightning flashes inside the darkened bedroom.

When the electric light flicks on, dread distorts the witnesses' faces when they behold the gruesome sight, while trembling fingers rapidly make the sign of the cross over their foreheads.

Max's lower body lies on the sleeper while his chest hangs from its edge. A cascade of blood flows from his slashed chest to flood the wooden floor.

By his side, Gumersindo writhes like a snake, his back riddled by bullets.

In the corner next to the side table, her face devoid of expression, Rosenda holds the still-smoking 9-mm. Parabellum.

Crippled by shock, Olga leans on the dresser, her mouth open in a silent scream.

"The boss is still alive!" Ricardo shouts, after examining Max. "Quickly, get the first-aid kit and help me get him onto the sofa!"

Dawn breaks at last and, behind it, a purple disk emerges from the ocean of blood in which the stars bathed.

"There it comes!" Alfonso yells, pointing at the sky.

"¡Máre! It cannot be. How so quickly?"

"Is it not?"

"No, bosh. That looks more like a Stinson. I hope Manuel does not take much longer, or the boss will die."

Just an hour and a half before, Manuel had left for Campeche to bring Dr. Lanz and the authorities, so it was premature to think he was back already.

"Look, Rico. The Stinson is lining up to land!"

"Maybe he is lost."

"Or it is failing."

The airplane lands, stops just long enough to deplane two passengers, and turns around to take off.

"You have good eyes, bosh. Can you see who they are?"

"It looks like... yes, it is them!"

"Who, caballo?"

"Chema and Capitan Calver. Chema!" Alfonso yells, running to meet him.

"Chema! My prayers were answered!" Ricardo murmurs, and then also runs to hug him cheerfully.

Their joy in seeing a long-lost friend once again, momentarily relieves their grief.

"Chema! I am so happy to see you again, I feel like crying. Glad to see you too, Capitan Calver."

However, Chema's desire to resolve his own situation prevents him from sharing his friends' happiness. His voice sounds strange when he asks, "Where is Cayetano? I need to talk to him!"

Ricardo's eyes cloud over.

Through a veil of manly tears, Chema looks down on the pale face for a long while. He experiences an orphan's bitterness – the same grief and desolation he went through when, as a child, he cried over another quiet face years before. It's not a son's devotion, however; this was simply a friend. Had been a friend. Help, advice, and sincere affection all lie there. If there's anything to forgive, it's forgotten now.

Sitting by the feet of the man he recognizes as mentor and benefactor, Ricardo surrenders to the pain of loss.

Nobody knows exactly how the multiple tragedies happened. The versions Chema hears are contradictory and confusing, especially those that point towards Olga's possible liaison with Gumersindo. His instinct warns him, however, that there are other hidden motives behind the carnage as he stares at Cayetano's closed eyes and lips that, although stiffening in death, seem determined to grin.

The arrival of the Travelaire and the ensuing clamor outside the storehouse draws Chema out of his trance. He sees Manuel, Dr. Lanz, and three strangers climb down from the airplane. Two of them look like foreigners. They all go inside the house.

In the storehouse, Bob places a hand on Chema's shoulder. "Come on Chema. Let's go, all is finished here."

Chema tells him, "No, *Capitán*. Not everything. There are some things I must clear up first. You see, Cayetano warned me about Wolff and Pallares. What happened to me was no accident, and Cayetano's death is murder. I cannot just let it go without punishment." He walks toward the main house, followed by Bob.

As they enter, the three strangers are arguing with a courtesy that is far from sincere. The Mexican, obviously a government official, is saying, "*Señor* Tamz, until I conduct a thorough initial investigation, I cannot allow the persons involved to leave the state."

"But we guarantee, with the endorsement of our diplomatic rank, that they will be confined in our embassy," argues the taller of the foreigners.

Chema approaches Manuel to ask him in a low voice, "What's going on? Who are these guys?"

"Chema! Where were you? We thought...."

"Never mind, I'll tell you later. What is it with these guys?"

"I do not know, *mano*. I think they are Germans, and they want to take the boss and the misses with them. When I arrived in

Campeche, they were looking for somebody to bring them over here. The other man you know – he is the Agent of the Public Ministry."

Chema turns his attention back to the argument. Tamz is saying, "*Señor* Görzten is a German subject and we must see that he receives the best available medical care."

"There you are, you see! You call him Görzten, and I know him as Wolff, a Swiss national. We need to clarify all this confusion."

"*Señor* Cámara," says the shorter German. "We would not like to take this matter to a higher level. Please allow the Görztens to travel with us to México City."

"There is no use in insisting, *señor* Walhörzt."

"We only want them in our custody," Tamz persists. "They will attend any proceedings they are required to."

"Look, gentlemen, I am going to be totally candid. Last night I was chatting with *licenciado* Varela, Chief of the Immigration Office, and he confided in me that he received a message implying that *señor* Wolff, or whatever his name is, came into this country illegally. Varela will be here today to investigate that report, which is another reason why I cannot allow these persons to leave Xkanták, except for Campeche."

"Who made this report?"

"*Capitán* Cayetano Rodríguez."

"And who is that man? Where is he?"

"He died last night! You see, all this is too dubious."

Assisted by Rosenda, Olga comes out of the bedroom.

Chema's first reaction is to reach for Olga and to claim her as his own, defying any man to dispute him this right. But Tamz hastens to her side.

"*Frau* Görzten, I am *Walter Tamz*, German Consul in Mérida. *Edwal Walhorzt* and I are here to help you in any way we can."

His voice snaps Olga out her stupor. Looking at them she panics, asking, "You are Germans?"

"Yes, *Frau* Görzten!"

In anguish he looks around and sees Chema and Bob.

"Darling!" she cries in English, rushing toward Bob. "Don't let them take me! They're Gestapo agents!"

Olga's reaction comes as a shock to Chema. His love for that woman kept him alive. He survived the jungle's harshness to come back to her. However, now that she clings anxiously to another man with better standing, looking for his protection, he understands he is out of place in her life and this cools down his jealously. He can't feel resentment or contempt for her, because despite her unkempt appearance, he is still aware of her beauty. It's just that now he recognizes her immense egotism.

"You're American, Bob. Tell them you protect me!"

Bob has a hard time rejecting her. He sees in her fear the desperation of a woman yanked out of her delusive past, into a chaotic situation she can't understand. Ruefully, he pushes her away, saying, "I'm sorry, ma'am. There's nothing I can do for you."

Olga seeks Chema's eyes and finds him aloof. She backs away, anguished, as Dr. Lanz appears from the bedroom rolling down his shirt's sleeves, to make an announcement without addressing anyone in particular:

"I'm sorry, I got here too late," he says. "*Señor* Wolff has just passed on!"

Bob looks at Chema, who asserts, "Now all is finished!"

Tamz goes to Olga and murmurs, "Frau Görzten, please accept our...."

"*Baronin* Olga Scheuermann!" she interrupts, reacting haughtily. "I am an Austrian citizen, and I demand to be delivered to my consul. I have no further ties with Maximilian Görzten!"

Holding Tamz back, Walhorzt whispers something in his ear. Tamz looks at Olga with sympathy and says, "You are right, *Baronin*. Your husband's death has severed your ties with him and with Germany. There is no reason why you should be aggrieved by the charges that existed against your husband. Given that Austria has joined the Third Reich, now there is only one diplomatic representation in México. However, if you do us the honor, we will extend you diplomatic immunity and will make sure that you are not subjected to any ordeal. If the Germans insist on giving you problems, Edwal and I will arrange political asylum for you in México. You see, we both are Austrians, like yourself!"

The sun shines again for Olga. She opens her teary eyes and asks in a quivering voice, "I will not be deported to Germany?"

"Absolutely not, *Baronin*. Edwal and I give you our solemn word of honor!"

Olga turns to Bob and arrogantly shouts at him, "You know what they said? That I don't need any of you! I don't have to go back to Germany. I can do as I please!"

"I am afraid that is not the case, Madam," a grave voice says behind her.

A thin man stands by the door. His sharp features look distressed. "I am *Eustaquio Varela*, Chief of the Immigration Office in Campeche."

Chema looks outside. There is a small airplane, whose arrival no one in the house had paid heed to.

Varela goes in the house. "I wanted to be here earlier, but an urgent matter kept me. May I speak with *señor* Wolff?"

"*Señor* Wolff just died, *Licenciado*." Cámara says.

"*¡Caray!* I feel deeply sorry, Madam. Being this the case, the news I have for you will be most regrettable!"

"What news, *Licenciado* Varela?" Tamz asks.

"Actually, they concern you too, *señor* Tamz. It has been confirmed by the Navy Secretary that the Mexican tanker Potrero del Llano and several other ships recently lost in the Gulf of México and the Caribbean Sea, were sunk by German submarines. This morning – and this is why I was delayed – General *Manuel Ávila Camacho*, Constitutional President of the Mexican Republic, has declared that a state of war now exists between Mexico and Germany, Italy, and Japan."

Bewildered, Tamz and Walhorzt exchange glances. The former asks, "What is our situation then, *Licenciado*?"

"You still enjoy diplomatic immunity, but you must go back to your consulate and leave the country within the next forty-eight hours."

"I assume the Baroness is entitled to equal immunity, is she not?"

Varela looks at Olga for a moment, and, chagrined, says regretfully, "I am afraid not. If she cannot certify her Swiss citizenship, and it happens to be that she is a German subject, she will be confined in a concentration camp presently being established in Perote, Veracruz. All her assets will be confiscated."

Chema looks at Bob, questioning him.

Bob nods. "Must be true!"

"*Licenciado*," Tamz begs, "you and I have been the best of friends. Surely there must be a way we can avoid this lady such inconvenience, widowed as she is, and especially being an Austrian citizen."

"Austria is now part of Germany. You will have to come to Campeche with me, Madam."

Olga, who has been watching them expectantly, walks back toward the door. She shouts, frightened, "No! I will not be confined. I don't want to go back to Germany and I don't want to be in a concentration camp!" She runs outside, down the path that starts at the *zaramullo* tree.

"*¡Señora!*" Rosenda yells, running after her.

"That path goes to the river! We have to stop her!" Ricardo shouts.

At the head of the landing strip, Chema sits at the controls of the Skyrocket, watching the Travelaire take off. In it, Manuel Torruco has as passengers Varela, who guards Olga, and Rosenda, who insisted on joining her mistress in her confinement.

Chema catches a last glint of Olga's golden curls and feels a pang in his gut; however, his passion for her has come to an end. Now his mind is set on going back to Mexico City, to the almond-eyed girl that he knows still waits for him. He waves at Alfonso Teja to go ahead and take off. In the Robin, Tamz, Walhorzt, and Cámara escort Max's body.

A hand on his shoulder makes him turn to his right, where he finds Bob's friendly smile. He turns his head to look back at Dr. Lanz and Ricardo, who hold Cayetano's body in place. Finally, he asks, "Are we ready, Rico?"

"Anytime, bosh!"

When the last airplane takes off, the men and women of Xkanták Central look up from Gumersindo's lifeless body, and exchange bewildered glances. No one is left there to tell them what they must do. There is no one to call the workers back from their *jatos*, where they still slash trees to extract gum.

Xkanták exists no more, but they ignore that...

PART VI - The Mayan Gods' Disappointment

Chapter 40 – The Message

Gucumatz, Heart of Heaven, looks at the Ahau Tepeu, and sighs. The men who were created with so much love have once again failed, defeated by the temptations that the Lords of Xibalbá, the inferno, have laid before them.

This time they had not been made of wood, they had not been made of clay. Gucumatz made them out of flesh and they worked well, but because their hearts were hard as rock, good sentiments could not permeate them, and their egotism vanquished their Creator.

Gucumatz recalls that, upon molding them, the men had asked of him: "Oh, beautiful Heart of Heaven, and Creator of Everything, listen to us. Give us descendants forever. When the sun comes up, give us wide and solid roads. Give us quiet peace. Give us good life and habits and being!"

All the blessings they had asked for had been bestowed upon them. Regardless, they had ruined themselves with their selfish deeds.

Gucumatz, being compassionate, rises from the cloud on which he has been sitting to regard men, and signals the Ahau Tepeu to withdraw, telling the men:

"Listen, my children. We have to go back to our heavens and we will not come back. The sign of farewell of the *Ahau of Deers* is manifest in the wind. The count of your days is finished. Take care of yourselves, dear children, and see what you have in your hearts.

I will not destroy you this time because you have done that to yourselves already. I will leave on earth and you can do as you please; but, from now on, without my blessings. Never-theless, I beseech you to remember that you cannot escape the consequences of your actions because every one of them will leave a wake, and for each trace they score there will be an outcome. Your actions will always bear effects. Whatever you do, shall come back to you. If you become selfish and ravaging, those traits will bind your fate. If you allow covetousness, irascibility or egotism rule over you, you will conclude in the hell named Xibalba. Conversely, if you contemplate encouraging deeds, spread love and behave faithfully with your peers, your life shall thrive. Remember, Xibalba is not the existing jungle, Xibalba dwells in your mind. You must realize you will be in charge of your existence. Myself, and Ahau Tepeu will not reward or chastise you any further since, from now on, we will only observe your demeanor. Now, farewell my children…"

Once that was said, Gucumatz and the Ahau Tepeu disappeared.

Nonetheless, Hurakan, Father of all the Gods, does not share Gucumatz's kind feelings. Men's ungrateful demeanor has made him very angry, so, gathering in his fists all the clouds in the sky, makes them tall. Then, as unpolluted white is not befitting, he dresses the clouds in black and wrings from them a squall of tears. The clouds cry for a long time over the jungle, washing away the offenses of the mortals that had sinned in it.

Then, to expel men from the confines of the sacred jungle, Hurakan lifted them in his breath and blew hard toward the four cardinal points, returning them to the places they had come from, leaving the jungle unsoiled again until other men dare enter once again…

THE END

GLOSSARY

German Language

Auf Wiedersen	= See you later.
Berliner Zeitung	= Berliner Daily.
Baronin	= Baroness.
Bis dann	= Until later.
Bitte	= Please.
Danke	= Thanks.
Danke Schön	= Thank you very much.
Dummkopf	= Idiot.
Du Bist Ja verrückt	= You are mad.
Du Bist mein mann	= You are my man.
Ein minute	= One minute.
Ein Glas Wasser	= A glass of water.
Feigling	= Coward.
Fraü	= Woman, misses.
Fräulein	= Young woman, miss.
Führer	= Leader.
Geben mir	= Give Me
GebenSie mir Irhe Hand	= Give me your hand.
Gestapo	= Secret Police.
Glück	= Good luck.
Gott sei dank	= Thanks God.
Gräfin	= Countess.
Hafenplatz	= Middle square, Central plaza.
Hauptmann	= Captain.
Heil	= Salutation. "May he live healthy and sound."
Herr	= Sir, mister.
Herein	= Come here.
Helfen Sie mir das Wasser su trinken	= Let me drink the water.
Herren	= Sirs, gentlemen.
Hör doch auf	= Get out.
Hundert und ein	= Hundred and one.
Ich habe	= I have
Ich bin krank	= I am sick.
Ich habe Schmerzen	= I am in pain.
Ich habe angst	= I am afraid.
Ja	= Yes.

Ja doch	=	To be sure.
Ja, die lamp	=	Yes, the lamp.
Jawol	=	Yes, indeed, to be sure.
Kaiser Wilhem	=	Emperor William.
Kommen Sie here	=	Come here.
Kommen Sie näher	=	Come closer.
Lebenwohl	=	Farewell, see you later.
Leutnant	=	Lieutenant
Lieb	=	Dear.
Lieben	=	Lover, dear.
Liebling	=	Darling.
Luftwaffe	=	German Air Force.
Machen Sie lampe on	=	Turn the lamp on.
Machen Sie die Vörhange zu	=	Open the curtains.
Major	=	Mayor.
Mein kliner lowe	=	My little lion
Mein liebe	=	My dear.
Meinem Mahen	=	My stomach
Nein	=	No.
Oberst	=	Colonel.
Österreich	=	Austria.
Postdammer Platz	=	Post Office plaza.
Prost	=	To your health
Reichmarshall	=	Field Marshall.
Sargeant	=	Sergeant.
Schlageter Staffel	=	Fighter squadron
Schnell	=	Quickly, hurry up.
Stuka	=	Dive bomber aircraft.
Scheren Sie Sich Raus	=	Leave immediately.
Setzen Sie Sich	=	Sit down.
Schmerzen	=	Pain
Um Himmles Willen	=	Interjection, For the sake of heavens.
Vaterland	=	Native country.
Verdammung	=	Interjection, Condemnation.
Warten	=	Wait.
Wasser	=	Water.
Wehrmacht	=	German Army.

Spanish Language

Afrodita	=	Aphrodite, Greek goddess of love and beauty.
Aeronautica del Sur	=	Southern Aeronautic, airline.
Achis	=	Interjection.
Agua, por favor	=	Water, please.
Ah, chingao	=	Interjection, fuck.
Ah, jijo	=	Interjection, ah son.
Ándale	=	Interjection, hurry up
Allá	=	Over there.
Atole	=	Breakfast drink made with corn flour.
Bola de pendejos	=	Bunch of fools.
Bosh	=	Buddy.
Buenas noches	=	Good evening, good night.
Buruna	=	Machete.
Caballo	=	Interjection, horse.
Claro, bosh	=	Sure, buddy.
Cabrón	=	Cuckold.
Cabróncitos	=	Little cuckolds.
Cantinas	=	Bars
Capitán	=	Captain.
Carajo	=	Interjection, prick.
Caray	=	Interjection, geez.
Carta Clara	=	Yucatecan beer.
Claro, bosh	=	Of course, man.
Cayito	=	Short for Cayetano.
Ceiba	=	Ceiba, Bubox tree.
Cenote	=	Pond fed by undercurrent water.
Coime	=	Billiars attendant.
Compadre	=	Godfather, crony, chum.
Compañeros	=	Fellows.
Cuate	=	Twin, friend.
Chachalaca	=	Wild bird.
Cuélele	=	Move on.
Chiapaneco, Chiapaneco	=	From Chiapas Estate.
Charro	=	Cowboy.
Chema	=	Short for José María.
Chicle	=	Gum
Chiclero	=	Gum platation worker.

Chiclero pilot	=	Pilot that flies gum out of the jungle.
Chicharrín	=	Piece of pork rinse.
Chicozapote	=	Gum tree (Manilka karazapota)
Chicharo	=	Pea, Barbershop apprentice.
Chichis trais	=	Spanich phonetic for Jesus Christ, meaning tits you have.
Chingao	=	Fuck it.
Chico	=	Interjection, small, little.
Chiquito	=	Small one.
Compares	=	Buddies.
Chirrion	=	Interjection, whip.
De inmediato	=	immdiately, right away.
Desgraciado	=	Ungrateful.
Diantre de gringo pendejo	=	Stupid gringo.
Digame, señora	=	Tell me, m'am
Enseguía	=	Right away.
El Gráfico	=	The Graphic, a newspaper.
Eitale	=	Interjection, hey.
El Pato	=	The Duck.
El Variedades	=	The Variety, a newspaper.
El Redondel	=	The Bullring, a newspaper.
Enguarumaos	=	Under the influence of marijuana.
Epa	=	Interjection, hey.
Esta bueno	=	All right.
Escuchen todos	=	Listen everyone.
Framboyan	=	A florid tree.
Gringo	=	A foreigner.
Gringo atarantado	=	Dumb gringo.
Guarumo	=	Marihuana.
Guayabera	=	A fancy shirt.
Güerco	=	Small boy.
Henequen	=	Pito plant's fiber.
Hola	=	Hi.
Hijo e puta	=	Son of a whore.
Hijole	=	Interjection.
Huy, manito	=	Uh, brother.
Joder	=	To fuck.
Juana	=	Jane.
La chingada	=	The fucked one.
La señora	=	The misses.
Las Ultimas Noticias	=	The Latest News, a newspaper.

Linda	=	Pretty girl.
Listo, Cayito	=	Ready, Cayito.
Maistro	=	Master, the expert, boss, chief.
Maqueta	=	A mold, a block.
Manito	=	Good friend.
Mano	=	Hand, friend, buddy.
Mande, señora	=	Yes, m'am.
¿Quiere que prenda la lampara?	=	Do you want me to turn the lamp on?
Mando cuatro	=	I send four, I pay four.
Máre	=	Interjection, short for madre, mother.
Marihuano	=	Pot head.
Me lleva la chingada	=	Interjection, the fucked takes me.
Métanle duro	=	Interjection, try harder.
Mis contlapaches	=	My buddies.
Mondao	=	Shaved head.
Montoneros	=	Gang band.
Morral	=	Bag made of ixtle fiber.
Muchacho pendejo	=	Stupid boy.
Mucho gusto	=	Pleased to meet you.
Negra Leon	=	Black Lion, a yucatecan beer.
Ni modo	=	No way.
Ninio	=	Child, boy.
Nivela	=	Level out.
No jodas	=	Interjection, don't fuck me.
Oh, que joder	=	Oh, what a fuck.
Órale	=	Interjection, come on.
Organo	=	Organ, a cactus.
Pago	=	I pay, I go.
Paila	=	Cooking caldron.
Pan de cazón	=	A seafood dish.
Panuchos	=	Yucatecan dish made with corn dough.
Pariente	=	Interjection, blood relative.
Pa'su Máre	=	Interjection, to his mother.
Pa'su mecha	=	Interjection, to its wick.
Patan	=	Evil goblin.
Patrón	=	Boss.
Pa su mecha	=	Interjection, this is tough.
Pendejo	=	Jerk, stupid.
Párate	=	Stop, wait.

Pérate	=	Wait.
Petate	=	Straw mat.
Picador	=	Slasher.
Prieta	=	Dark skinned girl.
Pulquerias	=	Liquor stores that sell pulque, agave plants' inhebriating juice.
¿Qué hago, señora?	=	What do I do, misses?
¿Qué hay, pues?	=	What's up?
¿Qué le pasa, señora?	=	What happens to you, misses?
¿Qué pasa?	=	What happens?
¿Qué tengo?	=	What do I have?
¿Qué tienes?	=	What do you have?
Quintal	=	Weight measure, 100 kilograms.
Quiubo	=	Salutation, short for Qué hubo? What is up?
Quiubo, qu jains	=	Hi, what's up.
Recabrón	=	Big cuckold.
Relleno negro	=	A dish, black stuffing.
Revolucion Cristera	=	Christian Revolution.
Santos Reyes de Tizimin	=	The Three Wise Men of Tizimin.
Saraguatos	=	Species of monkeys.
¿Se le ofrece otra cosa, señora?	=	Do you need anything else, m'am?
Si, pues	=	Interjection, yes, well.
Sirva la cena	=	Serve dinner.
¿Se siente mal?	=	Do you feel sick?
Sepa Dios	=	Only God knows.
¿Subimos más?	=	Do we go higher?
Si, Chucha	=	Interjection, yes, Chucha.
'ta bueno, ahí voy	=	All right, I am coming.
Tano	=	Short for Cayetano.
¿Tiene alguna medicina?	=	Do you have any medication?
Úchale	=	Interjection, Uff.
Újule	=	Interjection, admiration.
Valedores	=	Chums.
Vaya, pariente	=	Interjection, sounds good buddy.
Vamos	=	Let us go.
Voy a llamar a alguien	=	I am going to call somebody.
Viejo cabrón	=	Old cuckold.
¡Virgen Santa!	=	Holy Virgin!
¡Ya!	=	Enough!

Xic	= Evil goblin
Xtabay	= Witch of the cenotes.
Zócalo	= Main plaza in Mexico City

Mayan Language

Ahau	= Lord
Boa	= Pitcher.
Ha	= Agua.
Cum	= Jug.
Gucumatz	= Mayan god, creator of all there is.
Kache	= Sit down.
Nicte-Ha	= Water flower, Mayan princess.
Ppoc	= Hat.
Xibalbá	= Hell, abode of demons

CHARACTERS INDEX

Ahau Tepeu: Mayan Lord of the Earth.

Ahauabs of Xibalbá: Mayan Lords of Hell.

Alfonso "El Pato" Teja: Beginner pilot.

Baroness Olga Schewermann: Nobility Socialite, Maximilian "Max" Görzten's estranged wife.

Calixto Gómez: Beginner chiclero pilot.

Captain Karl Halder: Luftwaffe pilot.

Carmen Ortegón: Chema's sister.

Cayetano Rodríguez: Xkanták's Chief Pilot.

Chema: José María "Chema" Ortegón: Automotive mechanic and chiclero pilot.

Chinto: Chiclero farmer.

Chompipe: Airplane mechanic.

Don Melchor: Xkanták's bookeeper.

Don Nabor: Train Conductor.

Don Tacho: Barber shop owner.

Doña Fortina: Fonda owner and cook.

Doña Laura: Former wealthy landowner, Chema's mother

Doña Ticha: Xkanták's cook.

Dr Lanz: General physician.

Edward Walhortz: German Consul.

Enedina: Madam.

Galicio : Gumersindo's assistant.

Gucumatz, Heart of Heaven: In Mayan mythology, Gucumatz is the creator of all there is.

Gumersindo Pallares: Xkanták's Gum Central foreman.

Gustav Görzten: Industrialist, Max's father.

Hanahupu & Ixbalanque: Mayan Guardians of the Earth.

Hurakan: Godly creature, father of all the gods.

Ingrid Wolff: Baroness Olga Schewermann posing as Swiss citizen, Max's wife.

Ixpiyacoc & Ixmucane: Old soothsayers.

Jim Jones: Flight first officer.

Joan Stevens: Flight cabin attendant.

José María "Chema" Ortegón: Automotive mechanic and pilot.

José Pérez: Mechanical shop owner.

Josefo Martínez: Chiclero foreman, assasin.

Liborio de la Rosa: Chiclero farmer.

Lic. Cámara: Public Prosecutor.

Lic. Eustaquo Varela: Local Chief of Immigration.

Lieutenant Freda Leber: Colonel Görzten's secretary.

Ligia Cu: Prostitute.

Lt. Col. Hans Door: Luftwaffe officer, Max's co-conspirator.

Lysander Wynn: Chewing Gum Co. Executive.

Magdalena: Chema's cousin.

Major Harold Schultz-Hoysen: Luftwaffe officer, Max's co-conspirator.

Major Ludwig Heinz: Luftwaffe officer, Max's co-conspirator.

Manuél Torruco: Beginner chiclero pilot.

Margarita Ortegón: Chema's sister.

Maureen O'Leary: Flight cabin attendant, Bob's fiancée/wife.

Max Wolff: Maximilian "Max" Görzten posing as a Swiss merchant / investor.

Maximilian "Max" Görzten: Luftwaffe's Colonel, industrialist, Nazism oppositionist, plots to assasinate Adolf Hitler.

Neto: Airplane assistant mechanic.

Nick Harper: Airline Operations' Manager.

Nicolás Antonio: Old chiclero, looks like a living corpse.

Otilia: Enedina's apprentice.

Otto Halen: Chancelery auto mechanic.

Pepe: Cayetano's confidant.

Rafaél: Ramón's allied.

Ramón de la Torre: Field worker, looking to avenge his father.

Ricardo Quel: Airplane master mechanic, Mayan lore expert.

Robert "Bob" Calver: Flight commander, chiclero pilot.

Rosenda de la Torre: Maid, Ramón de la Torre's wife.

Sergeant O'Leary: Police officer, Maureen's father.

Teresa : Enedina's apprentice.

Tocho Pérez: Mexican airline pilot.

Tomasito "El Chicharrín": Airplane mechanic.

Vince Califano: Flight navigator.

Walter Tamz: German Consulate employee.

Willy: Flight engineer.

WORKS BY THE AUTHOR

In English:
- Pancho Villa's Mighty Air Force: The Golden Hawks
- Flying in Xibalbá
- Reds, the Saint Patrick's Battalion

In Spanish:
- Los Halcones Dorados de Villa (Bestseller)
- Esos Intrépidos Hombres del Aire
- Aventuras de Tierra Caliente
- La Nao de China
- Los Colorados del San Patricio
  (1998 Editors' Award)
- Nezahualcóyotl, Brazo de León
  (2009 Editors' Award)

MYSTIC BUDDHA TITLES

- The Fast Path: Adventures in Meditation and Self-Discovery
- Lifetimes: True Accounts of Reincarnation
- Total Relaxation: The Complete Program to Overcome Worry, Stress, and Fatigue
- Pancho Villa's Mighty Air Force: The Golden Hawks

For more information, please visit our website:
www.MysticBuddha.com